CALAMITY

THE DESPOT CHRONICLES #1

CALAMITY

ANDY T. HANSON

4 Horsemen
Publications, Inc.

4 Horsemen
Publications, Inc.

Published By: 4 Horsemen Publications, Inc.

4 Horsemen Publications, Inc.
PO Box 417
Sylva, NC 28779
4horsemenpublications.com
info@4horsemenpublications.com

Cover & Typesetting by Autumn Skye
Edited by Tabitha Saletri

Library of Congress Control Number: 2024906060

Paperback ISBN-13: 979-8-8232-0400-2
Hardcover ISBN-13: 979-8-8232-0401-9
Audiobook ISBN-13: 979-8-8232-0487-3
Ebook ISBN-13: 979-8-8232-0399-9

ACKNOWLEDGMENTS

To my big, wonderful family, for your love and support.

CONTENTS

PROLOGUE

JORDANA

Warning lights and blaring klaxons plagued Jordana Revere the entire flight. There had been a string of one sort of malfunction or another screaming their angry warning songs in a constant succession ever since exiting the exosphere. However, Jordana's innate sensible poise had not cracked in the face of the onslaught. She'd simply responded to each alarm as the on-board computer suggested, be it adjusting course, or closing a valve, or cycling the power reserves, and then cycling them again, and then once again for good measure. So the red light now flashing in her peripheral vision did not cause any undue panic in the former Royal Air Force fighter pilot. She'd spent four years flying some of the most cutting-edge aircraft Her Majesty had to offer. She did not panic. Jordana never panicked. Indecision and hesitation had been trained out of her completely, and training was everything.

Though of course, she had never actually trained on the ultra-advanced dirigible she currently piloted. Just before blasting off from the Earth's surface, Jordana had allowed herself a small moment of awed satisfaction over the incredible unlikelihood of ever finding herself in the captain's chair of one of these beautiful interplanetary ships. Flying this particular ship past the diaphanous barrier of Earth's atmosphere had placed Jordana among an extremely elite group of pilots, of which she imagined herself possibly the only living member. *I'll bet they were all just as gob smacked by the view as I am though,* Jordana told herself.

The state-of-the-art craft she currently stewarded toward that surreal view was awe-inspiring, in both aesthetic and capabilities; composed of five tons of high grade steel, twin collider repulsion engines, and roughly a hundred-million dollars' worth of AOA's most cutting-edge life support, artificial gravity and offensive targeting systems—all completely automated. The flight controls were automated as well, but to a lesser degree. A flesh-and-blood pilot was still required. A copilot was desirable, though not strictly necessary. All the ludicrously fast and ridiculously economical interplanetary craft of its class had been painted a solid matte-black for the basecoat and then tailored individually from there. The one Jordana currently helmed wore a thin orange stripe down its flanks, along with two huge silver and maroon AOA logos on either wing. The sleek craft appeared remarkably reminiscent of a hawk piercing through the sky in one of its legendary streaking attack dives, and thus were aptly named Star Hawks.

Jordana stretched out inside the cockpit of her Star Hawk as much as her firmly secured restraints allowed, craning her neck up and to the left in order to read the warning message flashing red on the critical systems console mounted to the cockpit bulkhead. "AUTOMATIC LANDING SYSTEM MALFUNCTION," it read, in bold, bright red font. "Bollocks." Jordana let loose the first curse of the entire ten-hour flight as she reached to her left towards an inconveniently placed operations console.

Testing the limits of her long, slender arm, she flicked the automatic landing system switch in the center of the console into the off-position. Jordana then turned her attention to the main display screen embedded in the starcraft's dash just two feet in front of her. Flashing red on the transparent touchscreen surface were her next instructions. Upon reading the message, she immediately whipped her head back and forth to clear any cobwebs that might've taken hold over the last ten hours. Only when she was certain of her lucidity did Jordana return her gaze to the screen to read the terrifying message once more. "ENGAGE MANUAL LANDING SYSTEM," it still read, in the same bright, urgent red.

Oh, you have got to be kidding me! You didn't train for a manual landing, Jor! Bloody hell! A sudden, desperate panic shocked her senses. *Hell, you barely trained for any of this, ya daft plonker,* she reminded herself an instant later. *You didn't have the time, remember? You rushed into this without thinking it through, without even bothering to train up a bloody copilot.* "Ohh, nooo, I won't need one, I can handle it alone," *you told them. Ha... well, you reap what you sow, don't ya, Jor?* Shaking her head back and forth vigorously, she broke free of her loop of useless thoughts.

Drawing in a deep, calming breath, she made herself reach back to her left and flip down the red plastic cover over the manual landing system switch. Jordana's finger hovered over the switch for a long moment as she expelled the nervous air she hadn't even realized she was still holding. "Well, shit. I guess I'm doing this," she spoke aloud into the spacious cockpit.

Without further hesitation, Jordana flipped the switch to engage the manual landing system. The craft's single-stick yoke instantly became sluggish and heavy in her hands. In no time flat, she found herself in a desperate and exhausting struggle with gravity itself. In the breath after the artificial gravity disengaged, the pressure inside the cockpit began to increase at a terrifyingly rapid pace, a cascading catastrophe resulting from an earlier emergency that Jordana must not have tended to as effectively as she may have hoped. After only a few short breaths, the immense G-Forces were almost too excruciating to endure. Each new second found her physical and mental faculties hurtling faster and faster toward their ultimate limits.

Her vision slowly began to tunnel, when suddenly, Jordana remembered that training she was always going on about. Fighting to slow her breathing, she regained her focus. Out of the corner of her eye, Jordana could see her current elevation flashing in that lamentably familiar, urgent red on the mounted systems console. The Star Hawk was sitting at around four-thousand feet, but she was spooling down quite rapidly. *Something's wrong,* Jordana knew. The craft was fighting her too much. She was falling at too steep an angle. One system failure was leading to another, hacking away, bit by bit, at the significant strength and focus she needed just to stay conscious in the face of the relentless pressure.

Manual landings were difficult, extremely difficult even, but not like this. *Something is very wrong.* The certain thought caused her to seek out her ship's status once more. She dropped her eyes to the dash-embedded display screen this time, and when she wasn't pleased with what she saw there, darted her eyes to the systems console to her right, hoping against hope it had a different opinion. Yet, cruelly, it spoke only gut-wrenching confirmation. She was descending way too fast.

Her every attempt at course correction seemed to send the Star Hawk careening wildly in the opposite direction. It took her a good deal of time—time she did not have—just to figure out the new subtleties of the ship's controls. No way would she be making a nice soft-dock landing on Cardinal's Nest's lunar dock like she and Arlo had planned so carefully back at Casper Station. She would have to perform an emergency field-landing. Jordana knew too that the field-landing would have to result in the Star Hawk being close to the station when it came down onto the dusty lunar surface. Her vacuum life support equipment (VLSE) had only a limited oxygen and power supply. It could not sustain a long cross-surface trek.

Jordana quickly analyzed her options and did not at all like the answer her brain spit out at her after its calculations were complete. Her situation was dire, but looking away from it simply because she did not like what she saw was no excuse, and it would help no one. She had to look her grim predicament square in the face. The ship would come down where it came down. That was that, at this point. Nothing to be done for it now. She simply had to stay focused on doing all that was within her limited power to ensure she was still conscious when the Star Hawk plowed into the powdery gray moon dust. She wouldn't have a second to waste.

All these thoughts and more ran through Jordana's head in the mere blink of an eye. And in the next eye-blink, she decided on a course of action, and although said course would be in direct conflict with the clandestine mandate of her current mission, she knew it was the right choice. Jordana had clear orders to avoid contact with the lunar station's few inhabitants until she had a better idea of what to expect from them. But that was always subject to early failure, in Jordana's opinion anyhow. *I mean, did The Bruderschaft really expect no one at the station to notice me landing a Star Hawk on their lunar dock?*

Jordana knew the hope was that whoever was operating Cardinal's Nest Lunar Station wasn't monitoring their docking ports. The tech guys seemed to think that was a possibility anyway, since they weren't operating their external communications systems either. They figured the station had only a limited power supply, with all occupants confined to a small section of the station to conserve power and resources. But as it was now, Jordana and the rest of The Bruderschaft knew precious little about whomever was up here turning on and off the station lights. Best guess they could come up with was that it must be a few dozen of Cardinal's Nest's earliest prep crewmen, doing their best to cling to life. It was operating. That was about all The Bruderschaft's tech guys knew for sure. At least none of those tech guys were able to make contact and learn anything more before Jordana had launched the Star Hawk from the dilapidated launchpad at Casper Station.

They had chased the myth of Cardinal's Nest Lunar Station across half the world. Every member of The Bruderschaft was eager to believe. It had seemed plausible, after all. When the infection spread, a lot of once-crazy conspiracies started to seem plausible. Add on the fact that they were all desperate for anything to believe in, desperate for some sort of hope to get them through those long, dark nights. And Arlo Bailey did not disappoint there. He gave it to them in spades. The bloke oozed charisma and charm. And boy, could he ever walk the walk as well, never leading them anywhere he wouldn't go first. Arlo was an easy man to follow.

Jordana sure as hell believed in him and his myth. And that belief had paid off in the end; everything Arlo Bailey had ever told them was true. They'd found an abandoned and half-decayed Casper Station right where he told them they would: twenty-five miles north of downtown Casper, Wyoming, alongside the Antelope Hills. There were no more doubters after that. Their brotherhood had taken on an even deeper kinship, for all of them, though all of them would've thought that impossible only weeks before.

And so, Jordana had more than a *want*, more than a *need* to contact that brotherhood now, her Bruderschaft, to relay her critical mission report; she had a *fateful purpose*. She would get that report out, and soon. The Bruderschaft would wait for her a few days. They would wait as long as they could. They were a brotherhood, after all, and took care of each other. But time was precious. The Bruderschaft had already been too long in one place. The infected hordes were thinning out more and more with each passing year, but there were still millions walking every corner of the planet. The Bruderschaft hadn't been sniffed out by any of those roaming hordes at Casper Station before Jordana had left them, but it wouldn't be long until one pack or another of the infected discovered them there and overwhelmed them with sheer numbers. They would move on before that happened, and abandon Jordana, assuming her obvious failure.

The Bruderschaft would most likely never get another chance to come back and attempt another launch either. They had found two other serviceable Star Hawks back at Casper Station, but again, time was not on their side. It never was. They had rushed to get this currently plummeting Star Hawk launch ready, probably rushed it a little too much, in hindsight. But that's what life on Earth was now, one seemingly eternal rush.

So none of them were naive anymore. They knew they couldn't stay static long enough to get another Star Hawk launch-ready. The Bruderschaft currently had all their manpower focused on bringing the E-11 Transport Cruiser they'd found alongside the Star Hawks up to a launch-ready condition, and even that was being done in a rush. Every member of The Bruderschaft knew that Jordana was their one and only chance. Jordana could not fail, would not fail, would not even contemplate the possibility; there were too many people relying on her. That was the heavy knowledge that led her to her ultimate decision. She had to reach out to whomever was operating Cardinal's Nest Station.

Jordana gritted her teeth, summoning all her available strength. With determination coursing through her veins, she quickly darted out her left hand at the main-display-screen to open a communications channel with Cardinal's Nest Lunar Station's Control Room. She nearly lost all her ever-shrinking management over the starship in the process. Struggling to right the ship while drawing in as large a breath as her lungs would allow, she shouted into the comms-mic embedded in the main-display-screen, "Mayday! Mayday! This is Captain Jordana Revere aboard the AOA Interplanetary Craft, Gallahad. Can anyone read me?! Is anyone there? This is the Advancement Operations Alliance interplanetary craft designate: AOA Ship Galahad, hailing Cardinal's Nest Lunar Station! Is anyone there? Mayday! Repeat, mayday! I am coming in hot! Automatic landing systems offline. I cannot approach Lunar Dock. Current onboard calculations have me landing roughly twenty miles northwest of the Kepler Crater. I'm going to need an extraction team immediately! I have very limited VLSEs onboard. Repeat, I need help! Please, is anyone there? Hello, Cardinal's Nest Lunar Station?! Hello?! Do you copy? Is anyone reading me? Hello! Is anyone receiving this?"

The elevation monitor on her display began flashing red numbers too small for even Jordana's otherworldly poise to withstand. She gave up on her seemingly useless pleas with the lunar station's control room to focus all her attention on the potentially catastrophic landing dead ahead. Waiting until the last possible second, she yanked back on the yoke with all her might. The Star Hawk's nose shot up past parallel, stalling out the main engines. Jordana lashed out with her left hand, smashing down the yellow mushroom-shaped emergency booster button on the top row of the operations console. After an agonizing second's delay, three oval-shaped boosters mounted in a horizontal line along the tail of the Star Hawk instantly flared to life. Jordana could picture them in her mind's eye: cones of red and yellow plasma shot through with streaks of cold blue. The boosters managed to halt the dirigible in a vertical rocket-launching position just a few dozen feet from the surface of the moon.

Then, just as a relieved breath escaped Jordana's lips, the boosters suddenly cut out, dropping the craft lazily as a bobbing buoy the remaining thirty feet. The orange-streaked Star Hawk impacted the surface boosters-first. The sound of crumpling metal and shattering steel came to Jordana as nails on a chalkboard. Swaying on end for an instant, the long black craft exhaled a torrent of disturbing pops and groans, before the nose of the ship, with the cockpit and a strapped-in Jordana, flopped forward. She had an instant to think herself weak for the sudden heave in her stomach just before the right wing of the Star Hawk burrowed into a dune of lunar dust, causing the ship to crash down at an awkward angle. The interplanetary craft was sent lurching abruptly to its side on impact, finally coming to a rest half-buried in the dust of a gently sloping dune. It was the last thing Jordana Revere was aware of before blacking out.

Slowly, ever so slowly, Jordana's vision came back into focus. Slower still, her visual sensory input began to crystallize inside her mind. She had bashed her head against the air recycling console mounted near the pilot seat when she'd impacted the surface. She remembered that now, and the memory brought with it a sudden throbbing pain on the upper right side of her skull. Jordana thought she remembered the boosters cutting out right before that. Everything seemed garbled and muddled. She started to shake her head to clear the cobwebs, as she had so often done in the past, but regretted it immediately. A red-hot needle seemed to be prodding her brain. "Ahh, bollocks that hurts!" Jordana shrieked as she reached a hand up to the source of the pain above her right ear. When she pulled her hand away to discover it smeared with blood, Jordana knew she was in serious trouble.

She had to act fast; time was not on her side. She had no idea if anyone at Cardinal's Nest had even heard her, much less sent out a response team. She'd never even received confirmation of signal reception. She might've been shouting into the void, for all she knew. Jordana couldn't rely on rescue. She had to take her survival into her own hands.

Letting her eyes once again take in the tremendous destruction inside the cockpit, this time with a much more lucid mind, she surveyed the carnage. It was a grim scene. Sparks arced out from nearly every console, some of which had broken free from their mounts and now dangled precariously from exposed wires. Through all the smoke and sparking chaos, Jordana located her VLSE container mounted on a nearby bulkhead. She pushed in her safety restraint release button on top of her stomach and felt enormous relief in her shoulders as the strap's pressure slackened. Fighting monstrous fatigue, Jordana then shimmied her way up and out of the pilot seat towards the wall-mounted container.

The ship's artificial-gravity generator had been damaged in the plummet, making it hard to balance in the extremely light lunar gravity. She nearly toppled forward, as she reached up to snatch her VLSE container from its mounts on the cabin bulkhead. The moon's gravity made cramming herself into the spacesuit an arduous exercise as well, but soon enough, Jordana was ducking through the cockpit hatch in her full maroon VLSE jumpsuit and silver helmet, with its polarized face shield. She managed to clear the fifty feet of empty cargo bay beyond in five long, slow bounds, finding herself standing in front of the emergency hatch with only slightly shaking hands. *Try not to breathe too much, Jor,* she told herself, with far less sarcasm than she would care to admit.

JED

Larry Holderman's snoring had all but lost its ability to irritate Jed Redding over the past decade of partnership aboard one of the eight serviceable collector modules Cardinal's Nest currently had in operation, but inevitably, there did come a limit that even Jed could not suffer through. There came a point where he could no longer simply sit silently by, allowing his friend and Collector Module Navigator to enjoy his *mid-ride nap*, as Larry so reverently referred to them. This was one of those few instances when Larry's clogged sinuses and heavy breathing were just too much for Jed to take. He could not believe the sight before his eyes, and Larry's snoring was making it impossible for his mind to settle down and make sense out of the insanity. So Jed lashed out across the roomy cockpit of his collector module to give the lantern-jawed, plump, middle-aged, pale, fair-haired, balding sot of a navigator a not-so-soft slap on one of his fleshy cheeks. It had the desired effect of both shutting up and waking up his navigator.

"What in the Sam-hell you think you're doing, Jed?!" Larry demanded in a puzzled and affronted voice while rubbing his cheek.

"Would you wake the hell up and look, for Christ sakes!" Jed responded, pointing out through the wide, sloping transparent windscreen of the collector module.

Larry gave his friend a confused look laced with more than a trace of indignation before moving to sit upright on the module's roomy bench seat. He slowly shifted his gaze from Jed to the windscreen before him and the impossible sight that lay beyond it. "What in the..."

"You got me, man," Jed said in answer. "I mean ... that's a goddamn Star Hawk, ain't it? But that don't make no sense The last Star Hawk is collecting dust on the lunar dock. Ain't it? The Commander blew up the other one ... didn't he?" His voice trailed off with that final question.

"Of course he did. We saw it, Jed, you damn fool. He put on a big goddamn spectacle, like the son-of-a-bitch does for everything. I remember the explosion." Larry broke off then to dig his trusty, old leather-covered drinking flask from the interior pocket of his Nomex module-crewman overcoat. He took a long pull of some of The Priest's harsh moonshine. The stuff tasted like ole-timey-triple-X-hillbilly shit to Jed, but Larry gulped it down by the gallon. "Christ, you remember," he added, wiping his lips clean of any lingering liquor residue, "the bastard had us all in the goddamn Meadow looking up through Stargazer Ceiling. It would've been a damn beautiful sight, if I hadn't known better."

"Yeah, I remember. I was there too, Lar. But what the hell are we looking at then? Did it survive the explosion somehow, ya think?" Jed asked hopefully.

"How in the Sam-hell do you suppo— Are you kidding, man?" Larry posited with rank sarcasm. "I suppose it's possible that the moon's gravity could bring it back down if it miraculously remained intact after that massive explosion we all witnessed engulf it, but we passed this exact same way on the way out yesterday, Jed. It sure as hell wasn't here then. Are you suggesting it took nine years to come back down for no good goddamn reason?" Larry didn't allow his collector-module pilot any time to respond. "And look at the emergency hatch, Jed. It's been opened from the inside. And I'm pretty sure I see footprints in the dust leading *away* from the Star Hawk."

Jed leaned closer to the windscreen to squint his eyes at the emergency hatch and the disturbances in the dust alongside it. *He may be right... No, no, what am I thinking, that's impossible. This is probably just some sort of elaborate Witenagemot trap. Whatever it is, it's trouble. You know that, don't ya, Jeddy old boy?* he asked himself before saying aloud, "Well, it's definitely not the collector module's tracks."

"Ha! No shit, Sherlock. Those are footprints, not giant tread tracks," Larry mocked his partner.

"I know that. I'm just not ready to call 'em footprints, is all," Jed responded in a shaky voice. "I mean ... what the hell are we saying here, Lar? Who the hell piloted that ship? And why did it have to be us that found it? As far as I'm concerned, I'm doing just fine keeping my head down and staying off The Witenagemot's radar. I don't need something like this in my life right now. This is gonna put us right out in front of all of 'em. They are going to want to hear about this, Larry! You know they are." Even as Jed spoke, he could tell his whining was fraying Larry's nerves raw.

"Slow the hell down, would ya?! We don't even know what we got here. Before we go reporting anything, we better damn well find out just what in the heck we're dealing with. Wouldn't you say?" Larry icily asked his long-time partner.

"What do you mean?! It's a goddamn Star Hawk crash-landed out here in the boonies!" Jed exclaimed. "That's enough. I'm sure the steward will send one of his survey teams out to inspect it. They'll probably just order us to stay here and keep an eye on it until they arrive. This is way too big to ignore, Lar. I'm calling it in."

Jed reached out for the communications hand-mic mounted on the central control panel. Larry slapped Jed's hand away from the mic before he even got close. "Hold your goddamn horses, Jed!" Larry yelled before tucking his flask back in his coat pocket.

Jed gave his navigator a dismissive headshake before once again reaching for the communications mic. He had to report this. It was a step too far not to. A step way too far, in fact. Jed and Larry were already pretty low on their supervisor's and warden's lists of favorite people, which was all Larry's doing, as far as Jed was concerned. Larry had been exposing Jed to enough trouble over the past few years just by association. Larry had always been friendly with the old rabble-rousing doctor's daughter, and even the damn trouble-making priest, but he hadn't been as outspoken, or as radically opposed to the Witenagemot as those two, at least not as overtly and blatantly as he had been lately. Jed was sure his friend's conspiratorial whispers and small seditious acts would land them both in a world of trouble, and sooner rather than later.

Still reaching for the mic, he spoke to his navigator in a calm tone that he did not at all feel, "I know what you're thinking, Lar. We ain't doing it. This is way too big. The commander and the rest of the Witenagemot are going to hear about this before we even get back to the station. You know they will. We can't keep this from them. And who's to say we even want to. That ship could bode just as ill for us as the illustrious reign of the commander and his Witenagemot," Jed pointed out. "Let's say those are footprints leading away from that Star Hawk. Who's to say we will like what's to come should we follow them? No, our best bet is to radio this into the control room and follow whatever orders they issue us, to the tee."

Jed had the mic ready to hand by the time he finished his rant. He was set about dialing in the channel for the control room when Larry once more slapped the mic out of his grip. "Like hell you are!" Larry shouted at him.

They wrestled for control of the hand-mic inside the cockpit, setting the large maroon and silver tank-like dirigible to rock back and forth on its ultra-sensitive shocks. After a few moments, Jed grew fed up with the struggle and released the mic over to Larry's control. "What the hell are you doing, Larry?" he asked him. "I am the goddamn ranking-officer inside this module, and I say we are radioing it in. Now give me the damn hand-mic."

"What am I doing?" Larry asked sardonically. "You know damn well what I'm doing, Jed. You know who I am with, and you know they would want me to find out what all this is about before I just hand it over to the goddamn Witenagemot!" Larry took in a deep breath before looking up into Jed's eyes with an earnestness written on his face that Jed had seldom seen in his friend. "I never wanted to drag you into anything, Jed. You're my partner and I respect you. I love you; you know that. And I know you like to keep your head down, but I'm past the point in my life where I can make excuses for that kind of shit. The commander is going down sooner rather than later, Jed. I know you can see the truth in that prediction. When he and the Witenagemot go down, we need to be on the winning side, and we need a way to keep all the crazies back in crazy-town from bringing the roof down on our heads once we've claimed the prize. If we are ever to be free again, Jeddy my man, then it's time to make a choice. No more playing the ostrich with your head in the sand. We have to be proactive, and that before us," Larry said, pointing to the crashed Star Hawk, "that's an opportunity, my guy. I know it is. Somebody must've piloted that Star Hawk from Earth, Jed! Don't you see what that could mean!? Finally, proof that it ain't just us left after all. Think of the implications of that. We have to follow those footprints, Jed. We have to discover who was in that ship, and where in the Sam-hell they came from, and we have to discover it before the Witenagemot and the commander do."

Jed was always helpless before the oppressive will of his navigator. It seemed as though Larry Holderman could talk him into trying to rope a calf with a pocket watch chain. He threw up his hands in acquiescence as all further protest drained away from him. He let his shoulders sag and looked across the cabin-bench to his navigator. Jed noticed the look on Larry's face and was almost afraid to ask his question, "So what exactly do you suggest we do, Larry?"

Larry looked over at his long-time partner and shrugged his shoulders. "Let's keep our options open. We'll just skirt past the wreckage, being careful not to disturb anything. That way, if we follow the footprints and don't like what we find, or if it turns out to be nothing we can use, we can come back to the wreckage and holler up the control room to report the crash site as though we've just found it. No harm no foul. Sound good?"

"None of this *sounds good,* but it's as good a plan as any, given the circumstances, I suppose," Jed reluctantly agreed. "I sure like how there is a chance to cover our asses if this takes a wrong turn. Which, knowing my luck, I'm all but certain it will."

Larry favored him with a knowing grin. Jed simply shrugged his heavy shoulders as he shifted the collector module into drive. The module slowly lurched forward a few dozen feet before completing its shift into high gear. Soon enough though, Jed had the vehicle maneuvered smoothly and carefully around the downed Star Hawk with the expertise of vast experience. Once clear of the wreckage, he glanced up from the few dozen yards of lunar soil before his module's path to take in an undulating white and gray expanse, as far as the eye could see. Floating just above the far-off horizon, spun a blue orb slashed with streaks of brown and green, set against a pitch-black star-freckled backdrop, appearing as a celestial satellite to the gray and ghostly barren plains of the moon, rather than the other way around. *Home,* Jed thought, pining. Then, with a bitter sigh for what once was, he refocused on the path before him.

CHAPTER 1

CARRIE

On any other day in Carrie Montrois' life, seeing a strait-laced, perfectly manicured, $100-hair-cut toting, fifty-something, white, CEO-class businessman in a thousand-dollar suit, dragging a black Coach rolling suitcase and bullying his way through a dense line of disgruntled and deeply confused people with an outstretched forearm, as if the very hounds of hell were nipping at his heels, would be an amusing sight, one worthy of a chuckle at least. On any other day, for sure. Today however, as that very sight played out before her eyes, Carrie was in no way amused. It only served to deepen her confidence that some looming darkness was edging its way closer to her own reality. For although she caught only the barest glimpse of the man's face, Carrie was quite sure she knew just who that fancy businessman in such an unseemly hurry was, and a man like that did not run anywhere. He had people to do his running for him. Whatever lit the fire under his ass could not be good, she knew that. Not good at all.

Carrie felt the faux poise wall she had built up today finally crack, a large, violent crack that she was in no way certain would hold. Mostly, she had spent today in a kind of detached daze, focusing on the immediate task before her. It was the only way she could cope, the only way she could gain enough outer calm to perform the duties motherhood demanded of her. Carrie did not have the luxury of grappling with the shocking and unprecedented nature of this warm autumn day in northern Maryland. She had Roxanna to worry about.

Her daughter needed a levelheaded adult for guidance during this time of crisis. It's true Roxanna had the knack of always appearing mature beyond her years. Every time she spoke to an adult, be it one of her and Monty's friends, her swim coach, or a school counselor, she would slap a look of unearned wisdom across her trustworthy, pudgy-nosed, round, bright-blue-eyed face and win all their undying praise. Carrie always tamped down her maternal pride whenever she witnessed these exchanges. She knew the truth: underneath the false understanding and bravado, there existed as vulnerable and naive a girl as any fourteen-year-old American kid who ever strode the continent. Roxanna needed her mother to keep her shit together and get them through this.

So Carrie had set aside her plethora of unanswerable questions— each a more unpleasant thought than the last— and focused all her attention on the things that were within her control. She had imme-diately set to packing bags for them, all the while speaking softly to Roxanna, "It's alright, sweetie. We are just going to visit your father a little earlier than we planned, that's all."

Roxanna's wary reply of, "But what's going on, Mom? I don't under-stand. The news said... it said those people were... it said they were... what was wrong with them, Mommy?! Why were they hurting those people like that?! I heard police sirens too, Mom! They were close. Are they hurting people around our subdivision? Wha- what... wha..."

Her daughter had trailed off at that point, and only thinking of a way to distract her, Carrie had pulled her teenage princess down alongside her as she zipped up Roxanna's well stuffed pink and yellow duffel bag and pulled over their heavily weathered and worn brown leather suitcase. "Help me pack, honey," she'd told her. "Don't worry about anything else right now. We have to move quickly though, okay? The shuttle is leaving in two hours. But it's okay, we have plenty of time, so long as we focus up and get it done."

Roxanna had wiped her tear-filled blue eyes with her shirtsleeve, smearing a streak of black eyeliner across her upper cheek. Carrie had almost chastised her daughter for wearing makeup. The words were nearly out of her mouth, until she had remembered there were bigger problems just then, truly bigger problems, not to mention her daughter's current age. *Duh. Hello, Car, your daughter's been wearing makeup to school for almost two years now,* she'd reminded herself. *My god, we have a true teenage girl, Monty. You and me. Can you believe it? The world really dropped the ball on that one, didn't they? I shudder to think about what karma has in store for the likes of us and our teenage daughter.* Carrie had shaken her head and cursed herself for wasting a moment on useless thoughts. And after completing a loud, wet nose-blow into a handful of Kleenex tissues, Roxanna had made a lackluster attempt to carry out her mother's request.

Carrie had realized within seconds that the hysterical girl was going to be more of a hindrance to packing than an asset. "Why don't you go around your room and gather up all your electronics and books and whatever else you want to take with us, and I'll take care of the suitcases. Okay?" she'd suggested instead.

"Okay." had been Roxanna's shaky reply.

"Just keep the TV and radio off for now. Let's just worry about getting everything together for our trip to see your father, okay?"

"Okay," was once again all Roxanna could muster. It was good enough for Carrie, especially when her daughter rose from her protective curl on the floor and began gathering up some of her things scattered randomly all about the purple and silver bedroom.

Only a few moments after Roxanna had calmed down and set to packing, Carrie's cellphone rang. It was the second time that day her husband Jasper "Monty" Montrois had called her. The first call had been what had set this day's events in motion. What her husband had told her in that first call in an unusual, frantic, halting fashion had been ridiculous. She had been so sure Monty was just playing some stupid prank. He was always telling fibs and outrageous whitelies just to get under her skin. Like all the times he'd told her the hard lump under the skin of his neck was really an embedded bullet, even though she knew it was just a benign cyst that his doctor had wanted to remove but Monty had kept in just for the stupid story. He tried to tell her— and anyone unlucky enough to ask about it— that someone overseas had shot him, but the bullet hadn't been able to penetrate the incredibly strong muscles of his neck. His skin had just healed over and absorbed it like some kind of mutant super-power or something. Or like the time he'd tried to convince her that a street back in Michigan where they grew up, named Tittabawassee, was a

Chippewa Indian word meaning *big titted squaw*. That was as crude as it was stupid, and Carrie had told her husband—then boyfriend—as much. Monty had a special knack for driving her crazy.

Yet somehow, the more he teased and messed with her, the more she found it endearing. To a point, of course. He could really drive her mad in the most literal sense of that word, and often had. Nothing pissed her off so much as his laissez-faire approach to his own health and general well-being, and basically every personal decision he'd ever made in his life—other than marrying her, of course. He was a good husband all and all though, and an even better father. Jasper always took great care of Roxanna and was ever attentive to their protection and particular needs. Though she did find herself more and more irritated these days by that reckless and impulsive behavior of his. *Like taking this damn security job on the goddamn moon. If that wasn't a quintessential impulsive Monty decision, then I don't know what is. Though I guess I've been too quick to judge,* she'd thought. With the shockingly strange turns this day had taken, that impulsive decision to accept the security commander job may end up being, in some weird, upside-down, accidental, ass-backwards sort of way, the very thing that saves her family's lives.

Carrie slowly came to realize over the course of those impossible seconds of that first phone call from her husband that Monty hadn't just been telling one of his stupid nonsense jokes after all. His unusual behavior was due to the pure, insane horror of the news he had relayed. She had turned on the television as Monty's story started to include details that were too intricate and weird to be any prank. Sure enough, every channel her expensive cable box offered was airing some slightly different coverage of the exact same story, an unbelievable and horrifying story. Those first few frighteningly gory images that flashed across her AOA ultra-thin 4D wall-embedded internet television were images Carrie thought would be haunting her dreams for the rest of her life. Realizing her husband had not been pulling her leg in the slightest had felt like being doused with a dozen buckets of bone-shudderingly cold ice-water all at once.

So when the second phone call from Monty had come across her phone, Carrie had answered it while drawing in a breath to steel herself to receive even more terrifying news. She'd been taken aback for a brief moment when her husband had no more horror to convey. Instead, he told her she needed to take the Sagal children with her and Roxanna when they came to the launch pad. Monty had told her in a rush that the Sagal's nanny hadn't been invited aboard the shuttle, so the woman had abandoned the children and left in an agitated rush. Monty had told Carrie the children's father, Dr. Sagal, was in a terrible panic about their fate.

The Sagal kids, Maisie and Elias, were the children of Doctor Perry Sagal, a former ER surgeon who had accepted a position with AOA to be the hospital administrator aboard Cardinal's Nest station. Apparently, he was renowned for his ability to manage a hospital and was head-hunted by the AOA for the monumental task of preparing the cutting-edge Newton Supreme Care Hospital aboard Cardinal's Nest Station to be ready to care for the three-thousand-odd station tenants AOA was planning to settle there by the end of the decade. Dr. Sagal had accepted the position and signed a legally binding contract, one he felt morally, if not legally obligated to uphold. Even in the face of the sudden car accident and tragic death of his wife of thirteen years, only two days after he had signed that very contract, the obligation was still a priority in the incredible man's life.

Carrie had tremendous admiration for Dr. Sagal. His ability to cope with trauma had amazed her. She couldn't imagine keeping it together like he had this past year, not if she had lost Monty in some freak accident like the one that claimed his Joan. Plus, Dr. Sagal had two young children to look after. Going with the advance prep crew and leaving them behind in their ultra-private subdivision with just a permanent live-in nanny to look after them must've been excruciating. But he had done that too. Carrie knew he video-chatted with both his children multiple times a week, but it wasn't the same thing.

She knew she could never deal with half the shit that family had been through this past year. Not with nearly as much grace, anyway. And so it made her happy to learn that Doctor Sagal and Monty had developed a casual friendship aboard the station over the last few months. The two men had first bonded when they discovered their families' condos relative proximity to each other back in the brand-new housing subdivision AOA had required the families of the advance prep crew to board up in. The Sagal kids were just five units down from where Carrie and Roxanna were quartered. That somewhat mundane anecdote had definitely played its part in the two AOA employees' early friendship, but mostly it was the fact that Maisie and Roxanna had developed a strong friendship of their own.

That friendship served as the foundation for all their interfamily relationships. The girls had become inseparable, with Roxanna playing the wise older sister role that the younger girl was so plainly desperate to have in her life. Dr. Sagal had told Monty and Carrie many times how ecstatic he'd been to learn of Maisie and Roxanna's friendship. He had moved both his children halfway across the country, abruptly separating them from all their friends and the only life they ever knew a mere week after their mother had been tragically and violently taken from them. Dr. Sagal had told her and Monty that he had been certain his kids would never make new friends, simply to spite him for his cruelty.

Knowing Maisie was in good hands with Roxanna, Dr. Sagal was then left with only his son's loneliness to agonize over. Dr. Sagal and Carrie had developed quite a friendship themselves over the last few months. He would call her up on video-chat quite often, mostly to talk about his son Elias. For some reason, the young boy chose her, of all people, to confide in. When Maisie came over to their house after school to hang out with Roxanna, Elias would sometimes tag along. He and Carrie would sit in the dining-room and have a few no-bake cookies and a Dr. Pepper. Carrie wouldn't press him. She could tell he didn't want that. Elias would sit across from her, sipping his pop, always with a crumb or two of cookie stuck to the corner of his wide mouth, his curly brown hair always spilling out from under the greasy old blue ballcap he jammed down on his head every morning as he rose to face the day, and then again mid-afternoon as soon as his last school-bell rang.

Carrie and the young boy always had very natural and organic conversations. Of course, it was mostly Carrie doing the talking, but the boy had been ready to contribute his part to the dialogue too. He never drifted or ignored her. He was never rude in the slightest. Never anything short of an extremely polite and respectful young man. Though he could never look you in the eye with those sad and broken hazel peepers of his for more than a few seconds, and then only if he really knew you. That closed-off nature made it difficult to know if you were getting through. There were times when Carrie couldn't be completely sure, but she assumed, with a high-degree of certainty, that just having someone to listen to did the boy a world of good. Even if all they spoke of was television shows, comic books, music and baseball. Carrie and Elias were both Detroit Tigers fans and spent many Dr. Pepper-fueled playful rages arguing over whether or not ownership would ever loosen their purse strings again to pay for a decent team now that the old man was dead. Carrie was of the opinion they wouldn't, while Elias was always the loyal fan, clinging desperately to hope. A little flutter of joy would beat inside her heart when she'd see the smile come across Dr. Sagal's face as she recounted those parts of her and Elias' latest conversations.

Helping soothe the Sagal family's trauma had been a pleasantly diverting undertaking for Carrie. It helped take her mind off the fact that living in AOA's high-security housing development felt a lot like living inside some kind of glass bubble. The cameras mounted on every house, lamp-post, and streetlight. The constant security patrols, up and down and back and forth. Not to mention the fact that everywhere she went and everything she did was monitored and scrutinized by AOA in one way or another. The amount of secrecy pledges, sworn oaths and non-disclosure agreements they'd had to sign before they were allowed to move into that ant farm were head-spinning. She'd always balked against someone scrutinizing the way she'd lived her life, or who she'd talked to, so living in that subdivision the past five months had felt a little like bugs crawling over her skin.

The Sagal family's desperation might have been the only thing that kept her sane these past few months. As cruel as that sounded, it might well be true. And on this day in particular, she welcomed any added distraction, and so had no qualms at all about bringing Maisie and Elias along on the forty-minute trek to the waiting transport shuttles poised for departure at AOA's top-secret launchpad facility. Carrie had told her husband that she would of course look after Maisie and Elias. She'd told him to pass on to Dr. Sagal her assurances that she would see them safely aboard the shuttle. Monty had then reassured her that everything was going to be okay in a soothing voice. They exchanged mutual pledges of love. Monty promised they'd all be together soon. And then, roughly an hour after she'd ended that last phone call with her husband, Carrie, Roxanna and the two Sagal children arrived at AOA's top-secret launchpad in the hills of West Virginia.

They had passed two separate security checkpoints where their AOA identifications—which were their passports on this day—were confirmed and then reconfirmed. With that hurdle cleared, they were unceremoniously hustled onto the launchpad tarmac, and loudly and rudely corralled into a milling line in front of a mobile staircase leading up into a hatchway in the belly of what Monty had told Carrie was called an E-11 Transport Cruiser. A second transport shuttle, with an identical staircase and restless line of people, was about 500 yards off to her right. The transport cruisers looked remarkably like big pop-bottles with the spout sliced off. The refuellable rockets clamped securely to the fueling hoses of the secondary launchpad even resembled the hexagonal arrangement you found on the bottom of most pop-bottles.

Did they do that on purpose?' Cause it's freaking uncanny, had been the ridiculous thought that had bubbled up in Carrie's mind just before that impatient businessman had stolen her focus with his rush through the line. She watched on as he plowed his way to the foot of the mobile staircase about twenty yards from Carrie's position in line. The familiar businessman swelled with rage and began hoarsely shouting at the security officer posted at the foot of the staircase after the officer moved to block the businessman's path.

"What does that asshole think he is doing exactly?" The woman directly in line in front of Carrie asked angrily. "Can't the moron see there's a line? Self-important bastard thinks he's better than the rest of us."

You may be more right than you know, Carrie thought, just as her previous sense of looming dread once again invaded her detached, single-minded focus. She knew for certain now who the impatient businessman was. He had turned and faced the line while shouting his displeasure with a wagging finger at the poor security officer, giving Carrie, and the rest of the families in line, a good look at his clean-shaven, square-jawed face. The confirmation brought no con-solation for the unease that permeated her every molecule.

The rushing businessman was none other than Hubert Richard Harrington, President and CEO of AOA International. She recognized him from that creepy *block party* the top brass at AOA had put on a few months back for the families living in their prison camp of a housing subdivision. Hubert Richard Harrington had smiled out at them that night with the falsest face Carrie had ever seen a man wear, as he assured them all of his company's loyalty to its employees and their families. The plain, smug, obviousness of the lies he had regurgitated at the families in attendance had disgusted Carrie to her core. He had a false, carpetbagger smile cemented to his face as he spoke to them about the necessities for the exclusive nature of their new homes, and just how truly important the confined and monitored living situations AOA were forcing upon them really were. It all tasted like such blatant bullshit that Carrie had nearly physically gagged. She had at least tasted bile in her throat, she remembered that much. So she had been shocked when the man finished his diatribe and all the sheep around her immediately began to bleat out their thanks and appreciation to the company for giving their loved ones such an amazing opportunity. Not one of them put up even a pretense of protest for what AOA had been expecting of them. Instead, they all bent down and kissed the ring.

Carrie had been worked up after that. She had felt all alone. No one seemed to be sharing her distress. Adding to her troubles was the fact that she basically knew there was little to nothing she could do about her predicament anymore. She knew her husband couldn't back out of his contract. He was already aboard the lunar station, 238,900 miles away. Plus, the Montrois family had needed this fancy new lunar station job just as much as the next family. Monty had burnt so many bridges along the way that their pool of options had been extremely limited. Carrie remembered being just as excited as Monty about the AOA job initially. The salary and benefits were greater than any job Monty had ever had, and by a lot too, a freaking whole heck of a lot. It definitely solved all of their financial worries. Still, it rankled her to have to be fed bullshit and expected to eat it and then ask for seconds.

The night she got home from that un-party block party, she had sent Roxanna to the Sagals' and drove herself to the library in Hillsdale.

She went all the way to Hillsdale, West Virginia, twenty miles from AOA's subdivision for a reason. It was a pleasant little shopping town she enjoyed visiting with Roxanna and Maisie, three towns over from the one AOA had leased space in for the prep crew families. Carrie had felt the distance was necessary to ensure no one would be monitoring her while she engaged in a research effort on AOA, and Hubert Richard Harrington in particular. She hadn't at all liked the multitudes of negative articles she turned up on Hubie Harrington and his cronies on the AOA Board of Directors. Even with her modest computer sleuthing skills, she was digging up articles from all over the country concerning gross malpractice following Hubert Harrington to every successive company throughout his career, leading all the way to the AOA. It was way too coincidental. Carrie hadn't been at all too sure just what Hubie and his friends were up to at AOA, but she knew it had to be no good.

And the AOA itself, that was something else. The more she had looked for specifics on the company, the less she found. It was impossible. It had to be. AOA was a huge corporation. They had investors from all over the globe and partnerships with cities and towns all across the country. How could there not be article after article on the international corporation that perfected interplanetary travel by inventing an unprecedented combustion technology light-years ahead of the next closest aerial technology developer, and then integrating that combustion technology into the propulsion systems of the Star Hawks and E-11 Transport Cruisers they then rushed into production at improbable speed. Not to mention the fact that they built an eight-million-square-foot, multi-trillion-dollar, self-sustaining habitation, equipped with mind-boggling new technologies, i.e. an artificial-gravity generator, a cutting edge solar power conversion system, a perpetual oxygen recycler/purifier and a water production facility that combined collected lunar dust with hydrogen and oxygen atoms brought in by colossal collector modules, and then, through some impossibly complicated process that Carrie didn't even try to wrap her mind around, made enough potable water to support three-thousand people indefinitely. And all this on the surface of the fucking moon. But nobody was talking about them? It made no sense.

The silence about AOA on the internet was as unsettling to Carrie as Hubie Harrington's unsavory past.

After that night at the library, Carrie had decided what little she had learned was enough to risk whatever fallout came from forcing Monty to back out of his contract with AOA. She was working on a tactful way to extricate him from Cardinal's Nest and get her family away from whatever repercussions would come from the Montrois' breaking their many sworn oaths and contract requirements, when she remembered how much Dr. Sagal, and his family, were desperately relying on her. And then, with them becoming her point of focus, in a matter of mere weeks, she was scolding herself for ever believing that backing out of their contracts wasn't just a fool's dream anyhow. Hubie Harrington and his AOA became a background concern in her mind. Lending a hand in mending the broken hearts of Maisie, Elias, and Perry Sagal alike, had forced her to unthinkingly turn whatever mental energy she had assigned toward planning her family's escape into repetitive and constant personal chastisement for not researching AOA before she let Monty sign that damn contract and get them in bed with the secretive corporate giant in the first place. *Not that you had a snowball's chance in hell of stopping him, Car.*

"My god, would you look at that! That son-of-a-bitch is going to get his way! Look … that security-officer is stepping out of his way," the woman in line ahead of Carrie complained once again as the businessman started to climb the steps in a huff.

"I think that security officer will be lucky to have a job after that," Carrie responded to the woman. "That was Hubert Harrington, the CEO of AOA. A real piece of work too, let me tell you."

"Oh, you know what? I think you're right. The son-of-a-bitch from that damn block party, right?" the woman asked as she turned around in line to face Carrie. She had a friendly face that was currently sporting a shaky grin. The woman had a rolling suitcase of her own beside her, though a great deal cheaper an item than the one Hubert Harrington had been dragging along. It was as neatly packed and put together as the woman herself though. She was about Carrie's height, at around 5'3", but she had a good ten years or so on Carrie's 35. Her hair was cropped short around her round, artificially tanned and chubby face. Carrie had worn hers in a similar fashion a few years back, though her strawberry-red hair made quite the contrast to the woman's sandy-blonde. *It looks better on her,* she thought, obscurely. The blonde lady's chubby, round face suited the style more than Carrie's longer, more aquiline one. Monty had said kind words to her back when she chopped it into the bob, but she'd seen the look on his face upon his first sight. The goof was easier to read than Dr. Seuss. His look was right in the end though, and she'd quickly grown it back out to the shoulder-length tangle of strawberry locks it currently was.

"Right," Carrie answered the woman. "You enjoyed that shindig as little as I did, I take it."

"Bullshit from the word go," the woman in the sandy-blonde bob said with a wry smirk. "That was my impression anyway. The food was okay though, I suppose. No one ate my tuna salad ... which was fine by me in the end. I brought it back home and ate it myself in front of the TV. Ughh ... the TV... I think I literally watched everything the internet had to offer on my damn TV these past five months. There wasn't nothing else to do in that concentration camp they call a housing subdivision they had us walled up in." The woman held out her hand towards Carrie as she added, "I'm Dolly Duchesne, by the way. My husband is part of the fishery crew that went up with the prep team."

"Carrie Montrois," she said after taking Dolly's hand into her own and shaking a few times. "My husband Jasper Montrois is head of the security staff up there. Maybe he knows your husband. There's only about sixty or seventy of them up there right now, I think."

"I think you're right. My husband Gabe is always saying it feels like some kind of creepy, futuristic ghost town up there right now. I can believe it. The goddamn station is a behemoth. I doubt it'll feel crowded, even at max-capacity." The woman finally looked to the three children huddled up close to Carrie. Her hand instantly flew to her mouth as it formed an oh-my-goodness pucker, "My apologies for the language, Carrie. I'm not myself today, I'm afraid."

"Believe me, I understand. This all feels a little surreal, like it's happening to someone else, and I'm just watching the show."

"What is happening exactly?" Dolly asked, abruptly taking on a more serious tone. "Did you speak to your husband at all?"

"He called as soon as he heard they were loading all the prep crew families aboard the shuttles," Carrie relayed in a rush. "He didn't have much information, really. I don't think he was holding back either. I'm not sure if that's a comforting thought or not. I mean ... who the hell does know what is happening out there? The news has been no damn help. Just non-stop clips of attacks, like that is helping at all. We're in some kinda apocalyptic crisis here, and all the news is worried about is click-bait."

"'Apocalyptic crisis' may be more right than you know," Dolly leaned forward to say in a conspiratorial fashion, being careful so the children wouldn't overhear. "Gabe told me everything he could which, as you heard from your husband, was little enough, but it tickled my curiosity bone, nonetheless. I mean ... it's almost like AOA was prepared for this. You know what I mean? Other than Mr. CEO man barging his way aboard the ship, all this seems way too orderly. Almost like it's been anticipated and prepared for in some fashion. I've been here at the launchpad for a while now; I was among the first of the families from the subdivision to arrive, in fact. We watched a meticulously organized and rehearsed act, or procedure, or whatever. They had the transport cruisers fueled up and ready for take-off before even I got here. I did see a huge bus pull up shortly after I arrived though. Now, this sounds like bullshit, but I swear to you that I shit you not," Dolly said, leaning even closer. "I must've spotted at least three world leaders—the Prime Minister of England for sure—pile out of that bus with what must've been their families and staff following behind them. They were all escorted immediately aboard this E-11 that we are in line for now. Now, what's that all about, I ask? How the hell did they all get here so fast? Before us even?! And the housing subdivision is only forty minutes from here. Whatever is going on out in the world, I'll bet AOA and these government leaders are in on it, or had something to do with it at least."

"Jesus, do you think?" Carrie's exasperated question was more rhetorical in nature, and she barreled over any response that may have come from Dolly, "I never should have let Monty talk me into letting him take this crazy job, not that he really ever actually asked me. I knew it though. I knew it. The secrecy around AOA never sat right with me. Jesus, what have they gotten us into?"

Roxanna must've noticed the unease on her mother's face, and so tugged Carrie's coat for her attention, "What's the matter, Mom? Aren't we going aboard the shuttle? Why are we waiting in line out here like this?"

"We're going aboard, honey. Don't worry. I'm just a little on edge. We all are," Carrie said as she bent down and placed her hands on Elias' shoulders. She held eye-contact with the boy for a long, reassuring moment before moving on to give Maisie and Roxanna the same treatment. "It's going to be fine; trust me, kids. We'll be having a meal with both of your fathers aboard the lunar station in no time. It's just an adventure, guys. One we are going to get through together. Right?" Once she got three affirmative answers to that question, she wrapped her arms around the kids, enfolding them all in a tight bear-hug.

"Yeah, I'm sorry if I've been scaring you kids at all," Dolly said to the children. "Nothing to worry about now. We'll all be aboard shortly, and everything will work out after that."

Carrie was busy treating Dolly to an appreciative grin when Maisie suddenly spoke up, "What about everyone else? There were people hurting people on the news earlier, I saw it. They said it's spreading. What about all the kids in my old school? What about all the people all over the world who don't live at our subdivision or work for AOA or the governments? What happens to all them, Mrs. Montrois? Are they coming up to the moon too?"

Carrie exchanged an uncertain look with Dolly. Neither of them made any attempt to answer Maisie's poignant question. The uneasy moment was forgotten quickly enough for Carrie when she looked down the length of the line of waiting families and noticed a large black bus pull through the heavily guarded entrance gates of the launchpad. The bus maneuvered in as elegant a fashion as a ten-ton passenger car on wheels could possibly maneuver, working its way across the launchpad toward the transport cruiser Carrie and her charges were currently in line for.

"More government people, I'll bet," Dolly said, turning as her gaze followed the bus on its creeping path.

And sure enough, Dolly was right. Carrie recognized the Chancellor of Germany, Abigail Hoffreyer, as she clambered down the steps of the bus. Hoffreyer was surrounded by the normal entourage of folks you would expect to see hounding the heels of a world leader. She allowed them to escort her directly from the bus to the mobile staircase leading up into the E-11's belly. Hoffreyer spared only a momentary look back to ensure that the people Carrie assumed were the chancellor's family were trailing obediently behind her. The chancellor had not even the merest glance to spare for the line of bemused prep crew families. And so, on and on it went for the rest of the passengers of the huge black bus, each passing the milling line of people as though it weren't even there. Carrie's incredulity had climbed to unprecedented heights with each new bus passenger trudging up that staircase as though they owned it.

"What the fuck is going on here?!" A deep-voiced woman a few yards back in line finally gave voice to Carrie's outrage.

"Who are these people?" The man a few places back from her shouted in a tone that demanded attention. "Why the fuck are you boarding them before us?! Seriously, what the hell is going on here? Hey, security man, I'm talking to you!"

The speaker might have been shouting at a lemon, for all the good it did him. The security officer kept right on ignoring the agitated line of people as he held one arm out, pointing up the stairs for any idiot among the bus passengers who couldn't figure out just where they were supposed to go. The whole thing drove home the point for Carrie that, to AOA, she and the kids were seen as no more than expendable assets. Sure, AOA would probably love to have a large compliment of people they could press into various labors and duties up at Cardinal's Nest to ensure the station ran smoothly, especially for all the bigwigs who were on their way up there, but it wouldn't be a deal-breaker for them. She understood with a cold certainty that they weren't truly safe until they were aboard. She knew now that AOA was not the wholesome corporation they claimed to be, and they definitely did not have the public-at-large's interests in mind. After the unflattering articles she'd dug up on Hubie Harrington, the utter lack of information she could find about AOA, coupled with all the utterly flabbergasting things she'd witnessed just now, and throughout this insane day, Carrie Montrois was left with no more doubts about the moral character of her husband's employer. She felt a wave of shame by association that hit her like a fastball to the chops.

Carrie felt Maisie stir uneasily at her side and looked down at the young girl as she once more perfectly articulated the unspoken thought Carrie and all the other adults in line were refusing to acknowledge, "Is there gonna still be room for us on the shuttle now, Mrs. Montrois?"

This unsettling question caused Carrie to snap out of her useless angst over bad life choices and once more focus all her energy on keeping her charges calm until they were all safely aboard the E-11. Carrie spoke to her small group in a soft, confident voice that she did not at all feel, "It's okay. I'm sure these people were just late. They had to board early 'cause they're important people. It's nothing to worry about. I'm sure there is plenty of space for all of us. We'll all get aboard. It won't be long now."

Her reassurances were having a positive effect that was obvious on both Maisie and Elias' faces. She could see the Sagal kids were taking comfort in a trusted source speaking to them with calm certainty. Their trust made the sight she watched unfolding at the entrance gate over their shoulders cause the wave of shame to smack her square once more, for Carrie was sure she had just lied to those trusting children. Judging from the sheer panic on the part of the security staff at the entrance gate, it was looking like a pretty safe bet anyway.

The gates were swung wide open as a handful of armored security Humvees screeched their way through the opening. Each Humvee had a fully armored security officer in black Kevlar vests and helmets standing behind a fifty-caliber machine gun mounted to the central turret of the vehicle. Each heavy gun was aimed behind their individual lumbering security patrol vehicle, straight out the gate and towards something Carrie could not quite make out. She could hear it though Even over the rumbling noise of the idling E-11 refuellable rockets, even through the panicked shouting of the security staff and prep crew families alike, through the throttling engines of the armored security Humvees, and the deafening sound of her own pounding heart, she could hear them coming. They were calling. They were moaning. They were growling. *How could it possibly be that loud?*

There must be hundreds of thousands of them, she thought in dis-believing horror. *My god, they're so close.*

She still couldn't see anything beyond the first fifty yards directly in front of the gates, where not much was happening. Dragging her attention away from the gate with a great deal of effort, she pulled all the children in close. When Carrie looked back up at the staircase, the last of the bus passengers was making his way through the hatchway. A moment after he cleared the portal, Hubert Harrington stepped back into the day's gloomy, gray sunlight. He hustled down the stairs, pulled the security officer at the stair's base a few steps up and whispered something to him that made the security officer nod. Carrie watched the exchange closely. The security officer didn't say a word. He just gave the one small nod and then walked shakily back down to the base of the staircase. She was still watching the man as he wiped his forehead with his shirtsleeve and drew in a deep breath. After a few seconds, he looked up at the first family in line. A few questions and answers were exchanged before he directed them to climb the stairs. "Okay, here we go, guys," Carrie said to the kids as she pointed towards the ascending family ahead of them.

"Oh, thank god," Dolly breathed out, sounding relieved. "Not a minute too soon either, eh, Carrie?"

"You can say that again." Carrie chose a moment when the kids weren't watching her and leaned in close to whisper discreetly, "Do you hear that noise?" Dolly glanced back at the gates before quickly returning her gaze to Carrie. She simply lifted her eyebrows, giving Carrie a look that seemed to perfectly convey the sense of fear and wonder that was currently pervading every single corner of Carrie's own mind. "I'll tell you what, Dolly, I'm going to want some answers from these people once we're up there, that's for sure."

"I'm right there with ya, Carrie," Dolly emphatically agreed. "I mean, these people have killed the world, haven't they? I mean ... that noise... My god, what've they done?"

After a few nervous moments in which the horrible, mil-lion-throated growl grew ever louder, Carrie and the kids had worked their way up the line. Only one family of three stood ahead of Dolly before their turn to climb the staircase arrived. The family of three, a mother and two young boys, quickly embarked on the climb after receiving the go-ahead gesture from the security officer.

Dolly stepped up next. The security officer turned to face her with a tablet in hand that Carrie assumed displayed some sort of passenger manifest. The man swiped the screen and then looked up at Dolly. He was about to speak when he suddenly looked back down at his tablet. He tapped his finger on the screen a couple times, then did a bit more finger-swiping, before finally lifting his gaze back up to Dolly. Once again, he opened his mouth to speak before quickly snapping it closed again. The security officer tucked his tablet under his forearm and stepped away from Dolly, climbing the few steps to bring himself alongside Hubert Harrington, who had rooted himself halfway up the staircase, making the families that boarded the shuttle edge their way around him. Carrie hadn't really noticed Harrington's strange behavior until now. She had just been content that the line was finally moving. But now that the security officer had run to his side to have a whispered conversation, just after darting away from Dolly without saying a word, all her earlier unease came flooding right back. "Something is wrong," she said, without even realizing she was speaking aloud. It just came out.

"What?" Dolly asked, looking back at Carrie with grave concern pervading her voice and body-language.

"I didn't mean... I think... I mean..." she couldn't find the right words for what she felt, but she knew a hammer was about to fall.

The security officer returned to the foot of the staircase as Dolly, Roxanna, Maisie and Elias were all staring at Carrie with confused and frightened faces. "Excuse me, ma'am," the security officer spoke up to get Dolly's attention. "Your name, ma'am?"

"Dolly Duchesne. My husband is Gabe Duchesne. He works in the fisher-"

"That'll do, Mrs. Duchesne. How many in your party? I have you down as a single occupant. Is that correct, ma'am?" The officer asked impatiently.

"Yes. My husband always wanted children. And we did try-"

"No need for all that, ma'am," the officer said, cutting Dolly off. "Go right ahead, Ma'am. Right up the stairs. Someone will help you to your seat once you reach the top."

Dolly reached back and took Carrie's hand into her own. She squeezed it reassuringly before taking her first steps up the staircase. As Carrie stepped up in front of the security officer, every ounce of hope left dangling on her heart leapt to its death upon her first glimpse of the consternation on the man's face. With seemingly great effort, the man began to ask a question, "H-h-ho-how... how... how many in your party, ma'am?"

"Four," she answered after a slight hesitation. "I'm Carrie Montrois. This is my daughter Roxanna. Her father is Jasper Montrois, head of security aboard Cardinal's Nest Station. This is Maisie and Elias Sagal. Their father is Dr. Perry Sagal, the station's hospital administrator. I'm responsible for them. Their father has entrusted me with getting them aboard."

The officer leaned in closer to Carrie and spoke softly, "I'm sorry, Mrs. Montrois, but we can only take two more. We've reached capacity limits."

"You what!?" Carrie said, loud enough for every man, woman and child left in line to hear. "What do you mean *capacity limits*?! We were promised passage to the station. My husband said you people assured him there would be passage for all the families of the prep crew. How can there not be space?! Is it because of those fucking government people you let board ahead of us?! That's it, ain't it?!"

"Ma'am, calm down, please," the security-officer pleaded while reaching out to place a quieting hand on Carrie's arm.

"Don't you touch me, goddammit," Carrie violently pulled her arm away from the man's grip. "Just step out of my fucking way and let me get these kids aboard this goddamn shuttle!"

"What's the problem down there, officer?" Hubert Harrington shouted down from his perch on the staircase.

"We've only got two slots left, sir. This lady has a party of four," the officer shouted back at Harrington.

"Well then, shout for a party of two and let's wrap this whole thing up," Harrington answered in a bored tone.

"What?!" Carrie screamed out, appalled. She was struck stiff with all-encompassing panic as she saw her disastrous premonition coming true before her eyes. The hammer had fallen. Things had definitely all gone wrong. "No!" She screamed, reaching to grab the security officer's shirt firmly in a balled fist. "We are getting aboard that shuttle. You hear me?" She told him.

The security officer knocked her hand loose of its grasp with relative ease and then looked back at her with what seemed like genuine empathy, "I'm sorry, ma'am, I really am, but there ain't nothing I can do. They ain't got room for me neither."

Carrie's response was lost under the noise of a new sound, a series of sharp, deafening crackles. She knew what the sound was before even turning to look at the entrance gate for confirmation. The machine guns mounted atop the security vehicles were firing through the chain links of the closed gate at a horde of infected and maniacal citizenry. The twin turrets perched fifteen feet off the ground at either end of the wide entrance gate added their fire to the thundering cacophony as well.

"That's it, officer. Pull the stairs away from the hull after I go through," Carrie heard Harrington shout at the security officer over the noise of the gunfire. Harrington cupped his hands and then shouted out at the worried mass of prep crew families, "The shuttle will return for you all shortly. Return to the main hangar and await its arrival there. You will be secure there. No need to panic, people!" He shouted, waving his arms for the line to disperse.

The security officer turned to execute Harrington's order and Carrie darted her hand out, grabbing the officer's arm just as the families in line behind pressed in close all around her, abandoning any pretense at an orderly cue. She nearly lost her grip on the security officer's arm in the chaos of the clamoring crowd, but she clamped down tight and dragged the man in close. "You said you had two slots, right?" The man gave the slightest nod of agreement and Carrie immediately thrust Maisie and Elias towards him. "Take them. They're a party of two. Just like you asked for. I was just looking out for them. Please take them," she begged. "You have the space. Please just take them. Please let them board. Please, you have the space." The officer gave another barely perceptible nod and gestured for Maisie and Elias to climb the staircase. "Oh, thank you, thank you," Carrie gushed as she gently pushed the Sagals toward safety.

Planting her feet firmly, Maisie Sagal would not be pushed another foot. "But what about you two?" She asked.

Carrie threw her arm over her daughter's shoulders and found a smile from somewhere deep within to favor the Sagal kids with. "Roxanna and I will be fine. You heard the man. They're sending the shuttle back down for us. But I promised your dad that I would get you two aboard *this* shuttle, and that's just what I intend to do. Now, get going before they close the hatchway." The Sagals were torn. Carrie could see that. Part of them wanted to run up the stairs and escape the carnage at the entrance gate, but a part of them must've know Carrie was lying about her confidence in the shuttle's return. That part of the kids was reluctant to leave their friends behind. "It's okay, kids, really. We'll be a few hours behind ya, that's all. Go on, hustle aboard now."

Maisie stepped up to Roxanna and engulfed the older girl in a final hug. Elias followed suit, wrapping Carrie in their first ever hug. They broke off the embraces simultaneously, and finding a brave smile of her own, Maisie took one of her brother's trembling hands. "I guess we'll see you guys soon then," she said in a quavering voice. The smile cracked a bit as they turned to march up the staircase.

"Hey! You can't just fucking leave us here!" An irate man shouted up at the hatchway as Elias and Maisie were being pulled through. The heavy spring-loaded hatch swung closed behind them and Carrie felt the fear level of the crowd around her swell to towering new heights.

"What the hell?! You can't just fucking leave us all here!" Another equally irate man shouted at the security officer as he drove the mobile staircase toward the hangar bays.

Carrie tucked her daughter into the cradle of her arm and bulldozed a path through the mob of abandoned prep crew families. She spied an open patch of tarmac and didn't stop trudging through the keyed-up crowd until she and Roxanna were standing inside its relative safety. Once there, she took the opportunity to ensure she and her daughter had escaped the tense mob without injury. Taking Roxanna by the shoulders, Carrie looked deep into her eyes, forcing her daughter to make eye-contact and hold it, "Are you hurt, Roxanna? Did anyone hurt you in there?"

After a long moment, in which Carrie could see a tiny bit of the fright drain out of her daughter's tear-filled blue eyes, Roxanna shook her head once, then thrust it deep into Carrie's bosom. Carrie wrapped her arms around her daughter and held her so tightly that she had to back off a little for fear she might've been hurting her. When Roxanna burst into a fit of muffled sobs against her chest, Carrie spat out all the useless platitudes: "It's okay, everything is fine, it'll be okay, don't cry, there is nothing to worry about." She hadn't even realized she was saying them, truth be told. She was as panicked and terrified as her fourteen-year-old daughter.

The second shuttle! The hopeful thought cut through the fog of terror clouding her mind. Carrie snapped her head around to look at the second transport cruiser. It was 500 yards to the south, but she could make out everything happening around its launchpad. The sight was just one more troubling, grim, hope-smashing view this day had given her. There was no longer a milling mass of prep crew families lined up next to the shuttle. There no longer was a mobile staircase leading into the E-11's belly-hatch. The hatch was all sealed up. It seemed that only the few dozen families in Carrie's line had been abandoned to the non-existent safety of the main hangar, where they were instructed to wait for the shuttle to return and collect them.

That proposition cemented its hopelessness beyond all doubt when Carrie looked back over at the gate. The massive chain-link entrance had an ever-growing mound of bullet-shredded corpses piling up in front of it, and as each new second passed, a new infected person was shot as they scrambled to the mound's top. To Carrie's horror, she realized the mound of dead would soon be so high the infected horde could just drop down over it. Which, in fact, was precisely what happened only a few seconds later. The first infected person to clear the gate fell to the asphalt tarmac beyond it, making no attempt to lessen his 15' drop. Carrie had no time to discover if the infected man's fall had done any damage to him, as a fifty-caliber machine gun tore him in half as soon as he plopped to the tarmac, sending up a red spray to join a low-hanging cloud of pink mist floating in the air just above the mound of shredded dead. The ferocity of the machine guns seemed to all be in vain however, for as soon as the first infected man who dropped over the gate was shot, two more plopped down beside him. And so, on and on it went. Carrie hadn't been watching for maybe thirty seconds before the first of the infected was clawing at the face of the nearest security officer.

The officer in question smashed her rifle butt into the infected man's face, winning her only the slightest respite in which to regroup and get her rifle pointed at the enemy. The barrel of the rifle was within a few inches from its target when the infected man cuffed it away with a clumsy swing of his arm. The security officer fired her rifle out of obvious panic and desperation. The rifle's fire struck two security officers a few feet away from her in the upper chest, neck and head. They fell to the tarmac like mangled and bloody sacks of potatoes. The horrible shock of what she had just done to her fellow officers must've been the cause of the hesitation in the woman, and what a deadly hesitation it was. The infected man suddenly lurched forward, sinking his blood-stained teeth deep Into her throat. The officer was dead within a few disgusting mouthfuls.

"Oh, Momma, they got her! They're over the gate!" Roxanna shouted out in absolute horror.

Carrie covered her daughter's eyes with her hands and pulled her back in tight to her chest. Whispering more of the mindless platitudes, she spun in a circle with Roxanna cradled tightly, searching for a refuge from the madness. Hubert Harrington had suggested the main hangar as sanctuary, but Carrie could see the it was only a few hundred yards from the swarm of violence at the entrance gate. It would be overrun within moments of the gate's collapse, she guessed. She needed a vehicle of some sort, a vehicle and an alternate exit off the tarmac to go with it. Getting away from this launchpad in a motorized vehicle was the only chance they were ever going to have to stay ahead of that heaving mass of mindless, infected monster-people. Unfortunately, after completing all 360 degrees of her spin, she saw no obvious egress, nor means of travel.

A dreadful new sound chose that moment to add its terrible notes to the odious symphony filling the air around her. Over the wretched shrieks and hungry groans of the infected, over the endless pulsing machine gun fire of the security officers, over the tireless wailing terror of the families, Carrie both felt and heard that new dreadful sound claim its place of primacy over all the others. It was the thundering rumble of the refuellable rockets of two E-11

Transport Cruisers blasting their respective crafts into the first stage of launch. A powerful burst of air, visible from the tremendous cloud of dust kicked up in its wake, hammered into Carrie, Roxanna and the rest of the abandoned families. Many people were thrown to the ground from the force of the impact, but Carrie and her daughter kept their feet.

"They're leaving us! Oh my god! We're all dead!" A voice called out in fear and grief from among the people still standing. "Look!" Another voice shouted. "They're over the gate! They're on the security men! There's nowhere left to go!"

The alarmed shouts quickly began to overlap each other, and in the space of a single breath, all out anarchy spread rapidly throughout the unfortunate abandoned. Those unlucky enough to have not yet risen back to their feet were trampled in the stampeding disarray. People ran away from the carnage at the gate in every direction of the compass. Carrie was forced to fall to a knee as the mass of fleeing people broke around her and Roxanna like a rushing stream around a boulder. After a moment, the press of panicked humanity around them thinned out and Carrie was able to shamble, with her daughter still clinging tightly to her chest, to a spot a few dozen yards away, relatively clear of the chaos enveloping the launchpad.

As she reached her new resting position, the twin shuttles had climbed to about a hundred feet off the surface of the tarmac. Carrie glanced up just in time to see their second-stage boosters engage. Powerful jets of super-heated fuel pounded down to the surface with an unbelievable intensity. She watched as a dozen of the fleeing people unlucky enough to be caught in that blinding blast disappeared instantly from existence in the blue-white jetstream. Dozens more were only a few yards from the impact-zone of those secondary boosters. Shock froze her stiff. She could do nothing but watch in horror as the clothes of those poor souls burned away with bright orange flames, disintegrating on their bodies before her very eyes to expose hideously burned torsos and legs, pock-marked here and there with scraps of smoldering fabric.

"Mommy. I'm so scared. I'm sorry, Mommy, but I'm so scared," Carrie's teen daughter shouted up at her in a frightful squeak.

"Don't be sorry, sweetie. I'm scared too. But we can't stay here." Carrie's mental fog cleared long enough for her to understand the importance of that simple truth. "We have to run, Roxanna. I need you to be brave for me. We both need to be brave." Carrie pointed towards the opposite end of the tarmac and used her other hand to push her daughter's chin a few inches to the left, dragging her line of sight towards the large gray hangar-like structure her outstretched finger was indicating, "Do you see that building, sweetie?" Carrie waited for a nod of acknowledgment from her daughter that came after a brief moment. "You and I are going to run there. Okay, baby?" Once again, a head nod from Roxanna. "We might find a way off this launchpad through the back of that building."

It seemed plausible enough. It was far away, but Carrie was still pretty sure it was seated right up against the launchpad's tall fence. Relatively few of the panicked people had fled in that direction too. Carrie counted that a point in their favor, especially if there really was a vehicle in that hangar-looking, gray building. Then she wouldn't have to deal with a struggle for control of the car. *If there was one in there at all,* her inner cynic whispered to her. There were a lot of ifs left for Carrie now, in truth, and very few immediate answers.

"What if the doors to that building are closed?" Roxanna shouted at her over the suffocating noise around them.

"Then we'll deal with that when we get there," she shouted back. And so, they would. Carrie took her daughter by the hand and waited for one more nod to be sure Roxanna was ready to run. With that confirmation, she hooked the duffel bag hanging off her shoulder around her head and neck so she could have one hand free for balance. Then she took off running towards the gray building.

Her daughter kept pace for the first hundred yards or so, but soon enough, Roxanna began to lag behind. The terrified teen was skipping and panting a few paces behind Carrie, struggling to keep up with her mother's frantic pace. Carrie was looking back at her exhausted daughter when the duffel bag hanging at her side entangled itself in Roxanna's legs. Roxanna lurched forward into Carrie, and thus, entangled her mother's legs as well. Daughter and mother both went crashing to the asphalt, their luggage scattering its contents onto the ground all around them.

Carrie was up almost instantly on her knees, stuffing clothes and toiletries back into suitcases, when she once more glanced towards the entrance gate. There were only a few Humvees left that the infected horde had not yet overrun. She watched as the tires of the surviving Humvees screeched and squealed, reversing at top speed away from the gate, still pouring lead into the raving horde from their machine gun turrets to little visible effect. A metallic snapping, groaning, wrenching sound at the gate cut through the concert of tragedy. Carrie looked over and saw the entire 50' swinging entrance gate collapse under the unstoppable weight and pressure of the infected horde. The mass of sick and crazed citizens crawled over one another to scramble through the now-open gateway, so many infected people they seemed like one living organism.

It wasn't just one monster, however. It was thousands of individual monsters. Though they did seem to share a single unified purpose: to kill and spread the infection. Some of the overwhelmed security officers seemed to have just been bitten or clawed a few times and then left alone. Other officers, the infected horde lingered over, pulling out giant handfuls of wriggling intestines and glistening organs to feast upon. She didn't understand why that would be. There was no pattern. No method to the madness. Just that alone, madness, utter madness.

Carrie suddenly realized she had been watching said madness for far too long. The infected were sprinting out in every direction towards the fleeing prep crew families. The nearest infected were now only fifty yards from Carrie and Roxanna. Abandoning the luggage, she ripped her daughter's duffel from her shoulder, tossing it to the asphalt at their feet. "Come on, baby. As fast as you can now," she stammered out between breaths.

The Montrois once again sprinted for the gray building at the opposite end of the launchpad. Each step Carrie took towards its possible safety seemed to push that distant building farther and farther away. All the while, the terrible growls and moans behind them grew ever louder. "Mommy, I'm scared! They are going to get us," Roxanna shouted out in a voice laced with inescapable fear.

"Just keep running, baby! We can make it!" The level of horror coursing through Carrie's body was indescribable. It was unthinkable.

It was unknowable. She was certain no human being had ever been so utterly, hopelessly, and absolutely afraid. And then Roxanna stumbled. "No!" Carrie cried out, struggling to drag her daughter back to her feet.

Roxanna regained her footing fully within a few stumbled paces, but after only a few dozen yards further across the asphalt surface of that tarmac of horrors, five or six of the infected fell on them from behind all at once. Carrie was shoved in the back and thrown so violently to the asphalt that her grip on her daughter's hand was knocked loose, along with all the breath in her lungs. She instantly scrambled and flailed her hand about, desperately seeking Roxanna's. All she found was pain. Jagged teeth locked around the flesh of her hand, viciously tearing away a huge chunk of what was once her soft, meticulously lotioned skin. She was just about to scream out in pain when a sudden sound pierced through all the others. Roxanna's pain-racked shriek was a torment far worse than the blood-crazed maniacs tearing Carrie's flesh away a chunk at a time.

The only thing worse than the sound of her daughter's screams was their sudden absence. Through the feet of her infected attackers, Carrie could see a gaggle of infected tearing loose, dripping red chunks of pink flesh from her baby-girl's lifeless body. Then a blinding pain in her shoulder forced Carrie to roll onto her back. The movement did nothing for the pain. The infected woman who had inflicted it only found a new patch of shoulder to sink her teeth into. Carrie watched with trance-like fascination as the woman chewed the chunk of her flesh, sending a gush of bright-red blood cascading down her chin.

She pulled her gaze from the infected woman to stare fixedly behind her at the twin transport cruisers, now just two barely perceivable dots in the afternoon sky. Carrie kept right on staring at those lunar-bound shuttles as an infected man went down on his knees beside her to sink his terrible teeth deep into her jugular. When he yanked back his head, a large chunk of Carrie's neck-flesh came away with it, spurting a bright-red spray across her eyes. The fleeing shuttles were the last thing Carrie Montrois ever saw, as her life was washed away in red.

CHAPTER 2

PERRY

The gathered crowd was densely packed and extremely agitated. *Damn, it's just a hair's breadth short of downright volatile around here,* Dr. Perry Sagal thought as he elbowed his way through the edgy lunar station employees and their family members. The task was proving to be a difficult one. Each of his hands were encumbered by one or the other of his two children, and there was no force in the universe that could pry free his grip now. After the ordeal Elias and Maisie had endured to reach the safety of Cardinal's Nest, and the previous nerve-racking day he'd spent wearing a path in the kitchen floor of Monty's living quarters with his incessant and compulsive pacing, the comfort of holding his children's hands in his own was one to which he was greedily clinging.

Yesterday had been horrible for Perry, possibly the worst day in his life, and he'd definitely had a few bad ones to compare it with. Losing his beloved Joan to that drunken asshole had been a bad one, for example. *But at least there wasn't the stress of wondering,* he thought. With Joan it had just been a late-night phone call and a blunt, just-the-facts report. It was brutal and it gutted him, but at least there was no ambiguity about it. Yesterday had been the opposite. All day long he went from one worry to the next, frustrated beyond all reason at the fact that he could do nothing to help his children.

If his trust in Carrie Montrois had not been as great as it was, Perry would have most likely crumbled to nothing from the ungovernable stress. He was pretty sure there were large clumps of hair missing from either side of his head. He never actually remembered seeing any of his graying black hair in his hands when he would pull them loose of the vise-grip they maintained on the thinning tufts of hair along the sides of his head, but that didn't mean anything. There was very little about yesterday he actually could remember clearly. It had become a blur of frustrated panic, right up until the moment the airlock hatch rolled open in the Lunar Dock Terminal inside Branch 2 and he was able to actually physically lay eyes on Elias and Maisie.

The euphoric relief of that beautiful sight had shocked its way through to the ends of his soul. Perry had paused only a moment to enjoy that comfort before bullying his way through the dazed crowd of passengers to wrap both his children in a bone-crushing hug. The nerves of the previous day poured out of him in heaving sobs drowned out by the chorus of similar reunions unfolding all around them. Perry finally had a hold of his beloved children, and he was never letting go.

Although, he did experience a brief pause of hesitation over dragging his children along with him to this make-shift town hall. He knew there would definitely be raised voices and curse-laced shouts at the very least, but the fear of losing track of his Maisie and Elias for even a few more moments overrode any hesitation he felt in dragging them along with him. And, judging by the look of the crowd, Perry wasn't the only one to make that calculation. He could see those prep crewmen aboard the transport cruisers when they blasted off from that secluded launchpad in West Virginia who were lucky enough to have their spouses, children, and significant others clinging to their sides as well.

Perry finished plowing his way to the front of the crowd and took up position a few feet from a makeshift dais that had been erected by pushing a couple of cheap folding tables together. They were in the Grand Rotunda, a cavernous, seven-sided central chamber at the heart of Cardinal's Nest station. The dais had been placed near the center of its humongous domed rotunda. AOA's logo was stamped in the center of the floor, gleaming with a polished beauty, twenty feet long, and done up in sixties-sci-fi stylized maroon and silver font. The dome of the Grand Rotunda was composed of dozens of giant curving white panels. Embedded in the dome directly above the logo, an oculus stretched seventy feet in diameter and was sealed over by a multi-paneled transparent screen. Sprouting off from the rotunda were the arcing mouths of seven capacious branches, each one twisting outwards from the Grand Rotunda in their own distinct fashion, according to the practicality demanded by the contents within.

The dais was centered just over the giant silver O of the AOA logo. Perched atop its precarious safety, stood Hubert Harrington. He was waving his hands wildly above his head in a vain attempt to quiet the cantankerous crowd. Perry looked behind the dais and saw American President Daniel Raferty; Derek Antoneson, the British Prime Minister; Abigail Hoffreyer, Chancellor of Germany; President of China, Zhang Yong Chen; and French President Andre Bergevin huddled up conspiratorially, speaking to each other in whispers. Perry couldn't be sure—he didn't keep up with politics as much as he should—but he thought he recognized a few other world leaders among the milling group of business-suited people gathered behind the dais as well. The fact that such illustrious dignitaries would yield the floor to Harrington seemed to say a lot about the dynamic at play aboard Cardinal's Nest. Though Perry couldn't be sure if it was the fact that AOA was truly running the show up here, or if it was just that all the world leaders were reluctant to associate themselves with the debacle that took place at the launchpad. *Debacle is far too soft a word,* Perry thought right before his friend Monty shoved his way to the front of the crowd right alongside him.

Perry looked over at the Cardinal's Nest's security commander, but Monty did not turn to face him. From Monty's profile, Perry could see he wore an expressionless look on his normally bright face. Monty was a tall, dark-complected, dark-haired white man. He was roughly 6'3" and about 260 pounds, Perry guessed. His frame was thick, but muscular. It wasn't what one would call chiseled. Instead, Perry would classify it as well-proportioned. His body was rough edged, yet somehow sleek-lined as well, and it showed its fair share of scars. It had the power of intimidation before a word was ever spoken, belying the man's nature. Perry supposed such a physique came in handy, however, in the security industry. He remembered their first meeting, and the sense of unease he'd felt as Monty wrapped his giant hand around Perry's own comparatively dainty and smooth paw. The strength behind the arm that shook his in that moment had put a definite and memorable impression deep into Perry's core. Though the feeling was almost instantly washed away by the wide grin that spread across the big man's face, and the genuine warmth in his greeting.

There was no warmth in the man that stood beside him now, however. Monty had been just as nervous yesterday as Perry was. While Perry was wearing a path in Monty's kitchen floor, a similar path was worn into the carpet of the living room by Monty himself. Neither of the men were the type to offer false hope to the other, so tho two relatively new friends spent most of the day only a few feet from each other, yet hardly a word had been exchanged between them after Monty finished his last phone call with Carrie. Perry had never seen the security commander with the sterling reputation in any state other than calm, cool, smooth, and unflappably collected. It gave Perry some solace for the shame he felt over his own pan-icked behavior to see his big, level-headed friend acting in much the same fashion.

Perry had been standing right alongside Monty as that giant bay door in the terminal rolled up ever so slowly. He didn't remember leaving Monty's side. His feet had just carried him, unthinkingly, straight to his young children. His euphoric reunion with them had caused him to miss the fact that half of the passengers who exited the transport cruiser were not prep crew families at all. It was only after those first few moments of jubilation elapsed, that Perry realized there were a dozen or so prep crew workers desperately searching among the passengers for their own family members. And then he saw his friend Monty among the frantic searchers. The look on the security commander's face had instantly shriveled a good deal of Perry's joy in his own familial reunion.

He was just about to run to his friend and aid in his search when Maisie had reached out and pulled him back by the arm. She'd told him about her parting with Carrie and Roxanna, and how she and her brother had been the last two people to board the transport cruiser. Maisie had told him of the horror unfolding at the gate as she and her brother climbed through the cruiser's hatchway. She'd told of a black bus pulling up and roughly a hundred people piling out to board the transport ahead of them.

Perry remembered looking out into the crowd as Maisie recounted to him what had transpired and seeing a kind of dual image. It seemed to him that most of the crowd delighted in their happy reunions, while a good portion were in an irrational, panicked and chaotic state, seeking their families, or some sort of answers. It wasn't hard for Perry to put two and two together and figure out what must've happened. *AOA boarded the government officials and their family members ahead of the prep crew families*, he'd thought, with sorrowful certainty. All around the Lunar Dock Terminal, the people around him slowly woke up to the reality of what had occurred. Shouts and demands for answers had soon filled the echoing chamber, and a few heartbeats before the boiling-point, an AOA representative shouted for their attention. The nervous man had told them to gather in the Grand Rotunda where AOA would address all their concerns and answer all their questions.

Perry had dragged his children right from their joyous reunion at the terminal to the chasmal Grand Rotunda, with what seemed like every person currently aboard the station walking alongside them. He'd kept an eye on Monty for most of that journey. The security commander hadn't spoken a word, or walked with any unseemly hurry. He wore the same blank expression for the entire length of the long walk to the Grand Rotunda that he was currently wearing right now in front of the makeshift dais. Perry found that expressionless face extremely troubling, and dug deep for some words of comfort to share with his friend.

He was spared whatever clumsy attempt at consolation he was about to voice when Hubert Harrington shouted out through cupped hands, "Ladies and Gentlemen, please, if you could all quiet down, all your questions will be answered. Please quiet down, folks. I understand you have a lot of questions and concerns, and we will cover them all. Just calm down now." It was then that Harrington noticed Monty standing in the front row of the crowd, "Oh, Commander Montrois, thank god you're here. Could you help me out and quiet this crowd for me?"

Monty did not move a muscle, nor change the look on his face one iota. He looked up at Harrington and held eye-contact with the CEO for a long moment but did not speak a single word. Harrington must've realized his mistake in asking a man whose family wasn't beside him for any assistance just then because he quickly turned from Monty and went back to his shouted pleas for silence. Slowly but surely, the crowd behind Perry began to settle down. The man slowly lowered his waving hands after the expansive hall quieted enough for his shouts to be clearly heard. "Okay, folks, thank you for your attention," Harrington began. "We realize you all must be worried about those family members who weren't aboard the transport cruisers. Let me first say that they are currently safe in a secure location at the launchpad. We are now in the process of refueling the cruisers to send them back to pick up everyone that we were very unfortunately forced to leave behind due to ship capacity regulations. However, there is no need to worry. The launchpad is well guarded by over seventy highly trained security officers and surrounded by a high-grade steel barbed-wire fence. They will be secure until the transport cruiser can return for them, I assure you."

"Bullshit! That ain't what I heard," a disgruntled voice called out from the crowd.

"Yeah, the launchpad was being overrun when the shuttles took off. I just heard it right from the lips of one of your own goddamn executives," another angry voice added.

"Oh, no! That's not true, is it?! Tell me that's not true," a lonely woman in the crowd cried out in horror.

One shout or cry began to overlap the next, and within a few moments, the entire crowd seemed to be wailing at Harrington. Perry saw a flicker of frustration cross Harrington's face, but it was gone just as soon as it came. He once again waved his hands over his head and shouted for silence. "I assure you, folks, your loved ones are perfectly secured," he promised. "The transport cruisers will return for them just as soon as the ships are refueled, and we gain proper clearance authority."

"What the hell does that mean? *Proper clearance authority?*" A confused man asked. "Who is left down there to grant clearance authority? The government is shut down. The fucking bastards are right there behind ya," the irate man pointed to the milling mass of important-looking people behind Harrington. "The fucking infection was spreading faster than syphilis in a goddamn whorehouse down there. There ain't no one left on Earth to give you clearance. Everyone is either running and hiding for their lives, or they've been killed by the infected, or maybe even become one of those fucking monster-motherfuckers themselves."

"Yeah, who the fuck do you think you're kidding, Hubie?!" A tall woman shouted out from the middle of the crowd. "Our fucking family members were down there when it was happening. They saw the horde attacking the gate with their own damn eyes. And we been watching the fucking newsfeeds up here too. There was only one of 'em left on the air before the shuttles arrived, by the way. Who knows if any are broadcasting now. We know shit went bad down there, Hubie. Now, quit bullshitting us and give it to us straight! You gave the prep crew families' places aboard the shuttles to those government fucks behind ya, didn't you?" The woman asked indignantly. "Have the courage to say it, you heartless fuck."

"They promised us our families would have a place aboard the shuttles. One of your AOA reps promised us yesterday morning when news of the infection broke that our families would have a place aboard the shuttles," a man a few feet further back put in. "They fucking promised us."

Harrington didn't like being spoken to like this. Perry could see that plainly on his face. To his credit though, he brushed off his anger quickly and let a patronizing smile wash across his lips. "I understand this is difficult for everyone, but a little trust is what we need from you right now. We promised your families would be with you, and we will do everything in our power to uphold that promise. We just need you folks to bear with us right now. There is a lot of confusion, obviously, but we are working to the best of our capabilities at this moment. We just really need you folks to bear with us. We need you to return to your quarters now. I promise that you will all be kept in the loop with any updates on the situation, but we cannot afford chaos to take hold aboard this station. We need you all to stay orderly and remain patient with us. Please, just return to your quarters and show your families their new living arrangements."

"What about the rest of us whose families you left behind?" Asked a solitary man in the crowd. "Are we just supposed to remain calm knowing our families were left back on Earth while some fucking apocalyptic plague is raging?!"

"Your families are being protected by our top-notch security teams," Harrington said, trying to placate the man. "There is no reason to panic, and no reason for the disrespectful language."

"You've abandoned my wife and daughter to the damned!" a deep voice shouted out, piercing through all the others.

Perry turned to see that the mournful, bitter, angry shout had come from Monty. They were the first words the big man had spoken in hours. His face showed its first signs of animation since discovering his wife and daughter were not aboard the shuttle. A silence fell over the echoing chamber in the wake of Monty's shout. Perry watched as Harrington looked down at his security commander with a puzzled stare. "I assure you, Commander, no one has been abandoned. Just as soon as we are granted clearance, the shuttles will return for your family. I would expect a little more professionalism and reserve from our security commander ... but, given the circumstances, I suppose I understand. And I'll go ahead and forgive you this one outburst. Why don't you go back to your living quarters and regain your composure, Commander? We will contact you when we need you," Harrington said in a tone dripping venom.

Monty held Harrington's gaze for a few endless, tense moments before abruptly turning away and barging through the crowd. Perry watched his friend head off down Branch 4, which lead to the living quarters, never once looking back at the dais, nor the dishonest businessman perched atop it. After the echo of Monty's retreating steps faded, the crowded chamber once again filled with shouted demands for actual answers. Perry could see they would get no more out of Harrington than they already had.

Cupping his hands to his mouth once more, the man shouted again for the crowd to return to their living quarters. After a few more barely audible entreaties, Harrington gave it up for a bad job and leaped down from atop the tables. He set his stride toward Branch 1 with no delay. AOA's corporate boardrooms, office spaces, and VIP living quarters lay within, as well as Cardinal's Nest Station's control room at the end of a long and lavish alleyway. The sycophantic world leaders and AOA executives knew then what was good for them, turning as one to follow closely on the CEO's heels.

CHAPTER 3
ABNER

Infection Event: Day 57

It was easy for Abner Normie Hyun to forget just how nervous he had been on his first recon mission, so he drew in a calming breath and reminded himself of the panic-fueled adrenaline he'd felt surging through every fiber of his being on that seemingly long-ago day before offering any advice to Nate Novocaine Calney Barker strug gling to strap himself into the jumpseat beside him. Once he was sure he could speak without sounding condescending, Abner elbowed Novocaine softly in the upper arm, "Hey, man, relax. Take a breath." Abner leaned as close as he could and pointed to the locking buckle of Novocaine's harness, "You have to click the green half of the buckle in before the red, or else it won't ever lock in place."

"I know that," Novocaine retorted hotly.

"Relax, Novocaine. I didn't mean to say that you didn't. I remember my first recon; that's all I'm saying. I was stressed out too. I didn't mean nothing by it, bro. But you are going to want that harness secure when we hit the atmosphere, trust me. If you ain't strapped in tight, you'll be tossed around the hull of this Star Hawk like a toddler shaking a moth in a Mason jar."

"I know that. I'm not an idiot. And I obviously know how to do it. I was buckled in during takeoff, you may recall. And I'm buckled in again now as well. See?" Barker asked, pointing to his recent accomplishment.

"Yeah, you sure are," Abner answered condescendingly. "You sure you're up for this? Ain't no shame in backing out and staying with the

Star Hawk with Gerwitz and Calvin. It ain't fun down there, Cainey. It's a fucking nightmare that can—and has—driven men mad. Better men than you, no offense."

"Yeah, why would I take any offense to that?" Novocaine asked sardonically. "I know what I'm getting into, Normie." Novocaine used the playful sobriquet Jasper Montrois had lovingly bestowed upon Abner in a tone reeking of condescension. "Just because I'm not one of you security dudes doesn't mean I'm not willing to do my part, or that I'm not as capable of doing just as good a job on these missions as any one of you."

"Well, I guess we'll see, won't we?" Abner asked with a grin.

"Just worry about your own duties, and I'll handle mine," Novocaine responded.

"Be sure you do that. We'll have enough goddamn worries to deal with down there without some newbie freezing up and getting people killed."

"Have you got some problem with me, Abner?" Novocaine asked.

"It's just ... I know your type, is all. You were full of big talk and chest pounding in the mission briefing room, not to mention around the living quarter's Rec District and cafeteria halls these past few days. You've been quite the big talker around there, I hear. Matter of fact, I hear you were saying it was going to be you that finds an Alpha Specimen from among the Damned to bring back here for the AOA science team to study. You're gonna be a hero, ain't ya, Cainey? We security officers are just fucking around on these missions, right? Isn't that what you said? It's our fault we haven't found any sign of one yet. Isn't that right? The only reason we haven't brought one back must be because of our gross incompetence, right? But now that you're with us, we're sure to find the secret to all of mankind's problems. You're the hero that's come to save us all. Ain't ya, Novocaine?" Abner paused for a moment, but it was clear Novocaine had nothing to say. "Yet, here you are struggling to fasten your safety harness while beads of sweat pour down your face. You're all talk, Cainey. You're a hollowman, a hindrance more than an asset, in my opinion, 'cause we don't need hollowmen patrolling with us down on the ground. No, when it's boots on the ground and you're hip-deep in the shit, you can't afford to have some hollow husk of a man out there with ya.

That's how teammates end up dead: one man not willing to play his part when the shit hits the fan. That's when it all falls apart, Cainey. We can't have tha-"

"I ain't no fucking hollowman!" Novocaine interrupted. "I know my duties down there, Normie. Thanks for your vote of confidence. Why don't you just worry about your crazy commander buddy and mind your fucking business about me. I can handle myself. I'm not afraid of the Damned. I will keep my shit together. Can you say that for sure about him," Novocaine said, pointing to the corner of the cargo hold where Security Commander Jasper Montrois was strapped into a jumpseat, his chin resting on his chest and eyelids pressed closed in heavy sleep.

"Hold your fucking tongue about the commander! You don't know shit about what he's been through... what all of us have been through," Abner said, indicating the ten other squadmembers strapped into jumpseats along the cargo hold's walls all around them. "Commander Montrois has saved every one of these people's lives on one or the other of these recon missions. Speak another ill word about him, and I will fucking gut you right here and now."

"Stow that shit, Hyun," Security Sergeant Marge Hamill shouted at him from her jumpseat across the hull. "Whatever the fuck you think of each other, or the commander, you can fucking save it until all of us are back safe on this Star Hawk with another successful mission under our belts. We are going to need each other down there. Abner, it ain't Cainey's fault that this is his first mission. He stepped up when no one else would. We owe him some thanks for that, I think. And Cainey, as for you, stow whatever opinions of the commander you may have right here and now. You've taken on a huge responsibility here, and none of us can afford you taking it lightly. The commander's orders are all there is down there, and you will carry them out without hesitation. You understand?"

Barker gave the smallest of affirmative nods, and Hamill raised her voice so all the squadmembers in the Star Hawk's cargo hold could hear her, "Turn all your focus toward your duties and trust your squadmates to carry out theirs. We all come back. Y'all hear me? Everyone comes back!"

"Everyone comes back!" All the veteran squadmembers echoed back, Abner included.

He wanted to be angry with Marge for scolding him, but he knew she was right. Sergeant Marge, as most of the squad called her, was a dark-haired, dark-eyed and dark-skinned woman in her early thirties, with a heart-shaped face and commanding eyes. She stood about 5'8" and had an athletic physique that did not, and could not know exhaustion, no matter how hard it was pushed. The moments during these recons when the shit was at its thickest, Marge seemed to exist in a state of otherworldly calm. Nothing broke her poise and meticulous professionalism. She mowed those snarling bastards down like she was hammering a nail into a piece of plywood in the comfort of her own workshop. Abner admired her for that, and for her often irritating ability to always be right. *Just like she is now, ya asshole, and you know it,* he thought. Abner hadn't meant to get into it like that with Barker in the first place. Marge was right, Cainey was the only one who volunteered, and, if Abner was being honest, he was holding out a little hope of finding an Alpha Specimen himself. He shouldn't begrudge another man that dream.

Most days Abner was certain that Monty, Eddie, Pedro, Donny, and all the rest of his like-minded teammates were right in thinking the Alpha Specimens was most likely just some myth the AOA scientists were propping up to give the community false hope. Most days he was sure it was all just a piece of propaganda Harrington, and the impotent world leaders, were spreading around to keep their workforce quiet, happy, docile sheep, mindlessly going about the tasks they'd all been assigned within a week of coming aboard station. Abner watched as AOA blinded them all by manipulating their predictable greed, waving food and entertainment credits for good work and civil conduct in their faces to keep them focused on their work, and not the fucking apocalypse just 239,000 miles away. It was obvious to Abner that AOA was trying to hide their culpability in the Infection Event in some way at least, and yet, he sometimes could not help himself from hoping the hypothesis of the Alpha Specimen was true, and that they might truly take the surface back someday soon.

Yesterday, in one of the brief conversations he and Monty had shared since The Event, Monty had been grumbling to him about how

AOA was just grasping at straws and making up lies to cover their asses. Abner had nodded his head and mumbled some non-committal nonsense, but inside, he wasn't sure he agreed. He had been thinking about the conviction on the face of that AOA scientist who had debriefed the team before that mission. There was no falsehood in his face when the mousy little dude explained his team's hypothesis about the Alphas. The man seemed to genuinely believe of their existence, and of the security team's ability to find one. Plus, the data they'd been shown, and the reasoning behind the science team's hypothesis, had seemed sound enough to Abner. In fact, it seemed way too sound, and a bit too exotic to have just been some tale AOA and the government heads cobbled together at the last second. And despite the evidence of his eyes, and the mutterings of his friends, he could not quite bring himself to believe that a global corporation, along with eight world leaders, could ever become so corrupted that they would use the lives of his team as some kind of toss away toys. No, Abner was not quite as jaded as Monty and some of the others, not yet anyway.

That wasn't exclusively due to his faith in the general decency of humanity, however. Most of the optimism that existed in his heart was there because of Stevie. Even now, strapped to his jumpseat, veteran of eleven recon missions, the thing he found most unbelievable about his life was the fact that he ever got an honest-to-God angel like Stevie Tremaine to marry his dumb ass. Abner knew his beautiful, redheaded, plump-lipped, freckle-faced wife was proud of him. She never failed to tell him so, but he couldn't help the urges he often felt to do something reckless in the hopes of impressing her. *Like taking this security job, ya damn fool.*

He had definitely come to regret that impulse lately. He hated leaving his wife's side for a second now. Being hundreds of thousands of miles apart during these recons, and not knowing if he'd seen her soft, warm face for the last time was getting damn near unbearable. He longed for mission's end and a return to the loving comfort of her arms. She was his everything. Abner dreaded this upcoming mission as much or even more so than any prior excursion down to the hell of Earth. He wished only to bury his head in her chest and let the madness of fate fade to oblivion.

Then the yellow signal light on the ceiling of the cargo hold suddenly began flashing. "Okay, everyone, grab onto something. Entering the atmosphere in ten seconds," Marge Hamill shouted out into the sudden silence.

Abner grabbed the harness straps that lay across his chest in either hand and tensed for the jolt and shudder that came with atmosphere entry in the belly of a Star Hawk. He let out a breath just as the yellow light stopped blinking and the red light in the row of ceiling-mounted signal lights immediately took up its pattern. No matter how well you managed to prepare yourself for the sudden immense pressure of massive G-forces pressing down on you, it always hit you harder than you were expecting. *Twelve of these damn trips now, you'd think you could control your stomach, Abner,* he thought, forcing his breakfast back down his throat.

The descent was just as rough as all the others. It even seemed to get a little worse than most as they hurtled through the sky. *Must be shitty weather over West Virginia,* Abner figured. *That's what comes from the lack of planning and the rushed nature of these fucking recons.* No one even bothered to check what type of weather conditions they would have upon landing. Abner figured all the planning that went into their recons was some AOA bigwig asshole sitting in a room surrounded by other bigwig assholes and closing his eyes to point to a random spot on a map. With the wild-goose-chases they'd been sent on so far, Abner figured it couldn't be much more scientific a process than that. He was afraid of where they might be sent when they ran out of places within a safe distance of the launchpad to explore. It was dangerous to stay down on the surface for more than a few hours, four tops. The Damned always sniffed them out, and they'd be harried by an ever-growing mob of them all the way back to the launchpad.

The Damned. The name always made Abner think of the day the transport cruisers arrived with the prep worker's families. Which was fitting, seeing as how the station residents had quickly adopted the moniker when talking about the infected after that day. It had become common jargon in no time. It drove Abner crazy. Whenever he heard it, he'd be reminded of that day and his old friend calling them *the Damned* as he blamed Harrington to his face for his wife and daughter's abandonment.

He had never seen Monty like that before, and they'd been through some emotional shit together in the service. Calling the infected *the Damned* kept reminding Abner that Monty had been a changed man ever since that day. He was still a great leader. *And that moron Novocaine Barker would see that with his own two eyes on this mission*, Abner was sure of that. Monty seemed fearless, and more than a little maniacal, in the face of the raving hordes of infected. But despite how vicious and ruthless he became when the hordes were on them, he had never shirked his duty for a moment. The man was unflappable, making all the right calls in just the right moments and only losing five security officers in eleven of the most intense and dangerous combat missions any paramilitary unit had ever faced before.

He was his usual professional and spectacularly talented self in that regard. But as for his old warm and inviting personality, Abner hadn't seen the merest glimmer since he cried out those words: *the Damned*. It seemed to him to be a cosmic insult for Monty's bright, magnetic personality to be taken away along with everything else that had been lost. It was too gratuitous a fate to add the shining soul of his dear friend to the daunting casualty list. Still, as much as it pained him to admit, he feared his old army battle buddy was lost forever.

A shudder of turbulence rocked the craft so hard that all clarity of mind was thumped out of Abner. His head slammed from side to side as his body strained against the tightly constricting safety harness. There followed a sudden weightless sensation that went as swiftly as it came, and he once again fought to control his flailing body in the violent turbulence. With no portholes in the cargo hold of the dirigible, there was no way to know their altitude, or what kind of weather the Star Hawk plunged through. The cockpit, with its large paneled transparent windscreen, was walled off from the cargo hold, and only accessible by a hatch in the bulkhead a few feet to Abner's right. All they could do was trust in the piloting expertise of Gillian Gerwitz and her copilot Barry Calvin. The crack duo hadn't failed the security team yet, and Abner felt a little guilty to doubt their skills even for a moment, but they'd never had a landing quite this rough. *It's gotta be a hell of a storm out there,* he thought with growing surety.

Then suddenly, the craft's shuddering ceased as the Star Hawk began to rapidly decrease its rate of descent. *We must be below cloud level. Good, should be no problems now ... short of a lightning strike, anyway,* he thought, because Abner was pretty sure they were landing in the middle of a thunderstorm. And judging by the violence of the turbulence, it was probably a big one. The craft slowly began to level out, and nearly all of the G-forces that had been sitting atop Abner's chest, gradually disintegrated. Followed closely on the heels of the pressure's release, Abner blew out a long, tense breath, then drew in a deep, fresh replacement of rich recycled oxygen.

This being his twelfth descent to the Earth's surface in the belly of a Star Hawk, he was able to tell the stages of their landing by the motion inside the craft and the accompanying sensations. Right now, he could tell they were descending in large looping circles towards one of the Star Hawk docking bays on the tarmac of Titan Launch Facility, AOA's secret launchpad in West Virginia. He knew it would only be a few minutes before they were unstrapping their safety harnesses, climbing out of their jumpseats and taking off on foot through the loading ramp in the rear of the cargo hold. Abner took the intervening time to mentally slap himself and dump all his unnecessary emotional garbage, leaving only his focus on the mission ahead.

A loud hiss of released compressed air filled Abner's ears just before the red signal light blinked off and the green signal light beside it took its place with a bright, solid glow. It was the sign from Calvin and Gerwitz that soft-dock with the refueling cables had been achieved and they were clear to depart the craft. One by one, each squadmember began disentangling themselves from their safety harnesses and jumpseats. Abner climbed from his seat along with all the others, immediately arching his back and stretching out the tightness that built up over the uncomfortable ten-hour flight from Cardinal's Nest Station.

Standing 6'1" when he stretched to his full height, Abner's head was only centimeters from scraping the ceiling of the cargo hold at his fullest extension. He placed both of his palms against the ceiling and tapped out a quick three-beat rhythm, a habit he'd started on their very first mission. And, being the superstitious bastard he was, Abner was now compelled to tap the beat before every recon. After one final stretch, he bent down beside his jumpseat to unstrap his M-4 semi-automatic rifle from its cradle. Once in hand, he pulled back its slide to examine the rifle's bolt before pointing the barrel towards a light fixture to peer down its length.

He saw no dirt, no carbon build-up, not a smudge, nor did he expect to. Abner had always taken good care of his rifle. It was the mindless repetition and attention to detail that the Army had trained into the very marrow of his bones that compelled him to keep his weapons in such pristine condition. Weapons inspection was a part of that repetition and detail attention, and Abner did it almost unthinkingly. But he did it nonetheless because you never really ever knew, not absolutely. You had to be as certain as it was humanly possible to be, about the little things especially. It was the little things that kept you alive out there. *Out amongst the Damned,* Abner thought ruefully, as he stuffed ammunition bandoliers into the cargo pockets of his black tactical pants, and into the ammo pouches attached to the front of his black Kevlar vest.

The vest seemed a bit superfluous to some. After all, the Damned didn't use weapons, and they never ran into anyone else out there. There wasn't anyone else to run in to. Everyone else was either a pile of rotting flesh, or one of the Damned themselves. So it started to seem unnecessary to a few of the squadmembers to carry around the Kevlar's extra weight. But Abner had been up close and personal with those infected bastards enough to know that the vest still had its uses. The Damned may be dumb as a pair of truck nuts, but they were impossibly strong. Their hands were iron, strong and brittle. And their teeth ... well, most of the Damned they'd fought had no teeth left. They'd all been broken off ripping away bites of flesh from their terrified prey. The ones they fought now all went for the stomach and chest with their terrible iron claws. His good friend Markief Almodi had been vest-less two missions ago when he was disemboweled by a half dozen of the Damned. Abner hadn't been more than ten feet away from his much-lamented teammate as the monsters pulled endless ropes of intestines from his belly. The experience was enough to happily consign Abner to the weight of the Kevlar vest forever.

Plus, it had an added feature, one his squadmates were adopting as well, each in their own fashion. In the back of the Kevlar vest, a leather sheath was sown on. The sheath held the item he had first been ridiculed for taking along with him on the ops, but now with which he'd become a trendsetter. He bent back down beside the rifle's cradle and plucked up his trusty metal baseball bat. He sheathed his Louisville Slugger in its custom-made holster and smiled when he noticed Eddie Sarkisian and Sarah Bristol across the hull mimicking his action with their own bludgeoning instruments, although they had their sheaths sown to leather straps that they wore as a sash over their black tactical jackets.

All three grinned. Eddie patted the barrel of the axe poking up over his shoulder while nodding at Abner with a raised eyebrow. Sarah and Abner laughed. They had to laugh, or else crack up. They'd all been amidst a raving horde of infected while running low on ammo. A good bat, or club, or axe—if you could find one, and many of the squad-members had—came in very handy in those situations. Most of the squadmembers now carried some sort of secondary bludgeoning weapon because of Abner's example.

"Listen up, people," Monty shouted. "Hey, hey, cut the shit. Focus up. We got a mission to accomplish, ladies and gentlemen. Gather round. Come on, everybody, bring it in."

Abner elbowed past a mildly protesting Novocaine Barker and found a good spot against the bulkhead near Monty to lean against while he gave them the final debrief/pre-game talk. Idiots like Novocaine Barker actually needed this kind of bureaucratic ritual, but Abner just wanted to get the mission over and done with. "Okay, listen up. We got a new squadmember with us on this mission. Barker, thanks for stepping up," Monty said to Cainey in a flat, bored voice.

"Thanks, Commander. I'm ready to do my part," Cainey said, irritatingly.

"Marge, you are going to take Barker with you and Fire Team 2. I'm going to be tagging along with ya as well. The numbers will be a bit skewed—five and seven—but that's the way it's gotta be. Pedro, Team 1 will have to be burdened with the extra cryochamber as well, but your guys can use all this extra exercise."

"No, yous guys is just lazy, boss," Pedro Alvarez, the young, handsome, intelligent and shrewd descendant of Mexican parents, and former Marine Corps infantry captain shot back while flipping a tuft of his thick black hair out of his eye.

"Don't worry, it's just from here to the garage, 200 yards across the tarmac. You'll barely break a sweat," Monty said, almost smiling. "So, we make our way from the Hawk to the garage, load up the cryochambers on the two personnel Humvees that we left fueled and ready to roll during our last mission. Then we roll out in convoy to this point here." Monty pointed to a spot on the map currently displayed on the tabletop touchscreen computer console bolted to the floor of the cargo hold. "AOA's satellite imaging suggests a large grouping of the Damned near the downtown area of this little Podunk town... Millstone, it's called. Christ knows why they're there, but, apparently, they are. One of the pointy heads even says he has reason to believe wo may find an Alpha Specimen there. Again, Christ knows why, but there you have it. So we dismount right at this point, roughly a mile outside the town limit. We split up the fireteams and close in on the downtown area from the East and West. Masterson, Woodson, you two will be driving the Humvees for your fireteams, so you will stay with the vehicles, and the cryochambers. Try not to scratch 'em. I'm told they're expensive. *Priceless* is actually what I was told, but you get the picture."

"We'll keep 'em secure, Commander," Hopkins Masterson, the gravely serious, agonizingly literal, short, frog-faced, boulder of a man, and driver for his and Sergeant Marge's fireteam, firmly promised.

"Good," Monty continued, "Our objective is capturing three subjects. We all know when we bag one of these fuckers they fight and shout like hell, so we are going to be as smart as possible when we do. We will move in and scout the area first. Keep your eyes open for small secluded groups of them. Call 'em out on the comms. No matter how juicy a target we see on the way in, however, we're going to keep on going all the way to the heart of downtown. We got orders to search for this Alpha they think might be there. So be on the lookout for any signs of a leader amongst them. Watch the Damned for any sign of them showing deference to a particular infected person. The science team didn't tell me why, but apparently, they have reason to believe those infected with this Alpha-strain are acting as some kind of queen bee for the rest of them. I was even warned that these Alphas may be able to make intelligent critical-thinking decisions. So, if you see anything like that, call it out over the comms." Monty paused a moment for the mutters of disbelief and complaints of futility to run their course. "I know how everyone feels about the fucking Alphas and all this shit, but that's above our paygrade. We have a job to do, and we are going to do it right, like everything we do. Don't think I'm letting the discipline of this squad slip just because of some silly little thing like an apocalypse." He paused this time for a few chuckles that came a bit tentatively. "Once we have made it downtown, I'll call for a sitrep and pick our targets. We bag our quota of the monsters and get the hell back here to the ship as fast as we fucking can. Gerwitz and Calvin will be here with the Star Hawk ready to go just as soon as we board. Barker," Monty called out, shifting his gaze to the new guy, "shit starts moving pretty fast once the Damned are on us, so just stay calm and follow the lead of your teammates. If you get confused or overwhelmed, call out for help. We don't need anyone playing hero. Just stick with your team and stay sharp. Okay, everybody got it?"

Everyone did. Monty tapped the computer display screen a few times to power it down, and then treated all twelve security squad-members under his command to individual nods of encourage-ment. Abner drew in a deep breath as Monty depressed the green mushroom-shaped button on the tabletop console in front of him. The button opened the main cargo hatch. And after another hiss of released compressed air, the rear wall of the Star Hawk fell away to become a loading ramp. Abner and his squadmates ran down the shallow ramp, hauling three seven-foot-long, rectangular white and blue AOA Model No. 793-D Cryogenic Suspended Animation Chambers along with them into the teeth of a raging thunderstorm. Lightning bolts arched across the sky in brilliant white-purple flashes. The rumble of thunder was so deafening it left no doubt that the heart of the storm swirled all about the launchpad. The driving rain came slashing in at a forty-five-degree angle and was quickly pooling in the dips and crevices of the tarmac.

Abner sprinted across the launchpad, splashing through puddles along with the rest of the squad, his hand clutched tightly to one of the forward handles of his team's cryochamber. He fought an epic battle within himself every time he made this journey to the Humvee garage to not look around and see the profusion of rotting corpses that littered the launchpad. The sight always reminded him of their very first recon mission.

They had landed at this same launchpad, the very same launchpad the transport cruisers took off from with the families. *Well, most of the families.* If Monty wasn't irreparably broken inside already by then, discovering what had remained of his wife and daughter sprawled out on the tarmac at the start of that initial mission had definitely sealed the deal. They'd found Carrie's watch still strapped to what had remained of her wrist and were able to confirm it was her through an engraving on the underside of the watch's face. *To my world*, it read, *my wonder, my wife. Yours forever, Monty.*

A piece of the light in Abner's heart had been chipped away in the wake of Monty's anguished wail upon that watch's discovery. Abner did not care to be reminded of that moment. He did not need his mourning for the friend he'd lost, and the life that was, to cloud his focus. He couldn't afford to get overwhelmed emotionally right now. They were out in the shit, and you never knew what was lurking behind every corner. So Abner dug deep and managed to keep his focus on the gray-blue Humvee garage in the cluster of hangars at the north end of the launchpad through the thick sheets of rain. And within no time at all, or hours on end—time always ticked by strangely in Abner's head during combat missions—they were outside the personnel door to the garage.

Monty cracked open the door and popped his head in to scope the scene. After a moment, he turned to his squad and gave them the all-clear. They all had to squeeze, shimmy, and re-grip the cryochambers a few times to get them through the narrow door and enter the garage. Once all the chambers were through, the squad gently set them down and spread out throughout the garage to confirm its security. That completed, Abner and his squad then loaded up the three expensive chambers and themselves into two pre-fueled Humvees. Monty rolled up the garage door in the rear of the building that led right to a side gate the team had left open during a previous mission. Masterson slowed the Humvee to allow Monty to jump into the passenger seat alongside him as they pulled out of the garage.

Forty minutes later, the rain had lightened to a constant drizzle. The low rumble of thunder could be heard only a few miles distant. Abner and his fireteam were spread out along a line about fifty yards wide, creeping their way through a forested area in the outskirts of the mountain town of Millstone. As they reached the edge of the treeline, Sergeant Marge signaled for the team to regroup on her location. Abner made his careful way to her side, arriving to see Monty and Marge crouched behind a giant oak tree and peering around either side.

"Whachya see, Commander?" Eddie Sarkisian gave voice to the rest of the freshly arrived fireteam's question.

A calm, patient hand held out behind him was all the answer they received from Monty for roughly thirty seconds. Then, abruptly, he turned around to face his crouching fireteam. "Looks like the corporate assholes can read an imaging map after all. The town square is right down the road, dead ahead of us about a half mile. Looks like there's some kinda park at its center, and it's as crowded as a Poison concert in 1987."

"There are pockets of them spread all throughout the town from what we can see, so stay sharp when we move in," Marge interrupted, cutting off Monty's flippancy.

"We want a good look at the group in the park before we bag any of these bastards," Monty continued, unphased by Marge's intrusion. "I spotted a three-story building with what looks like a flat, accessible rooftop. We make our way there as quiet as we can. I don't want to disturb any of the Damned motherfuckers on our way in. We need to take a look at what's going on in that park. We'll scout it from the rooftop and look for one of AOA's supposed Alpha Specimen motherfuckers. Once we are satisfied there, I'll contact Team 1 and call out our three targets."

"Any questions?" Marge asked, when it became clear that Monty was not going to.

No one had any, so they stealthily made their way to the tallest building in downtown Millstone. A few close shaves were avoided along the way, including one incident that required an axe-blow to the skull of an infected woman who stumbled out of a dark alley right in front of them. Eddie's swift and violent intervention had come just seconds before the infected woman would have cried out with that piercing, blood-curdling scream that all of them seemed to have. After that, it had been just a few detours and silent pauses before they were climbing over the ruins of the front door of the three-story building in downtown Millstone. The building had turned out to be an apartment complex. They avoided its halls and corridors by taking the emergency staircase and didn't encounter any Damned on their assent. Soon, they were spilling out onto the building's rooftop and back into the persistent, sprinkling rainfall.

Abner joined the rest of his fireteam in taking up a kneeling position behind the roof's eastward facing safety wall. To his left, Monty drew out the fancy, high-tech binoculars AOA had given him a few missions back. Abner thought them unnecessary. The park lay spread out right beneath them. It did not require any amplification to see from one end of it to the other, nor did Abner wish to amplify the unsettling sight in any way. Nearly shoulder to shoulder and covering almost every square foot of the modest two-acre park, stood an eerily silent, densely packed and slowly swaying mass of *the Damned*. As much as Abner tried to avoid that moniker for the infected, looking at them all together like that, the named seemed extremely apt somehow.

"What in the blue fuck?" Blurted out Donny McGuinness a few feet away to Abner's right.

"Quiet! Hold the chatter," whispered Marge. "Scan the crowd for any sign of an Alpha. If you spot anything, bring it to the commander and me ... but do it quietly," she implored softly, yet forcefully.

Abner scanned the swaying horde but saw no sign of any anomalous behavior. Every Damned in the milling mass seemed to be doing the exact same thing, to Abner's eyes anyway. He redoubled his efforts and focused hard to find any sign of leadership among them. He again found no evidence of that particular behavior, but what he did see in that overgrown, weedy park, he found more and more unsettling by the second. All along the edges of the swaying mass of infected, more Damned were joining them, even as they watched. The newly arriving mindless monsters were pressing their way in tight alongside their brethren and instantly adopting their strange behavior. The fireteam's perch atop the apartment building wasn't quite a birds-eye view in the truest sense of the word. There was still a great deal of the town they couldn't see, but the park was encircled by a turnabout with seven two-lane streets branching off that were clearly visible. Abner could see down each one for a good 500 yards. And down the length of every one of those rain sodden streets, dozens of the Damned were slowly stumbling their way to join the silent horde in the once proud park.

Abner shuffled over on his knees to within a few paces of Monty. Marge knelt a pace or two away to Monty's left. "Hey, Monty, Marge, you guys seeing this?"

"Seeing what, Normie?" Marge asked softly.

"More and more of these fuckers is joining in on this weird ass pow-wow by the minute. Look," Abner said, pointing to a street that branched off the turnabout to the north. The avenue had at least eight of the Damned spaced out down the visual limit of the road, all of them slowly but surely making their way to the park. "What the fuck is that all about? What the hell you figure is going on here, Commander?"

Monty slowly pulled the binoculars down from his eyes and looked over at Abner, "Some kinda weird ass pow-wow, like you said, Abbie Normal."

The instant joy Abner felt in hearing his old friend call him by the nickname he had stuck him with one fun, drunken night long ago, pierced through the misery of the weather and the strangeness of the gathering beneath them. He even saw a grin flash across Monty's face. Although, upon a closer look, there was something in the grin that Abner did not at all like, something sly, and even a bit devious. And just as quickly as the joy had sprouted in his heart, it withered back to dust.

Monty brought his hand up to his mouth and spoke into the communicator strapped around his wrist, "Anybody see an Alpha?"

Sarah Bristol, Donny McGuinness, Novocaine Barker and Eddie Sarkisian all responded with a negative report over their own wrist communicators in soft, professional voices.

"Okay, sit tight. Sergeant Marge and I will pick our targets," Monty told his squad. "You see any tempting subjects out there, Marge?"

"Down Main a few blocks to the west, I see a cul-de-sac and four milling targets," Marge reported in a flat, just-the-facts manner. "No sign of anyone else around them for at least two blocks. I remember I spotted a pharmacy parking lot on Green street—the street we first went down when we left the woods. There were a half dozen or so infected standing around a couple burnt out cars in the lot. No one within a few blocks of them either."

"Okay, sounds promising. Let me call up Alvarez," Monty declared as he tapped a button on his wrist communicator. "Alvarez, come in. This is Montrois. Give me a sitrep."

Over the comms, Pedro's voice crackled, "Yeah, Monty. Alvarez here. We spotted you enter that apartment building, so we took up position in the building on the northwest corner of Main and Washington, only a few blocks up from you guys. What you got for us, Commander?"

"Got a half dozen targets in the parking lot of a pharmacy on Green Street in the west end of town. Or at least there were a half dozen targets in that parking lot ten minutes ago. You and your team make your way there as quietly as you can and check it out. If they are there, bag two of them, and use your silencers and your bats and axes to take out the rest."

"Roger that, Monty. Hey, uh ... what in the hell is going on in this fucking park?" The fireteam leader asked, with obvious unease in his voice.

"Your guess is as good as mine, Pedro. Just be as quiet as you can and bag two of the bastards. Then get your asses to your Humvee and stuff 'em in the pods. Don't wait for us. As soon as they are loaded up, you head back to the Star Hawk. You hear me, Alvarez?"

"I hear ya, boss. Good luck. See ya back on the Hawk."

"See ya on the Hawk," Monty said, cutting off the intersquad channel. He tapped his wrist communicator once more to tune back in to the inter-team frequency. "Okay, team. Looks like the four sons-a-bitches in the cul-de-sac are ours. Let's get the hell off this roof and out of this pissing rain ... for a few minutes anyway." Monty got up off his knee and crouched low as he made his way to the door leading to the emergency staircase. Abner fell in line behind Eddie as he made his way through the door and off the wet roof.

The fireteam fell into a single-file line down the stairs. Eddie Sarkisian followed closely on Monty's heels. Abner was next in line. Behind him were Marge, Sarah and Novocaine respectively, with Donny McGuinness pulling rear-guard duties. Monty was just a step from the bottom of the staircase when the door that led into the lobby suddenly flung open in front of him.

"Jesus Christ!" Novocaine shouted from the staircase's second-floor landing as a shape burst through the doorway and into the stairwell, bellowing incoherently.

The voices of a few of Abner's other teammates filled the narrow space, joining together with Cainey's panicked screams, along with those of the howling shape. The figure at the foot of the stairs slowly came into focus in Abner's mind. He realized suddenly that it was a man, and not just that, but a shouting man, a man shouting coherent English words. "Don't shoot," the man was saying. In the same second it dawned on Abner that the man could not be one of the infected—for the Damned did not speak, they were mindless drones seeking only to destroy and spread—in that same moment, he watched Eddie leap forward, axe in hand, swinging the razor-sharp medieval weapon at the man's head. Abner meant to shout out but found his shock at confronting a genuine survivor in this small country town had frozen his voice.

Monty, however, was not diminished by shock in the least. He drove his shoulder into Eddie as he was moving past him on the final step. Eddie went sprawling to the floor of the stairwell in a thudding huff that marked the beginning of a sudden tense silence.

The thick quiet was broken abruptly by the survivor, "Please! Look! Please, God!" He held up his empty, cracked and dirty hands. "Don't shoot! I'm not one of them! I saw you guys from my hideout in the woods. I followed you. You gotta help me! You gotta get me outta here," the man began to plead with them frantically. "You gotta take me with you. You guys obviously came from somewhere safe. You all seem healthy and clean, anyway. Me, I haven't taken a bath in weeks. I haven't done anything but cower and hide for weeks, no time for anything else. The fucking monsters are everywhere, can't rest a fucking moment. Please, you gotta take me with you."

"Whoa, whoa, slow down, sir," Monty said in a flat voice. "Who are you? Have you been living in this town this whole time? What's going on with the Damned in the park?"

"What? The Damned? The infected monsters you mean?"

"Yeah. What is so special about this place? Why are they gathering here?" Monty asked once more in a flat voice.

"Wha... I don't... I... look... I don't know," the survivor spluttered. "I have no damn clue why they're all here. I just lived and worked in this town. That's why *I'm* here. I was a lawyer. My office is just up Main Street," he said, pointing to his left. "The infection spread ... it was chaos ... somehow my son and I were able to make it to a cave system in those woods you guys were traipsing through earlier. I've known about it since I was a kid. We've been hiding there since then. Just running back into town when it's safe to grab supplies from what's left of the Kroger and Kader's Pharmacy on Green when we need 'em."

"Where is your son?" Sarah Bristol asked the man as she made her way down the final steps to stand beside Monty.

The man looked like someone had slapped him. He reached up with a dirty sweatshirt-sleeve to wipe away the tears welling up in his eyes. After a long silent moment in which sorrow seemed to sit heavily in the atmosphere, the man spoke in a low, barely audible voice, "They got him. About ten days ago now ... I think. More and more have been coming to town over the past few weeks. I told him it was too dangerous for a supply run. I told him we had to leave the woods entirely and search for a more secure permanent location, but he was brave ... he... he... he said we needed supplies, or we'd starve. He... he went into town and... and ... he didn't," the survivor's voice cracked with emotion, "he didn't come back," he managed after a breath. "They must've got him. I should've went looking for him. I should've searched. But I knew."

"I'm sure you were right. There was most likely nothing you could do," Monty said, his voice on the edge of sounding genuinely sympathetic.

"But I was his father and I left him. I should've looked. What if they did get him, but didn't kill him? What if I abandoned him to become one of them? What if he is swaying along with all those other cursed souls in Concord Park," the survivor asked, almost to himself.

He looked a pitiful sight in the dim light of the stairwell. The well was lit by only the rainy day's meager light breaking through two tiny square windows set in the wall at the top of the stairs, but Abner figured the man wouldn't look much better in any light. The sweatshirt the man was wearing might once have been red, but it was soaked through and caked in layers of brown filth now, making it hard to be sure. His boots and blue jeans were in a similar wet and filthy condition. The survivor was most likely a white male in his late thirties, but with the layer of grime that covered his face, it was impossible to be sure. He was currently hunched over and overcome with emotion, but Abner figured he was of average height, probably 5'9". His body appeared wasted under his baggy, sopping wet clothes, but Abner guessed he probably walked around at about 220 pounds before the Infection Event. *Probably had a beer gut and a flabby ass from sitting in a chair doing all that clerical lawyer work,* Abner thought unkindly, being a bit prejudiced towards those in the legal profession.

"It's not your fault, sir. You've done an amazing job just to stay alive this long," Marge said in a pleasant, comforting voice. "You're the first survivor we've ever come across, in fact. We've been down to the surface twelve times now, and you're the first uninfected person we've ever encountered."

The man looked up with a puzzled face, "The surface? Came down? Came down from where? Where are you people from? Who... who are you people?"

"We will answer all your questions just as soon as we can, sir," Monty said. "For now, just stick with us and keep your head down. We have to make one stop and then we'll head to the Humvees and get ya out of here."

"A stop?! A stop for what?! Let's get the hell out of here now! There ain't nothing in this town. Trust me, I was born and raised here, there ain't nothing. Let's just all go to that Humvee you mentioned, straight away."

"I wish we could, sir, but we got a job to do," Monty answered with minuscule conviction.

"A job? What the hell are you talking about!? Who do you work for? Who are you people?"

"I promise, sir, we will answer all your questions. Just bear with us for now and try and stay quiet and keep up with us. It won't take long. We'll be on the Star Hawk in no time,"

"The Star Hawk? Wha..." The man seemed to run out of words as he stared at the fireteam with a slack-jawed expression.

"I know it must be overwhelming, sir, but we'll get ya out of here," Sarah told him with a bright, confident smile. "What's your name, sir? I'm Sarah Bristol." Turning to face the fireteam, she pointed to each member as she supplied their names for the survivor.

Once all seven of the teammates had been introduced, the survivor cleared his throat, "My name is Aponyaschefski," he told them, "Harclay Aponyaschefski. People mostly call me Schef."

"Well okay, Schef," Sergeant Marge said, stepping up next to the man, "you just stick close to me, and we will have you safe aboard our Star Hawk in no time."

"Uhh ... yeah, okay, whatever you say ... I guess," Harclay spluttered for an answer.

The cul-de-sac Marge had spotted from the roof was indeed bereft of any Damned, apart from the four she'd earlier identified as suitable targets. The four gray blood-stained monsters were hovering over a pile of rotting bones and viscera in the middle of the small turnabout at the end of the short cul-de-sac. The fireteam had all taken up their assigned positions. Abner and Donny, being the best two marksmen in the fireteam, were assigned the sniper duty. There was a running joke among the squad, which Abner was privately annoyed by, that he was Donny's long lost half-Asian half-brother, since they looked so much alike. Something had apparently been funny about that to a few of the guys. Some of the security officers weren't exactly the sharpest tools in the shed. Childish, rude behavior—fart jokes, locker room towel-snapping and lazy racism, had its appeals to such men.

However, Abner did have to admit he and Donny looked a lot alike. They were roughly the same height, with roughly the same long, lithe and athletic body types. They both had dark hair and wore scruffy beards. They even resembled each other in the face too. Which seemed to fuel the joke, since the only visible difference between the two men were the facial features Abner had inherited from his South Korean-born father. The joke was harmless though, and Abner had tough skin, so he let it slide. And Donny himself was not to blame. The guy was a prince among men. The type of dude who would never turn down a request for a favor. He and Abner had gotten on swimmingly since day one of joining the security team, and lazy racism aside, Abner figured there were worse things to be called than Donny McGuinness' half-brother.

The pretend half-brothers had taken up a position on opposites sides of the cul-de-sac behind a couple of conveniently placed burnt out cars. They'd attached suppressors to the ends of their M-4 rifles and were peering down their scopes, sighting in the hideous Damned at the end of the lane. Abner trusted that Donny would mirror his actions in this regard. Being the veterans they were, his trust and confidence in all his teammates—not counting Novocaine—was such that he did not need to visually confirm what actions Donny or any of them were undertaking to know for a certainty exactly what they were doing. This would be their eighth bag-and-drag mission. Each member of the fireteam knew their duties and executed them as unthinkingly as breathing.

For instance, Abner knew beyond all doubt that Eddie and Sarah were lurking behind the big green house to the left of the Damned, bag in hand, ready to jump out and drape whichever unfortunate creature he and Donny left standing after Marge gave the order to execute the plan. He knew too that Monty, Novocaine, Marge, and the survivor under her care named Schef were hidden behind the gray house to the right of the Damned. He knew as soon as he and Donny dropped their targets, the three team members would rush out and assist in the bagging effort. Once the Damned was completely stuffed inside the big black high-tech composite-fiber bag AOA had issued them for this specific purpose, they would knock the Damned off its feet, if it wasn't already, and then the process of dragging it back to the Humvee would immediately begin. Eddie and Sarah would be dragging, while the rest of them pulled security duty around the package all the way back to the Humvee.

I wish those damn Humvees weren't so frickin' loud. Would've been nice to pull in a lot closer to town than two fucking miles away. Abner was definitely not looking forward to that long foot journey ahead, dragging a wildly protesting bagged Damned along with them every step of the way.

"Okay, team, sitrep. Everybody green to green?" Marge asked softly over the comms. After Abner and the rest of his team responded in the affirmative, there was a momentary silence over the airwaves until Marge's voice was suddenly back in Abner's ear, "Okay, Hyun, you take the two on the right. McGuinness, you drop the one on the far left. Sarkisian and Bristol, be ready to rush and bag the remaining bastard." She took one deep breath, audible over the comms, "Okay, here we go, Donny and Normie, I'll give you a three-count. Ready ... three ... two ... one."

Blowing the air from his lungs slowly and steadily, Abner gently squeezed his rifle's trigger. He did not wait to confirm if his shot had hit its mark, he simply shifted his aim by mere millimeters and quickly squeezed off a second round. Abner lifted his head from his scope and saw that his two targets, along with Donny's, were indeed down and out. Head shots, all three.

A black blur flashed across his peripheral vision then, and instantly, his brain kicked into gear, telling him it was Donny moving to help capture the Damned. Thus reminded of his own duty, Abner immediately rolled over the hood of the burnt-out car and took off running towards the only Damned still left standing. He hadn't made it ten paces when Eddie and Sarah arrived in tandem right behind the infected man. In Abner's next pace, they had thrown the bag over its head and had it halfway down its torso. Then, in the next pace, Monty,

Marge and Novocaine came running from around the back of the gray house. Novocaine led them, running flat out with his head down, straight at the half-bagged Damned.

Abner blinked the rain from his eyes and reopened them just in time to see Eddie Sarkisian slip in a puddle pooling up in the street's gutter. Time began to run in the strange way it often did for Abner during crisis moments like this. He imagined he could see each of the thousands of individual raindrops surrounding him as time's pace slowed to a crawl. Dread rose up inside him as Eddie lost his grip on the black bag when his feet left the ground, coming right out from under him. Sarkisian began to topple backwards through an invisible lake of molasses.

The Damned wasted no time taking advantage of Eddie's fall. An eardrum shattering shriek from deep within its cold lungs jump-started Abner's internal clock into over-drive. In what seemed to him like the span of one rapid heartbeat, the Damned shimmied, shook and violently writhed its way free of the bag.

Then bam, the ticking of the clock inside his mind snapped back like a rubber band, instantly reverting to a helpless slowmo. He looked on uselessly, as Sarah made a lurching attempt to throw the bag back over the infected man's head. It was a deadly mistake. She over-extended herself and crashed to the cement on her hands and knees. The Damned had taken a clumsy step backwards and Sarah's bag had caught nothing but air. Painfully, agonizingly slowly, the seconds ticked away in Abner's head. *No!* His mind was screaming. Feeling as though he struggled against the colossal gravity of some gas-giant planet, he moved to aim his rifle at the Damned.

Someone beat him to the punch. The loud, sharp, cracking sound of an un-suppressed rifle crashed out a half a dozen times. It was Novocaine firing the shots. Abner could see in his periphery that he was still running madly towards the Damned. His bullets snapped and hissed all around Eddie as Sarkisian finally came crashing down on his back in the gutter puddle. Luckily, none of the bullets struck him, but unluckily, none struck the Damned either.

Abner nearly had the infected in his sights now, just as Sarah was turning her head up to face it. Her hand was held out before her in a protective position, but it didn't matter. The Damned latched onto her neck with one of its iron-claw hands. Officer and monster fell together to the road's cracked surface in a tangled heap. Abner no longer had a clean shot. He could do nothing to help her, nothing to stop it. The horrid sound of Sarah's esophagus torn, fully intact, from her neck under the unnaturally strong fingers of the Damned, and the sudden fountain of red that sprayed up into her tormentors face a short moment later, was bound to recur in his nightmares forever. Of that, Abner Hyun was dead certain.

"Oh, Jesus Christ!" Novocaine wailed, halting abruptly a few feet from where the Damned knelt over Sarah's limp corpse.

Abner watched with a mixture of disbelief and inevitability as Novocaine aimed his suppressorless rifle at the infected man. It sounded to him like every member of the team shouted "No!" at the same moment. It probably wasn't the wisest idea, seeing as how loud noises were exactly what they were hoping to avoid. It proved especially ill-advised when the Damned returned their unified shout with a thunderous bark of its own. The infected lurched back to its feet then, moving faster than Abner would've thought possible for one of them to move, right towards a frozen Novocaine Barker standing in the center of the street with a look of crippling dread. The beast got within a single pace of the fear-frozen man before Eddie Sarkisian's axe split a Damned's head in half for the second time that day.

"Oh, Jesus! Oh, dear Jesus. Holy fuck ... mother fuck," Novocaine babbled. The Damned's fresh dark blood looked poisoned, congealed and somehow grossly malign, splattered thickly across his face and chest as it was. The steady rainfall quickly went to work, washing clean the nasty substance, but the image lingered in Abner's mind, nonetheless.

"Shut the hell up, you goddamn moron. Fucking coward fuck! What the hell were you thinking firing your rifle like that?! Monty asked, bursting with rage. "Didn't you see the thousands of those infected bastards in that park, you asshole?"

"He-he ... The Damned was loose ... he would've ... he ..." Cainey spluttered.

"It doesn't matter. We just need to head back to the Humvee, *right now*," Marge butted in, saving Cainey from any further babbling.

"It's my fucking fault. I fucking slipped. I can't believe I fucking slipped," Eddie said, falling to his knees in the puddle of cold rain pooling around Sarah's limp body. "I'm sorry, Sar. I can't believe I fucking slipped. I'm so sorry."

"It ain't your fault, Eddie. It could've happened to any one of us. We will work out all the blame and pain later," Marge said, and not unkindly. "For now, let's just get her body back to the Humvee."

Eddie wiped his nose with his sleeve and then picked up the small, lifeless, blood-soaked body of Sarah Bristol. As Eddie was standing up with Sarah cradled in his arms, Schef, the survivor they'd recently found, stepped out into the street, getting a good look at the fresh carnage spread out around them. Just as Schef arrived, a guttural, phlegmy and spine-chilling howl filled Abner's ears. It combined in the heavy, damp air around them with an ever-intensifying rumbling thunder. The wind had shifted, and the storm was headed back their way. Abner's blood ran cold. He knew what that howl meant. It had come from the throats of the thousands of swaying drones in Concord Park. They had heard Novocaine's gunshots. They were coming for them.

"I told you we should've gotten the hell out of here. So much for your job," Schef said sarcastically. "Maybe you guys oughta stuff whatever is left of this guy in that big black bag of yours," Schef used his foot to softly kick the leg of the half-headed, gray-skinned corpse lying in the road in front of him.

"Not helpful at all, sir," Marge said, scolding the man.

The rumbling, hungry growl grew even louder, almost completely drowning out the fast-approaching storm now. "Everyone back to the Humvee. Hyun and McGuinness, you two have rear guard. Novocaine, you help Eddie with Bristol's body. Schef, you stay close to me and Sergeant Marge," Monty shouted orders at his subordinates over the rising calamitous symphony.

They stayed ahead of their pursuers for the first six blocks. As rear guard, Abner spent half of his time looking back down the street, and so far, no targets had appeared. That changed when Monty took a left on Green Street and started heading west towards the forested area they'd cross through on their way into Millstone. Novocaine and Eddie were right behind Monty. They were taking turns carrying Sarah's body over their shoulder. Eddie currently had the carrying duty, while to his left, Novocaine shuffled and stumbled his way down the middle of the street with his right eye glued down the sights of his M-4. He feverishly swung the barrel back and forth, coming awfully close to pointing it at Sergeant Marge and Schef who were walking behind him a few paces to his left. Donny rounded the corner of Green Street just before Abner, so he most likely didn't see the hope-sapping sight Abner glimpsed as he rounded that turn.

The end of Grant Street—the cracked and weedy lane they had just turned onto Green from—was packed by countless Damned spread out across the entire breadth of the two-lane road, and they had seen Abner too. He knew it by the cold hunger in their eyes and the slobbering grumble of their growls. "They've found us!" He shouted out, loud enough for Monty to hear him thirty yards ahead.

Monty stopped running and looked at Eddie. Sarkisian was breathing heavy from the exertion of hauling Sarah's body. Monty must've been judging whether the man needed a break. After a second's contemplation, he apparently concluded Eddie could hack it, because he shouted, "Okay, people, let's really frickin' run! Through the woods and straight to the Humvee. Follow me." He even waved his arm toward the forest to reinforce his order.

The judgment of Abner's commander was not as sharp this mission as had been the rule of the past. After only about fifty yards, Eddie began to lag behind Monty considerably, and Novocaine seemed in no great hurry to relieve him of his burden. In fact, the coward was sprinting like he was in the Olympic medal race for the 100-yard dash and gave no indication of slowing down. Donny was keeping pace with Abner. They were about twenty yards from Eddie, but the gap was shrinking fast.

"Slow up, boss!" Donny shouted through cupped hands, his rifle slung around his neck and dangling against his chest.

Monty heard the shout and came to a sliding halt in the wet road sixty or seventy yards ahead. He turned back and must've understood the issue at a glance. He held his long, scarred right arm, with its massive earthworm-veins bulging from every rock-hard muscle, stiffly out to his side. And like something straight out of WrestleMania, Novocaine Barker ran full-steam straight into it. It was the most vicious and effective clothesline-smash Abner had ever seen. It knocked Barker clean off his feet. He crashed to the cement with such a violent thud that Abner was sure all the air in his lungs had to be blasted loose.

Eddie had stopped running by that point. He stood in the center of the road, huffing and puffing with the water-logged body of his teammate slung over his shoulder. Abner and Donny arrived at Eddie's side just as Novocaine was rolling over onto his hands and knees. Abner watched as Monty stepped up behind their newest squad-member, placed his boot on Cainey's ass, and kicked out forcefully. Novocaine lurched forward a few feet, his face scraping along the wet cement all the way.

Monty went right on kicking the pathetic little man, shouting all the while, "Get back and help carry the body, you gutless fuck! She's dead because of you, you piece of shit, yellow, fucking pussy! Go back and help, or I'll fucking kill you myself!"

Donny took the precious load from Eddie as Abner watched Sergeant Marge arrive at Monty's side. Schef kept his distance from the enraged commander. Both he and Abner watched as Marge dragged Monty away from Novocaine, who was now crawling on his hands and knees along the cracked and puddled street. The volume of the collective groaning of the seeking horde of infected suddenly ticked up a deeply unnerving notch. Abner looked back down the road and saw the densely packed writhing mass of gray-skinned, red-smeared monsters turn the corner off of Grant Street.

Green was a wider avenue, but there were still plenty of the infected to fill in the gaps as they once again spread out across the entire breadth of the road; all the way from the shop fronts lining the north side of the street, to the large glass-walled restaurant spanning the length of the block's south side. Abner turned back to shout a warning, but there was no need. Monty had seen the horde as well.

The look on his face showed that plainly. Abner watched as Monty bent down and grabbed Novocaine's jacket in his fist, yanking him back to his feet. He shoved the soaking, humiliated man toward the woods and waved Abner, Eddie, and Donny to follow as he too turned and sprinted for the treeline with Marge and Schef running along at his side.

Abner locked eyes with Donny and Eddie for a long second before they too took off full-speed for the woods. They only made it a few yards when a pack of twenty of The Damned came stumbling out from around an abandoned moving truck parked on the street corner half a block ahead. Donny tried to stop, but Sarah's added weight must've thrown off his balance. He slipped on the slick cement and was forced to release her body or tumble to the ground with it. He chose to let the body fall. Blasphemous as it seemed, it was the right call in Abner's book because they had just run out of time. They were boxed in. The monsters were now clogging the road ahead and behind and were within 100 feet of their prey.

Their next decision might not have been a conscious choice, but it was a collective one. Abner and his two trapped teammates decided to disregard noise discipline and start fighting for their lives. Sarah's throatless body, laying crudely askew across the cement in front of Donny, soon had red-hot bullet casings raining down atop it as McGuinness, Abner, and Eddie began pouring lead into the relentless surging mass of infected. Abner emptied his ammo clip into The Damned, downing a half dozen and winging a dozen more.

Robotically, he executed the actions necessary for a flawless ammo reload. He slapped the bottom of his fresh clip to ensure it was seated securely, when the sudden realization that they were fighting a losing battle dawned in his mind. Abner risked a glance at the building on the north side of the street fifteen yards away from them. In a flash, he saw it had once been some sort of party store, and the front door had once been made of glass, but it was now a gaping hole of nothingness with jagged shards scattered on the ground all around. "Follow me, guys," he shouted over the noise of Eddie's cracking fire and Donny's muffled suppressed shots. Abner took off running for the party store and saw Donny move to follow him out of the corner of his eye.

"Wait, we can't leave her!" Eddie cried.

"We have to, Eddie," Abner said, turning back to grab his axe-wielding teammate heading the opposite way of the building, right toward Sarah's abandoned corpse. "She's gone. We have to leave her. We can't afford to carry her. She'll slow us too much. Come on, man, they're on us!'

Three Damned were taken out by Donny's quick trigger only a few feet from where Abner was trying to shout sense into Eddie. Their thick, dark blood spraying across Eddie's face seemed to help drive home in the man the good sense of leaving their teammate's dead body behind. He instantly stopped struggling against Abner's insistent tug and took off towards the hole where the party store's door had been. Abner followed only a step behind him.

Donny was first through the opening and into the ransacked store. He made his way behind the counter, kicking the cash register off the flat dusty surface as he leaped over it. An open doorway behind the counter led to a narrow hallway. Abner was last to hurdle the counter, running into the back of Eddie as soon as he cleared the obstacle. The hallway dead-ended only fifteen feet ahead. A closed door marked the hall's end. A second closed door was cut into the wall to their left, adjacent to Eddie. The sound of breaking glass caused Abner and his two compadres to turn back toward the store's entrance. Dozens of snarling Damned came shoving their way through the shattered doorway, and still countless more were crashing straight through the store's front windows, even as the serrated glass shards tore deep gashes in their sickly gray flesh.

"Times up, Donny," Abner said in a rush. "Choose one."

Donny chose the door at the end of the hall. He ran at it full out, smashing his foot into the door right next to the frame and just above the lock. It crashed open, falling away from its rusted hinges to end up on the ground of a dark and grimy alleyway behind the store. Abner ran over the ruins of the door with two grasping and growling Damned only a few feet behind him. The three teammates were immediately forced to turn right, as it was the only path available to them. They were in an alley that dead-ended to their left. To their right, the alley turned between two buildings a dozen yards ahead. So they went right, following the twisting alleyway, with Donny leading the way and Abner pulling up the rear. The monsters stayed just a few feet behind him all the while but were closing fast. Finally, one more left-hand turn and the three men burst back out onto a wide city street. They had no time to gain their bearings, with The Damned nipping at their heels. Donny turned left as soon as he entered the new street. Abner unthinkingly mirrored his action. Eddie followed suit.

They were running down the middle of the street, an endless pack of hungry Damned gaining ground on them with each passing second, when a treacherously disguised, rain-filled pothole ensnared the right foot of Donny McGuinness. Abner watched in horror from two paces behind as his friend spilled to the ground, screaming out in blinding pain. An instant later, Eddie and Abner were at his side, pulling him back to his feet. Abner studied his friend closely as Donny attempted to put pressure on his right foot. It was no good. Donny's leg crumpled under him, and he fell heavily into Abner's arms. *He must've busted the goddamn thing,* thought Abner, with a cruel and crushing certainty.

Eddie and Abner did their best, but they were only able to drag their limping teammate along for a few yards before the first of The Damned were on them, forcing them to release their supportive grips on the injured man and turn to face the enemy. Out of the corner of his eye, Abner saw Eddie draw out his axe from over his shoulder in the very same instant he went reaching for his Louisville Slugger. With a practiced, smooth motion, Abner drew out the metal bat to plant it firmly in the top of the skull of The Damned closest to him. The skull shattered on impact, caving inwards and shooting a fountain spray of brains and blood into the air. In his peripheral vision he could see Eddie swinging his gore splattered axe in wide, arcing loops, forcing The Damned to draw back from him. Abner copied the maneuver. A gap slowly opened up between them and the monsters.

Abner then glanced back at Donny. He was a few paces up the road, walking in slow, limping steps. Abner kept swinging the bat about wildly while Eddie did the same with his axe. After a few seconds, or a few hours, Abner couldn't have said for sure—even with a gun to his head—they made their way back to Donny's side.

And just as suddenly as they arrived alongside the limping man, he stopped and turned around to face the oncoming mob. "Get out of here, guys. Right now! "McGuinness shouted at Abner and Eddie. "I'll never make it … and I ain't slowing you two down and getting you killed along with me."

Abner wanted to protest, but before the words were formed in his mind, a grimy gray vise-like hand fell on his shoulder. Abner turned to thrust the butt of his bat into an infected woman's nose, sending it reeling backwards. He and Sarkisian made quick work of her and three other Damned who had raced out ahead of the horde.

No sooner had the last been felled, than they heard Donny shout out, "Just run. Get out of here, now!" McGuinness limped bravely with that, straight into the oncoming horde, holding both hands high above his head.

Abner saw, with detached focus, that each hand gripped a pinless hand grenade. He watched with dumbfounded shock as the horde completely engulfed his friend a second later as if it were a single creature, swallowing its meal whole. Eddie must've realized the implications of the pinless grenades Donny had been holding before Abner, because Sarkisian grabbed him by the strap of his vest as he ripped his axe clear of the chest of The Damned before him. Eddie kept tugging on Abner's vest, dragging him along for the first few paces of their headlong flight down the cracked road, before Abner finally snapped out of his crippling shock and began to run under his own power.

He glanced back after a few endless seconds, just as Donny's two hand grenades detonated. The sound of the explosion was muffled by the sheer mass that crawled atop McGuinness when the grenades went off. Time once more slowed in Abner's mind. He watched with unwanted fascination as a mass of infected bubbled up around the explosion. The rippling air of the explosion's shockwave was laced with a dark-red mist, and clearly visible to him. The spreading sphere of death rocketed past all The Damned nearest its epicenter, violently ripping their bodies apart and sending small chunks of flesh flying off in every direction.

Still looking back at the spreading carnage, Abner tripped on one of the myriad cracks in the aging cement, nearly losing his footing. Eddie reached out to lend him a steadying hand. He and Abner locked eyes before turning back in unison to glance at the explosion's aftermath. It might well have been a firecracker, for all the good it did slowing the hungry horde. Perhaps twenty had been annihilated in the explosion, but hundreds more crawled over their shredded remains, mindlessly seeking Abner and Eddie just a few dozen yards up the road. Abner looked back to Eddie and jerked his head to the left to suggest they continue their retreat. A return nod told him Sarkisian accepted the proposition to be their best option. Without another look back, they sprinted down the street.

Keeping a steady buffer of fifty yards between them and the infected, Abner and Eddie turned down one street after the next, searching for a path out of Millstone. Somehow, perhaps by the grace of God alone, they wound up back on Green Street, though they were still trailed by thousands of blood-crazed gray and red monsters. They headed straight for the woods at the west end of the craggy road, dropping a few hand grenades of their own in their wake for good measure.

The damage the grenade's explosions wrought increased Abner and Eddie's buffer enough so that by the time they'd made it back to Masterson, Monty, Marge, Novocaine, and Schef at the waiting Humvee, they were able to climb aboard free of harassment. Marge and Monty were even able to fire off potshots at their enraged pursuers with relative impunity as Masterson smashed the gas and peeled off back towards Titan Launch Facility.

CHAPTER 4

The red ceiling-mounted signal light had blinked off several minutes ago, yet Abner still sat strapped in tight to his jumpseat aboard the Star Hawk. He was trying—and failing—to process the events of that horrible mission. He was struggling for a way to make it make sense. Sarah Bristol, the young, whippy, energetic and lighthearted mother of three ... gone? Donny McGuinness, the professional workman with the soul of a philanthropist, and with whom he'd grown so close to in the last few months ... gone? And Novocaine Barker, that cowardly little shit, safe as houses aboard the Star Hawk?

It made no sense. The man had nothing but a few scratches on his cheek in penance for that shit-show he'd kicked into motion down there. Abner was seething as he watched him hovering over fireteam 1's two freshly occupied cryochambers, chattering in hushed, gossipy tones with a few of team 1's officers as though everything were fine and dandy, and he hadn't just gotten two of Abner's friends killed with his incompetence.

Finally, it became too much for him. Abner unbuckled his safety harness and stomped over to the cryochambers strapped against the bulkhead in the rear half of the cargo hold. Novocaine was leaning against the top end of one of the chambers, whispering with Dontavious Woodson leaning against the chamber to his left. Abner reached around to Novocaine's chest and grabbed a fistful of his jacket. He yanked the smaller man around, then leaned in close enough to kiss him. Abner was a deal bigger than the gangling, pig-faced little man, and so was able to toss him around with relative ease. Using his free hand, Abner poked Cainey emphatically in the chest two times. "Sarah Bristol, Donny McGuinness," he shouted the names in Cainey's face, "both dead, because of you, because you panicked, and then you ran. Did he whisper that in your ear, Dontavious?" Abner lifted his face from Novocaine to ask the officer. Woodson had no answer, at least none he cared to share with Abner right then. So Abner turned back to the pathetic little man quivering under his grasp, "Didn't bag the Alpha either, did ya, Novocaine?" Cainey still had no answer for Abner. "They're dead, you yellow bitch, and you're over here gossiping like some goddamn Celebrity Housewife. Go sit in the jumpseat in the fucking corner and don't fucking move 'till we're back at the station. Have some freakin' humility ... and show a little goddamn respect," he added, shoving Barker towards the opposite end of the cargo hold.

Cainey stumbled away from him a few feet, before quickly turning back to face Abner with a look of sheer indignation and bubbling out-rage written on his face. He opened his mouth to say something, but whatever it might have been was quickly swallowed when he got a good look at the faces of the men and women around him. Abner could tell Cainey realized he'd lost all the support he might once have had after that shouted retelling of his cowardly exploits during the mission. Cainey turned to his left to look at Monty seated in his jump-seat, picking dirt from under his fingernails with his black four-inch, AOA security team issue ceramic knife.

Monty looked up and stared into Barker's eyes for a few silent seconds before nodding his head towards the empty jumpseat in the front corner of the hold. Cainey's face flushed bright red. Abner was sure he must've reached his boiling point and was about to shout in protest, but Novocaine controlled himself. Meekly, he turned on his heels and marched off towards the jumpseat. The little bitch did take a swing at a yellow steadying bar on his way to the seat, but Abner noticed him pull the punch at the last second. *What a fake little fuck,* he thought, angrily.

The cargo hold was dead silent as Novocaine marched his way to exile, so a minor fright rippled through the squad when the cockpit hatch was suddenly flung open to smash loudly into the bulkhead beside it. Harclay Aponyaschefski ducked his way through the hatchway and into the still silent room. He'd must've felt strange about strapping himself into either of the freshly vacant security officer's jumpseats for takeoff, or any of the other five, because he had bypassed all of them in favor of the cramped little fold-out jumpseat behind the copilot station inside the cockpit. Abner didn't really blame the man. It had seemed to him like some sort of desecration to the memories of his departed teammates to have the dirty survivor strapped into one of their jumpseats. *Bad enough Cainey's bony ass is taking up one of their spots.* Schef must've understood that, and so, he had wisely elected to experience launch pad takeoff in heavy Earth gravity from a front-row seat. "Am I interrupting something?" Schef sarcastically asked the silent squad. When no response was forthcoming, the survivor sauntered his way across the cargo hold, stopping alongside the softly humming cryochambers.

He peered through the porthole embedded in the lid of the nearest cryochamber. Abner knew what he was seeing. He glimpsed it himself while he was haranguing Novocaine. Inside, lay a stiffly frozen Damned, though all that was visible was a frost covered black bag. And yet, Harclay stared intently through the porthole for a long, long time.

When he finally straightened back up, he looked over at Monty, who had set aside his knife to watch the survivor's strange antics right along with Abner and all the rest. "Cryogenic freezers, eh?" He asked Monty flippantly. "Straight outta some Star Wars, Trekkie, superhero space-opera, or some such ridiculous nonsense film. Except, I'm forced to believe it, aren't I? I mean, here the thing sits right before me, and I did just climb from the cockpit of some super spacecraft, powered by some unheard-of combustion technology. I sat there and watched two expert pilots fly her through the atmosphere and straight into space. Then I watched as they engaged some kinda artificial gravity—a thing those same two pilots, God bless 'em, couldn't even begin to explain the basic physics behind. So, I guess sci-fi space movies are the new reality. A man's gotta believe his own eyes, after all. Doesn't he? Somehow, this AOA company you all serve has managed to make inexplicably gigantic scientific leaps forward in absolute and utter privacy. I have to believe that. I mean, here I am looking at the proof, aren't I?"

"What exactly are you trying to get at, Mr. Aponyaschefski?" Monty asked.

"Oh, nothing much really. This is all new to me. I'm just trying to make heads or tails of it. Talking it out always helps me. It's how I prepared arguments for my cases back in Millstone ... back before the infection spread. Back before these *Damned*, as you guys call them, took over the world."

"What is it exactly you need to talk out?" Marge asked, slightly defensive.

"Well, that's obvious. Isn't it, Sergeant Marge?" Schef shot back with a grin. "I'm trying to figure out just what kinda welcome I should expect when we get to this Cardinal's Nest Station of yours. I'm trying to figure out just who the hell you people really are."

"Where I come from, it's considered disrespectful to insult your rescuers," Pedro said with acid in his voice. "We've shown you every courtesy, not to mention saved your ass from certain death, and we're repaid with doubt about our intentions?"

"You're right, of course ... uhh ... Pedro, isn't it?" Pedro gave a slight begrudging nod, so the survivor carried on, "I don't mean to insult you guys. I'm sure you're all good people just doing the best job you can, but all this seems far too coincidental to me." Schef spun slowly around with that, holding his hands out to point at all the amazing tech around him. "It seems to me this company you all work for had been planning for the apocalypse. Or was at least ready for it. I gathered from Gerwitz and Calvin that AOA built these Star Hawks and their lunar station in a matter of two years or so, with trillions of dollars of start-up money, pooled together from AOA and eight independent governments, and all right under the public's nose, yet completely hidden from them. And then, just as their super moon station reaches completion, some unknown, incredibly exotic virus spreads throughout the world. Yet, luckily for you guys, your bosses have the perfect place to ride out the horror in safety, and they were even kind enough to invite your families along, thus ensuring the habitat runs smoothly."

"You ain't the only one who thinks AOA knows more about the infection then they let on, if that's the point you're trying to make," Monty said blandly. "There's plenty of us who think they know a lot more about the infection's origins than they're saying."

"So then why in the hell are you carrying out their bidding on these suicide missions of theirs?" Harclay asked, as though he had been hoping someone would set him up for it.

Monty stared at the man for a few silent moments before ultimately shrugging his shoulders in a what-are-you-gonna-do fashion.

"To put an end to it all. That's why we do it," Marge said, with rare annoyance seeping into her voice. "The infection mutates too rapidly. If we can get the science team a sample from an Alpha Specimen, they can synthesize an antidote, and we can take the surface back."

"Right, right, Gerwitz told me about this Alpha Specimen y'all are looking for," Schef allowed, with disbelief obvious in every syllable. "Have you folks got one locked in one of these cryotubes?" He asked in an arrogant voice.

Abner watched Marge grit her teeth and bite back her swelling anger. She calmed herself in a breath and made her voice flat once again, "No. But the two in the chambers will help out a great deal. They've never been able to draw a sample of blood from a specimen with the infection still actively animating it. They'll be able to get some very useful insights from what we've brought them today." Marge cleared her throat and raised her voice to be sure the whole squad could hear, "Bristol and McGuinness can rest easy knowing their sacrifices were not in vain-"

"Why haven't they been able to collect a sample from an active infection?" Harclay patronizingly interrupted to inquire.

Marge had regained that inner calm of hers that Abner so admired. Her voice was flat and very matter of fact as she answered Schef's question, "Every Damned we've brought back before this mission became inert—with the infected carrier dying—just as soon as we were through the Earth's exosphere. The science team doesn't know why."

"Hence the cryochambers." Schef stated, pointing to the chamber he was still standing alongside.

"That's right," Marge answered. "The science team figures that if we bring 'em back a frozen one they'll be able to get one step closer to making the vaccine. They say it'll be really useful."

"And you believe them?" Schef asked in an amazed voice.

"Why shouldn't we?" Abner indignantly shot back. "They want to end the plague just as much as the rest of us."

"Do they?"

"I hate that coy, beating around the bush, fancy lawyer crosstalk, Mr. Aponyaschefski," Abner said in a growl. "If you got something to say, just say it already."

"Okay, Mr. Hyun, I'll get to my point," Schef stated professorially, as he strode towards the still seated Monty. Harclay Aponyaschefski sat himself down right alongside the security commander with a grace at odds with his appearance. "I understand I'm still getting my bearings here amongst you guys, but I did get a brief history of your lunar station, and the miracle company that built it, from those two fine pilots up in the cockpit. And after watching the distant moon grow ever larger in the windscreen, and reflecting on the day's incredible events, it occurred to me that this whole Alpha story is not the only lie AOA is stuffing down your throats."

"Is that right?" Abner asked with heavy mockery. "What else are they *stuffing down our throats*?"

"Well, for one thing, I don't think they have any idea how to synthesize some miraculous vaccine to save the world and cure the monsters, nor have they any real intention of even attempting that feat. It's become my certain suspicion over this eye-opening flight that your employer knows just who it was that released the infection in the first place. You see, I believe the same people responsible for the infection also gave AOA the blueprints to all their recent exotic technologies. Now, I'm not saying I know who that is exactly, or where they get their tech, or where they come from or whatever, but I am sure AOA owes their technological windfall to some sort of external source, or sources. So, you see, the AOA must then know that they can't do anything to cure this infection. They must know it's beyond their newly acquired technological capabilities to heal. You see? Because if I'm right about AOA having some mysterious benefactor, and if that benefactor is responsible for the infection, then they most likely sent the infection as a biological weapon, one that I'm sure they knew AOA would be powerless against, despite their recent tech boom." Schef patted the air in front of him with his outstretched palms to placate the officers around him emitting skeptical murmurs. "I know. I know. A little far-fetched when you first think about it, but apply a little logical reasoning—well, logical for this day and age anyway—and it's the obvious conclusion, my friends. It's right there for any unbiased, or un-indoctrinated, or un-propagandized person to see. They've been lying to you all. Feeding you hope and giving you seemingly vitally important missions to execute so you won't take time to sit back and think for a minute. I mean, what about this curse you all call an *infection* seems within the realms of any natural science's ability to fix? Does it seem scientific to you guys at all? It doesn't seem the least bit so to me. It seems *supernatural*. I mean, what about the infected themselves? Do they seem to exhibit any symptoms anywhere close to reminiscent of any infection, or virus, or pathogen, or illness, or whatever that you've ever heard the merest whisper of back in your old lives?" Schef paused at that point to gaze around the room, waiting for an answer that Abner could tell he knew was never going to come. "Like I said, I have no clue who AOA's benefactors may be, but for all intents and purposes, they may as well be ... well, magic, for lack of a better word. I mean ... you all have been on what, eleven missions now? You've been up close and personal with the infected. What have you noticed about them? Apart from the sickly smell of blood and rotting tissue they are usually covered in, that is. Their skin is a sickly gray color, right?" Schef paused to get a nod from a few of the officers near him. "Their eyes are a solid black, right? Like a pupil dilated well beyond maximum limit." Once more he stopped for nods of agreement. "And their blood—I'm sure you've all seen their blood—it's strange, right? All thick and congealed, like some sort of gross Jell-O after only ten minutes in the fridge. It's that strange dark red color too... almost black, it's so dark. Makes you sick to the stomach just to see it. Doesn't it? If you ain't too busy running from the bastards, that is." A rumble of low laughter accompanied more nods. "And they are unbelievably powerful, aren't they?" This time the nods he received were full of solemn remembrance of dread experience. "But how is that possible? How does an infection make someone stronger? Think about it. It's been two months since the infection spread, yet all the infected, regardless of when they were infected, aren't wasting away or decaying. Which means they must be feeding pretty regularly. Right? Feeding and drinking, don't forget. The human body shuts down, regardless of what it's infected with, after three weeks without food, and after just three days without water. Yet none of those bastards chasing us through Millstone today seemed to be struggling with dehydration or weakness from hunger, not to my eyes anyway." This time when Schef paused, there were exchanges of puzzled looks around him rather than nods. "Like I said, I've spent two months down there with those creatures, with the Damned, as you call them. Since day one, in fact, and back then, in the beginning, they didn't kill all their prey like they do now. Some of them were turned into other infected, other Damned. As the days and weeks went by, my son..." His voice caught as he spoke those words. An uncomfortable hush rippled through Abnor's enthralled squad-mates. Schef took another moment to gather himself before pressing on, "As the weeks went by, my son and I encountered fewer and fewer uninfected survivors like us during our supply runs. Then one day, about four weeks ago, I was returning from a Kroger supply run when I heard a scream. It sounded close, and by then I knew what the sound meant, so I hid behind a dumpster in a nearby alleyway. I was ducked down behind it, crouching safely out of sight, and I watched a young woman run down the street in front of me. She was gripping tightly to her torn backpack, still screaming in that high-pitched, fear-stricken way that I'm sure everyone in this Star Hawk is very familiar with. Then a dozen or so steps behind her, the horde came running down the street in hot pursuit. There were so many of them. As many as were chasing us today ... maybe... maybe not that many ... but a lot, anyway. So ... I just hid there. I wanted to help, I guess, some part of me did anyway, but I didn't. I waited it out in my little hiding spot until night fell and I could safely make my way back to our cave." Schef paused his story to fight an apparent battle within himself to ward off the obvious emotion attempting to seize control of his faculties. A few deep breaths brought back the calm and reasonable face that he'd been wearing moments before. "Up until this morning, when you folks went stumbling through my forest, that poor young woman was the very last uninfected person I ever saw in Millstone, other than my boy that is. After that run-in, a few days went by with no sight nor sound of another survivor. Then a few weeks. And, gradually, I began to think everyone else must be either hiding or dead ... or one of them ... one of the Damned. I started to fear that my boy and I might just be the last two survivors in the world. But then, upon some further reflection, for which I had an abundance of available time, it occurred to me that those conclusions didn't really make a whole lot of sense, not scientifically anyway. After all, there were still just as many Damned as ever roaming around town. So what were they feeding on? The animals? I've never seen one go after anything non-human. Never. Not once. I've seen them attack and kill a dog before, but only after the dog attacked them first. I've never seen one eating a dog after such a kill either. Have any of you?" His pause for a response was so brief and perfunctory it could barely be classified as one. "So basically, their prey is restricted to uninfected humans alone, and those have seemingly all but vanished. So, what are they eating? And how about drinking? Let's not forget about the importance of water. I've never seen one taking a drink. How about you?" After another perfunctory pause, he continued, "Unless they're chasing a survivor, the Damned all pretty much just mindlessly stand in place, just breathing and waiting, and not much else. So when do they drink? And where do they get their water? Are they walking down to the river at night to dunk their heads in? Is that it? Is that why none of us has seen one with a thirst? Or maybe they're looting bottled water off grocery store shelves like me and my boy. I never saw one at the checkout counter, if they have been. They don't drink, officers. That's why none of us has seen them do it," Schef stated with grave sincerity in his voice. "They aren't even human anymore. You have to see that."

"Zombies?" Marge scornfully interjected. "Is that really what you are implying, Mr. Aponyaschefski?"

"Call 'em whatever you like, Sergeant. It makes no difference to me. I just want you all to see the madness of these recon missions of yours. Just take those damn cryochambers, for instance." He pointed towards them for emphasis. "Why would you ever need something like that? Who here has ever heard of an infection that goes dormant in a person when it leaves the atmosphere? Not to mention, instantly kills its host when it does. There is nothing natural or scientific about your Damned at all. That behavior we all saw today, swaying together in that large group like that, what kinda fucking infection have you ever heard of that causes that? Or that completely overtakes a person's mind, erasing any trace of their previous humanity and replacing it with mindless, bloodthirsty malice. Does that sound scientific to any of you? Science has no dog left in this fight. There is a curse on the Earth, ladies and gentlemen. I'll bet that AOA's mysterious bene-factor released this infection curse as punishment for AOA's misuse of their great gifts. Maybe AOA and the governments were supposed to share their tech ... or maybe they weren't supposed to use it at all. Who can say? But in the end, what do your bosses care about their benefactor's wrath anyway? They don't need to fear any ravenous infection. They can wait out the horror in the modern utopia they've built on the surface of the goddamn moon, thousands of miles from harm's way. And since they are ever greedy for more and more unknown information, and since they have an expendable security team on hand at their beck and call, and fancy new interplanetary craft to send them out in, they've invented some elaborate lie about Alphas and vaccines and who knows what other nonsense, just to keep you all risking your lives on a bunch of fruitless missions back to Earth's surface. That's my point, Normie." he said, looking up to lock eyes with Abner once more. After a few seconds worth of tense stare down between them, Schef switched his gaze to Marge who instantly took up Abner's place in the staring contest. "You guys are taking me to the enemy's door, Sergeant, and you're acting like you're doing me some sort of favor by doing so."

A silence stretched out at the end of Harclay's diatribe, and just when it seemed to Abner that the mesmerized squadmembers around him would stay silent forever, Marge cleared her throat, "The AOA top-brass may have a few questions for you, Mr. Aponyaschefski, I have no doubt, but there is certainly nothing to fear from them, sir. Your theories are a bit farfetched for my taste. I'll stick with good sense and science for now. I hardly think it's time for any of us to go around embracing some magical-benefactor curse theory—"

"There is no scientific logic in the Alpha theory," Harclay cut in. "AOA's scientists told you there was, so you didn't question it, you just simply believed. They are lying to you, Sergeant. You are all being used, and for nothing noble. To them, you're just expendable couriers, bringing them intriguing *samples* to study, so they may slake their voracious curiosity while they patiently and comfortably wait for the curse to run its course."

"If you say so, Mr. Aponyaschefski," Marge humored the man.

"I do say so, Sergeant, I do. I know it's not what any one of you wants to hear. Discovering you've been serving an evil master is a hard pill to swallow. I get that. You all signed up to make a difference, and they're telling you that you've been doing just that. I get the resistance to hearing any argument against it, I really do. I understand it gives you a purpose, and much needed peace in your hearts, believing you're on a noble pursuit for humanity's cure. But I ask you: what is so noble about all those poor infected souls you've had to kill along the way on your quest to capture samples for your leash-masters? Can't you see the hypocrisy in that? If they're really going to develop a vaccine, then you've killed innocent people who otherwise could've been saved. Haven't you? What about *their* salvation through inoculation? If the vaccine is truly coming, then they've turned you all into murderers." Schef held out a placatory hand to stifle any rebuttals and barreled on, "Now, in my view, I, of course, see absolutely nothing wrong with doing what is necessary to stay alive. I blame none of you for anything you've had to do on your missions. That's not the point I'm trying to make here. I'm just trying to illustrate for you the obvious duplicitous nature of your employer. They are clearly willing to make any sacrifice necessary for the benefit of the corporation, short of risking their own skins, that is. It's fairly easy to see, with a step back and a bit of objective perspective, that they are, and have always been, lying to you."

"Well, thanks for your wildly inaccurate snap judgments, sir," Marge said in her calm voice. "But all of us already know damn well that we only do what is necessary to protect the team down there. I wouldn't expect you to understand, Mr. Aponyaschefski. You really think what we've had to do these past few months doesn't haunt every officer in this Star Hawk? We don't need you judging us from the outside, sir. Our own consciences take care of that well enough; we don't need your help. You've been with us for a half a fucking day,

Mr. Aponyaschefski. You don't know us, or AOA. So do us all a favor and hold your tongue about issues to which you have no grounds to an opinion." Marge nearly spat. Abner was certain she would, but she restrained herself, filling her lungs instead and releasing a calming breath, "I'll assign you a guard from among the squad to stick with you and keep you safe. Okay, Mr. Schef? Though, like I said, you have nothing to fear. Despite how much you need a villain to blame and hate—and believe me, I get that—AOA is not the evil corporation you'd have them be."

"I don't wish to give offense when I tell you I disagree, Sergeant, but I'm afraid I do disagree."

"I'll stick with him, Marge," Monty said, surprising Abner, and judging by their collective gasp, his whole squad as well.

"You, boss?" Marge asked, warily.

"I'll keep the brass out of his hair," Monty answered her with no emotion.

The commander turned in his jumpseat to face Schef. Abner watched as the two men exchanged nods of offer and acceptance. It somehow felt as though they had just become co-conspirators of a sort. Monty hadn't reacted much while Schef had articulated his wild opinions, but the way he'd quickly agreed to be the man's personal escort aboard station suggested Monty had been taken in by his crazy theories. Abner turned and slowly made his way back to his jumpseat, his mind abuzz with a million trains of thought, all of which mingled with a foggy, unfocused dire premonition.

CHAPTER 5

ELIAS

Infection Event: Day 58

The pitch floated over the heart of the plate slow enough to make the red-stitched white orb appear as large as a beachball. Elias Sagal knew it was a curve the moment it left Ricky Allanson's fingers. The boy was as predictable as the sun. Though, none of the other kids aboard the station had really been able to give him the challenge he craved either. Elias didn't find that fact very surprising, seeing as how there were only about fifty kids total in his age range aboard station. Elias had been a Little League All Star three years running back on Earth, while most of those kids in his age range had never even played tee ball, much less baseball. So his lack of suitable competition had been just one of the many things he'd been slowly coming to grips with over the past few weeks. It had sapped some of the joy from the game for Elias, but he still played as often as he could. Lately though, most of the fun he'd been able to get from the game was coming at Ricky Allanson's expense.

Ricky thought he was hot shit and top dog. Elias was overly familiar with his kind, to his eternal annoyance, and Ricky fit the stereotype like a sword fits its sheath. He was always running his mouth, relentlessly mocking any kid worse at the game than him. He'd even tried to bully Elias. *Tried and failed,* he recalled with pride.

Elias Sagal was a quiet kid. A lot of bullies mistook quiet for cowardice; he'd noticed that over the years, and Ricky was no different. The first time some of the kids got together for a pick-up game in The

Meadow, Ricky, for whatever reason, zeroed in on Elias as a suitable target for his derision. Elias had taken it in stride. He'd gotten quite good at that over the years too. He was one of the last kids picked for the game that first day. His team's captain must've shared Ricky's initial scorn for him as well because he proceeded to slot him in the eighth spot in the batting order. Elias didn't mind that either. He let it slide and waited patiently for his turn at the plate.

Finally, it had come. Then, as now, it was still just the first inning and Elias' team had already plated three runs. Then, as now, there were two outs, and runners at the corners, with Ricky toeing the rubber on the pitcher's mound. And then, as now, Ricky had brushed him back with the first pitch, only to toss the floating meatball he had the audacity to call a curve with his second. And, then as now, Elias kept his weight back on his right leg, not fooled by the off-speed pitch in the least. As the ball floated down over the heart of the plate at waist height, Elias corked his hips, both then and now, and pushed his hands through the strike-zone. His left foot lifted off the turf slightly, only a few inches, and once planted again, he dug his toes deep into the gravelly dirt around the batter's box. He used the left foot as a plant to stabilize the momentum of his follow through as he whipped the barrel of his bat across the plate. Then, as now, the meaty part of the bat's barrel contacted the ball at a rising angle and the sweet sound of flush bat-on-ball-contact reverberated around the massive indoor field. Though Elias could not see it, he knew the finely-stitched ball of worn leather contracted into itself, both then and now, and in the next instant was soaring through the air, stretching into a gravity-defying elongated oval.

That first hit had soared over the head of the befuddled center fielder. This pitch, however, was cranked over the leftfielder's head in a matter of mere milliseconds. Elias could have trotted around the bags twice before any member of the opposing team ever caught up with it. He didn't do anything so unsportsmanlike, however. Instead, he jogged around the bases with his shoulders straight and head held high. His teammates greeted him with plaudits at home plate, and as they jumped up and down in celebration around him, he stared out to the pitcher's mound. Once he caught Ricky's eye, he gave him a patronizing wink and a wicked grin, and only then did he saunter back to his team's dugout.

Elias sat down on the home team's bench and slid his Nike outfielders glove over his left hand. He used his right to punch the webbing, continuing the endless work of breaking in the glove. He should've been paying attention to Tessa Rodriguez in the batter's box, but the allure of the awe-inspiring sight that was The Meadow's Stargazer Ceiling distracted him. He was staring up at the high, transparent ceiling, full of dumbfounded disbelief as he unthinkingly kept up with punching the inside of his ball glove. He'd hit the snot out of that curveball and sent it flying at least 350 feet on a steep arc, yet the ball hadn't even come close to scraping the gaping, crystal-clear expanse above him. *It must be a thousand feet high,* Elias thought in amazement, and not for the first time.

Of all the incredible stuff Cardinal's Nest had to offer a young excitable mind, Stargazer Ceiling had been the one to captivate Elias' sense of wonder the most. He wasn't really old enough to truly understand just how far AOA's tech had advanced, and so, while most adults were talking about the gravity systems, power conversion systems and water filtration and collection systems, and of course, all the super-fancy interplanetary-ships, Elias found the gigantic transparent ceiling in The Meadow to be the most interesting thing about the station.

The Meadow itself was also pretty neat too, in Elias' book. He'd been afraid that having to stay aboard the station would mean the end of his baseball-playing days, so he'd been extremely happy when his father had first shown Maisie and him The Meadow.

At the end of Branch 5, a huge circular pale gray superstructure, trimmed in a dull orange, flared out from its end like a lollipop on a stick. The circular structure of The Meadow stretched some 600 yards in diameter. A lazy river flowed around the inside of the wall and encircled three distinct nature areas. Each of the nature areas were enclosed in a weird bubble that was nearly invisible, apart from a light-blue haze just on the edge of perception. Elias' dad had called the bubbles *magnetic suspensor fields.* They contained the three very distinct environmental conditions within, yet also allowed residents to pass through them with no resistance, save an ever so slight tingle. The entire facility was lit by two rows of angled stadium lights glaring down from atop the pale gray walls. The lights followed the path of the gentle river beneath them, encircling the three isolated nature areas inside the superstructure.

In the center of the chamber, and stretching from riverbank to riverbank, was the meadow that gave the facility its name. Its lush green grass was dotted with fields of lilac and lavender, daisies and sunflowers, roses and raspberry bushes, and a hundred other flora species besides. A trimmed, leveled and manicured section near The Meadow's towering archway had been set aside to use for base-ball, football, soccer and a few other sports. The meadow stretched almost 550 yards in length, from riverbank to riverbank, with a width of about 300 yards. The meadow rose up on either side to a gentle slope. At the summit of these slopes, two of the suspensor fields met, pressing airtight against each other to produce the light-blue haze.

The suspensor field bubble that was on the right side of the circle as you entered through the archway contained the warm, thin and arid climate that suited the rolling sand dunes of The Meadow's desert. The desert also ran about 550 yards at its longest, from river-bank to riverbank, but stretched only about a 120 yards at its widest, which was slope's summit to riverbank. A small oasis stood in the center of the desert.

On the opposite side of the meadow, another suspensor bubble contained the thick, wet and moderate climate most conducive to the green pine forest spread out within. The pine forest was roughly equal in dimensions to that of the desert. Towering elms, ash, maple and oaks were scattered among the thick pines as well. The trees were all transported—at great cost, and by some impossible engineering effort that baffled Elias' dad—from Tiger Mountain State Forest in the northwest part of the state of Washington. All three distinct environ-ments boasted a wide array of wildlife that The Meadow's entrance archway and its suspensor fields somehow kept contained.

Amazing as those achievements seemed to be to most folks, Elias found the transparent ceiling to be the true wonder of the place. There were other ceiling openings, along with large portholes, in nearly every corridor of the station, but all of them, including the giant oculus in the Grand Rotunda, were paneled in cloudy glass, not like Stargazer

Ceiling. If you didn't know that a glass ceiling was there, you'd assume The Meadow was open to the elements. It appeared seamless, with absolutely no glare. Elias knew it had a slight convex rise, but it was all but imperceptible to the naked eye. It was amazing, in short, and he was certain he'd never grow tired of looking up through it.

He was willing to drag his gaze away long enough to play the game he loved, however. Which he managed to do just as Tessa Rodriguez popped out to the right fielder to end the inning. Elias jogged past her on his way to center field, tugging on the bill of the plain blue ballcap his mother bought him on one of their excursions around town she used to take him on. He had only been seven during that particular day-on-the-town with his mother, and the cap was proof of that; snapped in back now on its very last button. Elias knew he would have to give it up soon, but the thought always made him so sad that he would immediately direct his mind away from it. This time he did so by offering up his honest enthusiasm and deeply felt praise for the lovely chestnut-eyed beauty named Tessa Rodriguez, encouraging her that the next one she hit was sure to drop in. He said it loud enough for Ricky Allanson to hear as well and was rewarded with a petulant look from the opposing pitcher before the prick turned away and slow-jogged to the visitor's bench.

Being the quiet introvert he was, Elias did not stay in The Meadow after the baseball game to hang, as most of the kids that played had. Contented with the trouncing he and his team had put on Ricky and his squad, and satisfied that no further games would be played that day, Elias decided to engage in his second-favorite activity aboard station: roaming the halls and tunnels of Cardinal's Nest on his own. He was pretty certain he'd seen everything the station had to offer by now, but he could never really be sure. After all, every time he'd thought that in the past, he'd been wrong; some previously unseen access tunnel, or hatchway, or narrow passage would suddenly reveal itself, and yet another of the station's secrets would be uncloaked.

I better check in with Maisie first, he thought, a little sullenly. His sister and he only had a few days alone with their father after coming aboard the station before AOA had come begging Dr. Perry Sagal for help. And of course, being the stand-up guy his father was, the good doctor could not refuse them. Maisie had told Elias not to be angry with their father for being so busy, though he really hadn't needed to be told. He was only eleven, but he knew that something really bad had happened on Earth. He knew it was some kind of infection thing. Which meant it was a medical problem. Which, in turn, meant his dad could help. And if Perry Sagal could help, he would. Elias had known that since he'd first known anything. So Maisie's appeal for understanding over his father's lack of family time was unnecessary, and a bit overbearing, really.

His father had been spending nearly all of his time in the corporate sector's science lab down Branch 1. He'd come back to their living quarters most nights around midnight, station-time. Elias stayed up every night waiting for him. Despite the half-hearted protests his father made about this fact, Elias figured his dad was really pleased to see him, and his demands to go to sleep had just been ceremonial. His father would ask if he was obeying his sister, and if he'd eaten dinner and brushed his teeth and done his chores. But once all that was out of the way, he'd snuggle up quietly beside his father on the tan couch in their living room and drift off to sleep beside him within a few minutes as his dad sipped at a glass of well-iced Pappy Van Winkle bourbon, his father's favorite. The old man had sneaked a few bottles of the expensive stuff aboard station in his luggage back when he'd first come to Cardinal's Nest with the prep crew. Those small moments in the wee hours of the night were just about the extent of his interactions with his father for weeks now.

Though Maisie was only a year and five months older than him, she had been responsible for looking after Elias for over six months back on Earth, so it had been no shock to have her in charge of him aboard Cardinal's Nest either. Sure, she could be a bit over-protective and excessively critical, but ultimately Elias figured he understood why she acted that way and had accepted her authority with little push back. Maisie loved him and his father deeply. She was determined not to fail either of them. And so, she kept a steadfast eye on her younger brother. She demanded Elias tell her everywhere he was going and check in with her every couple hours. Maisie was most likely helping out Boyd, the station's resident priest, at the half-assed storefront he'd turned his living quarters into. So, it was to Branch 4 and the Living Quarters, Violet Corridor beyond that Elias set his feet.

Maroon plastic folding tables were erected to either side of the entrance hatch to Father Boyd's living quarters. Recycled plastic and glass bottles of various sizes lined every inch of the tables' surfaces. The bottles were filled either with a clear liquid, or one of deep dark red. Elias had spent enough time around Father Boyd and his various customers to know that the clear liquid was something called moonshine, while the red was wine. The priest brewed and distilled a few other drinks in his living quarters as well, beer and mead among them. He had quite the elaborate operation inside his small, single-tenant chambers.

Most of his furniture had been removed, and he'd blocked off a small square area in the central chamber of his living quarters. Inside that area, he slept, ate, and tended to his business. Among the various bubbling pots and fermenting jars, two narrow openings had been blocked off, one leading to his bathroom, and the other to his automatic hatchway. Other than that, nearly every square foot of space was occupied with equipment of one kind or another. Including a brightly lit hydroponic garden where he was currently in the early stages of growing a half-dozen marijuana plants. Father Boyd hadn't exactly told Elias and Maisie that the plants were marijuana, but he didn't exactly deny it either. Elias and Maisie had both spent enough time around their stoner Uncle Jimmy, their mother's younger brother, to know what marijuana both smelled and looked like.

Maisie definitely knew it was weed. She was like the priest's little apprentice, running chores for him, helping him sell his bottles of alcohol and collecting the empties to be used once again, stirring vats and pots, filling bottles and then adding them either to shelves for further fermenting or to the display tables out front of Father Boyd's entrance hatch. She was a *Jack-of-all-trades*, as Perry Sagal might say.

Elias thought it was strange how much the priest seemed to trust his sister, but he supposed Maisie had a way about her that made adults trust her. *It makes everyone trust her.* She made the perfect salesman for the priest. Her rigid attention to detail, coupled with her tender care of his product, allowed him to focus on the thousand projects he had in operation inside his tiny chambers. Elias could certainly understand the priest wanting to take advantage of what his sister offered.

Their relationship still made him a bit uncomfortable, nonetheless. It seemed to Elias that Maisie was sounding more and more like Father Boyd every day. He didn't want to admit it to himself, but deep down inside, he felt Maisie was betraying their dad in some way. Seeing her and the priest bustling around in perfect coordination inside the cramped brew house that was Father Boyd's living quarters had been starting to irritate Elias more and more. So when the hatchway slid open, retracting smoothly into the wall with a soft woosh of compressed air, and Elias stepped into the cramped chamber to see that very picture, he immediately felt the agitation rise up within.

"Hey, Elias! How'd the game go?" Maisie asked as soon as she looked over and saw her little brother standing just inside the hatchway.

"Oh, it went okay. I hit a few good ones. We won, anyway," Elias answered after taking a moment to calm himself.

"Elias, my good man. How goes it? You didn't see anybody out front, did ya?" Father Boyd asked after looking up from the steaming vat he had been stirring.

"Nuh uh," Elias said, shaking his head.

"Want to lend us a hand, kiddo?" The priest asked with a grin.

"No, I bet he's just here to tell me he's going exploring again," Maisie put in. "My brother is done working for you for free," she jokingly told the priest.

"Well, here's to hoping you're never struck by that same principle," Father Boyd said, raising a wine bottle in his right hand.

Father Boyd was one strange priest. Elias had figured that out pretty fast. His father must've known the priest was a little out there as well. He remembered the first time his dad had introduced them to Father Boyd. He had pulled them aside before the introduction to warn them that the priest might seem a bit odd. The priest had, in fact, been odd, but he was also undeniably charming as well. Maisie was sure hooked after that first encounter, anyway. She'd spent parts of nearly every day since in the priest's company.

And so, Elias *too* had been often in the priest's company. And the more time he spent with Father Boyd, the stranger the man seemed. He wasn't like other priests. Elias had never been to church. And even if he ever had gone, his father would have probably taken them to temple, seeing as how Perry Sagal's parents had both been Jewish. So he'd never met an actual priest, or a pastor, or rabbi, or anything before. But even so, Father Boyd was nothing like what you would expect of a church leader. For one thing, he didn't seem very *religious*. He never talked about Jesus, or quoted scripture, or anything like that. He didn't look like what you expect a typical priest to look like either. He was a large, physically intimidating man, with broad square shoulders and a beer belly, and he didn't dress like the priests Elias had seen on TV. He mostly wore sweatshirts, jeans and sneakers. Every once in a while, Elias would catch him without one of his many hoodies on, and on those rare occasions, he would be wearing the classic priest's black dress shirt with that weird white square at the collar, right in the middle of the neck. But he had definitely been wearing that uniform less and less. Father Boyd never passed judgment either, or tried to reform anybody's evil ways, at least not that Elias had ever seen. Instead, the man seemed to be the kind of guy you'd expect to hear priests preaching against. His only real care seemed to be his make-shift liquor store. He did love to talk though, and people often stopped by to do just that. Sometimes they traded a few credits for a few bottles, sometimes they didn't, but all day long they came.

"Can I go?" Elias asked his sister, pointedly ignoring the grinning priest in the far corner of the open space.

"Sure," his sister answered with a sweet smile that seemed to convey she knew exactly what he'd been thinking. "Just be back to our living quarters by six-o'clock ST. I'm headed there in a few minutes to get dinner ready. I'm making pork steaks and fresh asparagus from the commissary. Dad promised he'd be home for supper too, so be sure you're there on time."

"I will," Elias quietly promised as he turned to exit the steamy, noisy, thousand-odored chamber. He didn't make it a single step before the hatchway swooshed open ahead of him. A large, dark figure filled the open portal, blotting out all but a few beams of light from the alleyway beyond, outlining his shape. Elias craned his head up to see the familiar figure of Jasper Montrois stride a long pace into the priest's living quarters. The security commander looked down at Elias standing a few steps in front of him. The expression on the man's face didn't even flicker. *Doesn't he even know me?*

He couldn't tell if Monty had been cold to him because he blamed Elias and Maisie for boarding the shuttle without Carrie and Roxanna, or if the pain of losing them, along with all the trips back to Earth he and his squad had taken had simply scoured the commander into an empty shell of his former self. Elias had never actually met him in person before Carrie had heroically gotten he and his sister aboard the shuttle just before they sealed the hatch on that E-11 and blasted off, but from what Carrie had told him about Monty during their Dr. Pepper chats, the giant, scruffy-faced, gorilla-shaped security officer had changed drastically. Elias had kept his distance from the dark, brooding man for the first few weeks after coming aboard the station, but eventually he'd worked up the courage to approach the leader of the security staff—those courageous warriors who risked their necks every day to fight monsters on Earth in an attempt to find the cure for the infection.

Perry Sagal had been trying not-so-subtly to get his son interested in medicine and science, but it was the black-clad soldiers Elias truly admired and wanted to emulate. He loved and respected his father for the work he and the science team were doing to find the cure, but it wasn't like risking your neck and battling the Damned back on Earth. Elias venerated the security officers more and more with each passing day and each new mission. And Jasper Montrois was the leader of that band of heroes. The man was on a different plane of idol, or icon, or whatever for Elias. He'd needed to offer him his condolences, to tell Monty how much he admired his wife and daughter, and everything they'd meant to him. He'd meant to tell him about the tremendous respect and esteem he had for Carrie, and how he'd never forget what she did for him, and how he would make it up to her someday, or earn what she did for him somehow, or at least pay it forward in some way.

He'd meant to say all of that. Instead, he'd just stuttered, spluttered and muttered out some incoherent nonsense. Just being in Montrois' immediate vicinity had emptied him of all his confidence, rendering him a babbling fool. In the end, he wasn't even sure Montrois had ever really even known Elias had been talking to him. After all, the whole time he'd been stammering, the Goliath of a man had never once made eye contact. He did, however, nod once at the end of Elias' stutters and give a grunt. Elias had assumed it signaled the end of the one-sided conversation. He'd run from the intimidating hulk and couldn't find the courage to look back.

And now he felt a strong impulse to do that very thing again, as Monty gazed down at him with that same cold, unfocused gaze. *Like he's deliberately not seeing you.* Elias probably would've run if it had been possible to do so, but there was no room to either side of Monty. Racks of shelves lined the narrow path on one side from the hatchway to the central space, while the other side of the path was lined with stacks of boxes, piles of discarded parts, tables of unusable bottles, and who knew what else, *bric-a-brac*, Elias' father would've called it. After a few tense and silent moments, which seemed to last an eternity, Elias began to back up into the room, allowing Monty to get by. Two steps into Elias' backtrack, Monty cleared his throat. "Excuse me, Father," he rumbled in a deep voice that seemed to boom inside his chest.

Although the notification was spoken at a relatively low volume, barely louder than the ambient noise of the room, Father Boyd was still able to hear it. "Commander Montrois, to what do I owe the pleasure?" the priest asked with genuine curiosity in his voice.

Monty turned his body, pressing his back against the shelves to his left to reveal a new figure now outlined in the fluorescent lighting of the alleyway beyond. "I'd like to introduce ya to the new guy," he said, giving said new guy an "after you" gesture.

The man took the offer, scooting past Monty into the open central space. Elias countered the new guy's move and found himself the one now standing in the narrow passageway. He paused there to take in the newcomer. The man was much smaller than Monty.

He had squeezed past him with relative ease, despite the limits of the cramped passage. Once the man had gained the comfort of the open space, he gazed around the room with slight amusement on his thin face. Elias watched as he finished his scan of the room and offered up a tiny twinkling smirk at Father Boyd as his only greeting.

Monty stepped a few paces further. "Father Boyd, this is Harclay Aponyaschefski," he said, indicating the slender man. "He's the fella we picked up down there on our last recon. I'm sure you've heard about it by now."

"We've heard a few whispers. Haven't we, Mais?" Father Boyd asked his apprentice with a sarcastic smile.

"More than a few," Maisie answered, staring the newcomer up and down with a suspicious eye.

"It's a pleasure to meet you, Mr. Aponyaschefski," Boyd said, struggling with the pronunciation.

"Call me Schef."

"Okay then, Mr. Schef, it's a pleasure. Anything I can do for ya to help you adjust, you just let me know."

Elias realized in that moment that no one in the room was paying any attention to him in the slightest. A sudden whim struck him so hard he found his legs moving without his conscious permission. Taking three delicate backward paces deeper into the passageway, he came up alongside the one and only gap in the tangle of wares. Beneath a table strewn with half-full boxes of one thing or another, lay the narrowest of gaps. If Elias were even a pound or two heavier, or an inch or two bigger, as he so often wished to be, he would've never been able to squeeze through, but thankfully, that wish had yet to be granted. Elias squirmed through the gap so quickly and deftly as to draw no attention. At least that's what he guessed happened due to the lack of reaction he heard in the room in the wake of his strange maneuver.

The first voice he heard after his scramble and squirm was Monty's, and it was as casual as Elias had ever heard it. "Your help is kinda why we are here, Father."

"Oh, is that so?" Boyd asked in a tone of slight confusion. "I can start you a tab for a few bottles, Mr. Schef, but I'm afraid everybody pays. It's the only way to keep it honest," Boyd said in a self-deprecating manner.

"I still got a few bottles I been sharing with him, Father," Monty cut in with the tiniest hint of humor in his voice.

"No complaints, I trust."

"None. You brew a fine ale, Father," Monty answered flatly.

"And the moonshine was so good it brought tears to my eyes," Schef put in with a chuckle.

"We just need a few minutes of your time, Father, if it ain't asking too much," Monty said in a way that made it seem like an order.

"Oh... uh... yeah, of course. Maisie," the priest called, turning to his apprentice, "why don't you go ahead and get that dinner of yours started a little early. I can handle the rest of this stuff tonight. Just turn down those burners behind ya."

"Oh... okay, Boyd, sure," Maisie answered, sounding wounded.

Elias squirmed and shimmied his way through the maze of discarded and surplus equipment, trying to find a vantage point offering both cover and a clear view of the people in the room. He stopped beneath a table near the back wall of the priest's living quarters that satisfied his requirements. The table held up two giant stainless steel pots, bubbling with some kind of alcohol, Elias wasn't sure which. There were stacks of brown boxes piled up underneath its tabletop, allowing him to completely conceal himself behind them. Elias rolled and scooched into a comfortable viewing position, achieving that aim just as his sister finished turning off two burners under two other bubbling pots.

After she stomped out of the quarters without a glance back or a shout for him to follow, he figured Maisie must've forgotten about him. Her loud and unhappy exit seemed to unnerve the three men for a few moments. All of them appeared somewhat nonplussed and thrown off their games a bit. At least, none of them had the presence of mind to remember Elias, anyway. He certainly heard no shouted demands for him to leave. They all must've assumed he left as soon as Monty and the new guy arrived, if they thought about him at all.

Elias had to lay flat on the ground to be able to get a good enough angle to see the faces of all three men now. It helped when the new guy, Harclay, sat down on one of the only two chairs in the room and Monty half-leaned, half-sat against the steel table behind him. Father

Boyd was clearly framed through Elias' looking gap, still stirring his steaming vat in the far corner.

"This is one hell of an operation you got going on here, padre," Schef broke the awkward silence.

"Why, thank you," Boyd said without looking up from his labor. "It started as simple necessity, but it's grown into something quite unwieldy."

"Necessity?" Schef inquired with apparent curiosity.

"Yeah, the AOA geniuses provided every imaginable amenity aboard this space town of theirs, besides the most important one," Boyd grabbed up the three-quarters-full wine bottle from the table next to him and took a long swig. When he pulled the bottle down, his lips were curled in a childish smirk and the bottle was only half full. "I was aboard the shuttle that brought the first prep crew workers here... What was that, Monty, seven ... eight months ago now?"

"Eight," said Monty.

"Eight," the priest repeated, shaking his head in astonishment. "So anyway, when I couldn't find any bars or liquor stores down in the Rec District, or anywhere else in this lunar monstrosity, I figured liquor must not have been a top priority for them—the damn fools—and I assumed it must be coming on a later shuttle. Only the shuttles kept coming and coming, loaded to maximum capacity with cargo every time, mind you, and much to my displeasure, not a one brought with it any liquor of any kind. I mean, I was close to raiding the kitchens for cooking sherry at one point ... at my wits end, so to speak. But then I remembered the internet. It's a hell of a thing that interweb," the priest broke off to laugh at his own statement. "I taught myself how to brew beer and mead, and how to distill wine and that moonshine that made you cry. The prep crewmen were awfully thankful of my newfound skills after those first few dry weeks, let me tell ya. You remember that, Monty?"

Monty acknowledged with a small nod.

"Why no alcohol aboard?" Schef asked.

"Don't know," shrugged Boyd. "There wasn't nothing about it in the contracts they made us sign, I know that. I'da never came aboard if it had been. I'd most likely be one of Monty's Damned right about now." Schef looked over his shoulder at the commander after that statement. The two men locked eyes without the priest's notice. "Maybe some temperance kooks are running the corporation. Or they were afraid we'd all get drunk and burn their fancy fishbowl down," Boyd added, indicating the station around him. "Who the hell knows. I just know that the liquor never came, and improvisation was necessary."

"Where did you get the hops for the beer and the grapes for the wine?" Schef asked. "I see you got a little hydroponics garden behind ya back there, but those look like pot-plants to me."

"Good eye, my man. I had the seeds for those bad boys, and the hops, snuck aboard for me by a friendly shuttle crewman about four months back. In exchange for absolution ... and a cut of the profits." Boyd once more broke off to laugh at his own quip. "The grapes I get from the greenhouse. They have a seed for every fruit and vegetable you could ever think of in the freezer vaults down there. Plus, the head botanist who runs the joint is partial to her wine and ale, so it was no difficult task to convince her to keep a small vineyard and hop field for me in a far corner of that gargantuan greenhouse. I got a few other mutually lucrative deals with various other crewmembers spread out through useful positions across the station as well. But I'll keep those to myself, if ya don't mind."

"Fair enough," Schef said, wearing what looked to Elias to be a false grin. "AOA is okay with you selling this stuff from here in your quarters, then?"

"I don't know really. They ain't said nothing so far," the priest answered. "They don't ever drag their asses out of their private, luxurious accommodations down Branch 1. Although, they do got all those damn flashing digital signs on every frickin' wall of every goddamn passageway, and those dumb fucking information kiosks at every alleyway junction warning us that their fancy AI program is monitoring us from their austere, creepy-ass, frigid frickin' Main Control Room, eager to hand out credits to the worthy. *No good deed goes unrewarded aboard Cardinal's Nest,*" Boyd parroted a ubiquitous flashing sign example with heavy sarcasm.

"Yeah, I think we saw a few of those signs on the way here," Schef put in with a chuckle.

"Ha, huh. Yeah, it may be hard to find a single square foot of this station that doesn't have one camera or another pointed at it. But what of it? In the end, Monty is their muscle. He and his squad are pretty much all that constitutes a police force of any kind up here."

"Luckily for you, Monty and his squad like a good drink," Schef said in a strange way, like this point had more import than it seemed.

"Uh... yeah, luckily they do," Boyd said after a slight awkward pause. "So ... what did you do before the Infection Event, Mr. Aponyaschefski?"

"Oh, I had a small law practice ... mostly divorces and wills and boring shit like that. It was a happy enough little life though, relative to current circumstances."

"How did you survive down there for so long?" Boyd inquired.

"My son and I hid out in a cave system in the woods just outside our town."

"Your son?" Boyd cautiously prompted.

"Yeah, he... he..." Schef trailed off, and just when it seemed he would stay silent forever, light came back to his face. "They got him in the end," he said in a strangely emotionless way that struck Elias as false.

"I'm so sorry," Boyd said, sincerity plain in his gravelly voice.

"They would've gotten me too, if not for Monty and his team," Schef barreled on as if he hadn't heard him.

"You were lucky AOA and that gang of nut-less world leaders sent the security team on recon to your little town, I guess," Boyd added off-handedly.

Schef didn't answer that right away. Rather, he made a big show of looking around the cramped room once again. The stranger spun around in place slower than Ricky Allanson's fastball, and for a portion of the revolution, Elias caught a good glimpse of his face. It wore a look that Elias figured even the fanciest, most expensive psychiatrists-ology-Dr. Freud-people couldn't hope to decipher. His right eyebrow was crooked up in a sharp, incredulous arch, while his lips were pressed thin, yet fighting the first hints of a smile threatening to spread out from their soft corners.

The man fascinated Elias. Here was someone different. Here was the dawn of some *thing* different. A soundless voice spoke to Elias from deep within his soul after that good long look at the stranger's coy face. It told him that his dull days aboard this beautiful prison were numbered. Although Elias couldn't say what it was exactly that the stranger presaged, he knew it was sure to be interesting. People like his dad were forever struggling uphill to set the world to order. Elias used to revere such folks for their fortitude, his father especially, but recently he'd found himself pitying his father's naivete, rather than admiring it, even though that wasn't really something he openly admitted to his conscious self. Elias had been slowly coming to believe, over these past few insane months, that a big damn mess was the world's true natural state. He found it exhausting now to even think about standing in the path of the unstoppable tide. *The mess will always find you in the end*, such was the recent experience of Elias Sagal, anyhow.

Despite the assured mess, he was still eagerly awaiting all the excitement that the stranger's face seemed to promise. Cardinal's Nest was almost completely explored already, despite how large and unending the station once seemed. Elias knew, with a panicked certainty, that he was nearing the end of the Nest's last few undiscovered secrets, and according to his dad, he had months, if not years, to look forward to up here. He was going to be one bored-ass kid soon enough. Elias wasn't looking forward to that in the least.

The excitement the stranger's appearance was sure to bring had Elias vibrating in his hiding spot with giddy anticipation. It was even making him scoot forward almost unknowingly along the floor. Elias bumped softly into the stack of boxes in front of him just as the stranger's circuit brought him face to face with Father Boyd. Elias' heart was in his throat for a heart-stopping second, but the box barely moved. It made no noise at all to speak of, much less one that could be heard over the room's ambient din, but Elias silently cursed himself for a clumsy fool, nonetheless.

"You surprise me, Father. I mean ... you are a priest, aren't you?" Schef's voice traveled clearly to Elias tucked under the table on the room's opposite side, and fast as lightning, all his focus was engaged once more on his self-appointed eavesdropping mission.

"What do you mean?" Father Boyd responded warily.

"Oh, I don't know. It's just ... being a man of faith, I would've thought you'd come to understand the same truth that I've discovered up here."

"And what *truth* is this?"

"Just the fate and destiny of all this, Father," Schef said, indicating the station around him. "Monty's team coming to my little out-of-the-way mountain town wasn't luck, Father Boyd, it was fate."

"Was it now?" Boyd asked with a skeptical grin.

"If you take it into account with everything else, there is no other possible conclusion," Schef answered in a tone laced with righteous certainty.

"What do you mean by *everything else*?" The priest asked, still sounding very skeptical.

"What made you become a priest?"

It seemed to Elias that Boyd must've been momentarily thrown off balance by the abrupt change in subject. He recovered quickly though. "A love of God and all his blessings," he answered, before once again taking a long pull from the wine bottle beside him. "Why do you ask?"

"Just curious." Schef stepped over to a nearby apparatus Boyd used to distill his moonshine. "You don't strike me as overtly pious, if you don't mind me saying. I know we've only just met, but I don't believe I've ever known a churchman quite like you before."

"Well ... I've always been a bit too impulsive, I suppose ... and a bit too stubborn to admit a mistake," Boyd answered him in a tone that gave nothing away. "It's a long story, Mr. Aponyaschefski. Maybe I'll tell it to you over a bottle someday."

"I think I'd like that," Schef stated in a matching tone. "How is it you came to be aboard this station? Is AOA's CEO Catholic, or something like that?"

"Ha, huh, you know what? I don't really know. It wouldn't surprise me though," Boyd chuckled. "I was sent here as a liaison for the church. The Vatican invested a bunch of cash into this station along with all those other governments, so the church was allowed to send a representative aboard, to protect their investment, I guess. In reality, it just ended up being a convenient corner to shove me into and forget about me. They must've figured I couldn't cause them any more problems if I was no longer actually on the planet," he laughed. "And truth be told, I was eager to get away from them too. And now, wouldn't you know it, I find myself the church's supreme authority left in the world, Mr. Schefski, as far as I know anyway." Boyd laughed at this irony for a good bit before looking up at Monty and Schef with a slightly more serious expression. "The whole liaison thing was just a big joke from the start, Mr. Schefski. I'm sure AOA didn't believe the church was actually going to take them up on their offer. So I came aboard to discover my duties were jack and shit. Which suits me just fine really," he chuckled.

"AOA is lying to everyone up here, Father Boyd. You do realize that, right?" Schef asked pointedly, still calmly inspecting the moonshine apparatus.

Boyd finally stopped his stirring to give his whole attention to the conversation. "Say what now?"

"The man who keeps AOA off your back and allows you to boil your brews here unmolested," Schef turned to point a shaky finger at Montrois, "he and his squad are being killed off, one by one, for a lie."

Boyd stepped away from the bubbling vat. Picking up a towel off a nearby shelf, he began to wipe his hands dry while moving to seat himself in a black leather rolling desk chair a few feet away. "That ain't much of a revelation, Mr. Aponyaschefski." he said, after a beat. "Most folks around here figure AOA and the world leaders are lying about what they know about the infection and its origins."

"Well, I'm glad most folks suspect they're lying, but I'm wondering why everyone is going along with it," Schef said, returning to the chair he had previously occupied.

"How do you mean?" Boyd made his question sound both casual and authoritative.

"I mean this whole Alpha thing," Schef said indignantly. "It's bullshit, father. I've been down on the ground since day one of the Infection. I've run from, fought with, and hid from thousands upon thousands of the Damned. I've never seen any signs of a leader amongst them. Never. Not once. They are all the same mindless horrors, Father. All they care about is ending us, humanity. Seek and destroy. It's all they know, Father."

"So, what are you trying to say?" Boyd asked.

"AOA knows they can't cure the infection. Set aside the impossible effort of synthesizing and administering enough vaccine dosages to inoculate the millions of infected souls down on Earth, there isn't anything scientific about the Infection in the first place. There is no vaccine that AOA's scientist can concoct to cure it, because the Infection isn't scientific, or natural, or whatever. It's not a plague, Father, it's a curse. And I think AOA knows that. Think about all the impossible technological advances AOA has produced in the past few years in unprecedented secrecy, despite a global multi-trillion-dollar cooperation effort. And then, just when their fancy lunar station finishes construction and is all ready to receive its inhabitants, a huge, unknown and unnatural plague—that is eerily reminiscent to human lore and legend—suddenly spreads across the Earth at lightning speed. Now, I ask: Doesn't all that seem just a little too convenient to you, father?" Schef plugged right on, not giving Boyd a chance to respond, "AOA knows exactly who let loose the Infection curse. It's the very same people, or beings, or whatever you want to call them, that gave them all their unprecedented tech," Schef said, once more indicating the station around him. "AOA knows they can't cure it, Father. That's what I'm trying to say." *My dad would definitely disagree with that,* Elias thought with certainty. "They know they can't get anything truly useful out of Commander Montrois and his squad's recon missions, but they're sending them out anyway," Schef continued with solemnity in his voice. "They are killing them off, one by one. And now they're even enlisting untrained clowns like this Cainey fella to tag along beside them, risking even more lives in the bargain. And all of it for samples of infected tissue to study so they may slake the very curiosity which I suspect brought the infection curse down upon us in the first place."

A palpable tension hung heavy in the air during the silence that followed Schef's rant. An awkward cough from Father Boyd shattered it. He grumbled in his throat for a few long moments, seemingly deciding how best to respond. Ultimately, he chose to direct his response towards Monty, who had remained silent as Schef spoke, giving nothing away with his body language either, "Has this man convinced you of all this, Monty?" Boyd asked him.

Monty slowly lifted his chin to lock eyes with the seated priest. "It was the crowd of them in that park that finally did it for me, Boyd. I've fought the urge to blame the supernatural and give up on the recons for a while now. I didn't want to believe it was hopeless. I didn't want to give up on all those people down there. I didn't want to imagine a world where we didn't succeed and find a cure ... but the truth of it all hit me when I looked down at that moaning and swaying soulless horde in the park. It would've convinced you too, Boyd, if you'da seen it. I understood in that moment that we were being used. I saw clearly that the infected ain't humans anymore, Father. They are unnatural beings. They are un-dead ... or at least un-living. There is no curing them, and no stopping them, and no hope of taking the surface back while they endure. I saw the whole thing clearly from that rooftop, Boyd. We had a safe refuge, an ark to ride out the flood, and we were rejecting it. I was leading my team into horror week in and week out, and it was all for nothing. I'm realizing now that a part of me knew, even as I looked down at that eerie and unnatural mass of the gathered Damned, that we were on our last mission. My conscience knew the only responsible thing for me to do, as the commander, was to refuse any further orders to return to the surface. And I know now that it can't stop there either. AOA and those corrupt politicians living the good life down Branch 1 cannot be trusted with the governance of this facility."

"They'll waste lives as they please," added Schef. "They've already shown their willingness to do just that."

Boyd took another long swig of his wine bottle and let out a slow, weary breath. "I don't know nothing about any undead. And I'm no fan of any corporation or government, never have been. I wouldn't put any such nonsense past any of 'em. Now, that being said, this *society* we got going on up here, it's fragile, to say the least. You boys go poking big holes in it, and our whole fragile system could collapse in a blink. Despite what I may think of AOA's corporate policies and endeavors, they understand the fragility of this station's survival. We are on the moon, boys, don't forget. This station has countless systems and facilities that need constant supervision and must maintain optimal operating conditions. Which, of course, requires a large workforce focused solely on maintaining said optimal conditions. AOA's credit system may be a bit crude and capitalistic, but to me it seems a practical necessity for keeping the people a happy and contented workforce, one that is able to maintain station operations, allowing us all to survive up here in this unnatural environment. Now, this revolution you are pitching me here and now, holds within it the seeds of our destruction, gentleman, should chaos grip the work-force in its wake."

"You've said it yourself, Father," Schef put in, once more wearing that fake grin, "Monty and his squad are the closest thing to a police force this station has. They already maintain the steady peace. It seems to me to be no big deal to simply have that police force stop taking orders from the toothless bureaucrats."

"And then what? Martial law?" Boyd asked in a disgusted tone.

"No, no. All that comes later. All we are talking about here is stripping everyone down Branch 1 of their power. We need to let all the station residents know that each and every one of us holds the fate of mankind in our very hands, Father. It is up to us to survive, to endure, so that we may one day take back the Earth after the curse has run its course. This station and its capabilities are fate, it seems to me. We have all we need to ensure the survival of the human race right here aboard this miracle lunar palace. There seems to me to be some divine purpose in that, one that I would think would be plain to a man of faith. And if we were to shirk that heavy purpose, there would be no greater failure from any group of people in all of human history. We need to instill in the residents of this station the awesome responsibility on all of our shoulders. We need to get them all to understand just how essential our enduring survival aboard this station is. We need to get them to understand that AOA and the world's *fearless* leaders are standing in the way of that supreme mission. And we need you there beside us when we make that plea to them, Father. To show them we are all in this together. And then, after we take AOA's power away, we can all decide as a community how to best govern ourselves ... a council perhaps. But yes, Father, revolution must come first."

The priest took another long swig from his quickly draining wine bottle. Afterwards, he plastered a sardonic grin across his face as he spoke, "Decide our own government for ourselves, eh? Well, I was always kinda partial to the governmental system Michael Palin outlines in Python's Holy Grail."

"In what?" Schef sounded slightly off his game for the first time since entering the chamber.

"The Holy Grail," the priest said in a way that made it plain only a fool wouldn't understand his reference. "You know, Monty Python, the British comedy troupe from the seventies..." After Schef responded with a flabbergasted shake of his head, Boyd's voice began to sound a little angry, "Oh, come on. Don't tell me you've never seen Monty Python's The Holy Grail."

"I'm sorry. I've never seen it, I'm afraid," Schef admitted.

"Blasphemy," Boyd said with outrage that sounded only slightly playful. He let the tension brew for a few heartbeats before snapping it with a chuckle. "Well anyway, near the beginning of the movie, Palin is playing a character named Dennis ... I think... ha, yeah, Dennis. Anyway, he goes on as this Dennis character to articulate to King Arthur—played by the late great Graham Chapman—he goes on to tell Arthur that he lives in an *anarcho-syndicalist commune and they take it in turns to act as a sort of executive officer for the week, but all the decisions of that officer have to be ratified at the bi-weekly meeting. By a simple majority in the case of purely internal affairs, but by a two-thirds majority in the case of major affairs* ... or something to that effect," he added with a long giggle that the other two men did not share.

"Huh, well that's one way to go," Schef said, uncomfortably. "Sounds a little like socialism to me, but whatever."

"Oh, you're one of *those*," Boyd said with an overt eyeroll.

"One of what?" Schef asked, sounding a little hostile.

"Never mind."

Monty stood up from his leaning position, drawing the attention of the two other men, "We just need you to help keep the peace during the transition, Boyd, whatever that transition will lead to. Can I count on you for that?" Monty picked up a bottle off a nearby shelf, making sure Boyd saw him do it.

After a slight pause, in which Elias could see tremendous calculation behind the priest's eyes, the clergyman slowly nodded his head, "You can always count on me to keep the peace, Commander. You should know that by now. But if you want this *transition* to go smoothly, you better get Mikkelson on board. You know he controls the credit distribution. If you want to avoid anarchy—and I'm hoping you do—you'll need him on your side."

"I know that, Boyd. We've still got a few more people to meet with privately before we bring our plans to Mikkelson. But rest assured, the credit flow won't be interrupted, whatever we do," Montrois guaranteed.

"And your protection and freedom to operate your liquor store won't be interrupted either," Schef added with a venomous smile.

"Just keep this conversation between us before we make any moves. Can you do that for me, Boyd?" Montrois asked in a tone that sounded a lot like an order.

"Mum's the word," Boyd answered with forced lightness.

"Good." With that, the bulky, bear-like security commander turned on his heel and exited Father Boyd's living quarters. Schef offered up the priest one last smile coupled with a knowing wink before turning to follow Montrois through the automatic hatchway.

They weren't gone more than five seconds before Elias heard Boyd call out, "You can come on out of there now, kiddo."

Elias was frozen stiff with shock and fear. *He knew I was here the whole time?* After a few moments, he realized the jig was up and lying prone on the ground any longer was just making an ass out of himself, so he stood up slowly and brushed the dust from the front of his sweatpants and t-shirt. "You knew?" He asked the priest in bewilderment.

"Of course I knew."

"Then w-wh-why..." Elias' childhood stutter suddenly came back, to his great shame.   Gracefully, the priest interrupted, "I don't trust Monty anymore, kid; trauma has corrupted him. And I only know that new guy from the stories I've been hearing about him today. And all that I did hear about him has me greatly concerned ... *very* greatly concerned." *You sure don't make it obvious,* Elias thought. "I didn't know what to expect when they came sauntering into my chambers," Boyd continued. "I figured a witness might not be such a bad thing. Your sister must've figured the same when she left without calling for you to follow. I'm sure she'll want to know all about this little clandestine meeting you've listened in on, so why don't you run on back to your quarters and fill her in. But only her, you understand me?" The priest demanded, with the first hint of steel in his voice.

"Yes," Elias answered quickly. He nodded his head vigorously as well, conveying to the priest he had understood the gravity and the import of what he had just overheard.

"Good," said Boyd. "Make sure you tell your old man as well. And tell him I want to see him too. Tell him tonight would be best. Can you do that for me, Elias?"

"Yes," was once again Elias' answer, along with the vigorous nod.

"Okay, good. Now, go on, get out of here," Boyd added with a sorrow-edged smirk. "Remember, not a word to anybody but your sister and father."

Elias omitted the verbal response this time, but his nod was just as vigorous. Halfway down the path that led to the hatchway, he turned back to see the priest had returned to his bubbling vat like a moth to the flame. Elias paused for a moment to watch the big and scruffy phony preacher-man slowly and methodically stir the concoction before him. Elias had been forgotten, quick as that, set aside by Boyd as easily as he tossed his towel back down among his table's assorted clutter. The false prophet was back to having only enough room in his mind for his precious hobby. Feeling insignificant in an upside-down world, Elias disappeared through the hatchway.

CHAPTER 6

JED

A solitary cinnamon roll remained nestled atop its wax paper on the third shelf of the sweets cabinet. It rotated ever so slowly, giving its white frosting an irresistibly tantalizing twinkle supplied by the cabinet's heat lamps glistening off the sugary surface. Jed Redding opened the door of the little cabinet perched at the end of the long, multi-segmented hot buffet line a dozen yards from the entrance archway of the Main Cafeteria Hall. He delicately removed the gooey treat, placing it carefully on his brown tray. It sat alongside a glass of orange juice, two pieces of white toast and a smoke-gray ceramic plate piled high with a healthy heaping of scrambled eggs along with a sensible portion of pork sausage links. *At least we're still eating well,* Jed thought as he cleared the buffet line and scanned the cafeteria for an open seat at one of the 143 tables dotting the hall's sparklingly waxed tile floor.

Jed had been spending a lot of time lately pointing out to himself all the things he should be thankful for. He was far from anything any sort of rational person would call religious, but knowing what his fate most likely would have been if he hadn't signed his contract with AOA to be a collector module pilot had shaken loose in his heart a new appreciation for each day and its little luxuries. The food really was good too, so it was by no means a struggle to force that appreciation. More and more folks lately had been buying their groceries at the commissary with their earned credits and preparing their own meals in their living quarters with their families. And although he had earned his fair share of credits over the last few months, Jed was still content seeking out one or the other of the cafeteria halls for his daily three squares.

A small collection of cafeteria halls dotted Cardinal's Nest's seemingly haphazard network of grand Branches, corridors, docking ports, colossal enclosures, and nest of alleyways, passageways, and access tunnels, making it easy for Jed to find a place to catch a quick meal no matter where he found himself inside the lunar station. Both the commissary and the cafeteria halls' fruits and vegetables were supplied, in most part, by the produce of the greenhouse. Their dairy, pork, beef, eggs, poultry and seafood were provided by the immense farms and the completely isolated fishery, all of which were located down Branch 3, with the farms right next door to each other at the Branch's end and the Fishery occupying a large space near the Branch's entrance. Jed had wandered down Branch 3 a time or two and always thought the place a rather comical sight for its juxtaposition of rural farming alongside space-age austerity. But for all its comedic value, it did operate with admirable success; they were keeping up with demand, as far as Jed could tell, and he was always one to keep his ear to the ground. The fresh nature of the supply chain, which, in Jed's opinion, was the epitome of the farm-to-table dream, had certainly been making for some tasty meals. He especially enjoyed the variety of the buffet line. Jed Redding had yet to be disappointed by a single choice.

Mostly though, it was the particular company one could find in the cafeterias which he enjoyed, with the Main Cafeteria Hall being the best bet on that end. He had no family and was thus duly assigned one of the single tenant living quarters secluded from all the decent family folk, back in Alleyway XVII, the short, dead-end alleyway tucked away in a back corner of Blue Corridor. So if he ever wanted to have a conversation with anyone other than his often tedious collector module navigator Larry Holderman, the cafeteria halls provided that opportunity. Although Jed himself wasn't much of a talker, he did like to stay informed. He liked to hear the gossip, if not be active in its spread.

And the cafeteria halls were always rife with gossip. Even more so since the security squad had returned with a survivor. The entire station had been abuzz with a thousand new rumors. Jed was eager to hear whatever new ones were passing from lip to lip today. He spotted an open seat at a table in a far corner of the cafeteria. The open seat lay between Dolly Duchesne and Helena Heathcoat, two of the most notorious gossips aboard station. At the table with them were Dolly's husband Gabe, Helena's wife Alice Stark, Dr. Sagal's young daughter Maisie, Jed's collector module navigator Larry Holderman, and lastly, rounding out the group to Larry's right, sat the immaculately groomed, mahogany-complected, dark-eyed, small and saturnine Collector Module Lead Engineer Aziz Patel, one of a very small number of non-U.S. citizens AOA had hired as part of the advance prep crew.

The way Jed understood it, the thinking had been that the secret nature of the Cardinal's Nest project would be threatened by going outside AOA's base country for its labor force, so very few foreigners were enlisted in the project. Aziz Patel had been one of those few exceptions. The collector modules' propulsion systems had been modified, in most part, by Patel himself, making his engineering expertise valuable enough to AOA to exempt him from their foreign labor exclusion practices. That spot of bad luck had landed the Indian man aboard Cardinal's Nest, and in the same boat as the rest of his mostly American counterparts. *Poor bastard,* Jed thought. He had come to know Aziz fairly well over the past few months. Patel spoke fluent English. It was that, and his calm, level-headed and grounded nature that made him easy to communicate with on any technical concerns or queries one may have about the modules. He was also a hands-on type of engineer. He had often gotten said hands dirty with the meticulous and greasy work of routine maintenance. That had certainly endeared the man to Jed.

He knew his navigator Larry Holderman was of the same mind about Patel as well. *The two of them have become quite close over the last few weeks, as a matter of fact, now that I think on it. My god, I'm a little jealous of that, aren't I? Get a hold of yourself, man. You know Larry's always got your back,* Jed thought, arriving at the open chair alongside Dolly. Loudly clearing his throat, he asked, "This seat taken?"

Helena was the first to look up at Jed, breaking out in a wide grin as the recognition dawned, "Jed! Of course, my big, handsome module pilot, sit yourself down."

"Looking good this morning, Jed," Dolly said with an admiring twinkle in her voice. Then she must've noticed Jed glance over at her husband Gabe with an apologetic look in his eyes, "Oh, don't mind him, Jed. He knows you are on my free pass list."

"Pay her no mind, Jed, she's just trying to get a rise out of you. Just do what I do: ignore her," Gabe Duchesne put in with a laugh.

"Oh, come on, you tall, beautiful, caramel Adonis, do as Helena says and sit yourself down," Dolly told him, patting the open seat.

Jed let the uncomfortable smile he'd been trying to fight off finally spread across his face as he took Dolly and Helena up on their offer. He got comfortable in the chair and forked in a bite of his fresh fluffy scrambled eggs before asking, "So ... what's the news this morning?"

"What have you heard?" Alice asked him.

"Last thing I heard before I hit the hay was something about Commander Montrois and that new survivor guy going around the station having some private meetings with some of the residents."

"One of those residents they met with was the priest," Larry told his module pilot. "Maisie was there when they came to his living quarters."

"What did they talk about?" Jed asked the group, scaring himself a bit with his eagerness to hear the juicy gossip.

"Maisie was just about to fill us in right before you arrived, my friend," Gabe said.

Jed turned his gaze to Maisie, who wore an unreadable expression. "I wasn't actually in the room when the meeting took place," she began in a qualifying tone, "but my brother was. He told me and my dad after, and then my dad went and met with Boyd late last night."

"Come on, kid, the suspense is killing us," Helena said in a playful manner. She had a way of making light of most situations. Though Jed, and a few others he had spoken with recently, had all noticed her usual chipper demeanor show more and more cracks of late. However, she apparently was feeling her usual playful self this morning. Jed looked over to her as a sarcastic grin took hold of her rosy red lips. Helena wore her sandy-blonde hair cropped short to her scalp in a bob near identical to that of Dolly's. Jed might have even confused the two from behind by now, if not for Helena always draping herself in a seemingly inexhaustible supply of knee-length turtleneck sweaters. Today the sweater was white with a pattern of wavy blue lines. She was a strikingly attractive woman, in Jed's opinion, in her mid-to-late forties and seeming to age like fine wine, as the saying goes. He was pleased to see her smile.

"My dad's the one who actually spoke to Boyd," Maisie said. "I should probably wait for him to get here before I say anything."

"Your old man is coming here for breakfast?" Larry asked eagerly.

"That's what he said. He told me he had a few people to talk to this morning and to meet him in the Main Cafeteria for breakfast around eight ST," Maisie answered.

The collected residents around the table seemed to glance at their watches or tablets in unison to check the time. Jed alone refrained from the impulse. "That's in two minutes," Larry shouted out, unnecessarily. He looked up from his AOA issued pocket tablet with utter panic spreading across his pale face as he realized there were no more empty seats at their table. "Shove over a little, Patel," Larry said, scooting his seat over and bumping into the skinny engineer. "Come on everybody, scoot. Make room for another place." The other residents all swiftly complied. Larry stopped his scooting and pointed a chubby finger covered in coarse black and gray hairs at the table behind them, "Alice, grab that empty chair behind ya and pull it up here by me." This time he used his gnarled index finger to indicate the gap that had opened up to his left.

Alice Stark gracefully extricated her sensuous, ample, short but curvy frame from her chair. She pushed her thick-rimmed tortoise-shell glasses back up the bridge of her nose with an index finger tipped with a pink and purple striped nail. She then used the same index finger to tuck away a few nuisance curls of her long chestnut hair behind her ears as she stepped over to the next table. She dragged from it an unoccupied white plastic chair with two orange gelatin cushions mounted at seat and back. The chair was one of hundreds like it, all of them made to a universal model that didn't deviate in design, pattern, or color. The white and orange chairs encircled every round matte-black communal dining table in the hall. Carrying on with the spirit of uniformity, every table in the hall was perched securely atop a central smoke-gray steel pillar firmly embedded into the tiled cafeteria floor.

Alice was dragging the chair into place across that shiny floor towards the newly opened gap to Larry's left when Jed noticed Dr. Sagal enter through the cafeteria hall's large entrance archway. The archway was trimmed with a wide band of neon pink and orange stripes. It was chiseled out of a corner of the cafeteria hall, adjacent to an equally expansive neon blue and green striped exit archway. Dr. Sagal was wearing a white lab coat that flapped around his knees as he made his brisk entrance. The lab coat made him easily noticeable even from where Jed sat, halfway across the cafeteria. Also notice-able was the fact that he did not enter alone. Dr. Sagal was hunched over as he walked, whispering in what seemed like an urgent manner to what appeared to be a member of the security team. Jed couldn't be sure which officer it was. He could only just make out the team member's uniform and little else.

"There is the doctor now." Patel's pronouncement, rendered in his flat baritone, beat Jed to the punch.

Jed looked around the table to see his breakfastmates all direct their attention toward the entrance. Glancing back, he saw that the doctor and the security officer had stopped abruptly after making only a few yards of progress into the dining hall. The angles were still too severe for a clear look at the security officer's face. The two whis-perers were leaned in intimately close to one another for what Jed took as apparent emphasis for the final stage of their hushed con-versation. Sure enough, after a few more beats, they drew apart and headed off in separate directions.

It was then that Jed caught his first glimpse of the security offi-cer's face. He recognized the man instantly. Although he knew him only vaguely in passing, it was enough to know his name and a few simple details of his life. After all, he did once share a meal at a table in this very cafeteria hall with him and his wife Stevie. The team member was the clever and affable Abner Hyun. Jed watched Abner as he headed from his huddle with Dr. Sagal on a direct beeline to a table populated by a handful of Hyun's fellow security officers about fifty meters across the cafeteria. Jed looked back over to see where

Dr. Sagal had gotten to. The man was on a beeline of his own. Dr. Sagal's tread was aimed directly at Jed's table, where his daughter Maisie was now motioning so vigorously for him to join them that she must've thought the very act itself might sweep the doctor to them all the faster.

Jed did his best to track both of the whisperers in the limits of his vision. He watched them arrive at their respective destinations at about the exact same moment, but his attention was sucked completely from Abner as Dr. Sagal seated himself in the vacant chair across the table. The doctor scooted himself in tight to the black table. He set his elbows on the tabletop in front of him and slowly leaned out over them, adopting a pose reminiscent of that from his whispered conversation with Abner Hyun at the cafeteria's entrance. The act seemed to have a hypnotizing quality about it. All the other residents gathered around the table began to mimic the posture. Jed found himself no match for the mesmerizing magnetism either. He leaned in, elbows on the table, head hunched low, and shoulders raised up in unconscious guilt for the conspiratorial nature of the posture itself.

Dr. Sagal looked quickly over his shoulder before turning to look in the eyes of each resident seated at the table around him, ending with his daughter. "How much have you told them?"

"Not much," Maisie answered. "Everybody already knew about the news of Commander Montrois and the new guy going around having private meetings with a few important people. I just told them about those two coming to visit Boyd, and how you went and talked with Boyd late last night. We were just making room for you to join our table when you walked in with Mr. Hyun. What were you guys talking about just now anyway?"

"Well, as it happens, Abner Hyun, it seems, was being deliberately left in the dark by his commander and squadmates about their upcoming plans," Dr. Sagal answered her in a strange voice. "So I was filling him in on some news I heard last night that I felt he would be grateful to hear."

"What are you talking about, doc?" Larry asked in a deeply puzzled tone.

"I went and visited the priest last night, just as Maisie said," Dr. Sagal began in a tired voice. "He told me what Montrois and the new guy, Aponyaschefski, had proposed to him, and to all the rest of the people they visited, we presume. A proposition that was so radical I knew the level-headed and rational Abner Hyun could never be on board with it. And believe me, with as many of the security officers as I fear *are* on board with it, we are going to need to employ every tool in our belt if we have any hope of stopping it. I figured maybe Hyun could speak some reason to those guys and maybe stop any madness before it's too late... I sure hope he can, anyway."

"What proposition? What are you talking about? Why are we whispering like this? What's going on, Perry." Alice asked one nervous question right on top of the other.

"Shhh," Dr. Sagal implored with his finger pressed firmly to his lips. "There's no telling how far it's spread at this point. We can't know who is spying for Montrois and who isn't. Best to just keep a semi-paranoid level of modus operandi from now on," the doctor told them in a manner entirely too unsettling for Jed's taste.

"Spying for Montrois? What the hell are you talking about, doc?" Dolly asked with light exasperation. "What did Boyd say to you exactly? I've never seen you like this."

"Yeah, you're kinda scaring us, doc," Gabe agreed.

"They've had enough with AOA's orders," Dr. Sagal answered pointedly. "They're gonna cut off their authority ... and replace it with god knows what."

"Who's had enough?" Asked Dolly, still only lightly exasperated.

"Montrois and most of the security team, and, if I can trust the rumor I heard on my way here, they got Mikkelson, the labor supervisor and head of credit distribution on board as well. Which is bad news. Control the money, control the world, so the saying goes. Apparently this Aponyaschefski guy has talked them all into joining in on some revolution pact. The way I hear it, this guy, who likes to be called Schef, is some slick-talking lawyer who has 'em all convinced AOA is lying about the Alphas and are ultimately responsible for the infection itself. He says they know it can't be cured. It's apparently a magical curse of some sorts that AOA has brought down upon us, and so, according to Aponyaschefski, science is powerless before it. And so the recon missions are getting security officers killed for no reason. It's all utterly ridiculous, of course."

"Is it?" Helena asked, so quietly that Jed wasn't sure she'd meant to speak.

"Trust me, Helena, I'm in the labs every day. It's just a natural, non-magical pathogen, like any other, a virus that can be inoculated against, like every one that's ever come before it," the doctor promised her with obvious sincerity. Jed couldn't be certain it had actually been any real comfort to the woman.

"It's not like any virus I've ever heard of," Gabe said. "Matter of fact, I hear it's more than just the mindlessness and the goddamn blood-crazed madness side effects that are strange about this infection. I heard a rumor last night from a guy who works in my department whose wife knows the wife of one of the security officers who says that the security staff thinks the Damned ain't even human anymore."

"Don't be ridiculous, Gabe!" Dr. Sagal scolded the dopey-faced, round-shouldered fishery crewman.

Gabe indignantly shook his melon face back and forth, flapping the long, floppy skin of his earlobes against his fat cheeks as he struggled to find a response. "I'm just telling you what I heard, is all."

"I'm sorry for snapping, Gabe," Dr. Sagal apologized after a calming breath. "I'm just a little sensitive about potentially inflammatory claims like that being passed around casually. I'm sure some of the officers have some pretty compelling anecdotal evidence that makes them believe what they do, but it's got no basis in reality. The way I understand it, the rumor about their super-humanity status is due to the fact that most of the Damned seem hale and healthy, apart from the sickly hue of their skin that is, and it's got everyone puzzled as to how they are feeding themselves anymore, since all the uninfected people are all wiped out now. Well, believe me when I tell you that there could be a thousand answers to that, you guys. Despite how much face time the security squad has had with the Damned, they've only ever observed them for a few seconds of their day at a time. Any sociologist, biologist, or zoologist worth their salt would tell you that is not nearly enough observation time to gather the necessary information to draw any firm conclusions about their feeding and drinking habits. Or to draw any conclusion about any of their behavior, in fact. The plain truth is we just don't know. We haven't observed them enough. The science team isn't very big. We've got every last doctor and registered nurse aboard station offering up whatever limited assistance they can, when they aren't pulling one of their regular sixteen-hour shifts at the hospital, that is. I promise you, my friends, we are working damn hard on synthesizing a vaccine. None of us down at the hospital, or in the labs, or anyone down Branch 1 for that matter, have had the time to study the Damned enough to debunk any of the ridiculous theories, but trust me, people, it's just a virus, nothing more. It is extremely exotic, I'll grant you that, but I do believe a breakthrough is close. The science team really is on to something with the Alpha theory. The data surrounding it is extraordinary. I can't really go into detail here, but I promise I will later. I'll put a layman's presentation together and set everyone's minds at ease. That might be a good idea right now anyway, with all the bullshit traveling around the grapevine." The doctor scratched at the thick graying stubble covering the lower half of his handsome, frank, and trustworthy face. "We all just need to keep our heads and not make any rash decisions right now. This station, and human civilization itself, needs us to persevere up here. We can take the surface back one day soon. I'm confident in that, my friends, but not if some reactionary elements up here decide to torpedo everything. Boyd tells me that Aponyaschefski is telling everyone we have a duty to humanity to resist AOA's missions back to Earth and focus on building a lasting society up here. Can you believe that? The damn fool. How does he expect humanity to grow up here? All we could hope to do is sustain, at best. It's a recipe for disaster, with a bleak and pointless future to look forward to. This place could go off like a powder keg at any moment along the way. It's a future without hope, people. We cannot give in to that. We need to stay the course, guys. I say *that* is our true duty, if such a heavy burden could ever really be defined by a word so trivial as duty. Look, don't get me wrong, I'm no fan of the way AOA has handled things up here, and I got more than my fair share of suspicions about their culpability in all this. I'm sure they know a little more about the infection's spread than they are telling us. And, of course, that disastrous evacuation, I'll be the first to admit that they are responsible for all of that. But I promise you, here and now, AOA will answer for that horrible day, and all the rest, soon enough. But right now, we need to stick with them and find a way to beat this mad disease. We can't go on vigilante streaks, spreading anarchy, no matter how just it may seem in the moment. This station can't afford one single, solitary second of chaos. We simply can't risk it. Our *duty* to humanity, the way I see it, is to cure as many of the Damned as we can and then take our fucking planet back." The doctor leaned in further over the tabletop. Jed, and the rest of the residents around the table, followed suit. "We can't give up on the vaccine, for the sake of all the loved ones we left behind down there to be engulfed by the nightmare without us. We must keep fighting for it, for all of their sakes. If AOA's executives are deposed, the missions stop, and the vaccine research and production along with them. We cannot let that happen."

"But maybe they're right to not trust AOA, doc," Dolly said in a low voice. "I mean … don't you remember the horror of that day? They abandoned the families of so many of your fellow prep crewmates. How are you still their advocate in the face of that? Don't you remember that day?"

"Damn sure *I* remember it," Helena said, putting conviction into her two cents this time.

"I remember it too," Dolly continued. "I'll never forget that day." Her eyes appeared haunted and full of shame as they became locked with Maisie's melancholy gaze.

"I haven't forgotten, ladies," Dr. Sagal answered in a somber tone. "Maybe this Schef guy is right about their villainous deeds, I don't know… but in the end, whatever they may have done, we are all in this together now, Dol. You know what I mean, Helena? Whatever games they may have been playing before don't matter anymore. We are all up here together now, and we can't afford to turn against each other." The doctor reached out across the tabletop to give Dolly's hand a quick squeeze. Helena withdrew hers just before he had a chance to offer the identical physical assurance. "We can't go rocking the boat now, you guys. Hell, she's in treacherous enough waters as it is. You know what I mean? Laws here aboard station, with all governments effectively collapsed … well, let's just say they are extremely fuzzy. And until the problem of finding the vaccine is solved, the bright minds who are best prepared to deal with the administration of a progressive, free, safe, secure, and just society are occupied with that much more prescient issue. So, for now, I think we ought to just keep relying on the system that's already in place up here. I say we ought to continue to let the organization that owns this facility, and also employs most of us, keep the reins of power for now. It's holding, after all. Ain't it? None of us are starving, and neither are we being worked to death—other than us in the labs anyway—and we haven't been pressed into any unsafe working conditions, or anything like that either, not that I've heard anyway."

"I guess you're right, doc," Dolly agreed with resignation. "Gabe and I left three brothers, two sisters, my mother and father, a dozen nieces and nephews and countless friends behind. Who knows how many of them got turned into a Damned? I struggle with leaving them all to that fate every single day, like I'm sure you all do. And I don't mean to sound weak, like I'm giving up on them or something. I just feel like everything has just been a lot more complex and bleak these past few months than my mind has been prepared to take. Ya know? I hardly know which way is up anymore." Dolly waved her hands at the other women at the table to shoo off the sympathies they showered upon her. "So you're right, Dr. Sagal, as usual. I certainly don't want anarchy reigning up here. None of us do, I'm sure."

"AOA has kept us safe this far. I say Dr. Sagal is right," Patel concurred in his distinctly accented baritone. "We can't afford to have anybody rocking the boat up here, especially not security officers."

Raised voices suddenly sounded out across the cafeteria, drawing their attention away from the uncomfortable moment lingering around the table in the wake of that statement. After Helena and Dolly leaned out across the table in front of Jed for a better view of the commotion, he stood up to gain an unobstructed sightline of Abner Hyun standing in front of three of his fellow officers seated alongside each other at a black dining table. He was shouting at them in sharp, angry, and demanding tones, wagging his index finger with great emphasis to drive home the fiery passion of his invective. Even as Jed watched, a female member of the security team stepped up alongside Hyun, hands up to indicate her peaceable intentions.

Jed looked down at the others gathered around the table and saw every last one of them, Dr. Sagal included, glued to the drama unfolding seventy meters across the pastel tiles. When he looked back towards the security staff's table, he saw the female security member now had her arms wrapped around Abner. She was struggling mightily to push him away from the table where the three officers were shouting back at him with curses Jed could plainly see their lips forming from half a cafeteria hall away. As the woman pushed Abner away from the altercation, Jed could make out the three chevrons of rank on her shirt sleeve. Her name popped into his head shortly after that. *Sergeant Marge. Yeah, that's it.* He'd only been in her company a handful of times so far, but they'd had a few quite memorable conversations on those occasions. Jed figured he had a pretty good idea about her character and had her pegged as one of the sane ones. She definitely appeared to be on Abner's side of the altercation, after all. Even now, their heads were huddled together as Abner, who was now somewhat cooled down, allowed himself to be ushered by the sergeant to the exit a few dozen meters away.

Jed watched them all the way through the giant portal and into the annex tunnel which connected the exit of the cafeteria hall to the echoing hustle and bustle of dozens of people trying to catch a trolley at the football-shaped black and gold checkered Trolley Depot Pavilion dotting the very center of the capacious domed Living Quarters Central Hub, with its bold silver walls adorned in an intricate pattern of large maroon diamond shapes of various hues and configurations.

"Well, what do you suppose that was all about?" Gabe suddenly asked no one in particular.

"I'd say all my fears are on the verge of becoming true. It's my guess that those two are on their way to an even bigger argument, and I'd say it's got the potential to be a pretty stormy one ... maybe even downright catastrophic," Dr. Sagal answered in a dry tone that did not at all jibe with the content of his words.

"What do you mean?" Dolly asked, her light exasperation replaced by deep worry edging her voice.

"He means they're headed to find Commander Montrois," Maisie clarified. "They're going to confront him about the coup he's planning, Mrs. Duchesne."

"Let's all pray they can still do something to stop it," her father added.

"Is that really all we can do about it, Perry? Pray?" Asked a flustered Alice.

"Where is that goddamn priest when you need him?" Gabe put in with a bit of humor that was entirely unwelcome at that moment.

Little by little, the tension in the cafeteria eased back to a semblance of normalcy. Then, one by one, or in pairs, according to their relationship circumstances, Jed's fellow residents got up from his table. They took their trays and culinary refuse with them, making a detour to one of the dozen black refuse bins with bright orange hoods that dotted the cafeteria floor as they headed out of the immense hall.

Jed alone hung back and soon was seated all by himself at the dining table. He hovered, fork in hand, over his still whole cinnamon roll, but found his appetite for the sweet treat had deserted him completely. His hunger had been replaced by a numbing sense of melancholy and foreboding. After a few lonely moments at the table, with just Jed and his special morning treat going uneaten for the first time ever, he mustered up the gumption to leave the cafeteria.

In his current mood, he found it a burdensome chore just to make it a few hundred paces across the pink tiles to the nearest refuse bin. Once there, he emptied his tray and then stood off to one side of the bin, out of the flow of the sparse pedestrian traffic. *Do you go back to your room and hide from the doom that's coming, Jeddy old boy?* He asked himself. *Shall I simply hope the whole mess just passes me by? Or do I need to satisfy that curiosity bug that's itching? Should I go see the priest and find out what kinda stories he's heard this morning?* The first option was the one that called to him, deep in his primal heart. He was a ride-out-the-storm-in-safety kind of guy, for the most part. But in the end, he knew his curiosity was the one thing his will could never tame. He knew he would end up at Father Boyd's hillbilly-liquor stand some time or another this day. *Might as well not fight it and head there now, my friend,* Jed thought, resigned.

On his way to the exit archway, he absentmindedly glanced back at the security team. Something about the look in the eyes of the three officers now leaving their table caused him to stop dead in his tracks. There was an imperious air about them, evident in the way they disregarded their considerable lunch debris, an air of superiority, evident in the way they pushed past their fellow residents on their march towards the exit, and an air of authority, evident in the way they locked eyes with everyone around them and refused to break it until the other person yielded first. Jed didn't know what it all meant, or if he was just seeing things, but it definitely deepened his sense of dread foreboding.

Suddenly, he realized he'd been staring at the security officers for far too long. They'd made it to within thirty paces of him. Fighting crippling panic, he dug deep and snapped some urgency into his weary bones. Jed fell into a swift, long-paced step within a few dozen feet. He stretched the gap between himself and the officers considerably after that, and before too long, he'd lost them completely. Nevertheless, worry still managed to dog his heels for every step of the short walk from the Main Cafeteria Hall to Father Boyd's Violet Corridor living quarters.

CHAPTER 7
MIKKELSON

Mikkelson held his mug of piping-hot coffee a few inches from his face. He blew on the java for a second before taking a sip. It was a fresh mug from a fresh pot, served to him with a polite, affable smile by one or the other of the grunt security officers currently leaning, sitting, or sprawling across the jumble of chairs and couches spread randomly throughout the rec room in the security staff's headquarters. He might've been able to recall the man's name if he thought about it, but really, he couldn't care less. A simple, "Thanks, officer," was good enough. Generic and to the point. Say it with a smile, like you actually give a shit, and it serves just fine. Besides which, his focus right now would be put to much better use aimed at the officer's commander.

He had known Jasper Montrois for over eight months now, since the very first of the prep crew workers had come aboard, in fact. They had countless run-ins over that period. Their positions of relative authority had even placed them in collaborative roles on more than one occasion. Mikkelson had thought he'd known the man well enough to have him pretty much figured out. He prided himself on his ability to read people, to figure out what they wanted and how best to move them, should the need arise, but this unprecedented step Montrois was planning to take made Mikkelson question whether the talent that had taken him to the top of AOA's dogmatic hierarchy was beginning to dull.

It wasn't a pleasant thought. He had few other marketable skills to fall back on. He didn't have a degree from some fancy Ivy League school like most of his asshole colleagues. He was a community-college-boy, and then an online-university-boy; a self-made man if ever there was one. A lifetime of out-thinking, out-hustling and out-maneuvering any unfortunate bastard that happened to get in his way had paid off big time. Even before this labor supervisor job aboard Cardinal's Nest, Mikkelson had himself a pretty damn enviable one. He knew it certainly made all his neighbors back in Scottsdale jealous, that was for sure. It had a fancy title: Chief Compliance Officer for AOA's Southwest Corporate Division. He had a corner office with a beautiful view, a cherry-red Ferrari parked in his specially reserved front row parking spot, a dozen tailored suits, a maid service, an unlimited-access membership to the lush fairways and greens of Whisper Rocks Golf Club and, best of all, forty desperate and pathetic corporate lackeys at his beck and call, day and night. He'd thought he'd known the sweet taste of power there in Arizona, but looking back now, he realized he was merely the biggest guppy in the smallest pond.

The power AOA had invested in him aboard this station made that old life seem like he had been managing a hot dog stand. He had literally hundreds of laborers and a dozen clerical support staffers under his direct authority now. Which, thanks to the apocalypse, was pretty much every human being left in the universe. And since the fools down Branch 1 had scorned the task of having to interact with their workforce in any way at all, they had placed the responsibility for the workers' governance almost completely on the shoulders of Mikkelson.

They had even named him President of the Credit Treasury Council. There was really no other qualified candidate other than himself when it came time to appoint a steward for the audacious new monetary system. It had been his ability to cook the books to the company's benefit that was the chief reason he was set on the corporate fast track in the first place. Couple that with his affiliation with the treasury project from its inception, as a founding member of AOA's development team for the Integrated Credit System, and he had been the obvious choice to oversee the burgeoning, independent, universally-integrated and self-sustaining economy. Both Mikkelson and AOA had known it. He figured it was why they had eventually caved to his *outrageous contract demands*, as they'd called them.

No time was wasted by Mikkelson after that in seizing total control of the Treasury Council—whether by hook or by crook—greasing the right palms, making the right threats and blackmailing the right compromised folks. By the end of that first month aboard station, before any of the infection shit had even begun, he had every other staff supervisor with a seat on the council in his back pocket. He resented the effort most of those proud, arrogant assholes had forced him to go to, but he hadn't hesitated to do whatever was necessary. Mikkelson had known securing all of their votes would be his golden wings over the final hurdle that might stand in his way when it came time to set his own grand plans into motion. He took a quick moment to revel in his glory. Mikkelson intended to ride a power high until the second he died, which unfortunate occurrence he was planning to delay for as long as physically possible. *I ain't never coming down,* he told himself with satisfaction and delicious anticipation.

He supposed it was possible that he might have felt a little bit dirty about some of the underhanded and shady dealings he'd been engaged in since taking control of the treasury, if it wasn't for the fact that the fucking idiot laborers didn't really need the credits to survive anyway. They got their three squares and their comfy quarters regardless of how many credits they accumulated. The credits were just for the station's perks, i.e., the commissary or the 3-D arcade, or any of the entertainment in the Rec District, such as the theaters, the interactive gaming system lounge, the swimming pool, the putt-putt course and what-not. So they didn't strictly *need* to carry out the demeaning tasks Mikkelson and some of his like-minded supervisors were beginning to demand of the residents for supplemental credits. Mikkelson didn't want any of his labor force to wise up to that fact, though.

No, what he needed was for them to stay stupid and willing ... *and spending*, because Mikkelson had known from day one of the credit treasury's creation that it couldn't truly operate independently from the economies of Earth for more than a few years, at best. AOA had swept the damning reports about their prized economic system's fated destruction under the rug as best they could, but Mikkelson had been privy to the data. He knew every chart and predictive model had projected an unrecoverable crash after 20-36 months, if cut off completely from Earth's major economic markets. So the credit well would run dry soon enough, and that's when he would *truly* have them. That's when he would truly taste power. He'd have it all under his control then, for if any of them wanted anything, they'd have to come to him.

But until then, Commander Montrois and his squad's unexpected plan seemed like the obvious horse to back. While it no doubt brought some unneeded uncertainty into Mikkelson's life, he could tell which way the winds were blowing, and he was a practitioner of the always-back-the-winner philosophy. Plus, it had some obvious perks that Mikkelson could immediately see. So all wasn't lost, as far as his grand plans were concerned. And a little martial law, for lack of a better term, wasn't such a bad thing, in his opinion. He didn't want any upheaval among the residents—anarchy isn't good for business—but the implied threat of a man with a gun watching over your shoulder while you work has a remarkable ability to keep the sheep in line. In such situations, people crave an escape. And if they wanted to use any of this miracle station's entertainment facilities to achieve that escape ... *well then, they were going to have to earn themselves some credits, weren't they?*

Mikkelson knew that the priest ran his operation unmolested by any of the treasury's various taxes mostly due to the protection Montrois and his team were providing him. It pissed Mikkelson off something fierce to have that fraud of a priest raking in his credits without a dime coming his way. He desperately wanted to take over Boyd's operation, and he figured teaming up with the security staff might get him one step closer to doing just that. And what difference did it really make to him who was calling the shots at the top? They were already living under a dictatorship now, for all intents and purposes. Besides which, he felt no specific loyalty to AOA. Mikkelson felt no loyalty to anyone, as a matter of fact. So, with only a few moments' careful consideration, he'd decided it was in his own best interests to throw in with Montrois and his officers.

Mikkelson had confidence that he could adapt his plans to fit any unforeseen circumstances. After all, he considered himself nothing if not adaptable. He believed that was how you survived in business, and in life: when a situation changed, you adapted, you did not dwell. Don't waste time worrying about how things changed, just go with it, search for an angle to take advantage of and make the situation work to your benefit. That was precisely what Mikkelson intended to do with the band of revolutionaries surrounding him. He had no intention of losing any of his newfound power.

I'll just have to prove myself indispensable to these gung-ho dick bags. The thought was hardly daunting. He knew they needed him to run this place. If they didn't see that now, they'd find out soon enough. Mikkelson knew the proper economic levers to push in order to bring whoever claimed to be in charge of the station crawling to him on their hands and knees.

Bringing his coffee mug back up to his lips for another sip, he peered over its rim through the steam drifting off the hot brew towards a seated Montrois. The man was rocked slightly back in a brown leather desk chair across the cluttered rec room. Montrois had his hands in his lap gripping tightly to a nearly empty plastic bottle of the priest's moonshine. He wore a blank look on his brutal and scruffy face as he brought the bottle up for a final swig, while leaning slightly towards the survivor Aponyaschefski as he did. The emaciated lawyer was leaning over his way as well, whispering something into his ear that must not have been very interesting, judging by the look on Montrois' face. *I'll have to watch that one too,* Mikkelson realized. *He must be the real driving force behind all this. God, I wonder what happened down there on that last damn mission? I'll need to get to the bottom of it.*

"Oh, shit," Mikkelson said softly as he snapped his fingers with sudden remembrance. He leaned over to where Rollie Cornwell, one of his staff supervisors—the one he trusted the most—was leaning against the wall beside him. "You got the recorder running?" Mikkelson asked him in a whisper.

"Yeah, just started it, boss," Cornwell answered with an even softer whisper.

"Good." Rollie was the only subordinate Mikkelson had brought with him to this meeting. He'd thought about bringing along a few other trusted supervisors, but in the end, he figured Rollie Cornwell was sufficient enough backup. The man had the kind of face you saw one second and forgot the next. He was quiet and unassuming, and easily overlooked. But Mikkelson knew what was underneath that plain, All-American face and quiet exterior. *An utter fucking madman,* Mikkelson thought, only half-joking.

It was Rollie's forgettable qualities, however, that would suit Mikkelson's purposes at the meeting that was about to take place. He thought having Cornwell beside him as a trusted second would send the right message, one that said he had nothing to fear and considered himself among trustworthy allies, yet also conveyed that he was no mere lapdog; important people answered to him, staff-supervisors could be brought along to serve as little more than his assistants. Mikkelson was so confident in his choice of companion that he had deemed the risk of the security team discovering he was having Rollie record them to be extremely low. They were still trying to officially win him to their side, after all. They wouldn't search him, or his unassuming assistant, or come right out and accuse him of something like that now. No, they were still in the wooing phase of their budding partnership, hence the polite smile and the warm cup of coffee.

Abruptly, the automatic hatchway a few feet to Commander Montrois' left and directly opposite the position Mikkelson was currently occupying in the interior designer's nightmare of a room swished open. All conversation in the rec room ceased. The only ambient sound to be heard was the gentle humming of the station itself. Abner Hyun and Sergeant Marge Hamill stepped into the silent room. Mikkelson could tell confrontation was imminent from the rage clearly etched across both of their faces. The two angry officers made it to the center of the room and began pacing around in circles, locking eyes with one of their squadmates and flaring up as if to shout at them only to move on to lock eyes with another squadmate and repeat the process all over again.

Finally, Abner must've gathered his wits enough to actually put words to his frustration, "What the hell, guys? Tell me it ain't true. Y'all ain't really thinking of doing this, are you? You can't be thinking of this, it's crazy. Have y'all gone mad? Somebody answer me, dammit!"

Monty stood up, with only the barest bout of alcohol-induced vertigo. Mikkelson noticed the empty moonshine bottle roll under his chair as he held out his hands in front of him and walked a few paces toward Abner and the sergeant. Mikkelson noticed the survivor a single step behind him, and always staying within whispering distance.

Looks like the real meeting is about to begin, he told himself with an inner smirk. The only two members of the security team who hadn't been in on the plan had found out through the station's lightning-quick rumor mill, just as they all knew they would. Now came their one chance, a chance Montrois had insisted upon giving them. He demanded they get to hear the full pitch and be given an honest and transparent opportunity to make their decisions on whether they would throw in with them, as Mikkelson had, or go their own way, or oppose them, even.

Mikkelson knew each of the two principled outlier officers. He'd met each of them on multiple occasions, each interaction more unpleasant than the last. They were lost causes, in his view. But Montrois had told him, "I want to do this right. We'll give them a chance, face to face." *Bunch of noble bullshit,* Mikkelson had thought. But Montrois had insisted, and so the drama must be played out. Mikkelson figured the commander was still trying to cling to the trappings of honor despite his seditious intentions. *Wants his cake and to eat it too. And they call me a glutton,* he laughed to himself.

Mikkelson had agreed to the security staff's plan last night, back in his own private office. He had shaken hands with Montrois and Aponyaschefski after their extended meeting, saying all the necessary pleasantries, and was given all the necessary warnings. Afterwards, they'd agreed to meet this morning to hammer out the fine details, but only after the charade that was about to play out before him had run its course. Montrois had explained he wanted to handle his two friends as delicately as possible. He wanted them to be able to have some time to hear it on their own terms and blow off whatever steam was necessary. Montrois had known they would confront the security staff eventually, and he figured it would be sooner rather than later. *And, evidently, he was right.*

"Calm down, Normie," Montrois' voice cracked as he spoke.

"Calm down?!" Abner returned with fury. "Just what in the hell is going on here, Commander?"

Mikkelson watched as Abner tore his stupefied gaze from his commander, his eyes landing on the toady lurking behind him. *Toady or puppet-master?* Mikkelson couldn't be sure yet. Abner extended an angry finger at the survivor, but he looked at his fellow officers as he spoke, "Just what has this poor, sick, traumatized man talked y'all into? And why do I have to hear about it from Dr. Sagal by way of Father Boyd? You let the priest in on y'all's plans before Marge and me?" He asked incredulously. "After all we've been through together?"

Thank god that fucking priest didn't throw in with Montrois' team, Mikkelson thought for the hundredth time in the past twelve hours. Boyd had given Aponyaschefski and Montrois some non-committal answer, one that had irritated Montrois, if his informers could be believed. The idea of the priest on the outside of the security staff's good graces was an even more pleasurable one than he'd expected. That was most likely due to that pretty little piece of meat the phony holy man kept as his operation's solo employee. Mikkelson hadn't sated his urges for the young, smooth, tight flesh of pre-teen girls since coming aboard Cardinal's Nest. He'd only actually bought himself a *session* with a young girl a handful of times over the last few years; most often after a big quarterly bonus. They were his special treats, his due. He worked damn hard and deserved a special reward. Mikkelson was a work-hard play-hard kind of guy. He knew when and how to treat himself.

But even still, he never thought his obsession with young flesh would turn into the intense craving it'd become aboard station. Knowing he was cut off from all his *special connections* seemed to send the urge to satisfy his nontraditional lusts skyrocketing to scary new heights over the past few weeks. Especially since the day his eye fell on Dr. Sagal's perky, bright-eyed, tight and fit teenage daughter. She might not even be a teen yet, truth be told. She could be twelve. Which was just fine, as far as he was concerned. Maisie, she was called. He shuddered as his memories of her hard at work, bustling around the shelves and vats of Boyd's operation, bending here and reaching there, flooded his mind. It was driving him a little crazy, in all honesty, but Mikkelson was able to calm himself with his steady assurance that he would have her soon enough.

He'd crush that pretender priest, and then, with the security staff's witting or unwitting help—it didn't matter which—he'd force her to stay on working the liquor operations. He'd be able to take care of her pussy-ass Jew doctor of a father easy enough too, if the man decided to be a nuisance. *Maybe I ought to go ahead and do that now?* He pondered. With Sagal out of the way, he could take the girl into his own personal care, maybe even tell everyone he'd adopted her when he discovered she had no one else. *The ignorant shits would eat it up. Some of 'em might even thank me,* he laughed. *Once I get these assholes on my side,* he thought with relish about the security squad surrounding him, *there'll be absolutely no one who could say boo about it.*

Mikkelson was shaken out of his pleasing thought process when the automatic hatchway once more swished open. The room went silent again as a few security officers entered the rectangular chamber. Mikkelson did not fail to note the stink-eye Abner shot at all three of the newcomers as they casually made their way to what must be their reserved seats spread throughout the rec room in the fresh silence.

"Why don't you two sit down." Montrois spoke to his two recalcitrant officers in an apparent attempt to cut the tension in the room. "Marge, no one is in your recliner. Take a seat and a breath and let us try and explain." Montrois stepped a few paces to his left and patted the back of what must be Marge's special recliner to punctuate his plea.

Marge couldn't seem to find the words for an appropriate response and resorted to a half-bemused half-irate shake of the head for an answer to the commander's invitation.

Mikkelson didn't know exactly when Abner had begun staring at him, but when he glanced back at the man, he discovered Abner's eyes were firmly fixed on Rollie and himself. "What the hell are they doing here?" Abner posed his question to his squadmates. He again received no answer, not even from his commander. Hyun physically seemed to manifest the act of surrendering his pride in order to lower himself into addressing a non-security officer within the confines of their sad and pathetic little clubhouse. "You're a part of this plot too, Mikkelson? What the hell do you hope to gain from throwing in with this coup my *trusted* squadmates are planning?"

Mikkelson plastered a smile to his face, doing his best to hide the strain of moving his considerable girth as he stood up from his comfortable leaning position against the back wall. Without even glancing in the staff supervisor's direction, he handed off his coffee mug. Then, throwing back his shoulders, he straightened out his spine. The act thrust out his beer gut, his shirt too threatening to untuck itself from his gray slacks and slide up a massive belly that would put any Buddha-statue to shame. But Mikkelson was never self-conscious about such things. Instead, he basked in the silence for a few moments, knowing every eye in the room had fallen upon him. They were on pins and needles, desperate to hear his response. Mikkelson absolutely loved the feeling. He milked those kinds of moments for all they were worth. And just before the udder dried up, he answered Hyun's insulting question, "I seek no gain, Mr. Hyun. I believe there comes a time and place for everything ... even revolution. My staff and I have been talking for weeks now about our horrible suspicions about AOA's executives and their foolish theories. I know there must be truth in Mr. Aponyaschefski's claims because of what I've witnessed firsthand over my time here aboard this station. In that time, they have revealed to me their deceitful and coldly indifferent nature. They take absolutely no responsibility in the operation of this station. They are useless, as far as I'm concerned, just a waste of our precious and finite recycled oxygen. If me and my staff took a break for just one hour of one day, this whole place would come crashing down on our heads. My colleagues and I want to avoid that, Mr. Hyun. I have worked too damn hard to make this station a comfortable habitation with a well contented workforce. I have bent over backwards to make that so, in fact, and I am willing to do whatever it takes to keep it that way. And it's clear to me and my staff that right now that means taking control of this facility from all the executives and government officials and whoever the hell else they got down Branch 1. Which I wouldn't know, by the way, 'cause I've never actually been invited down there, despite my *essential service* to their precious station's success." *Careful now,* he cautioned himself. *Remember, you want to sound like you are making the right moral choice here, not settling some petty grievance.*

"Mr. Mikkelson has seen the wisdom of our proposal," Schef said, snatching his spotlight, "and thankfully, he and his associates have agreed to cooperate with us. His knowledge of this station and its various facilities and operations will prove an invaluable asset in keeping life business-as-usual as we transition away from AOA's control into one of our own choosing. And I mean the collective *our*, as in every resident aboard this station's own choosing."

"Cooperate with you to do what exactly?" demanded Sergeant Marge. She slowly rotated in place, staring down each of her squad-mates in turn and ending with her commander. "Why have you allowed this man to corrupt the integrity of this staff, Commander?" Mikkelson couldn't be sure, but he thought he saw shame on Montrois' face after his sergeant's condemnation. "How have you all been taken in so deeply in just a few short hours?" she asked her squad, with desperation plain in her voice. "I don't understand why you're all doing this. Help me understand this."

"I don't know why you refuse to acknowledge the truth of your own experience." The survivor was determined to be the center of the meeting. "A truth that is now clearly seen by your fellow squadmates."

Marge stared the thin man down with a penetrating gaze that Mikkelson feared even he might've wilted under. "Shut up while we have a discussion among our squad, you've done enough damage."

"Cut him some slack, Sarge," the dark-haired, Latino soldier-of-fortune that Mikkelson was pretty sure was named Pedro Alvarez entreated his sergeant from a couch he was slouched in languidly along the back wall. "It ain't his fault he was able to see the truth that we've been blinding ourselves to. But we've all admitted that truth now, Sarge; we've let the veil drop. And now it's time you two joined the club. 'Cause we're all agreed, you need to understand that. This is happening; it's got to."

"What exactly is happening?!" Abner shouted out in exasperation.

Mikkelson watched the curious scene unfold before him. It seemed that they were all on board for the coup, but none of them actually wanted to say it out loud. Finally, Pedro spoke up, but it was only to pass the buck, "Why don't you tell him, Schef. It is mostly your plan, after all." *Fucking gutless phonies*, Mikkelson thought.

"No, I think it would be best for them to hear it from someone they know and trust. It should be one of you who tells them," Schef answered, breaking character to throw away his position as center of attention.

Pedro took a long moment to clear his throat and, presumably, arrange his thoughts. "We are going to move in force down Branch 1," he finally began, "we'll round up everyone we find back there cowering in their private little sanctuaries, then we take over the control room and shut down their AI video monitoring system. Once we can be sure we have control of the station, we gather the residents and inform them of our actions."

"Just like that?" Marge asked with disbelief clearly detectable in her tone.

"Just like that," Alvarez answered her with her own words.

Mikkelson knew what question was on its way next and Abner did not disappoint, "And then what?"

"Then we decide who rules us," Pedro answered flatly. "Schef and the commander have come up with what we've all agreed is the only fair way to decide who that person or persons should be, 'cause it needs to be fair, with everyone in the station given an equal opportunity to influence the outcome."

"You're going to hold a vote to decide who's in charge up here?" Marge asked, slightly puzzled and slightly hopeful.

"Not a vote ... not exactly," Pedro answered his sergeant.

"What then?" Marge paused to allow Pedro time to answer, but apparently the man was unwilling to clarify. "Why not just appoint a council from among the various staff supervisors?" she asked instead.

"Because that would exclude all the average laborers, and we need to do this thing right. It needs to be a fair process, one where every man and woman aboard this station is presented with an equal opportunity to influence the creation of their governance."

"So ... a vote?" Marge asked once more, clearly not getting the point the cocky officer was trying to make.

"No, not a vote. A tournament," answered Pedro. "Whoever ends up in charge of us, whether that's an elected council or a solitary man, they are going to need real power, real authority. We can't play around up here. We all know we exist on a knife's edge inside this station. There has to be unchallenged order. This station's operations need to run smoothly. There is no margin for error. So our leader ... or leaders, will need to possess real power. They need to be feared, in short. Fear is the greatest motivator in life. Any real military man or woman ought to know the truth of that." Pedro paused, in an obvious attempt to let that taunt's implications set in with the two officers still standing in the center of the rec room. "Mr. Aponyaschefski and the commander have devised an ingenious way to ensure our leader is feared, and thus, has that true power: A tournament ... two men, a fight to the death or a yield. Any resident may enter the tournament, but once they are in, they cannot refuse a challenge from any other contender. At the end, there will be one man or woman left standing, with no one willing to challenge them. That person will have real power, and they'll be able to keep the delicate order this station craves. Every man and woman in this room, short of you two, have all sworn a blood-pact to ensure this station's survival. We have vowed to serve whomever it is that wins the tournament and whatever form of government they decide to put in place afterwards. We are sworn to see this tournament through and to enforce its few rules. Sworn, you understand? We will honor those oaths."

"Wait a minute," Abner implored. "You're all in on this? Really? Every one of you?"

"That's right," answered a slender, pencil-mustached, young, caramel-complected officer that Mikkelson knew as Dontavious Woodson. "The squad is in this together, like everything we do, Abnormal Normie. Perhaps you and the sergeant have forgotten, but the commander never leads us astray. He knows what's best. And all of us have now come to see the wisdom and ... I don't know ... righteousness, I guess, in what we gotta do."

Abner asked his next questions in a much calmer and quieter voice, "So you're just going to abandon our mission and leave Earth to the monsters while y'all hide out up here? ... How could you even think about doing that? What about all our brothers and sisters we've left behind on our missions?" Abner stepped up to an officer Mikkelson had met once before and remembered as Eddie Sarkisian.

Hyun poked Sarkisian hard in the center of his chest with two firm fingers. "What about Donny McGuinness? Is this how you would honor his sacrifice? The man walked into a raving horde of Damned and fucking blew himself up for us, and you'd have his squad's legacy be cowardice and treason?"

Sarkisian did not look at all happy, but his voice was controlled when he answered Abner's accusations. "McGuinness and all the rest were sent to their deaths for no good reason, Abbie. I won't condemn another of our fellow officers to that fate. This needs to be done, Normie. We're all agreed on it."

"Well, not me!" The fire inside Abner was clearly reignited. "I'm not agreed. So y'all are going to have to try and do this on your own, 'cause you can damn well count the sergeant out too." Abner glanced over at Hamill who supplied a vigorous affirmative nod to show she stood with him. "So good luck trying to control a population of hundreds with just nine officers and one sickly lawyer as you try and overthrow their employers and then force some medieval tournament-of-champions on them."

"Well, we are the ones with the guns, after all. Don't forget that, Normie," Pedro answered, with a hint of a smirk on his lips.

"You can't use them inside the station!" Abner exclaimed in horror.

"Yeah, but they don't have to know that." Pedro still wore the smirk. "I figure the threat of the weapons themselves will be enough to keep things calm during the leadership transition."

Ah, yes, the weapons. That was, after all, the ultimate reason Mikkelson had decided to join the security squad's revolution. They had all the weapons. The rifles, shotguns, sidearms, explosives and bludgeoning weapons were all sealed up safe and secure behind a heavy steel security door set into the wall opposite of where Pedro Alvarez was currently seated. The door would only swish open, and allow access to the weapons racks beyond, once one of two security implant chips were read by the digital terminal embedded in the trim of the door halfway up along its right side. The two security implants were embedded in the right forearms of Commander Jasper Montrois and Sergeant Marge Hamill. Knowing this, it came as no surprise that Montrois and his staff were eager to win the sergeant over to their side. *I wonder if they'll cut it out of her if she doesn't agree to throw in with the rest of us?* Mikkelson pondered with pleasure. *I could use a little entertainment this morning.*

"And what about Cainey?" Abner continued his torrent of flabbergasted questions. "He's a security officer now, ain't he? Yet I'm not seeing him here amongst y'all."

"Cainey is weak-willed," Schef answered before anyone else could speak. "We can't afford a single weak link in the chain. He would twist our duty to his own gain. We cannot have that."

"This isn't as drastic a step as you two are making it out to be," Montrois addressed his wayward subordinates. "It seems like an extreme reaction to a possible theory from some random outsider—I get that, I do—but that's only true in relation to the world and the lives we've all lost... the before time. This is not extreme, my friends, it's *necessary*." Montrois reached out to place a hand on Abner's shoulder, but his willful underling pulled away from him with nothing but contempt and disgust on his face.

"Y'all swore oaths. Ya signed contracts. Y'all made solemn commitments," Abner reminded his fellow officers. "Have y'all got no honor? You say you've sworn yourselves to this madness. Well, why keep that oath and not the one you gave to AOA. The residents of this station expect us to protect them, to *save* them, to give them back their lives, or die trying, goddammit!"

"And that's a noble sentiment when the circumstances are just and righteous," Schef answered Abner's shout with enough condescension to make Mikkelson grin, "but there is no honor in serving a corrupt corporate regime, Officer Hyun. The only honorable action we can take on behalf of the people of this station is to remove the one great obstacle standing in the way of this habitation's perpetual success. And make no mistake," he said, raising his voice for emphasis, "what we do here today, and going forward, we are doing for the residents of this station, the last survivors of the human race. Let none of us here hold any other ill intention in their heart." Mikkelson cringed as Schef shouted out this last with a passion and flare fit for the stage, or even the political podium.

"Well, what about all our family and friends who've been infected and turned?" Abner asked, his resolve appearing to waver. "Are we just supposed to abandon them to a miserable and meaningless existence? Don't you think we owe it to all of 'em to keep searching for the vaccine?"

"Your friends and family are gone, Mr. Hyun," Schef said as tactfully as was possible. "I hate to be so blunt, but I lost just as many loved ones as the rest of you. They're not coming back, Officer. None of them are. We need to face that, for the good of humanity. We need to come to honest terms with that. I say we owe it to our unfortunate loved ones who've joined the ranks of the Damned, or been slain by them, to survive up here, so that their memories may live on inside each of us. We won't do that by following AOA's orders, my friend. They won't be happy until there isn't a single soul left aboard this station to send out on another meaningless suicide run."

"How could you possibly know that?" Abner asked with exaggerated exasperation.

"I see what's plain before me, Normie. It's a byproduct of my profession. Hope of curing the Damned is dead ... but hope itself is not. *We* are humanity's hope, and *we* must endure up here."

"If you're so determined to keep AOA in power up here, Normie, then wait for the tournament and try and claim your place as the undefeated and unchallenged," Pedro stated after a short silence had once again spread throughout the room. "Then you can go ahead and place the foxes back in charge of the henhouse, if you like. You can get your wish and watch each one of us die off around you, mission by meaningless mission, as we search for something that never existed in the first damn place. The tournament will be open to *everyone*, after all. If you think we're making a mistake here taking AOA's power away from them ... well then, the tournament will provide you with your chance to set things right."

Abner's lips were quivering with rage, but before he could put words to his fury, Schef spoke up to second Pedro's point, "That's right, Officer Hyun, if you win, and no one is left to challenge you, then you can install a hippy commune where everyone holds hands, or crown yourself king, or hand the reins of power right back to AOA, as Officer Alvarez suggests, whatever you like."

Out of the corner of his eye, Mikkelson watched Pedro lean forward from his slouching position on his couch and place both his hands on his knees. He glanced across the room with a look of sudden gravity etched across his face. "Don't you see how perfect this tournament idea is, Abner? It's like something out of the Middle Ages, but with like a real chance of actually working up here in outer-fucking-space."

"That's right," Schef once more voiced his concurrence with one of Pedro's statements. "It's a king's moot, only better, for there can be no bribery, or coercion, or playing of favorites in an honest battle. There are no politics in a fight to the death, only truth. And if it's truly a fair fight—which our solemn oaths ensure that we see to it that each match within the tournament shall be—then no man can deny it. The truth of the supreme authority of the tournament's champion would be plain to even the most stubborn of minds."

"I just ... I don't believe I'm hearing this." Marge sounded adrift from the pillars she'd most likely built her life around. "Seizing control of this facility? Betraying our contracts? Fighting to the death to see who's king? I mean, just listen to yourselves, for Christ's sake. Implementing your will on the residents of this station through fear and threats of violence? Have you all gone mad?" No response seemed quickly forthcoming, so she carried on, "There is no turning back from this. If you go through with this, neither myself nor Abner will be responsible for what happens to you. 'Cause like the man said, you can sure as hell count us out."

"Is that a threat, Sergeant Marge?" asked a redheaded and square-shouldered thirty-something female officer whose name Mikkelson couldn't bring to mind.

"I think it is, Poll," Marge answered the woman, whose full name, Apollonia "Polly Poll" Dobechek, suddenly came to him. "It's gonna have to be, I guess. You've left us little other choice." Marge turned towards the rec room's hatchway, grabbing Abner's forearm to pull him along.

The two hadn't made it five paces into their unceremonious withdrawal before Pedro stood up and leveled a finger at them, "Hold it right there!" He gestured towards the hatchway at two officers near that egress point, "Block that door, you guys."

Four officers on that side of the room actually got up to carry out his command. Abner and the sergeant immediately found themselves cut off and surrounded. Mikkelson could feel the tension in the room thicken with every breath, much to his satisfaction. *It'll be awfully nice to put whatever minor inconvenience these two shit-heads might pose in the near future to bed right here and now.* With all the uncertainties on the horizon, he was keen on eliminating as many problems as possible.

Marge looked over at her commander with abhorrence and bottomless disbelief written all over her face. Mikkelson scorned the way Montrois could not meet her eyes. *How pathetic,* he thought, disgusted. Abner faced the officers blocking his exit. He stepped a few paces towards the four officers who matched his progress with two steps forward of their own. "Get out of our way, you guys. I'm not going to ask twice," he told them.

The threat, however, did not land. The four blocking officers showed no hint of compliance. Instead, their crossed arms and tensed shoulders were a clear visualization of their intent to stand their ground. Mikkelson leaned back against the wall and smiled with both relief at the weight off his feet, and anticipation for the impending violence. It seemed, however, that Montrois was intent on spoiling all the fun, for just as Abner was drawing back his fist to officially kick off the scuffle, the commander spoke up loudly, waving his arms in panic as he did. "Wait, wait! Woodson, Polly, Hopkins, Schwambach!" He called to the four officers blocking the hatchway. "Step aside! Let them go. They've made their choices, it don't make them our enemies... not yet anyway," he added with obvious remorse.

The four blockers were still hesitant to abandon their new duty. Mikkelson watched with interest as they looked over to Pedro with confusion. "We can't just let them go, Monty," Pedro told his commander. "I mean, think about it; Sergeant Marge is the only other person aboard this station with access to the weapons locker. It's as disappointing and painful a thing for me to think about doing to any of our squadmates as it is to you, but they've already declared themselves our enemies, at least as far as our plans are concerned. We can't let them go out there knowing what they know, especially not with a key to the station's guns. They could arm some of the residents. And if anyone survives the firefight that would ensue from that, they'd be alive just long enough to watch this place blow up around them from all the damage that battle would inflict on this station's delicate machinery."

"Perhaps we ought to extract the sergeant's security implant chip and keep the two of them under guard until our plan has run its course?" Mikkelson suggested casually, not really caring whether or not his idea was acted upon. *Either way, I'm sure it will be entertaining.* This time he was unable to fight off his grin.

"The man is right, boss," Pedro assured his commander.

"No, he isn't!" The short, stout, frog-faced officer Montrois had referred to as Hopkins spoke up for the first time during the meeting. "We can't afford to spare a single man for guard detail. I say we do what we have to. I mean ... if we are willing to carry out a coup and ensure a deathmatch tournament gets played out, then it seems to me like we ought to have the stomach to deal with whatever problems get in the way of those two aims. Abner and Marge," the man said, speaking directly to his two blackballed fellow officers, "I'm sorry, but you both had your chance to make the right decision. What happens next is on your heads."

All four blockers stepped towards Abner and Marge with those words. Abner reacted almost too fast for Mikkelson to follow. Stepping quickly forward, he led with his right forearm, bashing it firmly into the bridge of Woodson's nose. Dontavious Woodson went down like a sack of meat, the blood already flowing from his busted nose. Woodson's body didn't make it a half dozen inches into its descent before Abner had twisted at the hip and used the momentum of his forearm's impact with Woodson's face to catapult a thundering fist into the side of Dobechek's head. Hopkins and Schwambach moved up beside him in the next instant and quickly latched hold of an arm apiece as Dobechek was launched into a nearby armchair from the hefty blow. She and the chair crashed to the floor in a tangled sprawl as Abner struggled to break free from his unyielding captors. He swung his head violently in a desperate, but ultimately fruitless effort to smash either man with a crippling headbutt.

Chaos gripped the rec room in its unforgiving claws. Marge raged as she ducked and dodged to avoid being incapacitated in a similar fashion as her counterpart. Every person in the room, short of Mikkelson and his man Cornwell, were shouting to be heard. However, only one man had the abilities to accomplish the feat; Montrois inserted a pinkie finger into either side of his thin-lipped mouth and let out a piercing whistle. It had the effect of silencing perhaps half of the shouting voices, allowing the security commander's growling demand to be heard above all the remaining shouts. "Knock it off, goddammit! Masterson, Schwambach, let the man go. Do it now!" He ordered them in a battlefield commander's voice, when it seemed they planned to disobey him.

Montrois marched across to them and shoved his two men off of Abner with frightening ease. He stared down Hopkins and Schwambach in turn. Mikkelson did not fail to notice the genuine fear that appeared in each man's face. Montrois then turned to Abner to point a long finger at the wayward officer as the chaos that had gripped the room only moments before ebbed away. "Get the hell out of here and don't think to come back. This was your one chance, the both of you," he added as he moved his finger to Sergeant Marge. "Just stay the hell out of our way. I don't want anyone getting hurt because you two don't have the stomach to face the truth. So go on, get the hell out of here! We catch you anywhere near the weapons locker, or even anywhere within security headquarters ... well then, we'll do what we must. I can only be so reasonable. My responsibility is too great to let old friendships jeopardize our plans."

Abner spat a thick yellowish glob of phlegm full into his commander's face. "Fuck you, whoever the fuck you are." His tone was as foul as his spittle. Monty seemed to wallow in the humiliation for a long moment before using his shirtsleeve to clean his face. Abner marched past him without another verbal or mucus-projectiled insult. Once in front of the automatic hatchway, he paused only long enough to hit the portal's controls. Marge had joined him, and the two left their former sanctuary in tandem with every one of their fellow officers, save perhaps Montrois alone, glaring icy daggers at their retreating backs.

CHAPTER 8

HELENA

The coughing man a few benches up from Helena Elle Heathcoat added a groan to his incessant hacks as the number seven magnetic repulsion trolley floated along a detour branch of the magnetic rail system. The magnetic repulsion rail and trolley system was a miracle of modern technology, deserving of reverent awe upon each encounter, but Helena had ridden them so often over the last few weeks that she was beginning to take it for granted, treating them with the same derision she would any old public transportation system. The system consisted of a single three-inch magnetic rail running down the center of nearly every passageway of every Branch inside Cardinal's Nest. The spider web of rails, and the public trolley cars gliding smoothly along them, were meticulously monitored. They were organized into a system that ran similar to any bus or train system you'd find in most big cities back in the States ... *back on Earth.*

Helena's trolley came to a hovering rest over a stop of the rail system at the end of Maroon Corridor, just a few short yards from the annex tunnel leading to the Living Quarters Central Hub. Unlike every other morning trip Helena had spent aboard the number seven, this stop would be the last the dependable trolley made for the rest of the morning. From here it was headed straight out Branch 4, and then nonstop all the way to the entrance of The Meadow at the end of the sepulchral and gloomy Branch 5.

The alleyway that cut down the center of that half-mile-long Branch had low ceilings and dim lighting that barely illuminated its cramped gunmetal-gray walls. Helena felt it added to the awe of The Meadow that such a bright and fantastical place could be discovered at the end of such a dreary alley. The Meadow had quickly become one of her favorite spots to unwind aboard station, so it made her sad, and a bit confused, whenever she thought about how that glorious garden of fantasies would be the stage for day one of the Final Tournament, as the residents had been encouraged to refer to the deathmatch contest with its grand-prize trophy of uncontested rule aboard station.

Helena sat in her usual spot behind the trolley conductor's cab this morning. Unusually however, she did not have a book in her hands, nor her work bag perched atop her lap. Today, each stop of the number seven trolley commanded Helena's full attention. She felt her nerves chafe raw with every second's delay each of the trolley's pickups caused. Normally, the trolley's multitude of stops passed Helena by in a barely noticed blur as ol' Number Seven zipped its way to the water recycling facility halfway down Branch 4's main alleyway. It was there that she *punched the clock* thirty hours a week to engage in the menial labor she had been assigned to perform ever since joining her wife Alice Stark aboard station.

The work she did there at the water plant was a far cry from her former career as a dental hygienist. Helena had hoped to be assigned a position at the fancy techno hospital and med labs down Branch 1 when she'd first been told that all the newly arrived family members would be assigned jobs aboard station, but she was informed by the fat asshole in charge of staffing that they had two full-time dentists and four full-time hygienists already on board and wouldn't be needing any others. He did say he would add her name to the hospital's auxiliary emergency list though, whatever the hell that meant. Then he mentioned that they did have a need for RNs, but she was a long way from anything like a registered nurse, having only gotten the limited education necessary to receive her hygienist's certification. The fat bastard harrumphed at her when she'd told him as much, then promptly assigned her to a labor crew at the water recycling facility without another question.

Helena had instantly begun to envy Alice's cushy job as a Greenhouse Technician, a position she'd held for two months before Helena had even come aboard station. The disparity between their two occupations aboard station had started to become a minor point of contention between her and Alice. *One point among many.* Although Helena knew she was being a little out of line. She was definitely lacking the PhD in botany that Alice had, after all.

Helena was eager to get to The Meadow's archway at the end of this trolley ride, and even more eager for The Final Tournament to begin. It wasn't for any morbid reasons, like lust for violence, or anything like that. The normally garrulous and easygoing Helena simply craved a distraction. She absolutely hated arguing with her wife, but they'd been doing so much more of it lately that it had her scared down to her very bones.

She was well aware of the dangers of dwelling on those arguments, not to mention dwelling on the rank bitterness in her and Alice's parting this morning. Unfortunately, all the trolley's stops were causing those painful recent memories to flood her consciousness. Helena had tried to push them away, tried desperately to focus on anything else: the gray-haired old woman at the end of the trolley who kept blowing her nose on the sleeve of her ratty green sweater, the young couple holding hands and whispering giggles back and forth a few rows up, the digital bulletin that scrawled across an electronic display band encircling the trolley's cream-colored ceiling and reading: "TOURNAMENT BEGINS TODAY. ALL RULES MUST BE OBEYED. VIOLATIONS MET WITH CAPITAL PUNISHMENT. NO PROTESTS ENTERTAINED. ENTER AT OWN RISK. BEST BEHAVIOR IS ENCOURAGED. YOUR ATTENDANCE IS ENCOURAGED. ALL LABOR OPERATIONS ORDERED TO SKELETON-CREW PROTOCOL." The scroll just repeated after that. And even the bizarre dissonance of seeing such a primitivistic and dystopian message scrolling digitally around the top of a magnetic rail trolley aboard an eight-million square foot moon base had not been able to distract Helena from her unwelcome ruminations. *God, get me to the tournament,* she thought, squeezing her knees and loudly grinding her teeth.

This morning's fight wasn't exactly the noisiest or fiercest she and Alice ever had during their eleven-year relationship, but they had never had an argument quite so consequential before. Even now, Helena could barely believe her significant other could be of such a polar-opposite mind over the issue of the security staff's takeover. It was truly baffling to her that Alice could not see the reality of their new situation. *Her head is still in the old world, God love her,* Helena thought, with both sadness and a little contempt. It was obvious to Helena that Montrois and the security officers were going to go through with their plans. Why risk standing in their way? Especially when no one could really say with any certainty whether or not they were actually wrong.

AOA had certainly lost all their credibility with Helena long ago. She remembered all too well the chaotic evacuation of the prep crow families. There hadn't been a day since when Helena didn't thank God she'd been in line for the E-11 shuttle that had boarded all of the family members in its queue. She always followed that prayer with one for the souls of those poor people left behind by that other transport ship, their places given to government officials and other VIPs without a moment's hesitation.

Helena knew that could very well have been her fate that awful day, and so, she rightly felt the utter joy of being alive when so many others could no longer claim that title. But she also felt the lofty burden that title placed on her shoulders, on all of their shoulders. She reflected on just how right that Schef guy had been the night he spoke to the assembled residents in the Grand Rotunda after the security staff had taken control of the station. He'd said, "We have a responsibility, a duty to mankind to endure, to put aside the comforts of the past, both ideologically and practically, and take whatever steps may be necessary to ensure mankind will survive to one day take Earth back after the curse of the Damned has run its course."

Helena understood just how delicate the operational systems aboard station truly were. She agreed with Schef and the officers that absolute authority was necessary if they were to keep the station operations running smoothly. Helena was a realist, unlike her beautiful wife, who was an eternal optimist. Or what Helena's father would call *a goddamn moron*. Helena was well aware that a population of any substantial size, as the population currently aboard station surely was, would have a fair number of bad eggs rotting away inside of it. People like that would always take advantage of any lulls in power and twist them to their own gain, even if it was to the detriment of everyone else. Knowing all that, she had at least agreed with the logic behind the tournament, though she shuddered at thoughts of its possible violence.

Alice's reaction of outright refusal to attend The Final Tournament, and then her disgust at the revelation of Helena's concurrence with the security staff, and their means, had genuinely taken Helena aback. Alice had always been at least practically rational in the past, if not a little naive. It had been one of the myriad things Helena had loved about her. Alice had conviction and could be a bit overzealous at times, but she wasn't a radical, by any means. In fact, their moral compasses had always seemed firmly aligned in the past. This time, however, it seemed that Alice was unable to get past the violent nature of the leader selection process. She was still trying to live in the past, in the old world, and Helena had told her as much. She hadn't been expecting Alice to counter with, "You've let the horror of the past few months make you morbid, Elle. You must be sick. How can you think a death tournament is the best way to decide our fate? Do you even hear yourself? I seriously think you're sick, Elle."

It was that final sardonic statement, posed with such raw condescension, that caused Helena to snap and say the words she now regretted most. "Maybe I am, Alice, maybe. I just don't know. Mostly, I just think that the men with the guns believe that a death tournament is the best way to decide our fate, and I don't think it's a good idea to disagree with them. You're too weak to understand hard decisions, Alice. The old world is dead. We need to survive in the new. The security officers are going through with this thing. We have to be seen as people they can trust. And likewise, for whoever ends up winning this damn tournament. That's the right thing to do here, Alice, for us. And since you don't have the strength to do what is in our best interest, I'll shoulder the load and swallow my pride and attend their little macho blood matches, for us. You can thank me for it someday, though I doubt you'll have strength enough to swallow *your* pride to do so."

The words were out before Helena had even realized she was saying them, but with a moment's reflection, she'd found she really did believe in their truth. So she had turned and marched out of their living quarters without another word. It was an extremely hard thing to do, especially as the sound and tempo of Alice's sobs had grown with each step she took toward their automatic hatchway. She had made it to the trolley stop a few hundred feet from their quarters in Blue Corridor, and a few moments later, managed to board the number seven trolley. And all without bolting back to her living quarters to fall to the floor at Alice's feet and beg her forgiveness, as so much of her had wanted to do.

I should've seen this difference of opinion coming, Helena chided herself. *You did tell her not to go to Dr. Sagal's stupid Alpha presentation, remember? But did she listen? No, she went ahead and let that ego-soaked doctor man fill her head with AOA's propaganda.* Sagal and Alice had been spending an awful lot of time in each other's company recently. Helena didn't think much of it at first. After all, they'd both spent a great deal of time around the station with the doctor and his family over the last few weeks. Plus, the doctor had been the loudest voice of opposition to the security staff's actions over the past ten days. So really, it only made sense that Alice would be listening to the man who was speaking the most, a man she had known since they came aboard together with the first of the prep crew. She was like that, often swayed by the last person to pitch her an idea. Alice thought she was enlightened and principled, but Helena knew the deeper truth, one she would never say to her dear wife's face: Alice was a sap. Helena's bleeding-heart wife was utterly lost in this new fast-changing world. She needed to be led. So, Helena had seen nothing strange with her wife seeking out a loud voice to guide her through all the craziness.

But after a few days, she had noticed Alice was spending more time with the doctor than any of the other nervous residents who hovered around him. She'd even sounded like him during this morning's argument, making all the same points Sagal had been shouting at anyone who'd listen over the past ten days. Helena had not liked that at all. She thought back on previously dismissed strange moments between the doctor and her wife, things she had quickly brushed off as nothing at the time: a seemingly accidental touching of the hand, or an odd flirtatious look. Such things were suddenly seen in a darker, more objective light. Helena realized she had been pushing away the truth in Alice and Perry's odd interactions since the day she came aboard, out of loyalty, trust and love. Those emotions drained inside her heart now. Pure bitterness slowly filled the vacuum.

The son of a bitch won't be happy until he's stirred up a counter-revolution to the security staff's, Helena told herself with furious certainty. *Well, I'll be goddamned if I let that slick-talking fancy doctor man lead my baby into danger. I've got to protect her from him, from everyone, from her own damn self, even. And it starts today, Elle. If any of these security officers see me in the crowd, I better look like I approve of their little masculine theater.* Fear that she might cringe at some of the violence she was sure to see today began to nag. Helena didn't want to send the officers any mixed signals about her approval. Alice was already giving them enough cause to blacklist them both. Helena shook her shoulders and set her mind to the task ahead. *Alice will understand that I'm doing the right thing someday. But for now, for both our sakes, you need to put her out of your head and focus on the road directly in front of you.* With great effort, she forced herself to study each letter of the trolley's scrolling digital bulletin as it passed her sightline, and not think about Alice, nor that bastard, rabble-rousing doctor for the rest of the trolley ride.

Helena crossed The Meadow's footbridge just inside its grandiose archway, feeling the vibrations of the smooth gunmetal-gray surface resonate up her legs with each new footfall. However, it was the excessive size of the crowd gathered a few dozen yards beyond the bridge that grabbed most of her attention. It both surprised Helena and simultaneously affirmed her convictions about the necessity in her attendance. Neither the softly ringing bridge beneath her feet, nor the incessant chatter of the residents surrounding her, nor even the teeth-rattling roar of the rushing river churning beneath the footbridge could distract from her amazement at how many of her fellow residents had made the same decision to attend.

Helena was not usually immune to the alluring call of the rushing rapids either. She would stop beside one of the footbridge's glass rails to peer over at the rushing river below, nearly every visit she made to The Meadow. For most of its length, the river was a daintily rippling flow, but under the footbridge, the path of the stream was significantly narrowed and strewn with jagged, artificial boulders to produce a roughly twenty-yard stretch of white water rapids. Just one more wonder for The Meadow's visitors to marvel over. Today however, the sound of the powerful current was out-intrigued by the shockingly massive crowd. It pulled Helena forward like its own magnetic force.

The security staff had ordered three sets of bleachers erected, ten rows high and horseshoeing around the center of five tennis courts positioned in the middle of the meticulously groomed recreation fields that dotted the lush and startlingly green meadow. *The goddamn bleachers are already half full, and the tournament ain't even set to begin for another twenty minutes yet.* The astonishing event left her breathless for a moment. Helena could clearly see the central court, where all the day's action would take place, mown as short as possible, though she could still make out the faint outlines of white paint splatters around its former boundaries, atop the very tips of grass blades here and there.

Despite the anxiety coursing through her veins, Helena had to marvel at her new habitat. Even at fifteen percent capacity, the station was so ordered and adequately staffed that they could afford to assign a team of laborers from among the residents to groom and garden the grounds of The Meadow. *I wish I got assigned a job like that,* she thought. *I might not feel like shooting myself for thirty hours every week. That's another reason to be sure to be seen on the side of The Final Tournament's champion, Elle. You can try and land yourself a nice cushy assignment alongside Alice.* Helena couldn't help but smile at that thought.

The Number Seven trolley had dropped its human cargo just outside The Meadow's archway right alongside several other full cars just like it, leaving Helena surrounded by dozens of her fellow residents as she made her way across the bridge toward the bleachers. She never much cared for big crowds, and was always more than a little impatient, even in the best of times, so she shouldered her way as forcefully as her meager courage allowed, in a mad rush to claim a quickly vanishing seat in the freshly erected bleachers. Helena had overheard, yesterday morning in the Main Cafeteria, that a team of the station's welders and engineers had been hastily assembled by some rather insistent, and then ultimately persuasive members of the security staff to cobble the viewing stands together as fast as they could. The hastiness was a bit worrisome to Helena. So she was pleased after her first step onto the bleachers to discover a sturdy construction. Helena quickly found a spot near the boundary rail of the lefthand set of bleachers, four rows up from the court's turf.

Once there, she settled in for a long day. Removing her cardigan, she revealed one of her famous turtlenecks underneath. This one was navy blue with three large gray lines running diagonally across its front. It was one of her less flamboyant options, which she found suited the occasion. She folded her cardigan into a neat square before placing it under her ass as a make-shift cushion. She had a feeling it was going to be a long, long day, and it may just save her a bit of discomfort, because although the bleachers were sturdy, they were anything but comfortable.

Two middle-aged men with the look of maintenance workers about them waddled up and sat down next her, causing her to once again marvel at the amount of people that had come out for this gore-fest. All week it had seemed that at least half of the residents were vehemently opposed to The Final Tournament, but as Helena looked about her, she grew certain that there were more than half of the Nest's residents in attendance already. She saw with horror and righteous indignation that there were even some children in the crowd. *I guess all the fear those officers and supervisors stirred up over the past few days worked its magic pretty goddamn well in the end,* she bitterly told herself.

"Well, hey there, Helena. I didn't expect to see *you* here," a woman's voice interrupted her introspection.

Helena looked down at the woman sitting on the bench directly in front of her. She forced a smile to spread across her face when recognition dawned. It was Maddie Aranzono. Helena and the nosy bitch worked the same shift at the water recycling facility. Helena was known for her bubbly personality and fast-friend-making ways; despite this, she and Maddie had clashed from day one. The rolled and folded, flabby-bodied, flat-nosed little troll of a woman had adopted the teacher's pet role with their staff supervisor, while Helena had slid into the goofing-off-in-the-back-of-class-passing-notes part at the water plant. So they'd inevitably had a few disagreements over the weeks. However, they kept any overt animosity toward one another bottled up for the most part. During their shared shift, the rivals had usually treated each other in a cordial enough manner, though one layered in a medley of sarcasm and repugnance.

Of course Maddie is here, Helena thought. Considering how strongly all the staff supervisors had been pushing for their workers to show up, it was certainly no surprise to see the royal suck-up in attendance. With a bright colored sweatshirt and an approving smile plastered to her face, no less. "Oh, Maddie, how lovely to see you. This must be the husband you talk so much about," Helena said, nodding to the thin gray-haired man with Charlie Brown ears seated to Maddie's left.

"Oh, yeah. This is Carl. Carl, Helena," Maddie introduced them. "We work the same shift at the water recycling facility."

Carl gave only a brusque nod as acknowledgment while Helena muttered, "Nice to meet ya."

"I'm surprised to see you here, Elle," Maddie said, pissing Helena off with her use of the nickname that was reserved only for Helena's closest friends.

"Surprised? Why surprised?" Helena responded, trying to sound like she couldn't care less.

"Oh, I don't know ... I've just seen Alice with Dr. Sagal a lot, is all, especially these last few days. And I know how vocally against The Final Tournament he has been ... so I just figured you two girls must be with him, I guess."

"Oh, no, Maddie, don't be ridiculous," Helena answered in what she hoped was her usual easy-going voice. "Alice and I are no fools. We both understand the necessity of this Final Tournament, that's for sure."

"Oh, well, I don't mean to pry or anything," said the woman who lived to do just that, "I've just noticed Alice with the doctor a lot lately, like I said. And—"

"He's our friend, is all," Helena interrupted her coworker's shameless unwillingness to drop the subject. "He and his family are friends, and they've been there for us over the last few months when we've needed a hand. We owe him. Alice and I thought it best to humor him for a while, is all. That's why you've seen them together so much lately. She is trying to bring him around to the right conclusion. It's been a slower process than we'd hoped—don't get me wrong—but out of respect for the good doctor, we are forced to go at his own pace."

"Oh ... so ... I guess you and Alice are on the same page about The Final Tournament then?"

"That's right, Maddie—though it's hardly any of your business—my wife and I are most definitely on the same page."

"Oh, of course, of course." Maddie made a show of looking around as she added, "Is she on her way here then? Are you saving her a seat? 'Cause I think that gentleman just took the last one open beside you," she added with a vixen's grin, pointing to the 280-pound light-skinned black man in a green silk shirt who had just sat down to her left.

"No, Maddie," Helena responded, struggling to tamp down her rage. "Crowds aren't really Alice's thing. She doesn't do well in them. Agoraphobia, you know. Perhaps you've heard of it. I myself am not a fan of large gatherings either, but we thought it best that one of us be here for this momentous occasion. Mine is several degrees lower than that of Alice's, so I was the obvious choice."

"Right," the witch said with a sneer. "Well, I won't distract you from the show then. I'm sure Alice will be upset to miss even a single second of the action. You better focus up and absorb every last detail so you can tell her all about it."

"Thanks so much, Maddie. I sure do appreciate the advice." Helena growled out the sarcastic retort as the skanky nark turned around on her bench to face the makeshift killing grounds. *My god, Alice, you see what you've already done? We're marked out as dissenters, goddammit.* Her fears threatened to overwhelm her outer calm. She wasn't lying about her discomfort with crowds either. The two large residents to either side of her were causing tingles of panic to shoot down her spine, over and over again. *God, just start this fucking tournament already,* she begged her benevolent creator.

Speak of the devil and he appears, was the cliché that jumped into her head as Schef, the survivor who broke the news of the security staff's takeover in the Grand Rotunda, chose that moment to saunter out to the center of the one-time tennis court. Helena once more spared a glance for the crowd around her. She couldn't find an empty seat left on any of the bleachers. There was even an overflow crowd milling around, jostling with one another for the best view.

Schef made it to the center of the court and started flapping his arms up and down in what looked like some weird mockery of a disturbed penguin. Apparently, he was trying to get the crowd to settle down, but it wasn't very effective. Helena watched as the overflow crowd pushed up against the thin line of armed security officers trying their damnedest to keep them from trampling out onto the court. There were a few dreadful seconds when Helena was sure chaos was about to erupt in the midst of the gaming fields, but before too long, Commander Montrois rose up from his perch in the center of the first row of the righthand set of bleachers. He shouted in his booming, authoritative voice, magnified ten times over by AOA's handheld silver and maroon bullhorn pressed snugly to his lips, "Silence! We will have order here! This is your one warning. Calm down now, or we shall be forced to make examples of some of you."

The threat definitely had teeth. The officers were all conspicuously armed. Helena figured they had nearly every firearm in their arsenal on display around those tournament grounds. Each officer had a semi-automatic rifle slung over their shoulder and at least two sidearms in holsters attached to body armor, utility belts, or strapped around their thighs and calves. Each one also had an axe, or a baseball bat, or some other kind of long blunt instrument sheathed at their backs. The determined and fearless looks in each of their eyes added to their threat as well. Clearly, they were all very serious about this. After a few moments, the crowd seemed to get that hint and began to settle down. A silence was slowly gripping the gargantuan chamber. Helena's eyes fell back to the survivor at center court, and in that moment, she could almost feel the eyes of everyone else in The Meadow do the exact same.

Schef pulled a cordless black microphone out from his back pocket and started tapping its windscreen. In the heavy silence, muffled bangs from his tapping blasted out from a long black speaker set in a rectangular silver and maroon frame. The volume the speaker produced was surprising. It seemed to have much more power than its size would suggest, being roughly the same dimensions as most household cedar chests. The speaker sat on the flat turf three feet in front of the center set of bleachers, and about five yards from a curious black line painted across the court. There were four black lines freshly painted on the court, she realized. Three ran parallel to each set of bleachers. The fourth line sealed off the box where the horseshoe of bleachers ended, enclosing a large rectangle of shorn and soft green Bermuda grass.

Schef was apparently not satisfied with the speaker's volume. He motioned to a security officer seated next to Montrois with a tablet in her hand. The officer must've gotten whatever message the survivor was attempting to convey because after another finger-tap against the windscreen, he smiled at the woman and offered her a thumbs-up. Schef then brought the microphone to his lips and blew softly into it once more before looking up to the silent crowd all around him. "Welcome, residents of Cardinal's Nest." He paused there, maybe expecting applause. The silence continued instead. "Today we embark on the first chapter of the next age of man: A Tournament. Two men. Two weapons. A fight with no rules, save one: If a man yields, his vanquisher will honor the submission and spare the man. The man who yielded will be eliminated from the tournament and disqualified from challenging in any future matches. If no man yields, the fight ends when one man is dead. Now, I have sworn an oath that eliminates me from eligibility to challenge in this tournament. It was a condition my new colleagues asked of me before agreeing, unanimously, to elect me to be this tournament's Supreme Officiant. When I deem a fight has reached its end, I will hit a button on one of our fancy little tablet thingies and you will hear this noise..." A sound much like that of an angry alien yowl blasted out from the court-side speaker. A few people around Helena reached up to cover their ears. Although the sound was indeed loud and obnoxious, she thought they were being overly dramatic. "An annoying sound, I know," Schef's voice came as soon as the sound faded away. "And loud, definitely loud. But that's the point. This way there can be no excuse for not hearing the final bell and delivering an illegal blow. Because this is where it gets truly serious, folks. My adopted brethren and I are fully committed to carrying out this tournament according to its few strict rules. Indeed, we have even all sworn sacred oaths to see this unfortunate but necessary deed through to its end. And we are also sworn to serve whoever claims the title of Champion of The Final Tournament. We are all fully committed to the champion's authority, with oaths of honor. Which still mean something to us, by the way. All of us," Schef said, spinning around and pointing out all the security officers around the court, "through horrific experience, have come to realize the tremendous responsibility being a resident of this miraculous habitation places upon us. The great span of human history has rested its lofty weight upon all our shoulders, and we have agreed to take up the call. We do not expect you all to come to this clarity of mind as seamlessly or as quickly as either myself or any of these brave officers before you have. And perhaps it's good that you don't. We need to keep our humanity, after all. We need to keep our independent and inquisitive spirit as a species. That, to us, is just as important as ensuring our security. But ensure our security we shall, ladies and gentlemen. Violations of this contest's few rules will absolutely not be tolerated. One of my unfortunate brothers- or sisters-in-arms will dispatch the violator without hesitation. I say this to you not as some crude attempt at martial intimidation; it is simply something that must be said, something that must be known by everyone here today because it's the truth, and we are too far into the endgame of our mighty and illustrious species to not look truth square in the face. So before you offer yourself as a combatant, or attempt to disrupt these proceedings, be sure you know and trust our commitment. Once the fights begin, do not, under any circumstances, cross the line of officers around the tourney grounds, at any time whatsoever. You will be dealt with, and again, without mercy or hesitation. You will receive one warning, and only one warning, for unruliness from the officers, after which, they have the discretionary authority to deal with you in whatever way they deem appropriate. Point being people: We ain't fucking around here. I'm aware that all of this might sound a little medieval and regressive to some of you. But those of us who have seen what the world has become, know that the willingness to face the threat of victory or death is precisely the kind of trait we need in the leader of this precious and fragile ecosystem around us." Schef stopped to gesture up at Stargazer Ceiling and the inky blackness beyond speckled with a billion flecks of dazzling silver and blue. "We need a leader we can all trust with our survival when everything is on the line," he continued, "because we all know better now. None of us are virgins to catastrophe any longer. That wariness that I'm sure you all feel, it needs the comfort of a strong and capable leader to set it to ease. It has to be a deathmatch for our leader, my friends, for that is the only way to ensure that no weak-hearted fools like Hubert Harrington, or President Rafferty, or any of their cronies cowering back in their luxury suites are ever able to place their corrosive hands near power again. Look around you and you will notice every last one of them is conspicuously absent today. And we know why, don't we?" The question was apparently rhetorical because he immediately provided the answer, "They all lack the strength of will to submit themselves before the people and prove whether or not they are worthy to shoulder the responsibility of leading humankind's last hope. They bought all their so-called *power* with money and influence, with politics and backstabbing. They do not deserve your respect. If they deserved their authority, they would be here right now, ready to challenge for that honor. But not a one of those *VIPs* is here to earn their titles. We have gone to extremes here, it's true. I'll be the first to admit it. But the officers and I all believe that these extremes are commensurate with the demands of our current unprecedented circumstances. You see, my friends, no coward or self-interested bureaucrat can manipulate a simple fight to the death. A coward, by definition, lacks the heart to prove themselves in the crucible of combat. This tournament assures our safety from the traps and snares of humanity's past."

Schef paused just then, letting his words sink into a silent crowd on the very edge of their seats, soaking up the sermon. Helena was leaning forward with all the rest. *The man can give a speech, that's for sure*, she thought, remembering his fiery oratory in the Grand Rotunda ten days back. *Although, what's with all this "he" and "man" bullshit? What, does he think no woman could ever defeat a man in a stupid fight? Asshole.* Helena had a secret hope, admittedly low on her priorities at the moment, but a hope nonetheless, that at least one woman would enter and kick the ass of some of the cocky, thick-headed male assholes that were sure to fight. Somewhere deep inside her, Helena actually wished she had what it took to be the woman to do that ass-kicking. *Sadly, Elle, you fool, you barely have the courage to raise your voice to your wife*, she laughed sadly to herself as she watched Schef bring the microphone back up to his lips.

"Soon, I will ask for the first competitor. Once that person is selected, I will then ask for a challenger. The two combatants will then choose one weapon apiece from this bin..."

Just then, one of the security officers rolled a large gleaming silver metal barrel to the center of the court on a dolly. The barrel was filled with various weapons of differing lengths and shapes. There were long wooden staffs, some plain, others tipped with a leaf-shaped spear blade. There were baseball bats, a few metal and a few wooden, with the wooden bats all having long nails hammered through their barrels. There were axes too, both wooden-handled and graphite, a few double-headed. All the edges on the blades in that barrel of killing tools gleamed with oily reflections of The Meadow's bright lights, offering testimony to their razor-sharp points. There must've been other smaller hand weapons stuffed in the barrel that Helena couldn't see as well, judging from the struggle the officer had in moving the dolly out from under the clearly heavy bin.

"Once the weapons are chosen, a second choice will not be allowed. So choose carefully, would-be combatants, for if your weapon breaks, you'll be left with your hands alone to save you. Or, of course, you may also yield. Once we have a winner of the first fight, I will call for a challenger. And once we have that challenger, we shall pause for thirty minutes to allow the victor to recover. No man shall fight more than three matches in a day. After his third fight, we will break and resume the next day. If a fight ends after 1900 ST, then we break for the day, after another challenger declares himself. When we break for the night, the two combatants who will start the next day's fights will stay in the security staff's rec room, under guard of the officers. They will be provided meals and a comfortable bed but will not be allowed contact with anyone else." Schef drew in a deep breath and his face grew even graver, even though Helena hardly would've thought it possible. "And then we keep going, on and on like that, right up until we are left with a victor that no one present is willing to challenge. That's when we will know we have our leader. I long for that moment, ladies and gentlemen. And I hope that if you don't feel the same in your hearts right now, you will come to cultivate due reverence for it in time."

"We are with you, Schef! I feel it. I long for it," Maddie shouted out over the rumblings that quickly rippled through the crowd.

"Yeah! Let's get this fucking show on the road," the maintenance worker to Helena's right shouted, lurching to his feet. "Come on, call for the first challenger!" In the man's exuberance for the impending violence, he knocked his arm into Helena's shoulder. It wasn't a hard blow, and purely accidental, but it did cause the man to drop the plastic mug in his hand, spilling its contents all down her turtleneck.

Instantly, Helena knew said contents had been brewed in the priest's cramped workshop. The pungent, stinging aroma of alcohol quickly flooded her nostrils. "Hey! Goddammit! Watch what you're doing!" She shouted at the man whilst attempting to brush some of the liquid off her sweater before it could soak in.

"Oh, damn. Sorry, lady, my bad," the maintenance man answered in a mildly sheepish tone.

"Your bad?" She asked with acid sarcasm.

"Yeah. Relax, lady."

"Relax?!" Helena jumped up from her seat on the bench to look the man dead in the face. The crowd was now shouting at Schef, half of them a good deal more passionately than their counterparts. Despite the noise of the crowd, an officer decked out with a pistol on his hip and one on his calf, and a casual hand resting cocksure on the stock of a black semi-automatic rifle with a handle-mounted short scope noticed their argument. The jackboot took a step towards them as his free hand wrapped around his rifle's barrel stock. There was no doubt to Helena that it was her and the asshole beside her to whom the gesture's menace was intended. Immediately, Helena sat back down, ignoring the man she had meant to chew out. The man, for his part, waved both his hands at her, as if to toss off the nuisance she represented, and went back to his shouting. *Goddammit, Helena! You are so blowing this,* she scolded herself. *You need to calm the hell down and get through this. If these assholes are drinking, then you can expect further spills as the day goes on. So what? Get over it ... for Alice's sake.*

"I'm sure everyone here today has heard about this tournament and the many rumors—both true and false—surrounding it all week long," Schef broke in through the shouts. "Indeed, you've most likely played your own small part in their dissemination. The rumor mill up here is shockingly swift, I've discovered. So I'm guessing you're all well enough up to speed that I don't need to waste anymore of our time with further verbose declamation pertaining to this sacred tournament's rules or provenance," Schef declared to a quickly quieting crowd. He turned to face Montrois in his front row seat. Helena saw Montrois' nod from her spot all the way across the court. It must've been a cue Schef had been waiting for. Raising his hand to quell the final lingering shouts and magpie conversations, he at last attained a quiet sufficient enough to suit him. Only then did he raise the microphone back to his lips, "Well then, fellow residents, my colleagues and I, with dedication and ample solemnity, declare The Final Tournament officially begun."

The scratchy yowling noise burst from the speaker straight into Helena's ears once more but was mercifully cut short. She thought she may come to have a bitter association with the wretched sound in the very near future. That really scared her, since she already felt like shoving a fork in her ear whenever she heard it. Looking around her, Helena was sure she was not in the minority on the matter either. It seemed a little bit sadistic somehow, almost like they deliberately picked such a painful sound to prove a point. Like torture for the sake of torture, just to prove they can.

Jeez, I sure hope whoever wins this fucking thing isn't a security officer. As soon as the thought popped into her head, Helena knew what a fool she'd been, what a fool they'd *all* been. *Of course a security officer is going to win this tournament. All of this is nothing more than an elaborate game to ease us into their rule. You watch, Elle, it'll be one of them winning the crown here for sure.* Helena reflected on that for a long moment before ultimately sighing with reluctant acceptance. *Hmm, maybe it's just as well. At least I can be assured they will take care of the station and keep it running safely and smoothly. And men as smart as Schef and Montrois will also know taking care of the station means taking care of the workers. And a safely operating station might be the best thing to hope for here, Elle, now that I think on it. It could be one of those hairy meat-head maintenance workers, or collector module garage morons, or some other dirty-job-having blockhead that wins this thing. Like these louts beside ya, Elle.* A shudder ran up her back at that thought. *This place would wind up looking like a biker bar in no time, complete with brothel and pawn shop, no doubt.* The vision was as sick as it was clear. *No, no, we can't have that. I guess it's just gotta be a security officer. No one else stands a chance here. None of these soccer moms and tech-nerd dads filling out the remainder of the resident roster could stand a damn chance against the meatheads and professional killers. Oh well, Elle, like you say, at least they will take care of the station.*

"I call then for the first competitor," Schef interrupted her inner monologue to say. "Who will that brave man ... or *woman,*" the jerk added as an afterthought, "who shall that person be? Your name will forever have a place of honor in the history of our new society, here in the portentously named Nest. Who among you believes themselves not only capable, but *worthy* of leading us into a brighter future? Is that man here today?"

"He sure as hell is," a surprisingly nasal voice that didn't jibe with its authoritative subject matter shouted out in response to the call.

Helena couldn't see who had spoken, but from the way the crowd around her behaved, the shouter must be seated on the same set of bleachers as her, only on the opposite end. She didn't bother standing to see who it was. She doubted she would see anything, with everyone else in the bleachers standing as well. Not to mention the fact that she had no desire to be face to face with the fat, clumsy, dick bag standing to her right. So she had to wait until the crowd finally reclaimed their seats before she saw The Final Tournament's first competitor. The nasal voice had left her doubting, but she shouldn't have bothered; she was right all along. It was a meathead, if ever there was one.

He was a gigantic meathead. This was the kind of guy other big guys would call a *big guy*. She figured him for a mechanic of some sort, judging from his grease-stained hands that she could clearly see as he passed near her on his way to Schef's side. She pegged him for either the collector module garage down Branch 6 or the transport craft garage and lunar dock down Branch 2. Although, upon further inspection, the guy didn't look like someone they would allow near aviation machinery, especially not AOA's fancy rocket ships. He looked like some kind of big dumb ape, one you might be able to train to push a big button if you worked at it really hard for a few decades. His protruding brow shadowed his beady little eyes. His long, thick, tattooed arms hung so low his knuckles were in danger of scraping the turf. Unlike most apes, however, this one had a bald white scalp, with here and there a few clumps of graying, brown hair. He smiled just then, revealing a missing front tooth. The moron must've thought the deformity some sort of resume testifying to his toughness. And apparently the crowd agreed; shouts of encouragement and super-lative plaudits rained down on the Neanderthal as his grin grew ever wider.

"The honor of first competitor is yours, good sir. I commend you," Schef said with an obviously fake smile. "Your name?"

"Scott Osentoski. I work at the maintenance depot," The ape responded confidently. "This place would fucking fall apart without us. We're fucking tired of shoveling all y'alls trash and fixing all the shit y'all break at your quarters and are too fucking stupid to fix your damn selves. We tired of all of it. And lucky for the depot, they got a fucking beast like me to champion them. We already running this fucking place. Now I'ma make sure we get the fucking credit for it. I'm ready to kill any of you motherfuckers. This is my time, bitches."

He tried to execute a mic-drop, but Schef was too quick, snatching it from the air after only a few inches of plummet. Cool as ever, Schef moved the microphone slowly back to his lips, "Do you understand the rules, Mr. Osentoski?"

The ape tried to snatch the microphone back, but Schef was having none of it. Helena could see Osentoski wanted to take it by force, but he glanced about him at the ever stoic and watchful armed officers surrounding him and must've thought better of it. He spoke his agreement into the un-amplified air, so Helena was only able to go by his nod as proof that he understood.

Schef took a step away from Osentoski and once more motioned for the crowd to settle. "So, we have our first combatant. Do we have a challenger?" He asked the fresh silence. "Is there a man here willing to risk life and limb for a chance to prove Scott Osentoski is not the man to lead us? Surely one of you believes you are better for the job than this man?" He pointed at the ape, who was turning an angry shade of rouge in the middle of the court. There were a lot of derisive shouts aimed at Osentoski, but it seemed no one had the courage to walk their talk. Osentoski's frown quickly straightened, and with each passing second without a challenger announcing themselves, it stretched and twisted into a smile in the style of the Joker himself.

"I challenge! Hey, hey, Mr. Official man!" The shout cut short Osentoski's smile, sending it snapping back into a pressed, thin line. Helena didn't need to wait for the man to step out onto the killing grounds to be able to see who had spoken this time. She need only turn her head to the left. The shouter had been seated right beside her; the huge man in the green silk shirt. He was getting to his feet even as she looked. As he stood, the people in the crowd around him sat down or scooted themselves away, as if to proclaim they weren't with him. *No one has a wish to get on the maintenance depot's bad side,* she laughed bitterly to herself. A path through the bleachers opened up in front of the man, as though he were Moses before the Red Sea. The man strolled down the path with just as much confidence as Osentoski had displayed, though this man lacked Osentoski's flair. Helena found herself liking him a little for that.

The man had good reason to be confident, in her view. He was a large, intimidating sort of fella. At first meeting, when she was already feeling the pangs of agoraphobia, all she noticed about the guy was how fat he was, and how much space his ass would take up. Watching him make his way to center court, she could see that, although he was indeed fat, with that aforementioned large ass, he was also quite tall. Not quite as tall as the ape he would have to fight, but at least 6'4". He had bulky shoulders, at least three feet wide, and a neck so thick and squat it was hard to say for sure if it was actually there or not.

Jesus, these gotta be the two biggest guys aboard station. As soon as she thought it, she knew it must be true. The two combatants dwarfed the scrawny lawyer standing between them at center court. The black man slowly and methodically removed his green silk shirt while keeping eye contact with Osentoski. Helena could tell from the scars and tattoos that covered nearly every curve of muscle and fold of fat on the man's torso that he was definitely the real deal. The ape must've realized the same thing; all the color drained from his face in a heartbeat. A flush returned quick enough, however, after Osentoski began to visibly work himself into a rage, jumping up and down and slapping himself in the face. Schef placed a hand on Osentoski's chest and pushed him back a few paces when his antics landed him within a few feet of the challenger. He yielded to Schef's control easily enough. The survivor then turned, microphone in hand, to face the challenger. "Your name, sir?" He asked.

"Charlie Dutton," the challenger responded, still staring down Osentoski. "And I ain't living in no world that this fascist, douchebag, racist-ass motherfucker is in charge of. Yeah, that's right, mother-fucker," Dutton spoke directly to Osentoski, "I heard what you been saying about me and my niggas up here. I heard your dumb ass running that fucking mouth of yours 'round the cafeterias. You think you're a hard motherfucker, but you ain't nothing. I ain't letting you and your fucking Klan homies run this place. No way. I ain't gonna stand for it. No fucking way." *Well, I guess these two have some history,* Helena thought. Dutton pointed a long, fleshy finger at Osentoski as he made his final point, "I been looking for an excuse to beat your bitch-ass to death for a while now."

Helena was hoping for more of a reaction from Osentoski, but he simply waved his hands at Dutton, brushing off his threats with casual disregard. "You understand the rules then?" Schef asked, reclaiming sole control of the microphone. Helena saw Dutton's nod, but she once again missed the audible confirmation. "Well then, we have two willing combatants. I won't ask you two to shake hands. Just select your weapon from the bin and make your way to either end of the court. Mr. Osentoski, as first competitor, you have the honor of first choice."

Helena watched Osentoski walk to the silver barrel, as rapt as everyone else, if the silence in The Meadow was any indication. He deliberated for only moments before withdrawing a long double-headed axe with a black head and gray graphite handle. Osentoski delivered a few test chops into the empty air as he swaggered his way to one end of the one-time tennis court.

Dutton stepped up to the barrel next. He was not as hasty as his opponent had been in his weapon selection. Dutton withdrew more than a few weapons, one at a time, testing their balance and weight. He had no need to inspect their edges, in Helena's opinion. From her vantagepoint, it was obvious they were all deadly sharp. But Dutton must be a meticulous fellow, because he made sure to run the ball of his thumb down the edge of every blade he picked up. After a couple more selections were found lacking, and thus discarded, the crowd began to grumble a bit. Helena couldn't be sure if that was what made Dutton finally make up his mind, but he did accept the metal bat with its yellow taped handgrip that he was holding at the time the grumbling had reached its pinnacle. Dutton swished the bat through the air in shallow arcs, rotating it back and forth with his wrist as he plodded towards his end of the court.

The dolly-toting security officer shuffled back onto the field to collect the barrel-of-death. He wheeled it away in a hurry and left Schef alone at center court. The survivor's hand shot up once again and the crowd quickly hushed. *He's getting pretty good at that,* she reflected. "Ladies and gentlemen, I want to remind you of the reverence you need to maintain in your hearts here today, and the appropriate demeanor with which you should comport yourselves while viewing these matches. The stakes for you—for all of us—have never been higher. Combatants," he said, switching his focus toward the two fighters, "you know the rules and you've accepted them." The survivor flipped his gaze between them as he spoke. "In so doing, you have sworn yourselves by your very lives to abide by them. And so, with nothing left to be said, we've come to it at last. Are you ready?" He asked them in the sober tones of a pope reading scripture. Osentoski and Dutton nodded their heads in unison. They kept up with the synchronization as they then jerked them side to side, stretching out any lingering kinks. "Very well th— Oh, I almost forgot! Stay inside the black lines as best you can, gentleman. Or you can expect to be shoved back in the square by one of the officers." That seemingly important rule, added in an off-hand manner, rattled both competitors for a brief moment. Schef didn't let them stew over it, "Okay then, that's it. Begin," he shouted at them. Instantly, the thin man tucked away his microphone and sprinted out of the killing box to an open seat in the front row of the bleachers, right alongside Montrois.

Schef needn't have sprinted. The two combatants had barely made it five yards from their starting positions by the time he was seated. They were walking in slow and shallow zigzags, sizing each other up, neither one in any hurry to be the initial aggressor. Helena figured she could understand that. If it were her facing gory death at the end of a wicked axe or a crushing metal bat, she'd be in no big rush to meet it either. Osentoski suddenly cut off his forward motion to raise his arms toward the starry expanse above his head. The double-headed axe held aloft in his right hand reflected the countless, twinkling fireballs. He motioned for the crowd's support, bellowing requests for their encouragement. The return cheers quickly echoed into the modern-age coliseum, though they were accompanied by an equal number of derisive taunts as well. Osentoski didn't seem to care. Instead, he reveled in the attention, as if there wasn't a large, angry, tattooed man on a vendetta and armed with a pummeling tool walking straight towards him.

His arms came down just in time to block Dutton's first swing, which came whipping in towards Osentoski's ribs on a flat arc. The shaft of Osentoski's axe fell just in time to parry the blow, though it nearly cost the cocky man his grip on the heavy weapon. He gave himself time to recover his hold on the axe by darting away from Dutton a few feet up court. Dutton moved quickly to close the gap but was forced to break off pursuit to parry a one-armed overhand slash that Osentoski somehow managed to hurl down with cat-like speed. Dutton turned the blow with a two-handed smash that clanged off the axe blade and sent a piercing metal jangle into the air, making Helena realize how quiet it had become all around her.

Despite Osentoski's early efforts to rile up the crowd, the unreal sight they were all witnessing caused Helena and her fellow residents to drop their jaws and hold their breaths.

The metal clang, however, had broken the spell. The crowd around her quickly began to take back up their chants and boos. The men on the court must've been too focused on the immediate situation to notice the crowd one way or the other. They didn't miss a beat. After the metal-ringing parry, Osentoski had gone with the force of the impact and spun around 360 degrees to deliver a two-handed slash toward his opponent's chest. Dutton saw the blow coming and was able to dart backwards out of the axe's considerable reach. Osentoski must not have been expecting the man with the flabby beer gut in front of him to be able to move as quickly as he had; Helena certainly wasn't. He had over-extended himself too far on the slash and couldn't whip the axe back in time to fully deflect the crushing counter-stroke Dutton aimed at his left shoulder. The shaft of the axe arrived in time to somewhat lessen the blow, but even so, the impact with Osentoski's shoulder could be heard clearly above the noisy crowd.

Osentoski reeled away from Dutton while the crowd murmured a collective and perverse anticipatory "oooh," at the sight of his left arm hanging limply by his side. Osentoski jogged a dozen yards across the court before turning back to face Dutton, who had not chased him. He shouted some unheard goading insults at the shirtless man while pointing the axe at him with his one good arm outstretched and baleful.

At first the insults failed to move Dutton, but a few paragraphs in, Osentoski must've plucked the right chord. Dutton began to slowly make his way across the court, swatting the metal bat in his open palm every step of the way. Dutton stopped right in front of the injured man, getting within a few feet. He must've wanted to say something in response to Osentoski's taunts, but he never got the chance. Osentoski slashed the axe down at Dutton's left leg, cutting short the insult clearly forming on the fat man's lips. Dutton reacted remarkably quick, despite his surprise. Twisting at the hips, he swung his leg out of harm's way just as he lashed out weakly in defense with the bat. Dutton continued his twist and dodging maneuvers to evade the next few axe slashes that chased him backwards six or seven paces. Finally, Osentoski whipped in a forehand slash looping down at Dutton's chest that even his uncanny quickness was unable to avoid. The axe scored a long crimson gash from his left collarbone to midway down his bloated abdomen.

A gasp rippled through the crowd as Dutton stumbled backwards with a hand pressed to his fresh wound. He opened up a dozen yards of space before stopping to pull his hand away and discover it soaked in his blood. The wound looked deep and painful; sheets of bright-red blood pulsed from its gnarly chasm, soaking Dutton's colossal stomach. Helena wanted to look away. Oh, how badly she felt the pull to shield her eyes and run away from this place. But she didn't. With a strength of will she never knew she had, Helena Heathcoat kept her eyes locked onto the necessary catastrophe.

Dutton shook out his bloody hand and wiped it clean on his pants. Then he pointed the bat directly at his foe, releasing a howl of rage that silenced the crowd. Helena could feel its pain and anger and intensity reverberating in her bones. Dutton suddenly broke into a flat-out sprint at Osentoski. Helena registered a moment of shock on the maintenance worker's face before he raised his axe and charged forward to meet his challenger. Both men aimed mighty one-handed slashes at their opponent's chest. The shaft of the axe collided with the meat of the metal bat so hard that Helena was sure she could see a ripple of air jet out, as if from a sonic boom. After the ripple—whether mirage or reality—a crack echoed out into the crowd. An instant later, Helena watched the top half of Osentoski's axe sail through the air and bounce dully to the turf five yards from the combatants.

Another gasp rippled through the crowd, then. Something about it sent a chill down her spine. Helena felt more detached from life, from reality, from herself than she ever had. The events taking place upon the death court seemed like a television show. She needn't put any effort into watching it now. Helena had gone to somewhere deep inside, allowing her to let the world happen around her, detached from it all somehow. Like staring through a porthole floating through the sky that no one else could see. Through this porthole, she found she could make it all a fiction.

She stared into the fiction and watched Dutton's face stretch into a wide smile when Osentoski reeled back from him in sheer panic. The panic cost the man. His feet got tangled up within a few steps and he stumbled, falling to his ass. Dutton charged, raising the metal bat high over his head, ready to strike. Osentoski still clung to the lower half of his broken axe shaft. Realizing its futility against the bat, he chucked it at the charging man and rolled to his left. The broken shaft bounced off the crimson-soaked chestnut belly of Charlie Dutton, doing nothing at all to halt his forward motion. Osentoski was scrambling to his feet when Dutton reached him. The bat came flashing down to impact Osentoski's back and send him sprawling back to the turf. He quickly rolled over and made a desperate grab to snatch the next bash Dutton swung down at him, but Osentoski's dexterity failed him, and the blow caught him square in the belly. Osentoski curled up to protect his injured gut, opening himself up to danger in many other vulnerable areas. All of which Dutton pointed out to him, most unkindly.

After five or six pummeling wallops, Dutton stepped back from his clobbered foe and began to play a little to the crowd. He motioned for some cheering, and the sheep were happy to oblige. Osentoski managed to roll away a few feet in the meantime. Then he seemed to give up the struggle all at once. He lay there on his back, breathing heavily and staring up through the majesty of Stargazer Ceiling. Dutton approached and stood over him, bat in hand. Helena could see his lips form the obvious question: "Do you yield?" Osentoski didn't respond.

Helena wasn't sure that he could. She could see Dutton ask the question once again, but with much more menace. Still, Osentoski gave no answer. A great many loud voices in the crowd offered their advice on how to deal with the recalcitrant man. "Kill him! Smash him! Kill him!" they shouted. After a few more times fruitlessly shouting the question at Osentoski and demanding an answer, Dutton must've realized that was indeed what he must now do. He ended his demands and slowly raised his dented bat high over his head.

He paused there in that position and glanced over to where Montrois and Schef were watching with expressionless faces. He seemed to be asking for their permission. Neither of the men broke their stoic gazes to so much as nod. Dutton looked back down at Osentoski and shook his head in obvious regret. He began to swing his arm down to deliver the coup de grace, but it never got there. Osentoski, when he'd crawled away from his attacker, had managed to get within grabbing distance of the top half of his axe, the blade half. And so, axe in hand, he rolled with what appeared to be the last of his strength right into Dutton. His axe-equipped arm trailed behind the roll and the sharp, heavy blade landed with a good deal of force into the meaty part of Dutton's thigh.

The bat fell from Dutton's hand in a blink, and he tumbled to the turf, favoring his chopped thigh and writhing in pain. He started yelping out howls and shouts in a high-pitched, petrified tone. And soon enough, some in the crowd began to mock the injured man. Through the porthole, Helena watched them too. They seemed just as artificial and surreal as the fight itself.

The mocking laughter seemed to encourage Osentoski though. A smile came to the battered man's face as he climbed to his feet with a good deal more ease than he had any right to. He shook his head back and forth vigorously, only breaking off to slap his face a few times. Apparently, the ritual was effective. He broke it off and walked over to the still writhing Dutton. Osentoski went down on a knee beside him, free from any obvious pain. Without a word, he jerked the axe free of Dutton's thigh and tossed it a few feet away as a fountain of blood sprayed up from the wound to soak Dutton's pants and complete his red ensemble.

Osentoski snatched up the metal bat lying near the bloody man's feet before rising. He staggered back to his feet, bat in hand, and hobbled a few paces until he was standing at the head of his challenger. Dutton managed to pull his attention away from the pain of his leg just in time to see Osentoski raise the bat to strike. Dutton's hands shot up to protect his face and he looked as though he meant to shout something. Helena could clearly see a plea forming on his lips, but the world would never know his intentions. The bat came whipping down, smashing into his face and cutting short the shout in its infancy. The metal club buried itself in Dutton's face, which instantaneously squashed, shattering inward. When Osentoski withdrew his weapon, all that remained of the once strong visage was a void, dripping with globs of white bone and gray brain matter, and red, red blood. The sound of Dutton's moment of demise managed to reach Helena, even through the porthole. That sound, and the sadistic exclamations from a few meatheads in the crowd immediately after it, would stay with her forever, despite the detached fog of the porthole, she was sure of that.

Osentoski looked as though he wanted to deliver a few more blows, but the ugly sounding alien screech bursting out from the speaker made him think twice. He dropped the bat and raised his one good arm high above his head. Osentoski pointed to the stars with an outstretched index finger, alternating between that gesture and waving for the crowd to shower him with praise.

Schef made his way to center court, microphone in hand. The crowd's volume lowered with each step he took, so that by the time he arrived he didn't need to quiet the crowd before speaking, "We have our first winner, my fellow residents. Let's hear it for him." Schef followed his own instructions, launching into a modest congratulatory clap. Those few bigoted buffoons in the crowd who had been rooting for Osentoski followed suit, throwing out obnoxious hoots and whistles. Most in the crowd didn't seem to care one way or another about the victor or the vanquished. They seemed to be clapping simply because they had been told to, like some ill-omened automatons. But there were also a few folks with appalled looks on their faces, shoving through the crowd on their way to The Meadow's archway. Helena did not fail to note all the officers, Montrois included, watching them all leave. She could tell they were marking them down in their minds. *Well, what did these people expect to see here today?* She asked herself. *It's their own damn fault for bringing their damn kids along.*

"And now, I call for the next challenger," Schef shouted in a showman's voice. "Is Scott Osentoski to decide our fate? What say you all?"

"No," a calm voice called out in response. Two rows up in the middle of the center set of bleachers, a hooded figure rose to their feet. With one wide pace, the hooded figure cleared the first row and stepped out from the fevered crowd forming around them. The figure pulled back the hood of a dark-gray zipped up hoodie to reveal the square jaw, thick neck and crew-cut hair of yet another of what Helena suspected was going to be an endless parade of meatheads.

However, the whispers Helena was hearing around the bleachers quickly disabused her of that assumption. It even drew her out of her detached safe-room-of-the-mind. Once more, her intrigue was peaked, despite her belly-roiling disgust at this spectacle of violence. Maddie's nasal shrieks played a large part in pulling her back to herself as well. The royally irritating woman could be powerfully loud when she had a piece of juicy gossip to spread. So Helena clearly heard her co-worker exclaim, "Oh my god! I know that guy. He works for those government bastards! He's like their special security guy or something."

"Yeah! That's the Secret Service agent HMFIC!" A man two rows back shouted in agreement.

"Right," Maddie barked back. "Secret Service, that's what I said. He's like their leader or something. Trust me, I know these things. I know everything up here."

Helena didn't doubt that. The bitch had her nose in everyone's business. More shouts of recognition rained down from the crowd as the tall, cocoa-skinned, athletic possible government agent made his way to Schef at center court. Once beside the survivor, he unzipped his hoodie and tossed it out of the court with a casual grace. He wore a black cut-off Under Armor workout shirt underneath. And when he ripped his tearaway sweat pants off, Helena saw his matching black Under Armor gym shorts. His black Nike tennis shoes matched as well, in style if not brand.

"Give us your name, challenger," Schef demanded, his even expression never flickering.

The short-haired G-man grabbed the microphone and pulled it close to his lips. He tried to wrestle it free of Schef's grip but gave up after only a momentary struggle. Then he smiled at the survivor with a twinkle of menace as he began his speech, "My name is Special Agent Seth San Marron, United States Secret Service."

"See!" Maddie shouted out in triumph.

"I was hoping my services wouldn't be necessary here today," San Marron continued. "I was really praying y'all wouldn't go through with this here madness. But, sadly, The Commander in Chief's worst fears have been proven true here today. I am a contingency that both myself and President Rafferty did not wish to have to implement. But here we are. Sadly, here we are. I am entering this tournament of yours because no other choice is available to me. I cannot—*we cannot, meaning your rightful leaders*—allow anarchy to spread its evil wings in this station. We cannot give up on the world, my brothers and sisters." *He ain't too bad a speaker himself. Seems more like a politician, rather than a babysitter for one,* Helena thought as the man drew in a deep breath. "I am here to set this madness to rights, and to get back to our duties," he continued, still clinging firmly to the microphone. "The world is in the grips of a terrible pandemic. But the world has not ceased to exist, ladies and gentlemen, nor has its laws, nor its rightful leaders. So, I will win this barbarous tournament and return us to our sanity, and reaffirm the old, and one true order."

"Very well then," Schef said into the microphone once San Marron released his grip. "Good luck to you, Special Agent San Marron. You know the rules then, I trust?"

Schef shoved the microphone back at San Marron, so Helena was able to hear his acceptance, "Yeah, I understand the damn rules. Let's just get on with it."

"Very well," Schef said with a hint of a smile. The dolly-and-barrel officer made his way back to center court. Once more he plopped down the heavy silver barrel and set off a clanging rattle of death within. "Choose your weapons, gentleman. Then we pause thirty minutes for recovery time. Mr. Osentoski, you still have the honor of first choice."

Helena could see that Osentoski was not at all content with the relatively short reprieve. He was itching to argue over it. She could see him restrain outburst after outburst and force himself to limp his way to the barrel. He paused over it this time, breathing heavily, and looked up after a few moments to stare at his new opponent. After a brief locking of eyes, Osentoski looked back to the barrel and drew out an axe quite like the one he had wielded in his previous match. This double-headed axe had a wooden handle, however. Perhaps Osentoski was hoping the wood would prove more shatter resistant. His peacock nature was all but absent as he limped and stumbled towards the end of the court he had started on before.

San Marron then stepped up and immediately began running the ball of his thumb across the edges of three spear-headed wooden staffs in the barrel. He must've decided which weapon was sharpest because he plucked out one of the long staffs with righteous confidence. He had no flair to speak of in his march toward his end of the court either. None at all. He made it within a few quick strides and immediately turned to face the court with the staff gripped in his left hand, hanging low around his hips. His expression shouted both impatience and intrepidity.

"The cafeteria staff have been kind enough to set up food stalls just outside the archway," Schef's voice boomed out once again from the small speaker. "I encourage everyone to avail yourselves. No credits asked. Restrooms are directly to the left of the archway, right behind you," he said, pointing through the righthand set of bleachers. "Whatever you got to do, do it with dignity. And be sure and make it back to your seats within thirty minutes. The match begins, regardless of whether you've finished shitting or not. So hustle up." He marched off the court and back to his seat after that, leaving San Marron and Osentoski to puzzle about what they were supposed to do in the meantime.

CHAPTER 9

Helena hadn't moved from her seat in the bleachers for a single second of the thirty-minute recovery time. She hadn't had anything to eat today, but despite this, felt anything but hungry. She had peed right before her fight with Alice and hadn't drunk anything since, so she didn't require a liquid release at the moment either. Truth be told, she was in shock. She couldn't bring herself to get in line for a hotdog and a pop after all she'd been through and all she'd seen this morning. Unfortunately, remaining in her seat had meant she was there when three security officers dragged Dutton's corpse from court. She watched as they tossed it, with an upsetting lack of the reverence that Schef kept demanding of everyone else, onto the back end of an electric cart with a big red cross painted on both of its white sidewalls. The cart took off and her mind raced, imagining all the nightmarish places it was off to. The break had passed by in a blur after that. Helena had spent it slowly settling back into the comfort of her special porthole. She felt good and detached from her impulses as the last few seconds of the thirty-minute break ticked away and the next match of The Final Tournament was set to begin.

Schef slowly made his way back to center court. The crowd, picking up on the routine, quickly quieted to hear his pronouncement, "Okay, victor and challenger, the thirty-minute recovery time is up. You both know the rules and you've accepted them. In so doing, you have sworn yourselves by your very lives to abide by them. And so, let your battle begin."

Once more, he jogged off the court but needn't have. San Marron began a slow, deliberate march toward his opponent, while Osentoski didn't move at all. The maintenance worker planted his axe handle on the turf and leaned all his weight against it, his legs shaking under him. The crowd's gasp came as predictable as sunrise when San Marron closed the gap. The agent darted a jab with his spear as soon as he got within range, but Osentoski had merely been playing the old rope-a-dope. He spun and lashed out lightning-fast, chopping his axe down on the spear's shaft and splitting it in half with ease. A shocked gasp in a different octave rippled through the crowd at that sudden twist of fate.

San Marron, caught utterly off guard, stumbled forward into the range of a killing chop from Osentoski's axe. The chop came promptly from the effectively-one-handed, bald and battered maintenance worker. San Marron fell quickly to a knee and somehow managed to get his hands up to catch the axe's handle just centimeters before it sunk its wicked edge deep into his skull. With a vicious roar, he lurched back to his feet, driving the axe backwards into Osentoski's face. The back blade of the double-headed axe carved off a three-inch chunk of flesh from Osentoski's forehead before San Marron ultimately held the axe jammed up against the bleeding man's shoulder.

He's spent now, Helena thought from behind her porthole, with a certainty that both excited and appalled her. San Marron released his hand from the axe, using it to slam a back fist into Osentoski's ugly face. Helena couldn't be sure, but she thought his nose was broken. The blood that quickly began to pour out gave testament to her belief. The headbutt San Marron delivered next into that nose settled the issue beyond all doubt. Osentoski crumpled to the ground after the wicked blow, releasing his hold on his axe entirely. San Marron moved to stand over his head in a jinx-evoking duplication of the last fight's ending. The special agent offered the fallen man a chance to yield, much like Dutton had.

And again, Osentoski refused. Unlike the last fight, San Marron did not look to Montrois and Schef for approval though. He kept his eyes on Osentoski as he raised the wood-handled axe high above his head. With only the barest hesitation, San Marron whipped the axe down, and somehow, from somewhere deep within, Osentoski found enough strength to roll away just far and fast enough to avoid the mortal swing.

San Marron attempted to dislodge the axe from the green turf that had swallowed it but gave up after a few tugs. He stood up straight, shoulders back and let a smirk wash over his face. Then he walked a few yards, bent down with deliberate movements, and picked up the top half of his spear from the court's turf. He slowly approached Osentoski, crawling away at a snail's pace on his elbows and knees. With no further appeals for the man to yield the match, San Marron drove the leaf-shaped blade down through Osentoski's back. He kept on driving the razor-sharp spear until the boastful maintenance worker was pinned to the turf of the court and soaking the lush green around him in a spreading pool of dark red. Only the buzzer's harsh call stopped San Marron from driving his weapon even further through the man. He straightened up and released the spear before spitting a glob of green phlegm towards Schef and Montrois to demonstrate, with contempt, his acknowledgment of the fight's completion.

Schef slowly rose to his feet and gave the smallest of bows to the bout's victor. Agent San Marron spit once more, although this time it was merely into the turf at his feet. He followed it up with a slow and contemptuous shaking of his head. Montrois appeared perturbed for the first time all day. His stoic facade had finally cracked, only slightly, but it had cracked. Helena watched as Montrois grabbed Schef's arm and pulled him close to whisper something in his ear. Schef nodded after receiving Montrois' message and then stepped up to the nearest security officer, apparently to pass along the whisper. That battle-ready security officer nodded after receiving the message, much as Schef had, and then walked towards one of her fellow patrolling officers. Meanwhile, Schef began another slow, sauntering journey to center court. The crowd hushed accordingly.

Schef stopped right alongside Seth San Marron, standing like a statue, with crossed arms, a furrowed brow and a judgmental frown. "Congratulations, Special Agent," Schef told him with a false smile. San Marron didn't let the boos and sparse nervous applause that followed crack his steely-eyed focus. After a long moment, Schef raised his hand to settle the crowd. The riveted masses complied with unsettling unanimity. *He's getting pretty damn good at that, indeed,* Helena thought, with capitulating admiration. "Two matches fought. Two men dead," Schef reflected. "Have we found our leader then, my fellow residents? Shall we let Special Agent Seth San Marron hand his leadership back to the people responsible for landing us here in the first place? Is that what you all want? More of the same? Or is anyone willing to break the loop? Is anyone willing to risk their lives for the honor of the selfless service that leading this society shall be? Does anyone have a vision for our future they are willing to fight for, to die for, if necessary? Or is it truly more of the same you all crave, more of President Daniel Rafferty and his quippy little campaign slogans, and entrenched and stagnant partisan bureaucracy. The same bureaucracy that classified themselves as more valuable than all those family members of so many of you here today that got left behind during their evacuation. Those mourned loved-ones' rightful places here aboard station have been usurped by the elitists down Branch 1. And this man here stands for them, their champion," Schef said, holding out his arm toward San Marron. "Is there anyone here today that will stand for your abandoned family members?"

Long seconds stretched without a single voice breaking the eerie silence. Helena studied the miracle survivor, Harclay Aponyaschefski, standing alongside a fresh killer. He gave nothing away with his expression, but the glance he darted towards Montrois confirmed his unease. Helena moved her focus to Montrois and clearly caught the nod the security commander aimed at a young Latino officer a few yards away from him. The man returned his commander's nod before starting in on the long process of unstrapping his body armor. He was midway through peeling off one of the Velcro straps of his vest when a soft voice broke the heavy silence, "I challenge," was all it said, and only once, but despite its brevity and volume, the pronouncement could be clearly heard.

Heads darted back and forth throughout the crowd, seeking the speaker. After a few suspenseful moments, Helena saw a man emerge from the righthand set of bleachers a dozen paces from where Montrois was seated. A puzzled look flashed across the security commander's face upon his first glimpse of the new challenger. And in a few seconds, it was swiftly replaced by an out-and-out scowl.

Well, well, this is certainly interesting, Helena thought. *Now, who could this be?* She turned her attention back to the new challenger and took him in. He was nothing special, really. *Ordinary* would be the word Helena would use to describe him. Put him in a gray suit and a blue tie and stick a briefcase in his hand, and he'd blend into any nine-to-five rush-hour crowd in any major city in the western world. But he wasn't in a gray suit. He wore black chinos and a navy-blue Henley shirt. He looked to be average height, with pale skin and short, dark brown hair covering his head and face. He was perhaps a few pounds overweight. A beer gut in its earliest stages was clearly out-lined beneath the soft fabric of his shirt. Nothing about his physique spoke to any martial skill, yet he strode towards center court as if he were out walking his dog through Central Park.

The new challenger treated Schef to a slight nod and a look that gave absolutely nothing away as he arrived alongside him. Schef looked from the unremarkable man back towards the place in the bleachers that the man had come from. Helena followed his line of sight, and though she had no way to be certain, was pretty sure she spotted the man Schef and many of the officers were now staring at with fire in their eyes. He was hard to miss. If Charlie Dutton had been fat, then she didn't know what to call this repulsive son-of-a-bitch. It was Mikkelson, the labor supervisor; the wheezy asshole that had stuck her at the water plant. He was staring right back at Schef with a devious grin, only breaking eye-contact to treat Montrois, a few rows below and to his left, to the same treatment. Obviously, the new challenger must be Mikkelson's man. But that confused her. Helena was under the impression that Mikkelson and his staff supervisors were loyal servants to the security staff's cause. But if the look on the officers' faces were any indication, the labor supervisor had just gone rogue.

No way Montrois and his men were expecting this, she thought with certainty. Personally, Helena was anything but surprised that a creepy slimeball like Mikkelson would betray his co-conspirators. *They should've known the type of guy they were getting in bed with,* she scoffed at the security staff's poor judgment. Their clear anger at Mikkelson for using a puppet to make a play for the title that he'd been claiming all week long to have no interest in, through his staff supervisors, was definitely understandable. But even so, she thought the rage clearly bubbling up inside of all of them was a bit overblown, considering the man Mikkelson had chosen to act as his puppet. The challenger's sagging shoulders and downcast eyes seemed only to further exaggerate the madness of the mutinous act. Except that Mikkelson's impish grin never once wavered.

Schef finally broke off his icy stare at the labor supervisor to raise his hand for quiet. "So, challenger, give us your name," he requested of the cat's paw, with only a minor hint of irritation in his voice.

"Rollie Cornwell, Lead Staff Supervisor," the man answered in the same soft voice he used to declare his intent.

Schef pulled the microphone back to his chest after it was clear that would be all Cornwell would say. "Very well, Supervisor Cornwell," he said, glancing back once more at the grinning whale in the bleachers. "You understand the rules?" Schef asked, trying not to sound begrudging, and failing miserably. Rollie Cornwell gave one slow, exaggerated nod as answer. Then the dolly-and-barrel officer took up his charge once again. The officer kept his burning eyes locked on Cornwell all the way to center court and stopped to spit at Cornwell's feet after stepping away from the barrel. "Choose your weapons, gentlemen," Schef commanded. "Then we shall break for another thirty minutes. Agent San Marron, as last fight's victor, you have first choice."

San Marron seemed a bit off-kilter, like the situation had taken a detour he wasn't at all prepared for. He shuffled a few steps and stared about him in what Helena took to be a search for friendly faces. She couldn't be sure if he'd found any or not, but he shook his head quickly to help regain his earlier composure as he stepped up to the barrel. San Marron didn't hesitate to snatch out one of the two remaining spear-headed wooden staffs, forgoing any inspection of the blade's sharpness this time. He sauntered off towards the end of the court he started on previously, and once there, took a seat on the turf with his legs folded under him, placing his spear across his lap and shutting his eyes.

Cornwell approached the barrel almost timidly after that. He bent over its side to peer at what lay unseen within. Hands clasped behind his back, he made a circuit of the barrel, running his eyes over every one of its armaments. A hand came from behind his back to cup his chin in contemplation while his other hand came out from its casual perch to clutch the taped grip of a wooden baseball bat. He held up the bat and flicked it back and forth with his wrist a few times before nodding in approval. Cornwell held the bat out at a safe distance from his body, as its barrel was a hedgehog of long, twisted and expertly sharpened nails. The bat swung at his side as casually as sensible precaution allowed on his way to the unoccupied end of the killing court.

CHAPTER 10

The line for the women's bathroom had taken nearly every last second of the thirty-minute break, leaving Helena little opportunity to cue up for any of the half dozen concession stands along the dank alley wall. She was regretting that now. She was feeling better despite herself, and her appetite had come crashing down like a thunderbolt. Despite how creepy and unethical the idea of the concession stands had at first seemed to her, the hang-up was overcome fast enough when she realized she was definitely in the minority on that opinion, and when her stomach pangs reached a point of intense discomfort. But the lines for every stall were long slow snakes, and Helena simply didn't have enough time to navigate them. There was a taco stand among the many stalls too, which sent an extra lash of disappointment whipping across her back on this day. Helena loved the Mexican food aboard station. The cafeterias made an excellent tamale, not to mention their taco salads. But she didn't have time to enjoy either The immense pressure of staying in the security staff's good graces was still keenly felt.

She'd made it back through the unyielding crowd with barely a few breaths to spare, and despite her fears, Helena's spot in the bleachers hadn't been snatched from her after all. Her cardigan lay untouched, still folded neatly, the impression of her ass, formed over the course of two matches and roughly two hours, was still visible and undisturbed. It had even remained unsoiled by the moron to her right and his pungent drink, though the big galoot had remained in his seat during the entire break. She'd somehow found the humility to nod at him in appreciation for that when she returned, as though he'd saved it for her despite their earlier altercation. He'd returned the nod cordially enough, so perhaps he had.

Sitting there, perched atop her sweater on the newly constructed bench as the last seconds of the break ticked by, Helena realized she was actually looking forward to this upcoming match. At first she was a little afraid of that. Her initial instinct was to rush to her porthole and extract herself from all feeling or critical thought. But she held back. She stayed. It didn't even seem all that difficult to do, really. Something had happened inside her during that last match. Helena couldn't say what it was, even with a gun to her head, but she did feel it. She was different somehow. A master of herself, for once in her life. No longer just a ditsy, gossiping chatterbox, riding life's anxiety express train. She felt a resolve to face the darkness, a resolve to see the evil thing through for the sake of the light lurking at the end of the tunnel. There was no longer any fear about the prospect of keeping a calm, somber, but ultimately approving face, during this next match because she knew a part of her, most of her in truth, actually truly felt that way. She was having trouble remembering exactly how she'd been feeling only an hour before. It felt almost like those feelings and memories belonged to someone else now. Helena Heathcoat felt new somehow, and yet in touch with an ancient and central part of herself that somehow she'd always known, without ever really knowing.

It was all strange, hard to explain. The source of her new clarity was difficult to chase down. It disintegrated like fog whenever she got close. She felt emancipated from everything and everyone, and yet truly part of the world for the first time ever. It was a calm, more than anything. A patient calm. She found she wasn't even afraid of the anxiety's return. Its prospect seemed too remote to entertain. Riding a wave of courage never before known to her, Helena even tempted the panic, daring it to come back. She stared around at the officers in their full battle rattle. Nothing. She focused on the crowd pressing in all around her. Nothing. She glanced over at the weapons barrel, bristling with instruments of war. Nothing. Then, the porthole began slipping away in her mind's eye. No accompanying impulse came to reach for it before it faded forever. In fact, she watched it go with an inner grin.

The crowd hushing all around her brought Helena's attention to Schef, who had once more taken up residence at center court. "Okay, victor and challenger, the thirty-minute recovery time is up," he said. "You both know the rules and you've accepted them. And in so doing, you have sworn yourselves by your very lives to abide by them. And so, let your battle begin."

Schef wasted no time embarking upon his ritual jog back to his seat at Montrois' side once he had repeated his pre-fight edict. San Marron began a long-paced quick march towards Cornwell the instant the survivor was clear. The ordinary-looking man's countering maneuver matched the charge, skewing the combatant's angles. San Marron didn't miss a beat. Planting his left foot at the end of one long stride, he pivoted to his right, correcting his angle, now squarely in line with his foe once again. San Marron then raised his spear to his chest and held out his left arm in front of his body. He leaned forward, completing his ready posture, and quickly closed the gap. Cornwell decided to abandon forward motion and stand his ground. Holding the bat low in his right hand, he thrust his left arm out defensively. His legs were in the classic runner's pose, left leg out and right slightly back, ready to explode forward as needed.

Helena felt a wave of pity for Cornwell as San Marron darted in with his first spear jab. The man appeared utterly helpless against a clearly physically superior opponent. It wasn't that she wanted Cornwell to win, specifically. Her rooting allegiances for this match were pretty well torn and jumbled into something she had no urge to try and untangle. She knew she didn't really want President Rafferty, Hubert Harrington, and their ilk to take back power and have all this blood and death be meaningless. Her fight with Alice, and the serious strain it had placed on their otherwise sublime relationship, would've been all for nothing, and so too the overthrow, and all the violence that took place that day after a few of the operators in the control room resisted the security staff's incursion with two pistols stored in the room for emergencies—pistols that the security guys weren't aware of. A lot of people got hurt and three operators had died, despite all of the security staff's promises and apologies. And then there was

Charlie Dutton and his brutal death, even that stupid ogre Scott Osentoski; it would all be for nothing. She didn't want to examine what amount of culpability of all that fallout would be on her shoulders.

So Helena definitely wasn't eager to see San Marron win again. But almost equally so, she did not want Rollie Cornwell to wind up the victor either. Nothing against him; she didn't really know him. Now that she knew his name, she'd remembered hearing some people talk about him before, but couldn't remember if the talk had been good or bad. It was his puppet master she hated. Mikkelson was the king of all creeps, the epitome of a male predator. Helena desperately dreaded living in a society with him at the helm. So, with no good options, she was steering clear of rooting for one man to prevail over another.

Through that neutral lens, Helena studied the combatants a bit closer. San Marron appeared focused and graceful, while Cornwell displayed a semi-casual posture. It seemed to her a perfect visualization of the disparity between the pair's fighting skills. Therefore, Helena was caught off guard at how quickly Cornwell dodged his head away from the spear thrust San Marron had aimed between his eyeballs. Cornwell followed the dodge with three rapid and smooth steps up court. If San Marron was surprised at his enemy's quickness, he gave no hint. Whipping the spear blade to his left, he followed Cornwell for every step of his evasion. His blade swished through the air only inches from Cornwell's face. As soon as it was past, the challenger spun 180 degrees. His back was to Helena, so she had no way to be sure, but she thought the ordinary-looking man must've been smiling at San Marron after the Secret Service agent twisted back to shadow the speedy change of direction. The G-man had stopped dead in his tracks and a menacing frown quickly darkened the light-brown skin of his face. San Marron barked out a growl after a few seconds of stewing rage and charged at Cornwell, spear thrust out strong in front of him.

The mighty thrust was dodged by Cornwell, this time by twisting his body sideways. A mirror-image maneuver avoided the follow-up thrust. San Marron crouched low and held his spear ready, scanning his opponent with brand new eyes. It was now apparent to everyone, San Marron last of all, that Rollie Cornwell was not what he seemed. He was clearly quick, crafty and elusive. Helena and the rest of the residents in attendance were now eager to discover if his offensive game was equally impressive. As yet, he hadn't swung his cruel weapon once. San Marron apparently wanted to test that theory as well, darting in quick probing thrusts aimed at Cornwell's torso. The man still never lifted the bat, not even in defense. He simply ducked and dodged up and down the court, avoiding the thrusts by mere centimeters at a time.

San Marron tired of his probing tactic after a bit and took up a stationary pose a few paces in front of his foe. Helena glanced across the court to where Mikkelson sprawled languidly across the bleachers. The man still wore the same knowing grin. *He knows Cornwell is just toying with him,* she thought, observing the asshole's smirk. She glanced down to Montrois and Schef and saw them watching the action on the court with a dark intensity. Helena looked back to the action just in time to catch San Marron suddenly charge forward two steps and lean into a hard spear thrust. Helena knew she'd have been caught flat-footed by the abrupt offensive, but Rollie Cornwell was made of different stuff. He pivoted slightly at the hip, and the gleaming blade shot past his side with barely a finger's breadth to spare. Cat-quick, Cornwell clamped his left arm down on the spear shaft, capturing it firm between arm and body. San Marron gave the spear a panicked tug, but found Cornwell had surprising strength as well. The spear was clamped tight. Not to be outdone with clever thought and quick action, San Marron gave up the tug-of-war to step into a snapping headbutt that landed on the upper cheek of the much shorter man.

Helena—and she figured everyone else as well, judging by the anticipatory hush rippling through the crowd—were expecting to see Cornwell's legs buckle and the man collapse. Instead, his head rocked back only a few inches from the impact. It was San Marron who appeared to suffer the worst effects from the blow. His eyes were crossed as he pulled his head back and retreated a wobbly step. Cornwell didn't wait for an invitation. His attacking speed was equal to that of his evasive maneuvering. He closed the gap with one long stride, while clutching tightly to the spear between left arm and side. Cornwell launched a headbutt of his own, with an upward drive from his toes. The blow crashed squarely into San Marron's jaw.

The agent reeled backwards, only stopping his rearwards flight after nearly losing his grip on the spear.

San Marron shot his free arm up to cover his face from another devastating headbutt. It was then Cornwell finally delivered the first blow of the match with his wicked weapon. He swung the bat on a flat arc, slamming the barbed barrel with crippling force into San Marron's left hip. The razor-sharp nails protruding from the barrel buried themselves so deeply into the man's sinews that Cornwell was forced to twist his hips for leverage in order to tug his weapon loose from his enemy's flesh. San Marron yelped out a sharp, pained screech as his arm fell futilely down to his side in defense.

Launching another driving headbutt from his toes, Cornwell caught San Marron off guard, landing the blow in what appeared to be the same place as the first cranial smash. The agent's head lurched backwards. Helena could clearly see his jaw was shattered. It sagged loosely; attached to his skull by a few layers of thin skin. Blood quickly pulsed from the injury in hot waves. San Marron brought his free hand back up to his face, uselessly. Helena couldn't believe the man was still on his feet, and judging from the gasps, and *ooohs* and *aaahs* coming from the crowd, they couldn't believe it either.

Both men still clung to the spear. Cornwell had a firm lock on its shaft while San Marron's grip looked to be slipping. The Agent staggered and fought to stay afoot, so Cornwell stepped in, once more launching from his toes, and clearly aiming another headbutt at San Marron's jaw. The agent's free arm darted out defensively to ward off the blow, but it had only been a feint. Cornwell broke off the launch and swept his bat down at the bigger man's legs. The bat's barbs pierced San Marron's left calf and, with another pain-fueled screech, Branch 1's champion tumbled to the turf with the tangle of steel shards lodged firmly in the meat of his calf muscle. He'd lost his grip on his spear in the fall, to boot. Cornwell, now in sole possession of the weapon, tossed it away with disinterest. Then the ordinary looking man yanked free his gruesome bat from his enemy's deep tissue.

San Marron, despite the hideous pain he must be in, was no fool to his plight. Instantly, he began scrambling on his hands and knees, dragging his now useless, bloody leg. His feeble scramble to where the spear had landed on the turf broke through Helena's new poise for a moment. Her heart went out for the sad, desperate man. But only for a moment. Her steely determination returned in time to witness Cornwell's two-handed overhead swing smash, with a sickening thud, into the small of San Marron's back. His sad scramble came to an abrupt halt and the agent's pitiful whimpers could be clearly heard over the crowd's low awed murmuring. Cornwell then elicited more groans from the agent as he rocked and jiggled his weapon free from the man's mangled back. Blood and muscle sprayed out from the bat's glistening daggers as he whipped it back for another blow.

Helena could see San Marron's right hand lift slowly from the turf, reaching towards Montrois and Schef, his fist slowly opening and closing in some strange sign language of the weak and dying. But neither the security commander nor the survivor seemed to speak the new language; their stone-faced expressions were never broken in the slightest. Then, the final swing dropped down, cutting off the silent plea forever. The blow thwacked into the back of San Marron's skull. And although the noise it made was comparable to when the bat had crushed Dutton's face, the skull this time remained largely intact. At least until Cornwell placed a foot on the center of San Marron's shoulders, once more for leverage, and extracted his savage weapon from his foe's head. The pulverized gore left in its wake proved beyond any doubt that the final blow had been instantly fatal.

The ugly noise suddenly blared from the speaker just as Helena began to feel impatience and panic invade her newfound calm. Mikkelson's man had won. What did that mean? Surely the security staff had someone to match the labor supervisor's madman of a champion. *Oh, God, I sure fucking hope so,* she thought. *It sure as hell cannot be Cornwell and Mikkelson. Come on, Schef, get out here and call for a challenger. There's gotta be somebody that can beat this guy. He can't really be that good, can he?* Helena asked herself as Schef did indeed stand up and begin his journey to center court. *Thank god,* she thought. *Just in time. I was starting to slip away from my new self for a few seconds there.*

"Congratulations to our newest victor," Schef proclaimed with a goading drawl, adding a weak little golf clap. The previously silent crowd quickly mimicked the action. It all seemed so obviously forced. *I guess I ain't the only one here who knows what Mikkelson is, or who knows what having his man win means for us residents,* she thought, with a small degree of consolation. "Is Rollie Cornwell our champion then?" Schef asked the crowd in a plaintive, almost desperate tone.

Anonymous jeers of various types, along with cries for the victor's head, rained down from the crowd, one over top of the next, but Helena heard no clear declaration of challenge among the shouts. Schef turned almost completely around to face Montrois. He didn't quite raise his arms up in the classic what-now pose, but he definitely came close. Montrois did not seem at all pleased with the survivor's lack of decorum. He didn't acknowledge the impatient behavior with a response. The security commander maintained his dark and empty thousand-mile stare as his predator's eyes fell once more on the handsome Latino officer. The man seemed to be expecting this non-verbal order from his commander. Immediately, he nodded and embarked upon the tedious task of unstrapping his tactical gear for the second time that day.

He was on the very same strap he'd frozen on before the last match when a hand fell on his shoulder from behind. The handsome young officer turned around to face a redheaded female officer. She stood an inch or two shorter than the slick-looking warrior. She had just as stout, and perhaps even a little wider, shoulders than her counterpart too. Leaning her modestly weathered face forward, Helena saw a visage speckled with darkly ominous maroon freckles which echoed some sort of native warpaint, and flattered her carrot-colored hair. She began to whisper something into the Latino officer's ear. Helena watched as the man's head shot up within the first few words of the whispered message. He pulled his head back to better look the redheaded woman square in the eyes. Helena could clearly read his lips. "Are you sure?" He asked the new-age shield maiden. Helena could clearly see the words "Trust me," form on her lips in reply. The handsome officer gave a glance back over to his commander, and once he received an ever so small approving nod from Montrois, the Latino officer turned back to the female officer to treat her to a larger and more deliberate gesture of approval.

"I challenge," the woman then shouted out through a widening appreciative smile. The smile stayed as she set to work stripping free her cumbersome gear.

Helena had no way to be sure exactly what the woman had whispered to the Latino officer, but she thought hard on it as the redheaded Valkyrie marched across the court. Helena came to figure that she must've told the Latino officer that whatever game Mikkelson was playing with them, it would send him a better message if it were a female officer that defeated his champion because everyone definitely knew now that it would be a security officer that would have to challenge Cornwell. No one else present had the necessary skills for victory. That explanation had made the most sense to Helena. It went a long way towards explaining the quick capitulation by the handsome officer too, especially considering he had twice now appeared more than eager to fight. Helena focused on those kinds of safe speculations, trying hard to not think about how her small wish of having a woman enter the contest was being fulfilled. She was afraid that dwelling on it might just jinx the situation.

On the court, Cornwell moved to stand along Schef's left side just as the freckle-faced officer arrived at his right. Cornwell still held his reaping tool down at his side, its nails dripping dark-red blood, with here and there a clump of flesh clinging to its jagged needles. Schef made a point of looking down at the bat, with distaste plain on his face.

The unassuming madman could've cared less. He had eyes only for his next opponent. The woman stared him back down with a casual contempt that boosted Helena's confidence in a positive outcome for the upcoming match, positive in relation to the current crazy world she lived in, anyway. *She ain't afraid of this guy. I knew there was someone here to match this fool.* The woman definitely seemed a physical match for him, if not a match in skill, at least. She had an inch or two and about twenty pounds on Cornwell. And it was twenty pounds of muscle, too. There wasn't an ounce of flab to be seen hanging anywhere from the bulky woman. Helena watched with gob-smacked awe as she removed her black tactical blouse to reveal well-toned arms laid bare under a black tank top. The freckle-strewn bodybuilder's arms sprouted out from wide shoulders and a bull's neck. The impressive looking fresh challenger stood up tall and sturdy on long, bulky, yet limber legs. She looked the part, in short, and Helena once more took heart. As she tied up her shoulder length hair in a ponytail, the crowd suddenly began showering the warrior woman with praise. Slowly, Helena began to understand, with a timid, uncertain sort of satisfaction, that it wasn't just her who had been taken by the casual-mannered gladiator, and the security staff she represented.

"Give us your name, challenger," Schef demanded of the Amazon.

"Polly Dobechek," she said, crossing her arms and smiling.

Cornwell returned her grin with one of his own, along with a wink for good measure. There was no fear to be seen on his face as he jerked his head left and right to crack his neck. "And do you understand the rules here, Miss Dobechek?" Schef asked.

"I understand and accept them," Polly Dobechek answered into the microphone with solemnity.

Schef turned in time to see the dolly-and-barrel officer put in appearance number four. The officer did stare down Cornwell for this entire trip too, though he did manage to omit spitting at the man's feet. "Alright then, combatants, choose your weapons," Schef said, regaining some of his earlier prestige. "And then we shall break for thirty minutes. Mr. Cornwell, as last match's victor, you have the honor of first choice."

Cornwell slung his bat casually over his right shoulder. His smile became a thin line as he marched off silently toward his end of the court after the smallest of scoffs. "I guess the little guy is sticking with what works," barked the big man to Helena's right. The laughs and taunts that followed the observation showed that the crowd was definitely not with Rollie Cornwell. *Have we all truly consigned ourselves to the security staff's rule so fully that we're actually cheering for it now?* She was pretty sure she knew the answer, but Helena was currently trying to avoid any more troubling thoughts, so she did not pursue it.

Dobechek strode towards the weapons barrel, providing Helena with a much-needed escape from the heavy thoughts. Almost as soon as she arrived over the barrel, Dobechek drew out a long steel rod that had been beneath the barrel's rim, and thus, unseen to all beforehand. The crowd gasped out a long echoing *oooh* as she drew the weapon out to reveal its full dimensions. The steel rod was wrapped in the same trusty old yellow athletic tape that she'd seen on so many of the weapons. It had a three-foot-long, slightly tapering shaft, and at its end, a metal ball as big as a gorilla's fist was welded firmly in place. Welded to the ball itself were six or seven steel spikes, gleaming wetly in the harsh lights. Helena figured Polly must've known the weapon was in the barrel. She'd grabbed it out so deliberately that it only made sense, especially when you considered the fact that it was the security staff who supervised the construction of the weapons for the tournament, forcing the welders and craftsmen to cobble as many death sticks together as they could manage between the construction of the bleachers. So Helena figured the choice of weapon was a direct and well thought out answer to Cornwell's choice of armament. That too gave Helena comfort in Polly Dobechek's ability to defeat Rollie Cornwell. And so, she was feeling pretty good about the coming match as the brutal-looking ginger gladiator stomped towards the unoccupied end of the court.

CHAPTER 11

The food stall lines had been thinner this break, the taco stand especially. Helena had arrived at the mobile Mexican food cart with only three or four other residents lined up ahead of her. Most folks had stayed in their seats this break. They must've been eager for the next match to begin. Or, with this being the third thirty-minute break over the last three hours, they'd probably already filled their bellies. So before she knew it, she had been standing before the cart and ordering the grilled chicken taco salad, one of her station cafeteria favorites. Standing behind her set of bleachers, Helena ate the overflowing tortilla bowl. She had enough time to not be in an undignified rush during the ingestion process, but nonetheless finished the delicious meal in no time flat. With both contents and bowl devoured, Helena had made her way back to her seat.

It was there, belly full and feeling all the better for it, that she once more found herself. Helena sat nestled atop her cardigan cushion, watching Schef saunter with an ever so slight hitch in his step towards center court. The microphone came up slowly to his mouth once he'd arrived, but for a long time Schef's lips didn't move. The hush of the crowd was absolute. Still, no words came. He turned his head to look at both combatants. Still, no words. Schef started to rotate in place, staring intently into the encircling crowd of residents all the while. Finally, he spoke, but it wasn't a preamble to another lecture like she guessed; it was the pre-fight edict, "Victor and challenger, the thirty-minute recovery time is up. You both know the rules, and you've accepted them. In so doing, you have sworn yourselves by your very lives to abide by them. And so, let your battle begin."

Schef had a lot less urgency in his jog this time and, ironically enough, this was probably the first fight where a hasty departure was most necessary. Polly had instantly darted up court along the boundary line to her left, and Cornwell wasted no time in countering the charge and was only a pace or two away from colliding with the retreating Schef as he made his way off court. The crowd let out an awkward groan in reaction to the near miss as the combatants finished their charges and found they'd just flipped positions. It seemed the game would play out once more as Polly instantly darted back up the court, again keeping the boundary line just to her left. Cornwell seemed content to dance the dance again as well, but three or four steps into his charge, he pivoted and darted across the court to intercept Dobechek.

She spun to her left just as Cornwell cut her off, and his wild swing zipped harmlessly through empty air. Cornwell was left off balance from the swing and retreated a couple steps to regain his composure. Polly had planted her feet at center court by then, and they both paused there to draw in a few heavy breaths while staring each other down.

Helena couldn't quite read the look on Rollie Cornwell's face, but she thought it might've contained a pinch of fear. Helena glanced at Cornwell's pale leviathan of a benefactor in the crowd to see if she could see that same fear on *his* face. Mikkelson disappointed her in that. The same shit-eating grin as before was glued to his big round moon-face. Helena figured it was just a really good act, a calm, unaffected disguise. There was no way he could actually feel as confident as he looked. *Even if his man defeated Polly Dobechek, surely the security staff would send out another officer to face him.* Though the more she thought about that, the more Helena figured it was probably precisely the thing Mikkelson was hoping for. *He must think his man can defeat everyone here. The fat bastard must be planning on his guy taking the whole security staff out, right here and now. That way there will be no one to threaten his rule. He's using this tournament as a tool to eliminate his adversaries and ensure unassailable power.* The certain thought chilled her.

Then the action on the court supported her dreadful hypothesis. Cornwell looped in an overhand smash aimed at Dobechek's shoulder. Polly darted her weapon up to block the blow. Helena had overheard Dobechek's wicked steel rod-and-ball weapon referred to as a morningstar while in line for her taco salad. The morningstar looked heavy and ungainly, but Polly Dobechek seemed to wield it with an effortless grace. She had the weapon held out horizontally in front of her, ready to deflect the blow with plenty of time to spare. But Cornwell's swing had merely been a feint. He broke off midway to thrust the bat forward toward Dobechek's chest. The end of the wooden bat crashed its three-inch-diameter point just above her right breast. The impact sent Polly spinning off to her left. Cornwell charged after her, swinging his wicked weapon with awful speed and strength. Somehow, Polly was able to avoid the blows. She stumbled more and more with each retreating step, yet somehow, *somehow*, she stayed on her feet, avoiding each and every one of them. Cornwell finally abandoned the onslaught, pausing to draw in a deep breath.

The crowd must've been just as captivated and bereft of comprehensible speech as Helena. The labored breaths of both combatants came clear to her ears through the tense silence gripping The Meadow. Helena dared not breathe. Those past few seconds, watching Polly Dobechek narrowly duck and dive her way out of certain death had taken their toll on her calm. Helena Heathcoat finally knew who she was rooting for. It had taken four death matches to straighten out in her mind just where her trust and allegiances lie on this day, but she'd come to terms with her acceptance of the security staff's rule, unconsciously at least, and she knew without a doubt who she wanted to prevail in this match: Polly Dobechek. The woman was an answer to a prayer Helena never even realized she'd been praying. Imagining one of those razor-edged nails tearing through the female officer's flesh was bringing all her earlier fears flooding back. So while the two combatants circled each other a few paces apart, Helena took a few moments to stare down at her feet and suck in a few deep, shaky breaths of her own.

"Kill the fucking guy, Polly!" A shout pierced the silence from somewhere in the crowd Helena couldn't place. It was followed by a few more supportive concurrences. And after four or five breaths, so many residents in the crowd were shouting that no discernible statements could be clearly comprehended.

Back on the court, the combatants were catching their breaths and listening to the jeers and shouts of the crowd rain down on them. In the next blink, they were simultaneously exploding towards each other. They each had two hands on the grips of their weapons. Both had them drawn back over their right shoulder to strike. They arrived near center court simultaneously and both launched devastating blows aimed at the other's head. Each fighter drew their head back to avoid the blow as their weapons clashed in front of them with a loud metal on wood twang. The recoil from the impact sent each fighter reeling backwards a single step. Instantly, they began to pace around in a slow, shuffling circle. Helena glanced at Cornwell's bat, held out ready to his side, and saw one side of its barrel's protruding nails were bent back on themselves. Cornwell then aimed another swing at Dobechek's side. She parried it with relative ease, and another half dozen of the bat's nails were bent sideways.

Cornwell glanced down at his bat to inspect the damage and Helena could clearly see the curse form on his lips. "Fuck!" He screamed, though she did not hear it. Dobechek saw the momentary despair on her opponent's face and moved fast to take advantage. A looping overhand smash sent Cornwell retreating a couple paces, forcing a feeble counterstroke. Dobechek easily bashed it aside, stepping in with one long, fast stride and thrusting her morningstar out before her. Cornwell was able to twist away from the jab, though a few of the weapon's metal spikes raked across his shoulder before he was able to retreat to safety. Just how pleased Helena was at the sight of Cornwell's blood leaking down his arm was a tad shameful.

Dobechek shadowed Cornwell's flight and was perfectly set to deliver a two-handed slash towards his head as soon as he settled his feet, but Cornwell showed off some of that cat-like speed he displayed during his first match. Ducking his head clear of the blow, he turned his dodge into a looping swing aimed at Dobechek's calves. Polly Dobechek had herself a reaction time to rival anything

Cornwell could bring to bear, allowing her to jump clear of the swing only inches ahead of the tearing barbs of Cornwell's bat. Mikkelson's puppet followed the momentum of his swing and looped around 360 degrees. At the end of his spin, he aimed a two-handed smash at Dobechek's chin. Polly flicked her morningstar up one-handed to parry the blow. The slick shaft of her morningstar rode up the splintered shaft of Cornwell's bat before becoming entangled in its twisted nails. Dobechek tried to draw back her weapon just as Cornwell was attempting to wrench his own loose. The ensuing tug-of-war lasted a few agonizing breaths until Cornwell seemed to abruptly relinquish his grip. Dobechek was still trying to haul her weapon free, and so was sent lurching backwards from the sudden release. The wooden bat went flying several yards across the court.

Helena watched the bat land and almost missed Cornwell's quick reaction. Hands free, he dashed in at Dobechek, who'd regained her balance after a few steps and was ready to swing a one-handed overhead smash down towards her charging opponent. Cornwell halted mid-charge and reached up to grab Dobechek's weapon arm. He pivoted his hips, hauling Dobechek's arm over his shoulder, and kept right on pivoting his hips until Dobechek was pulled off her feet. She went flying over Cornwell's back, smashing hard to the turf, flat on her own back.

A hush rippled through the crowd fast enough for Helena to hear the actual release of air smashed free from Dobechek's lungs. The shield maiden still had a grip of her medieval weapon, but Cornwell had a grip of that same hand clinging to the cruel steel. He held it firm while leaning into a downwards smash with his free fist. The punch landed squarely between Dobechek's eyes. Her free hand shot up to guard her face in the same instant she attempted to sit up and wriggle loose of Cornwell's grip. Mikkelson's man wasn't having any of it. He dropped his right knee down onto her waist, pinning her to the turf. Then he leaned his full weight down as Dobechek tried to smash her hand into his face. Cornwell paid the flailing hand little attention until it clamped a firm grip around his neck. He grabbed the offending arm by the wrist then, and after a considerable struggle, was able to extract it from his throat. Cornwell seemed to draw in a big breath after that, and in the very next moment, smashed his head down into Dobechek's face.

Seeing the morningstar drop loose from the Valkyrie's limp hand sent cold daggers piercing deep into Helena's heart. The writing on the wall did not spell out a pretty story, and Helena knew it. Her wish had gotten an innocent woman killed. She felt more heartsick than she ever had in her relatively long life. Dobechek had no place inside that black death box. Helena had wished her there and killed her. When Cornwell's follow-up headbutt smashed home, she was certain she would be seeing her taco salad once again.

She was turning her head to fulfill that prophecy when Dobechek bucked her hips forcefully enough to toss the smaller man off her, bringing an abrupt end to the roiling of Helena's stomach. Both fighters scrambled to their feet at about the same moment and paused there to look one another up and down. Dobechek was pouring blood from a shattered nose while Cornwell was sporting a slightly surprised look at how the big woman found the strength to toss him off after those two tremendous smashes. Then, in unison, their gazes fell on the morningstar a few yards away, exactly halfway between each combatant. Cornwell reacted first, diving forward and reaching out with both hands to scoop up the match's superior tool. Dobechek must've been hoping he'd make the move, stepping one long, confident stride with her left leg as a smirk stretched across her face. Cornwell's hands brushed against the shaft of the morningstar just as Dobechek's right foot came driving up into his chin. The morningstar went skittering a few feet one way while Cornwell's body went flying limply the other.

Helena's inner turmoil broke like the sun slicing through a bank of dark clouds. She watched on with genuine glee as the female officer fell atop Cornwell, who was now the one sprawled out on the turf. Dobechek sat astride the man's stomach and dropped down blows at his head as he flailed, deflecting them only slightly. Lightning quick, Dobechek trapped both his arms against her chest with her left arm. His face was now free and clear. Needing no encouragement, she dropped hammer-fist after hammer-fist into the exposed area. After ten or twelve blows, Helena could see the man's arms go limp. *His lights are out, finish him,* she thought with barely any worry about the morbidity in it, even after she remembered morbidity was the very thing Alice had accused her of that morning.

Dobechek must've felt the man go limp beneath her when she flung his arms from her chest to lurch back to her feet. Breathing heavily, she stomped towards her discarded morningstar. Helena wasn't watching Cornwell. Her eyes were locked in awe on her feminine superhero striding towards her super-weapon. So she didn't know when the man had gotten to his feet. First thing she knew, Dobechek was crashing to the turf. Helena had thought she'd tripped, until she looked down to see Cornwell wrapping his arms around her legs. With a practiced wrestler's skills, Cornwell shimmied on top of Dobechek, and in no time flat, found himself in the power position once again.

Helena's head and heart were spinning. The emotional rollercoaster currently had her plummeting deeper and deeper as she watched Cornwell smash his own hammer-fists down into Dobechek's face. The blows weakened her resistance to the point where Cornwell could swing his right leg up over her left shoulder. He worked his left leg up behind her head, and though Dobechek did her best to prevent it, eventually Cornwell was able to lock his legs together around her neck.

Dobechek must've been panicking now; Helena sure was. Polly's right hand shot up to the man's head and latched onto a clump of his hair. Cornwell brought his left hand up to knock it away, and Dobechek slammed her left hand into his face. Desperate for air, and all but blind to the world around her, Dobechek's left hand found Cornwell's right eye. She drove her thumb deep into her attacker's socket and Cornwell cried out in pain. He quickly reached up to pull the offending hand away, but never relinquished his leg-lock around the female officer's neck in the slightest. If anything, the eye gouge only caused the man to tighten his deadly grip. He did lean backwards at the waist though, once he pulled Dobechek's hand free, in order to take away any future threat the arm could pose.

Helena could clearly see Dobechek's face turning purple. Each second brought with it a new and contradictory thought. *Give up, you're dying. Don't quit, shake him off you. It's not worth your life, let him win. No, Mikkelson cannot rule us, you have to get him off of you!*

The thoughts raced by, though time on the court seemed to have slowed. Cornwell held tight to Dobechek's right arm while leaning far away from her left. She gave up trying to hit him to get free and focused on prying loose his grip from around her neck. When that yielded no results, she bashed fists into his thighs and stomach. And when that too yielded no results, Helena was sure the end was near.

"Tap out! Yield and I'll let you live! Just tap!" Cornwell shouted out over the chirping crowd. "Tap out! Tap out now!" He screamed this last over and over as he raised his eyes to find the puppet-master to whom he owed his allegiance. Mikkelson was smirking down at him. Helena watched as the disgusting hippo of a man slowly and deliberately nodded at his puppet. She knew what the nod meant. *Kill her*, he was saying. And in that moment, after she'd thought the idea impossible, her hatred for Labor Supervisor Mikkelson grew even stronger.

Cornwell squeezed his legs tighter, and though the crowd had not quieted, Helena swore she could hear multiple bones in Dobechek's chest and shoulders cracking. Dobechek's left arm fell limply to the turf above her head. Cornwell leaned forward, rearing a fist back to pummel Dobechek's helpless face when Polly's fingertips brushed against the taped grip of her morningstar. Helena thought she could actually see the hope shoot across the trapped woman's face in that instant. She must've been on the very edge of unconsciousness, so perhaps she didn't really believe what she was feeling, but she had enough presence of mind to wrap her fingers around the grip and swing it at the man draped around her neck. The morningstar slammed into the right side of Cornwell's torso. The blow didn't have a lot behind it, but the spikes of the weapon's ball were sharp enough to pierce deep into his flesh.

Cornwell rolled off Dobechek so violently that the metal spikes tore loose a chunk of his shirt, along with three square-inches of meat from his lower chest. The man howled out in shuddering pain as he rolled away from his recently rearmed foe. Helena's soul brightened a notch with every movement Dobechek made to climb back to her feet. Once she'd regained her footing, she paused to draw in several large, gulping breaths.

Cornwell took advantage of the delay to clamber back to his own feet. His bat was behind Dobechek, so if he wanted it, he was going to have to go through her. Dobechek must've realized that too. She spread her legs out wide, ready to strike. Cornwell held his right arm pressed to his side, favoring his fresh injury. Helena knew he must really be in a lot of pain, but she still figured the pose was a feint. Dobechek apparently had the same thought because Cornwell's sudden dash to his left didn't catch her off guard in the least. She seemed to be expecting the exact maneuver, in fact. Dobechek stepped forward just as Cornwell darted left. After two steps, she'd cut him off and slashed in a looping one-handed swing aimed at the head of Mikkelson's stooge. He ducked just in time but wasn't able to completely avoid the backhand swing Dobechek whipped in as a follow-up. The morningstar's spikes raked across his stomach, tearing the navy-blue fabric of his shirt once more and leaving three long and jagged red slashes in their place.

Dobechek kept the morningstar swinging, whipping back a forehand slash towards Cornwell's head. This time he dived down into a somersault as the heavy weapon slashed through empty air. Cornwell sprung to his feet and found himself behind Dobechek, the wooden bat unobstructed ten yards in front of him. Cornwell dashed towards his weapon while Dobechek pivoted into a one-eighty spin, aiming a backhand slash at Cornwell's legs. Three paces into his dash, the morningstar crashed with a nauseating thump into his left knee. His leg bent at a wicked unnatural angle. He toppled to the ground instantly, landing hard on his uninjured knee. The crowd's hush mirrored that of Cornwell's momentary silent shock. After he began screaming in unknowable pain, the crowd noise came back with a vengeance. There were the regular sickos, happy to see a little blood and laughing at another man's pain, then there were those just ecstatic that somehow Dobechek was going to end up winning this thing. Helena was firmly in the latter camp.

Dobechek took a step back from her fallen enemy, pointing the morningstar at Mikkelson while Cornwell writhed on the turf in agony a few yards away. "Do you yield?" She shouted the question out at the pain-racked Cornwell but stared down a now smirk-free Mikkelson all the while. Helena doubted that Cornwell heard her questions. He was in a world of pure agony. There could be nothing else for him. After a few more shouts for her opponent to yield went unanswered, Polly

Dobechek dropped her morningstar down to her side and turned to face her once stoic, but now frenzied opponent.

Cornwell must not even have been able to notice Polly step up alongside him, so out of his mind with pain as he was. She stood over him where he sat curled up on the turf, clutching his demolished knee to his torso. Her killing blow was a one-handed arcing slash that collided with the side of Cornwell's head. The dull thud of a collapsing skull was followed by the loud snap of a breaking neck. The gruesome sight and sound did not touch Helena in that moment, all she felt right then was pure relief.

Cornwell's head lolled against his chest as his body crumpled to the turf. Dobechek raised her morningstar high over her head and gestured for the crowd to give her some love. They were more than happy to satisfy the request, few more so than Helena. Dobechek thrust her weapon up in celebration and leaned her head back to gaze up at the humbling, brightly-speckled black expanse above.

Mikkelson drew Helena's attention from the victorious fighter at center court. The pale-skinned fat man in the bright colored shirt was hard to miss, especially when he was the only one trying to clamber out of the bleachers. Well, he did have a gaggle of lapdogs trailing in his wake, but the fool waddling his way down the rows was what held one's attention. The crowd quickly fell silent. No one was ignorant to the fact that Mikkelson was embarking on the final act of his betrayal of the security staff. Apparently, with his man dead, he wasn't going to keep up the pretense of respecting the security staff's authority. He was making a grand, defiant show of leaving. Helena figured it was all that the perverted whale had left to him. And so, make a big show of it he did. He made his way down the bleachers even slower than was necessary for a man of his size. Once he reached the turf, he walked directly towards a still-seated Montrois. The handsome Latino officer and two of his compatriots moved to cut the fat man off before he arrived.

Montrois looked up at Mikkelson with rank contempt. Mikkelson held his gaze, defiant as ever. A pin drop could've been heard in that long, tense moment. Abruptly, Montrois broke off his death-stare and motioned with his head towards the Latino officer. Apparently the nod meant step aside because that's precisely what the handsome officer did. The two officers behind him followed suit, and Mikkelson and his pack of sniveling supervisors marched past them without a word. The crowd's hush persisted until the fat bastard and his toadies crossed the footbridge and stepped through The Meadow's archway.

The tension went out of the atmosphere like a needle piercing a balloon. Once more, the cheers rained down. A large majority of the women in The Meadow were on their feet clapping and hooting for joy, along with a great many men as well. There still seemed to be a few, however, who were only there for the same reasons Helena had originally come for. Their applause was lackluster, and for a moment, she feared for them. If she could tell their enthusiasm was false, then surely the security staff could see it too. Helena almost wanted to go to them and warn them but felt the act itself might cause her to be singled out, and after all the good work she'd done today proving she was on their side, she didn't want to take that risk. So Helena Heathcoat just kept clapping.

Dobechek still held her morningstar above her head at center court as she began spinning in a slow circle and making eye contact with each of her fellow officers. Her smile grew ever wider as she completed the circle. Dobechek ended with Montrois. Helena would've thought the battered woman's smile couldn't grow any larger, but she'd have been wrong. Montrois stood up slowly and Schef, seated alongside him, followed suit. Montrois stepped out towards his victorious subordinate with a great big smile of his own etched from cheek to cheek. Helena was shocked to see it. The man hadn't smiled once in the entire time she'd known him. But he was smiling now as he strolled out to meet her.

Schef and the handsome Latino officer, along with three other nearby officers, tagged along. Montrois began a slow clap as he approached Dobechek. A few of the other officers took up the clap while a couple of her compatriots stepped up to either side of her, allowing her to lean against them and get off her feet. Dobechek did just that. She threw her arm around the officer to her left and leaned heavily on the man. He took her weight with a grin, while tapping her on the shoulder and barking out praises.

"I challenge!" The shout could barely be heard above the applause, but it was heard. A second shout came from the same voice, louder this time, "I challenge!" The crowd hushed with practiced rapidity. Helena looked to center court, where a complete one-eighty transformation had come over the officers. The elation that had permeated all their faces just moments before was nowhere to be seen. In its place was astonished anger. A dark, heartbreaking anger, the kind of anger only those we love most can cause. And when the challenger stepped clear of the gawking crowd and Helena gained a clear line of sight to the man, she understood why that black rage could be seen in the officer's faces.

The challenger walked with an obvious reluctance, hounded every step by jeering officers and trailing onlookers. The challenger made it to within five paces of Montrois, Schef and Dobechek when the two officers who had been holding up Dobechek moved to block his path. The challenger halted his march, and the two approaching officers stopped two paces in front of him. No one at center court said a word or made a move. With each silent second's passing, the crowd around them grew ever quieter. Finally, Schef broke the spell and pulled out the microphone from behind his back. He made a move to step away from Montrois and give himself the spotlight he seemed to crave, but the security commander placed a hand on his shoulder to stop him.

Schef looked back towards Montrois in puzzlement. The microphone had apparently been switched on already, however, so Helena and the rest of the residents could hear most of what was spoken next. "Traitor!" The shout came from multiple angry officers' voices crowding around the lone man.

"You fucking traitor! You'd kill your own sworn sister?" she heard the Latino officer yell above the other shouts.

The rage boiled off the crowd of officers. The chaotic atmosphere that had been absent since the first moments of this crazy day came flooding back into The Meadow. All of Helena's earlier elation was washed away. Now, as the crowd grew more and more restless around her, she found herself squeezing her fists to ward off panic. It was the challenger who'd caused it all. Helena knew him on sight, as did nearly everyone aboard station. He and his fellow officer, Sergeant Marge Hamill, were the only two dissenters the security staff had. They had stirred up a lot of trouble during the takeover and had almost got a lot of people hurt. The man was dangerous. It was true that she had never actually met him in person, but Helena knew in her bones that Abner Hyun was bad news. The memory of the irate Hyun wagging his finger and berating his fellow officers in the Main Cafeteria floated its way back into her mind's eye. *He is going to ruin everything.* She just knew it.

"The hell are you doing, Normie?" Montrois asked Hyun in a tone of genuine heartbreak that made Helena's own heart go out to the security commander for the first time ever.

"What you've all made me do," echoed his response from the speaker. A response that did not please his fellow officers one bit; Helena could see that plain enough. Montrois was even forced to restrain a few of his officers before they could attack Hyun. The security commander shoved his subordinates around with a disquieting ease Helena could tell Hyun did not fail to note. The officers around center court quickly calmed down when they understood their commander's conviction to see the moment through with words alone.

"You can't do this, Abbie," Montrois said, once his officers had calmed.

"You changing the rules, Monty?" Hyun asked in return. "I thought The Final Tournament was open to any challenger present," he said, spinning around to look his onetime coworkers in the eye. "Well, here I am, and I challenge. I just can't let y'all do this, I'm sorry. But there doesn't need to be a fight. I loathe the idea of fighting you, Polly, more than you could ever know," Hyun said to the last fight's victor. "I dread it more than I could ever figure out how to even begin to say. But I will do it. I'll fight you, if that's what I have to do. You can avoid all of it though, Pol. Do the right thing here and yield. Then we can end this psychotic farce y'all are playing. It's not too late. Stress has pushed us all to unspeakable limits. We can all get over these past few weeks together. But we must end your madness. Y'all cannot have power. We are the power's security, not the powerholders themselves. We can't be both and expect to endure peacefully up here. Y'all are kidding yourselves if you believe otherwise. I love Commander Montrois as much as any of you," Hyun said to the gaggle of officers but looked directly at the security commander, "but grief has broken him. He seems steady now, but he'll snap soon enough. And if you give him power, which I'm certain is the very thing y'all are planning to do, then that snap will destroy all of us. It will destroy humanity, my friends."

The hush of the crowd was still absolute. Montrois looked about him and seemed to realize that everything that had been said was broadcast out to the masses. He glared at the survivor until Schef sheepishly shrugged his shoulders in apology. Montrois took one giant step towards the now cowering emaciated man and ripped the microphone from his hand. "Okay, Abner, okay," he said into it in a slow, rumbling voice. "We have no power to deny your challenge. So, if that's what you want, then that's what you shall have. But you'll have to wait 'till tomorrow," Montrois added with rough command. "The fights are finished for today. We will pick up again tomorrow morning, same time as we began today. You hear that, people?" Montrois now addressed the crowd directly. "Disperse for the day. Be back for the Final Tournament: Day 2, tomorrow."

"You can't just do that," Helena heard Hyun's plea faintly through the microphone clutched firmly in Montrois' grip.

"And yet, I have," he said, barely audible over the speaker since he was now holding the microphone away from his mouth. A patronizing grin stretched across Montrois' face as he brought the microphone back to his lips. "Both of tomorrow's combatants will spend the night in our rec room ... under guard, as the rules clearly state."

"Oh, so now you care about the rules again. I didn't know it was a pick and choose kinda thing." Hyun's response once more came faintly over the speaker.

Montrois looked fit to spit. He calmed his rage after a few breaths, forcing a placid look to his face. Then he once more addressed the crowd, "Disperse now, ladies and gentlemen, and be back here tomorrow." With that, Montrois tossed the microphone back at Schef and barked a command to his officers. Two officers stepped up to Hyun in the next moment and began to march him off towards the archway. The other officers all took up positions around tomorrow's two combatants, clearing a path through the milling crowd like a hot knife through butter.

Helena's fellow residents began to gather up their things and head for the archway shortly after. She remained rooted to her seat, however. So much had happened this day, so many emotional swings, Helena wasn't sure where her head had ended up and she wanted to take stock. She replayed the day in her mind, spooling backwards to when she first awoke this morning. Exhaustion seeped into her shoulders with each memory's passing. When she turned her thoughts to having to repeat the whole thing over again the next day, sorrow and dread added their weight as well. Finally, Helena knew there was nothing for it but to put aside tomorrow's uncertainty for the moment. She knew she had to head back to her quarters. It was time to face Alice.

CHAPTER 12

ABNER

"Are you sure your place is safe, Normie? Maybe we ought to head over to my unit in Blue Corridor." Barry Calvin's nervous suggestion was the only noise to be heard in the living quarters alleyway, yet it still barely registered in Abner Hyun's overloaded mind.

"They won't be coming for me," Abner organized his cluttered thoughts enough to say.

"With how you left them, they sure as hell will be," Gillian Gerwitz demurred with a certainty in her voice that brought Abner fully back to the present moment.

Just a few minutes earlier, Gerwitz and Calvin had been milling around in the Living Quarters Central Hub, swapping hushed gossip with some residents near the trolley depot. He had spotted them right away. They were easy to pick out in a crowd. They seemed to always be at each other's side, and for some reason that Abner never could quite put his finger on, they seemed to always be wearing their matching silver and maroon Nomex flight suits too. Today was no exception.

The pair of Star Hawk pilots both stood roughly 6' and sported similar lissome physiques, which the flight suits flattered. Gillian's was a tad curvier, admittedly. However, her curves were in just the right places, in Abner's humble opinion. Both pilots made for a handsome sight in their snazzy suits, no doubt about that. Even so, it seemed unnecessary to him to wear the things at all times. The flashy jumpsuits made them look like stock photos of astronauts a few hours before launch. Gerwitz and Calvin's short cropped haircuts were also very similar, right down to the color and shape; the color being a rich brown with shades of auburn, while the shape was the classic military style high-and-tight, though Gerwitz left hers a good deal longer on the sides and top. It's the hair that sealed the deal for Abner in believing their mirrored looks to be intentional. Even their matching sandy-beige skin tones served as a further approving stamp on the theory of their mirror relation. True, the two longtime partners did display yin-and-yang type personalities, but even that aspect of their relationship seemed to scream *twins* to a befuddled world. Abner never once brought up the issue of the odd uniformity in their appearance to either pilot though, for despite all the evidence to the contrary, Abner Hyun was actually very much averse to confrontation.

The twin aviators had broken off from their whispered conversation with a group of five residents in the overalls of collector module garage maintenance workers as soon as they'd seen Abner enter the Central Hub. They had rushed over to join him without a single parting word. Abner had been taking long, Evil-T-1000-Terminator strides towards his and Stevie's living quarters off a back alleyway in Silver Corridor at the time. The pilots had been struggling to keep pace ever since. It was just now sinking in that he was being a bit rude and inconsiderate. After all, Gerwitz and Calvin were the source of none of his current rage and turmoil. They deserved his cordial, mannerly attention, even despite this morning's prospects. *They may in fact be some of the last few people you can trust up here anymore, Normie,* Abner realized. *It's just you, Sergeant Hamill and these two pilots against 'em all now. Better not be so short with the last few allies you got left,* he scolded himself.

Slowing down, he allowed the two Star Hawk pilots to fall in alongside of him. "Montrois knows I'll be there. He's got no reason to send anyone after me," he told the pilots in a voice so calm it even surprised himself a little.

"Yeah ... well ... I don't know. They ain't exactly very trusting these days," Gerwitz responded warily.

Abner and the two pilots came around a bend in the weaving alleyway system inside Silver Corridor, and finally, his unit came into sight. Abner couldn't help but pick up the pace once again. "Nobody got hurt. Well … not too bad anyway," he told them. "I made Dirks and Schwambach look like a couple of fools on the way out of the rec room, and maybe gave 'em a few bumps on the head, and maybe a black eye or two, but that's just justice in action in my book. I'm sure those two morons will be all hot to come snatch me back into their bullshit lockup, but Montrois won't let them. They won't want the bad publicity. They wouldn't like their incompetence being whispered about," Abner explained to his friends, now hustling just a pace or two behind and to either side of him. "I get that Montrois ain't the man we all once knew, but I believe I at least still know him well enough to guarantee no one is coming for me. He knows who I am, even if we no longer truly know *him*. He knows I'll show. Besides, they only said I had to spend the night under guard, nothing was spoken about this morning. If they want to invent rules and laws at a whim, then I'm free to interpret them how I choose. That seems only fair." Abner looked at both the pilots walking just behind him after that remark, hoping for a chuckle or two. Sadly, he received only wary silence. He was in dire need of a good laugh right about then. As it was looking, his prospects for such a thing happening anytime soon seemed mighty slim.

"This is all so fucked," Gerwitz muttered after a moment.

"*Sooo* fucked," Calvin concurred with his aerial partner. "I cannot get over how many of the security officers are going along with all this shit. I mean … after yesterday, with that fucking gore-fest on that fucking tennis court, not to mention those poor operators they hacked down in the Control Room last week … all this madness, and they're all still just as committed as ever? … I'm sorry, it's just … it … it fucking boggles my mind! I just cannot believe all this shit is really happening up here. It's so freakin' surreal."

Abner would've spoken a firm concurrence if they hadn't just arrived in front of the hatchway to his living quarters. He busied himself instead with the door code while Gerwitz and Calvin darted glances up and down the empty alleyway behind him. Abner smashed in each number of the code and felt his panic rise with each new digit. *Prepare yourself for a slap or two, Normie,* he told himself, feeling wholly deserving of a few good ones.

Normally, Stevie wasn't the type of woman to raise her hand in anger, but, over the years, Abner had said and done enough truly bonehead things that his wife was forced to smack a little sense into him. He had no doubt she would be waiting for him just inside the hatchway so she might do that very thing now. *Maybe she'll hold off for Calvin and Gerwitz's sake, but I'm sure to get it eventually,* he thought with an inner begrudging smile.

In spite of the cold reception Stevie was sure to have in store for him, he nonetheless felt the same tingle of anticipation flutter in his chest that he felt every time he first laid eyes on his gorgeous wife after a night or two apart. Last night's separation hadn't exactly been planned, and the flutter seemed all the quicker for it. Abner had bonked those two moron officers in the head back in the rec room and bolted out of there before anyone knew what was happening, all for a chance to see Stevie before his match began. She was his source of strength. He needed her love before he faced death.

Abner did feel extremely awful about risking his life once again, but he had solace in knowing he had no other choice. Even so, he knew his missions back to Earth had been trying enough for Stevie. This had the potential to be a bridge too far in her eyes. Abner resigned himself to taking his medicine and enduring his wife's anger and vitriol with a penitent silence. And when she ran dry of rage, Abner would explain his reasons, and she would just have to come to understand in her own time. *Same as Calvin and Gerwitz, and Sergeant Marge too.* Abner knew that Stevie couldn't send him off to face his death without her love. *She wouldn't.* If she was a bit stiff, that would be understandable, but she'd give him what he needed in the end. He knew that. And after today, things would all be okay. Winning would solve everything. Stevie would forgive him then. She could never stay mad at him for very long.

With that firm belief giving him strength, Abner punched the last digit of his door code. "Speaking of that gore-fest Barry just mentioned, do you really think that volunteering to be a part of it was the best idea, Normie?" Gerwitz posed the very question Abner knew Stevie was surely just about to ask him, albeit with a deal less hostility than he was sure to get from his wife. The hatchway swished open in front of him, offering Abner a momentary escape from the gravity of the question.

Abner had to appear confident for not only his own sake and sanity but for those who both loved and doubted him. He didn't want to let Gerwitz throw him off his game before he'd first spoken to his wife. The decision was made now, and he couldn't see how it would do anyone any good to appear uncertain about it. *Never let 'em see ya cry*, his Grandpa Richter used to say. Abner took the mantra to heart. He was a firm believer in putting on a brave face. And anyway, he was, in fact, extremely confident in his decision. So the brave face didn't seem like the false bravado that it had so often been in the past.

It might not have been a long stretch in real time from the moment after Rollie Cornwell's head imploded and neck snapped, until the moment Abner voiced his challenge and *volunteered to be a part of it*, as Gerwitz just characterized it, but it sure felt like an eternity. Abner had played out every possible scenario in his head in that short time, from beginning to end, imagining every possible challenger left in the gigantic space dome, and what that would mean for the station, its residents and his own and Stevie's lives. Even at the end, he hadn't really wanted to challenge. He was begging on the inside for someone else to scream out instead, or for someone to shake him awake from this month's long nightmare. He'd held those pleas in his heart right up until the moment before he barked out his challenge over the noise of the crowd.

Looking around him in the instant preceding his cry, something in the faces all about him brought about as clear an epiphany as Abner Hyun ever had in his life. He knew in that moment that it had to be him to challenge, that no one else would, and that Jasper Montrois and his fellow officers could not be left in charge. He understood a collective madness had spread through the security staff and was even now rapidly coursing its way through the station's impressionable population. He knew that somehow, despite their better angels, a good number of them had reverted to some primitive belief in power. And despite how medieval and mad it all was, they were all fully committed. In that moment before his shout, Abner had known his only way to end the madness was to dive into it.

The last hesitation he had struggled through before that dive—other than what Stevie might have to say about his entering a death tournament, that is, which was a whole can of worms that Abner had pushed firmly to the back of his mind—had been his fear that even if he, or anyone else did win the Final Tournament, the security staff would simply ignore the victory and fudge the rules so they could keep the power, for Abner was finally certain that power was in fact the very place where their hearts were all now set.

But then he'd seen the fear, fervor and fanaticism in the faces of the residents around him. It had persuaded Abner in that instant that there would be no way Montrois and the officer's fragile power could last in the face of the backlash that would surely come if the security staff were to betray the oaths they had promised everyone they all swore by disregarding the champion's wishes. Abner figured the spell would be broken if that were to happen, and he figured Montrois, and especially the survivor Aponyaschefski, were smart enough to realize that too. He understood then that the security staff would be forced to respect the winner and his authority, even if the winner was someone they all now hated, someone who would turn the power right back over to AOA and the world leaders. Abner knew, and he was sure Montrois and Schef knew as well, that the monster the security staff had created would turn on them in the blink of an eye if they did anything less. And so, Abner had issued his challenge.

He'd done it, and there was no turning back now, and for all those reasons, it had seemed right at the time. He wasn't keen on arguing the point now, even with friends. So Abner didn't respond to Gerwitz's question. Instead, he darted inside his cramped quarters. The pilots were forced to hang back in the alleyway when Abner drew up short in his tiny little foyer with its small wooden bench, coat rack, and small closet that housed their vacuum and cleaning supplies. Stevie was nowhere to be seen. He'd expected to find her in the living room, seated in either his custom recliner or on the edge of their dark brown Ikea-special coffee table, waiting impatiently for him to come home, but the room was dark and empty. There were no sounds or vibrations of habitation of any sort emanating from any corner of the 1150 square foot living quarters. *She ain't here,* he slowly came to realize. *Where the hell could she be?*

Stevie was an early riser, and she never went to the cafeterias for breakfast. *She should be here.* Confused as he was, Abner did not shout out for her. He was still trying to maintain the brave face for his comrades' sake. Swallowing his disappointment, he made his way through his low-ceilinged apartment towards the dining room. The two pilots followed close behind like little ducklings.

Once there, he pulled out a black chair from the thin black dining table and plopped himself down on its soft gel cushion. The austere blue-gray dining room's single concession to ornament was a 36" x 36" painting by Stevie herself. It showed a single-masted, black-hulled sailing ship. The ship's charcoal sail was pictured full and billowing to reveal a misshapen white circle painted in its center. The ship was positioned in such a way as to make it appear to slice swiftly across a calm sea. The horizon painted halfway up the canvas bloomed with a richly colored sunset, full of violets, purples, oranges, and pinks that blended and spread their way across the placid waters.

Both pilots paused before the painting. They were powerless not to. It drew the eye. Abner suppressed a grin. *People really do like that painting.* No surprise really, people liked anything and everything Stevie Hyun ever did. His wife seemed to have a natural talent for almost everything. But of all her masterpieces, Abner liked this painting in particular. He couldn't say why exactly. He knew as much about art and paintings as a dog knew about filing taxes. Maybe it was how much other people especially seemed to like the painting that made it so extraordinary. Whatever the painting's draw was, it was an easy choice to include along with all their other trifles when AOA offered cargo space aboard a Cardinal's Nest bound E-11 shuttle a few months before the Infection Event. They had been informed that shuttle would make a solo trip, with all five of its cargo bays stocked only with whatever items the workers might care to have aboard to remind them of home for the five-year experiment they were set to embark upon.

Finally able to wrest the attention of the two pilots from his wife's painting, Abner gestured to the empty seats across from him. They quickly plopped down in the offered chairs. "Coffee?" He asked them, after a few silent and awkward seconds.

"Sure," Calvin responded with a cheerful grin that was doing its best to fight the day's grim atmosphere.

"Yeah, I'll take a cup. Two sugars. Just a little cream," Gerwitz said as Abner popped up out of his chair, making for the coffee pot.

"Just black for me, thanks," Calvin added as Abner crossed through the arched doorway into his simple kitchen.

Abner had a clear view of his friends seated at the dining room table as he prepared their drinks. The kitchen was only a few paces deep, and maybe only a few wider. It did house all their necessities, despite the space. *Got to give it props for that*. Still, whenever he spent any amount of time in there, be it preparing meals or grabbing his morning coffee, he was always reminded of the pristine and placid waters of White Fish Lake glimmering in through the sliding glass door in the kitchen of their first home together back in Montana. That bittersweet thought led directly to more thoughts of the beautiful wife Abner loved so very much. *Where the hell is she? And just what in the hell am I going to say to her exactly?* Abner wondered as he finished stirring the coffees.

Emerging from the kitchen, he had to quickly shoo Calvin back to his seat when the man rose to grab his mug. Abner slid the two drinks across the smooth surface of the tabletop to their respective guests as soon as he arrived at his seat. He took a small, delicate sip of his own heavily-creamed, heavily-sugared concoction before seating himself back down on the comfortably cushioned chair.

"So, let's hear it," Gerwitz prompted as soon as Abner brought his coffee back up for another sip. "What were you thinking? How could you challenge in that fucked-up tournament?"

"Go easy on the guy, Gillian. I'm sure he had himself a pretty rough night," Calvin said with a grin. "Pretty rough morning too, from the sounds of it," he added with a laugh.

"Not as bad as Dirks' and Schwambach's morning, I'm sure," Abner pointed out with a laugh that was somehow both composed and jovial.

"This is serious shit here, guys," Gerwitz said in tones that cut through all the bullshit. "I got no wish to be the party pooper here, but you were both at the Final Tournament yesterday. You saw what happened. You saw what they've become. You guys need to be taking this shit a whole lot more seriouser."

"Seriouser?" Calvin asked with a sheepish grin indicating he couldn't help himself calling out his copilot's gaffe.

"You're the talker, Barry, not me," Gerwitz answered, as the start of an unbidden smile was killed before it could quite reveal itself on her lips. "I'm just trying to save your guys' lives is all, don't mind me."

"Believe me, Gillian, I know how serious the security staff have become. I've seen it for myself, up close, twice now," Abner said in what he hoped was a reassuring voice. "I know what I *volunteered for*, as you so eloquently put it, and believe me, if I thought there was any other choice, any other possible way to stop them from taking total control of this station, and the entire course of human history along with it, I would make that choice. I'm in no way looking forward to fighting a woman to the death whom I once fought beside, back-to-back, shoulder-to-shoulder against countless Damned. I would take any road that averted that fate for me—that is, any road that didn't hold the doom of humanity at its end. I looked for such a road, Gill. I searched, I really did, but this is it. There's just ... there's no other way, Gillian. This is how it's got to be." When Gillian Gerwitz didn't seem likely to respond to his preaching, Abner changed tack with a question. "Have you ever read Machiavelli's The Prince?"

"What?" Gerwitz and Calvin asked in unison, and with deep puzzlement.

"I don't read enough," Calvin hurried to offer in a self-deprecating manner.

"I think I remember it a little from college," Gerwitz allowed. "Why?"

"Well, I don't know, it just seems kinda relevant to my point just now is all. The book extols the virtues of learning from your enemy and then using that knowledge to beat them at their own game."

"Yeah, so?" Calvin asked, though his words were almost drowned out in the coffee mug he mumbled them into.

Abner seized on the question even so, it being the very one he was hoping for. He only wished Stevie was here now so he wouldn't have to make all the same points twice, "Montrois and that fucking worm Aponyaschefski have whipped the people of this station into a madness, we know that," he began. "But the madness starts with the officers. They're the true zealots in all of this. Right now, they got the residents under their thumb because of the united and committed front they're displaying. It's a powerful sight, a strong piece of propaganda indeed, especially in a closed environment like this. It can have a real impact on fools and believers. But you see, that's a double-edged sword, the way I figure it. Schef told everyone there yesterday—before any of the killing even began—that he, along with every one of the officers—apart, of course, from the sarge and myself—he said they all swore oaths to respect the authority of the Final Tournament's champion. I heard the bastard with my own damn ears. So as soon as they show the slightest sign of wavering from that commitment, what little hold they have over the people will be ripped away like the false veil it is. Despite what a colossal douchebag and cowardly asshole this Aponyaschefski guy has turned out to be, I can't deny that the son of a bitch is clever. He and Montrois are both more than capable of seeing what is so obviously plain to the likes of us. They'll know they can't go against the commands of the champion and expect to keep the people in their pockets. There just aren't enough officers for that. And we all know they ain't really going to risk using their guns, even in an uprising. The panic in all the officers' faces when Rollie Cornwell won his first match ought to be evidence enough that they know that if they want to keep the power, they're gonna have to win this goddamn Final Tournament or else bow down to whoever the hell does. So I will use against them the very fear mongering, fanaticism and sycophancy Schef and Monty have stoked up to snatch control of this station. I'll use the people's and my former squadmates' own irrational passions to set things back to rights. Then I will ensure irrational passions can never rule us again. So yes, I *volunteered* to play their stupid little game, deadly as it is, because I know I can beat them at it. When I win, they'll have to respect my wishes. They'll have no other option. They've made that their reality, not me. I'm just taking advantage of it, though it makes me sick to do it. I am playing their game in order to *end* their games forever, Gillian. Before they even start."

"Ha, tell that to those three poor operators they beat to death in the Control Room," Calvin mumbled once again into his coffee.

Abner ignored this mumble, as he was certain Calvin was hoping he would. Instead, he stared across the table at Gerwitz. The tall, svelte and handsome pilot gave nothing away as to what she might be thinking. She seemed calm as ever as she slowly sipped her coffee. Finally, it was too much for Abner. He found himself blurting out, "What good would it do us to stay out of the Final Tournament? What good would it do us to just sit back and allow Monty to install himself as Lord High Tyrant?" When Gerwitz still did not respond, he plugged right on, "I don't agree with the Final Tournament—its ends nor its means—but if I want to have any say in my freedom and governance, then I have no choice right now but to play their god-damn game."

"Well, that there is the problem, the way I see it, Normie," Gerwitz finally responded. "You only have a plan to *play* their game, not a plan to *win* it. You're just trusting in your admittedly admirable fighting skills to get you through, but that's not a plan, Abbie Normie my dear. It could all fall apart with just one misstep. One slip, or stray beam of light, or broken weapon and it's all over. That's what I think you are refusing to face here. I think you're angry and you've made an impulse decision and now you're trying to justify it, to yourself as well as Barry and me. And despite my faithful partner's silence, I'm not the only one who thinks that's so. Sergeant Marge is also of the same opinion. Barry and I were over to her living quarters last night. She wouldn't shut up about it. Wait till she gets a hold of you, my friend. She's gonna tear you a new one, for sure. Help me out here, Calvin, goddammit!" Gerwitz lashed out a backhand slap across Barry Calvin's arm for added emphasis as she broke off her rant, "Tell Normie what Marge was saying last night."

"She wasn't exactly *saying* anything," Calvin responded with an arched brow. "She did *shout* a lotta shit though. And I'm afraid my dear partner is right, Abbie, Marge is super pissed at you."

"I knew she would be," Abner conceded. "It's only because I wouldn't go along with her plan. She's just bitter because I pointed out how ludicrous it truly is. Down deep, she knows as well as the both of you that what I'm doing is the only hope left to us now. Slim as it seems, this is it, you guys. The sarge will come around to admitting that soon enough, believe me. So did she attempt her fruitless plan after all, as she warned me she would? Did she say?" he asked his guests, hoping to disguise the nerves he felt coursing through him. *It ain't the coffee, Normie. Don't kid yourself.*

"She went to the rec room," Calvin confirmed.

"And what did she find?"

"There wasn't no one left to guard it, just as you suspected," Gerwitz stated, begrudging every word.

"And what did she find in the weapons vault?"

"A few sidearms and some ammo cartridges, nothing more," Calvin reluctantly answered, after it was clear Gerwitz would not.

"Exactly like I told her," Abner said with a shaking head. "One look at my former squadmates yesterday at the tournament was all I needed to confirm that suspicion. The sons-a-bitches had every long-range and automatic weapon in the security staff's arsenal strapped to their bodies in one place or another. I told her they would move and hide the PRZVL-33's too, though she had no way to move them herself, even if they had been in there to steal. I knew they wouldn't risk the sarge leading a break in to raid the vault while they were all gone. It was just so obvious."

"Well, she thought they might not send 'em all to The Meadow," Gerwitz said, making excuses. "She thought it was possible, likely even, that they would leave a few guys back to guard a still stocked weapons vault. Then the two of you could've overpowered the guards and raided the vault. And then we could arm the people to get our AOA benefactors their power back. She thought it was worth the attempt anyway."

"I know all that," Abner said with slight exasperation. "She told me her plan, and I told her it was hopeless."

"You left her high and dry!" Gerwitz exclaimed. "What if there had been officers left behind to guard the weapons vault after all? You could have very well gotten her killed by abandoning her!"

"But I didn't, did I, Gill?" Abner asked the flustered pilot, and not unkindly. "I suppose a part of me knew even before the Final Tournament began that I was going to have to end up challenging in it. I think Marge saw that truth somewhere deep inside her as well, but rather than give into the inevitable and go, ready to challenge if necessary, like I did, she decided to reject the truth calling out to her.

She was still clinging to an empty hope, a beautiful hope though it be, a hope in the return of our once venerable commander. A hope which I've only very recently felt completely wither and die in my own heart. The man is dead, you guys. Grief and Harclay Aponyaschefski have constructed some Frankenstein's Monster out of the shell of what was once our beloved battle buddy, commander and friend. He's gone and he ain't coming back. We have to stop him. *I* have to stop him. It's my fault. I couldn't reach him. I should've kept Aponyaschefski away from him. I knew the man was deranged, after surviving on the surface for so long. So it's on me to step up and set things right. And that's exactly what I intend to do."

The color faded from Gerwitz's face, as did the tension in her shoulders. Neither of the pilots were able to verbally communicate their acceptance of Abner's decision, but after a few silent beats, they both wearily nodded their heads. Abner took it as a victory, probably the best he was likely to get, anyway. He decided to change the topic from the death match he was just 57 minutes away from fighting to something a bit lighter, "So where is the sarge then? You say you were with her last night."

"She told us she was headed to the rec room this morning to plead with Monty to release you and put an end to the Final Tournament once and for all," Gerwitz answered with wry irony. "She's probably there now. Though I can't know for sure, of course, because the stubborn fool can't be hailed over her tablet. She's paranoid that the security staff's been able to track her through it ever since they took over the control room."

"Yeah, I know. She told me that a few days ago too. The bastards took my goddamn tablet last night before tossing me into the pitch-dark rec room. God knows where Polly got to spend the night. Comfortably in her own bed, would be my guess. And then this morning, I left there in too big a hurry to try and get the goddamn tablet back. I feel like I'm going to regret that," Abner gushed in a nervous rush.

"I just hope she don't do anything crazy and go pushing her luck with them guys," Calvin interjected with a response much more appropriate for the situation. "They ain't playing no more, especially since they're all likely to be upset after the way Abner left them in the lurch this morning. Maybe we ought to go down there and see if she's okay."

"The sarge is a big girl. I think she can take care of herself," Abner's voice failed to mask the very real fear he felt for the safety of one of his last true friends. There was nothing he could do for the sergeant now. No matter how much he hated it. He couldn't make it back to the security staff headquarters and then on to The Meadow before the Final Tournament resumed. If he wasn't there exactly when his match with Polly Dobechek was set to begin, Monty, Schef and the security staff would seize on that as a reason to disqualify him. Marge was on her own now, little as he liked it. Abner could do no more than hold a prayer for her safety close to his heart.

I can't help her, but maybe these guys could get to her in time to lend a hand, if need be. Maybe I ought to second Calvin's idea of them trying to find her, Abner thought, staring the two pilots down with a more critical eye. *Although, if she is in trouble, I may very well be condemning 'em to their deaths by sending them seeking after her. I sure as hell don't need any more bad karma like that on my conscience right now.* Those, along with a good deal more such anguished thoughts, bounced around Abner's head for a few protracted seconds, until Gerwitz abruptly broke the lull in conversation, "We'll go find her. We'll make sure she's okay," she promised with determination. "Don't worry, Abner. Just focus on what you got to do today. And don't lose, for God's sake," she finished, rising to her feet.

"I won't," Abner solemnly swore. Her promise to find Marge, unprompted by him, eased his fears for his wayward sergeant, as well as made him feel better about the pilots going after her. If they did get into some kind of trouble, at least he wouldn't have to feel guilty about sending them. "I better start heading to The Meadow, so I'll follow you guys out," Abner said before draining the dregs of coffee from the bottom of his mug.

Abner then popped up posthaste to get himself in front of the pilots so that he might lead them to the door. He had a desire to be the first to the hatch; it seemed more hospitable to him to be standing beside the portal with a gesturing arm to direct his guests to exit ahead of him. Abner took the duties of a good host seriously and knew he'd already dropped the ball on that account several times over. He wasn't so lost to decorum that he would allow things to end as they began. So there was no one ahead of him when he stepped onto the chaotically embroidered, hand-knotted rug sprawled across the floor of his small foyer and the hatchway before it suddenly swooshed open. In the next instant, Stevie darted into the chamber, nearly barreling straight into him. Pulling up short at the last second, she brought her hand up to her mouth to cover her fright-filled shout.

"Oh, Jesus!" Stevie shrieked as she drove her fist into Abner's chest. "You scared me!"

"Sorry, baby," Abner said, grabbing his wife by the shoulders and steering her further into their lunar domicile.

"Sorry?!" she screamed at him with indignation, before adding a few more thumps for good measure.

Abner began to realize just how distraught his wife truly was. She was in one hell of a state. Her lush red hair was unwashed and unbrushed, with fly-aways galore. Her crystal-hued blue eyes, normally as welcoming as a mountain spring, were brimming with tears and inflamed in a savage red that clashed with her normally ondearing splash of amber freckles. Stevie was draped in Abner's old man's ancient University of Michigan Football sweatshirt. The petite, redheaded little firecracker was drowning in the old, well-worn garment. It hung loosely everywhere, sagging off her narrow shoulders and drooping all the way down to her knees. She completed her obviously hasty ensemble with black joggers and pink Crocs that did not wholly conceal a purple sock on her left foot and a light blue one on the right. "What is it, baby?" Abner asked her with rising panic. "Did someone hurt you? Did the security staff send someone after you?"

"What?" Stevie asked in bafflement after a few slow, calming breaths.

"Where have you been?" Abner pressed. "Why were you out like this? I came back home to see you before I ... before the Final Tou— Why weren't you here? Where have you been?!"

"Looking for you, you big ass!" Stevie shouted just as she plopped herself down on the coffee table. "I've been running all over this god-damn station trying to find you! I got a message on my tablet from Alice Stark this morning, telling me she'd overheard people talking about you escaping the security staff's rec room during her breakfast in the Main Cafeteria." When Abner had no quick response ready for that, Stevie finally looked away from him and noticed Gerwitz and Calvin for the first time. "Barry. Gillian," she said to them, with a nod for each in turn, after a moment obviously spent regaining her composure. "I hope you two are here to convince my husband that he's an idiot. Or, at the very least, I hope you've softened him up enough for me to get that job done."

"We gave it our best shot, Stevie," Gerwitz quietly conceded after a few moments.

"We better get going," Calvin cut in graciously. "Sarge may be needing us."

"Right," Gerwitz agreed.

Abner turned to look both of his friends in the eye. He ultimately could give them no more than a shrug of the shoulders to mark their parting. A similar shrug was all they had for him as well. The twin pilots plodded out of his living quarters with firm determination written in each stride. When the hatchway swished closed behind them, Abner was left all alone in his living room with Stevie, and even though it was the only thing he had been craving in all the world just minutes earlier, Abner suddenly felt a strong urge to be anywhere else. He knew his wife. He could read her moods. She had many, with many nuances. And it was clear now that Stevie was a great deal more upset with him than even his worst fears had allowed him to imagine.

"What were you thinking?" she asked, breaking the silence with an icy chill in her voice.

"I had to, baby," Abner said, turning to face her.

"Don't you dare say that!" she shouted suddenly. "You did not *have* to! This is not on you. You've already defied them enough. You've done all you could to stop the Final Tournament, and the overthrow. None of this is your responsibility, Abner. Don't tell me you had to."

"There was no other way, baby. If I don't act now to take advantage of what could be the last opportunity this community—and maybe the human race itself—might ever have, then we may never get another chance of any kind ever again. And if I drop out now, then maybe we postpone my possible death for a few days, or perhaps even a few years, but they'll come for me in the end. They'll come for us both, Stevie. At least this way I got a fighting chance to prevent all that. I'm doing this to protect you, baby. Don't you see that?"

"Oh don't you dare use me as your excuse!" His wife's barbed words were starting to sting now. "You're angry at Monty and the rest of 'em, that's all. And believe me, so am I, along with a lot of other folks around here. But you don't see any of us rushing off to join their stupid fucking games, giving them the very validation they crave in the process, do ya? I mean ... Jesus, Normie, what were you thinking?"

Abner didn't trust himself to speak just then. He bought time by drawing in a few deep breaths on his way to seat himself atop the armrest of his custom black leather recliner. Once there, he stared down his wife, who was refusing to make eye contact with him. Abner outlasted her, and eventually she turned to face him. "I know you don't want to hear it, sweetie, but I do believe, deep in my heart, that I had no other choice," he explained. "I know this is our only way to stop Monty and that Schef bastard's madness." His voice turned both earnest and plaintive, but Stevie turned away from him once more. She began shaking her head rapidly while her knees danced. Clearly, she was bursting at the seams, but she couldn't seem to find the words to properly convey her apparent jumble of emotions. So Abner continued his defense before she could parse through enough of her jumble to reply, "Whether you choose to believe it or not just now, I really did not want to have to challenge. I am not looking forward to having to hurt Polly. I'm still clinging to a hope that she'll withdraw, and we can still work this all out peacefully and sanely. But I do warn you, my love, it is a very small hope. I have to kill a friend soon, and that burden would be a lot easier to carry if you could find your way to seeing the truth and necessity in why I gotta do it."

"I know what you want from me, Abner, but I'm not gonna give it to you," Stevie told him. "I fucking love you, Abbie," Stevie paused to fight back emotional collapse. Then she continued, "I love you so goddamn much, and that is why I can't give you my blessing for this. I won't put on a happy face just so you can feel good about betraying me again."

"Betraying you?" Abner exclaimed in a wounded voice.

"Yes!" She screamed back at him. "You swore to protect me, to spend your life with me, and then, since day one, Abner, you've tried to break that oath. You've run off toward one danger after the other, like you crave it or something. It's a sickness. And you're about to do it again! And you want me to be happy about it! Well, I won't do it. If you love me, you'll abandon this delusion you have that you, and you alone, can save the fucking world. It's egotistical madness, and it's a betrayal of the promise you made to me when you gave me this!" Stevie thrust her left hand towards his face, giving him a good look at her nuptial band alongside her over-sized proposal rock. "You promised to love and protect me when you slid this on my finger, Abner. You promised me. How can you do th— How are you supposed to keep your promise if you are nothing more than ashes by dinnertime?"

Abner had no answer for that. He thought about promising to survive, promising to win, but somehow, he thought the assurances would fall on deaf ears. So he said nothing, only reached out to clasp one of Stevie's shaking hands. When she recoiled from the contact and pivoted on the coffee table, so she was facing completely away from him, he felt his heart physically crack, and a large chunk of it break off and crash to the bottom of the deep, black chasm of his soul. "Don't do this, Stevie, not now," he pleaded in a pathetic voice.

"Say you're staying. Say you'll go nowhere near the Final Tournament, Commander Montrois, Harclay Aponyaschefski or all the others. Say you'll stay beside me and never run off into danger again. You've given your fair share, let other people carry their portion now," Stevie pleaded while still refusing to look at him. "Say all that, and I'll shower you with all the love you crave. Say it, and you'll have all of me forever. We can find a way to let go of the world's big problems together. We can leave them to the next generation. We've given our fair share. It's our turn now to try for the kids that we've only ever dreamed of before. We won't put off our lives any longer. We can live happily in this place, together till the end."

Abner rose to his feet, taking a few drawn out breaths to steel himself for what he feared was going to be the hardest thing he'd ever have to say. "If I don't go through with this, Stevie, *the end* won't be very far off, not for any of us. God forgive me, baby," he said, struggling not to crack up, and failing miserably, "God forgive me, but I have to do this. And I'll just pray that he'll let you see the plain truth of that before too long."

Abner turned to take his first step out of his living room and towards the hatchway when his wife's voice came softly to his ears, halting him in place, "If you step out that door, Abner Hyun, don't bother coming back. Even if by some miracle you survive today, our family dies here and now if you walk out that door. If you leave me all alone one more time to battle the crippling worry and fear over your safety, then I'll know you were never worth worrying over to begin with."

"You don't mean that," Abner said sadly, after a time. He waited for a few silent seconds, but Stevie had no answer for that, beyond a few muffled sobs. Drawing on every last ounce of courage and resolve left to him, Abner Hyun marched, quietly and dejectedly, out of his living quarters. He barely lifted his head the entire hike across the station to the glowing neon orange archway of The Meadow.

CHAPTER 13

Final Tournament: Match 5

"**S**hit, Normie, sure sounds like all these good people don't like you very much. Lord knows they ain't alone in that." Hopkins Masterson delivered his taunt only a few inches from Abner's ear. Regardless of the range of delivery, he still barely heard the snide comment. The noise level inside the massive nature preserve was suffocating, making it hard to focus, much less hear anything. The five security officers encircling him at the center of the black-lined rectangle of the Final Tournament's killing grounds, clutching cudgels of one type or another in one hand and the handle of a pistol in the other, and clad head to heel in semi-automatic weaponry and ammunition, were certainly contributing to his clouded and claustrophobic feeling as well. All of it added up to not caring very much what a fool like Hoppy the Frog—as the officers all called Hopkins Masterson behind his back—might have to say.

Hoppy figured that out after a bit longer than it would've taken most, backing off to reclaim his original position, chock-full of undisguised disappointment over his goading attempt yielding no results. That left Jasper Montrois and Harclay Aponyaschefski as the only other station residents sharing a place alongside Abner inside the intimidating circle of dead-eyed officers, the former being his old friend of more than a decade and countless combat missions, and the latter, a creepy, withered, little, scarecrow-looking, fear-driven, slick-talking country lawyer bound and determined to corrupt all remaining human sanity until everyone was just as fearful and irrational as himself. The security commander stood to Abner's right inside the circle, rigid as a woman in a Victorian-era painting, with arms crossed firm and brow furrowed. While Schef, microphone in hand, hunched slightly at the shoulders as he wheezed and hacked just two feet to Abner's left.

The crowd pressing in close all around them seemed, unbelievably to Abner, even larger than yesterday. He couldn't tell if his mind was just playing tricks on him, or if that were indeed the case. They were definitely loud, Abner knew that much for sure, at the very least. His former squadmates, and that son of a bitch, Aponyaschefski, didn't appear the least bit interested in attempting to calm their unruly fervor either. The security staff had demanded calm obedience from the residents yesterday. Today, however, they appeared content to let the rage steaming off at least half of them continue to scorch Abner's resolve with their scalding spray. He let most such nonsense wash right over him, but the sheer mass and volume of the vitriol couldn't help but wear on his already wounded psyche. Abner knew it wasn't everyone. He knew half the crowd were only there out of fear. Nonetheless, it scared him. It was making it hard to keep up with the brave face and proud shoulders.

Abner could've hopped aboard any one of five trolleys along his way to The Meadow and arrived in a more timely and dignified manner. Perhaps he should have, if only to allow himself more time to stretch out and loosen up, but Abner had needed that long walk across the station. He'd struggled its entire length to find his way to the right headspace for this upcoming bout. By the time he made it to the threshold of The Meadow's dazzling neon-orange archway, he'd been a deal more centered than when he'd first left Stevie in their living quarters, but was far from certain he'd found anything close to the proper state of mind he truly needed.

However, one look at the packed bleachers and surging crowd had forced the appearance of confidence into his demeanor and stride, in spite of his apprehensions. Knowing there was no way out but through, Abner had sauntered past the jostling crowd, and then beyond Dontavious Woodson without even staring at the man's newly crooked nose. Woodson had averted his eyes as soon as he had seen Abner. It was easy enough for the young officer to pull off without seeming petulant, as he had been doing his best to hold back the rowdiest among the rambunctious crowd. His next step after passing Woodson landed him on the close-cropped Bermuda grass of the Final Tournament grounds.

And there he stood at center court, surrounded by a martial ring of his former family and present foes. Abner dug deep within himself for some spark, some flickering ember to reinvigorate his passion and confidence, but with each new second's passing and no intervention from any member of the security staff to quell the crowd's rowdy and contemptuous behavior, Abner felt the confidence drain out of his body language. He couldn't help it. The brave-face-mask had just grown too damn heavy to bear any longer. Schef must've seen it too, for even as Abner watched, the survivor's scowl shifted into a satisfied grin.

Abner was on the point of lashing out. He felt all his grand plans crumbling out from beneath him. *They ain't even gonna let me fight,* he thought with sudden certainty. *Polly ain't even here.* At least, he hadn't seen her yet anyway, although he'd been immediately descended upon by Masterson and the four other encircling officers as soon as he stepped onto the court. She could've been lurking just out of sight this whole time, for all he knew. *More likely though, they're just going to kill me here and now in front of everyone to make a point,* he told himself sardonically.

And just when Abner was on the verge of really starting to believe that to indeed be his fate, Schef finally brought the microphone up to his lips, "Ladies and Gentlemen, my fellow residents, please calm down. Take your seats and let's have quiet, please."

It was eerie how quickly the assembled masses, who only moments before seemed on the edge of riot, complied with that order, for expertly couched with pleasantry or not, it was, in Abner's opinion, still an order. *Maybe they got these people too far under their sway already,* Abner thought in a panic. *Maybe I'm already too late for winning to mean anything. Shut up, Normie, you goddamn panicking POG, get a hold of yourself. There ain't no backing down now. Don't let these guys intimidate you anymore.*

Schef let the silence settle for a few heartbeats before glancing toward Monty. The security commander issued one of his slow and silent nods. Schef instantly brought the microphone back to his lips, "Welcome to Day 2 of the Final Tournament," he said. "We start this morning with a carry-over match from yesterday. Unfortunately, Polly Dobechek's injuries are just far too severe for her to continue in the Tournament any longer."

"What's this now?!" Abner shouted loud enough for the microphone to pick up his voice and amplify it through the speaker out to the enraptured crowd.

Schef treated him with a stink-eye while quickly covering the microphone's windscreen with his free hand, though Abner was finished shouting. With a flare of his nostrils and curl of his lips, Schef seemed to dismiss him as a nuisance before once more raising the microphone. "There is no need for outbursts, Mr. Hyun, we have an opponent for you. One of Polly's true and loyal squadmates has agreed to take up her mantle."

"So you just choose the fighters now?" Abner spoke in a flat, even tone that the microphone was only barely able to pick up. "I thought the fighters are chosen here, in front of everyone. You'd deny the assembled people here today the right to challenge in Polly's place?" Abner figured something like this would happen, in truth, but he felt obligated to object, as it was clear no one else would. The treasonous officers couldn't be allowed to just steamroll the rules of their own damn tournament without any push back. They were already flexing their authoritarian muscles enough as it was.

"You're right, Mr. Hyun. Let's do this properly," Schef said with a condescending sneer. They both knew what was coming, and it seemed Schef was happy enough to play out the charade. "Is there anyone here who would like to replace your heroic champion, Polly Dobechek, and fight this treacherous waste of space before me?" If Schef was hoping for some reaction to the insult, Abner disappointed him. He stayed silent, as did the crowd. They both knew no one would challenge. Every soul present knew a member of the security staff was about to. And they all either knew they couldn't beat any of the officers, or they thought it a bad idea to kill one of them, as it would most likely upset all the others. So there were no declarations of homicidal intent tossed down from any corner of the ever-swelling crowd. "Well, I guess no one else here is interested in challenging," Schef said, still wearing his pompous sneer. "So then, I suppose no one would object to the aforementioned officer taking his sister-in-arm's place in this sacred tournament?" The survivor stared Abner down while shouts of *No*, and *Let them fight*, and dozens of variations of such damning nonsense came rolling down from the bleachers in hoarse waves. Schef raised his arm and the trained sheep immediately quieted back down. "Very well then. Mr. Sarkisian, would you care to come forward and voice your challenge so that all present may hear?"

No, not Eddie, Abner thought in sudden horror. *No, God, tell me I didn't hear that right. He wouldn't. He couldn't. No way he would fight me, after all we've been through*, he reasoned. Then he saw his former teammate, Eddie Sarkisian, the man who'd been alongside him for countless unimaginable horrors over the past few months, the man with whom he'd barely escaped the Damned-infested streets of Millstone West Virginia, edge his way between two of his encirclers.

One was Burger Gregson, who didn't budge his barrel-shaped, 5'9", 280-pound frame a single millimeter to help the would-be challenger squeeze inside the circle. Millicent Dirks, with her scowl failing to draw attention away from a fist-shaped purple and yellow bruise below her pale-blue right eye, was the other, and was a little more accommodating to Eddie's intention. She shifted her stance to a side-on position, allowing Eddie Sarkisian to lean heavily her way and accomplish his squeeze and shimmy into the tight security circle. Unlike the rest of the officers at The Meadow that morning, Eddie was free of tactical gear. He was dressed head to toe in the black Under Armor gym wear issued by AOA to every security officer upon coming aboard Cardinal's Nest. His long, broad feet were encased in black running shoes. Black sweatpants clung tightly to his burly legs, while a black hooded sweatshirt rounded out the ensemble. Each garment was stamped with a small white Under Armor logo and an equally sized AOA insignia, with its trademark maroon As and silver O pressed tightly together in their sixties-sci-fi bold font.

Abner watched on, frozen with disappointment, as Eddie rocked his head back and forth in a pantomime of someone loosening up their neck, never once making eye contact with him. As he stood there, frozen and disbelieving, while he watched his former friend prepare himself to fight him to the death, Abner felt another chunk of his heart crash against his soul's black bottom. *How could it have come to this?* he asked himself. Abner was ready to fight Polly. He'd come to terms with that in his mind. He'd known too that after that fight was won, he would most likely have to face Monty as well, and even though the man had once been his closest and dearest friend, he'd made peace with that eventuality. But for whatever reason, this betrayal that Eddie Sarkisian appeared determined to carry out, felt like a blind-side smash delivered by a full-speed Mack truck.

Maybe they're making him fight me to prove his loyalty, Abner thought with a sudden, desperate hope. *Eddie's no genius, but no one has ever been able to pull the wool over his eyes neither. He wouldn't go along with all this willingly. He's just following the pack, like he's always done. He can't be as much of a zealot as the rest. Maybe this won't be such a bad thing. Maybe I can get him to yield without a fight.* Eddie finished his neck loosening ritual and stepped up alongside Schef just as those hopeful thoughts struck Abner.

His attention was fully on Sarkisian now, as the tall, black-bearded, hawk-faced officer bent down to the microphone. The tone in Eddie's normally smooth and melodic voice quickly disabused Abner of all his hopes about the motivations of his old battle buddy. "I challenge," the officer said, with heartbreaking conviction. "My name is Edward Sarkisian. I will take up my battle-sister Apollonia Dobechek's mantle. For the good of the people of this station, and the very sake of all of mankind, I challenge the traitor Abner Hyun, and do so pledge, with my very life, to make of him an example for all coming time."

The declaration sounded scripted. Surely they were Schef's words in his friend's mouth. However, that certain belief did not lessen their venomous bite. Sarkisian still couldn't bring himself to look him in the eye. Abner wished he knew if it was because Eddie was ashamed of what he was saying and doing or if he was just too disgusted with him to even grant that simple respect. Although Abner supposed it didn't really matter all that much in the end. Regardless of the truth or falsehood of Sarkisian's conviction, they were still going to have to try and kill one another now. Maybe it was better that the man hated him.

Maybe I ought to try and hate him back, he thought, with only partial sarcasm. *It sure would make what comes next a whole lot easier.*

"Very good, Mr. Sarkisian, well said," Schef lauded the recitation after pulling the microphone back. "I take it you understand the Final Tournament's few rules then?"

"I do," was Sarkisian's short and direct response.

"Well then, I suppose we should get to it." Schef turned to face Abner with a mockery of honest sincerity stretched across his features. "If that's alright with you, that is, Mr. Hyun?" He asked with obnoxious sarcasm.

"If we must, Harclay, then let's get on with it." Abner was in no mood to trade banter. He wanted this whole business over and done with.

"Alright then, Mr. Hyun, alright," Schef said, waving the weapons barrel officer to center court.

Dontavious Woodson was the officer who had pulled the dolly duty today. With Alvarez joining Dirks, Masterson, Schwambach, and Gregson in the circle of officers around Abner, Woodson was the only one left to handle the task. Abner realized as he watched Dontavious wheel out the barrel that he should've known Eddie was to be his opponent a whole lot sooner. He wasn't one of his encircling officers, and it had been Woodson who he'd brushed past to get out on the court. Only Sarkisian was left unaccounted for, once you factored in the fact that Polly Dobechek must be laid up in Branch 1's hospital. A part of Abner probably did know his opponent was to be Eddie as soon as he stepped onto the court and the officer's descended upon him, and that only he and Polly's faces were absent from the gathered staff. But some vigilant sanity monitor in his head had not allowed that knowledge to register in Abner's consciousness.

Abner looked around at the crowd, and out of the corner of his eye watched Dontavious Woodson struggle a deal more than Gregson had with the barrel's weight. He might've expected some of the residents to take advantage of the lax security and press closer toward the court. Every armed officer in the station was currently crowded together, yet no one in the packed crowd seemed the least bit interested in challenging the strict rules imposed upon them at the start of yesterday's matches. The officers surrounding Abner did not so much as glance about them. Not one of their eyes ever left him.

Not even Woodson's. His death stare nearly cost the whip-thin, high school long jump champion though. Dontavious lost control of his dolly midway through setting down the barrel, and it snapped free from his grasp, rocking back and forth, the weapons inside clanging with agonizing shrieks against the metal sides. As it teetered on its edge, Dontavious Woodson finally managed to grab hold of its rim and bring it down safely atop the turf. A red blush flushed its way across the dusky skin of Woodson's face, accentuating his busted nose, as he then struggled with prying the dolly out from under the abundantly laden silver death barrel.

"Okay then, combatants," Schef rushed to say, hoping to bring back a previous solemnity, now tarnished somewhat by Woodson's gaffe. "Okay then," Schef added, looking to Monty for a confirming nod and instantly receiving one, "Mr. Hyun, seeing as how our true champion has been forced to step down, we suppose it is only fair to award her challenger first pick," Schef told him before gesturing toward the barrel.

Abner hesitated for a moment, but only a moment. With one mighty breath, he trudged the half dozen yards to the weapons. At first glance it looked to Abner like every tool inside the wicked toolbox was sticky with the blood of his fallen comrades, and the viscous sludge of the squad's countless slaughtered Damned. He gave his head a good, hard shake and shut his eyes. After another deep breath, he peered down once again into the barrel. The red was gone, both the dark and the bright. All that remained were the tools themselves. *The death tools. Which one shall I pick?* He asked himself. *Which of you shall I use to murder my friend?* Abner stared down intently into the barrel but could find no easy answer to that question. One glance back over towards Schef and Monty told him that regardless of the difficulty, he was going to have to come up with an answer real soon. With a half-whimper half-sigh, Abner pulled a war hammer free from the barrel and held it out firm before him. The hammer's shaft was an inch and a half thick at the handle and two and a half feet long in total. Protruding from the slightly tapered end opposite the yellow-taped grip was a coal-black four-inch thick, six-inch long, blunt-nosed steel hammerhead. Jutting out from the back of the hammerhead was a tapering six-inch long steel spike, two inches thick at its base, a quarter-inch thick at its tip, and finished in the same coal-black as its inverse end. *This'll do, I suppose,* Abner cheerlessly thought of the pleasantly balanced killing instrument in his outstretched hand.

"If that's your choice, make your way to your end of the court," Schef shouted at Abner without the use of the microphone.

The survivor kept the black mic tucked close to his leg, and even cupped his free hand around his mouth to ensure his order carried only to Abner. Apparently, he didn't want to air his impatience over the loudspeaker. Abner rolled his eyes at the interceding interloper before striding off towards the end of the court. The war hammer swung freely in his dangling right hand, just inches away from scraping the delicately manicured turf every step of the way. When he finally made it to the boundary line, he turned back to center court just in time to see Schef gesture once more towards the barrel.

Eddie Sarkisian stepped up to the silver barrel with no delay and barely hesitated once alongside it. Abner figured he must've decided on the brightly polished, 6', steel staff with the five-inch, leaf-shaped spear blade grafted to its end before he was even invited to approach the barrel. Eddie slid the weapon free with an elegant, determined sort of grace. The steel sliding out along the barrel's rim sent an eerie ring rippling out. As it washed over Abner, it left in its wake a cold finger of unknowable misfortune tickling slowly up his spine.

As soon as Sarkisian stepped away from the barrel, Woodson quickly set to work reloading it onto his dolly. After a fair bit of effort, he had it loaded up and wheeled back off the court. Once Dontavious Woodson and his taxing load cleared the hallowed boundaries, Schef gestured with overt grandiosity for Sarkisian to take up position at his end of the court. Sarkisian wasted no time in complying with the gesture, sprinting to his end. Once there, he quickly turned away from a knot of residents showering him with praise and admiration. The small group were obviously bound and determined to ingratiate themselves with the security staff. Abner stared the fanatics down for a long moment and soon felt more of his already vulnerable heart crumble off into the black abyss, for, even as he watched, he knew that should he lose, their gross, fawning behavior would quickly become the norm up here. *And that'll only be the tip of the iceberg of indignation, old boy,* Abner thought with ever mounting dread, mixed though with a rising certainty of purpose.

Then Schef's pompous voice drew Abner's attention back to center court, "You both know the rules and have accepted them. In so doing, you have sworn yourselves by your very lives to abide by them. And so, let your battle begin." With those words, the five encircling officers spread themselves out to take up sentry positions around the Final Tournament's boundaries. Schef and Monty, meanwhile, jogged softly to their usual front-row seats. The two spots had been reserved for them somehow, despite any obvious signs to indicate how that feat was accomplished in the face of the eager and ever-growing crowd. *Fear mongering,* Abner dolefully told himself, after small reflection.

It didn't really matter now. Nothing else mattered anymore, not while an armed and cruelly serious Eddie Sarkisian was slogging straight at him across the court. Abner gave his head one last hard shake before snapping into action. He darted to his left, quick as a mouse, heading up court a few yards. Eddie adjusted his march and moved to counter. "This is madness, Eddie," Abner yelled out at him over the surging roar of the crowd. "You have to see that. Are you really going to shove that thing through my heart, my friend? Think about it, Eddie," Abner pleaded while shuffling up court to keep Sarkisian at a safe distance. His once-teammate moved quickly to mirror his shuffle. "Look at what they're asking of you. How many times have I saved your life down there? Christ, how many times have you saved mine? Are you really going to kill me after all that?!" Abner asked in a cracking scream.

"I'm prepared to, Normie," Sarkisian finally responded. "You're asleep, my friend. I ain't gonna let your slumber doom us all. Just hold your tongue now, Normie, and prepare yourself to kill me, 'cause you best believe that's what I'm trying to do to you. There ain't no more warnings, man. That time is all gone now. So just shut up and fight!" Sarkisian darted in to deliver a firm two-handed thrust which Abner was only just able to dodge.

"God damn you for this, Eddie. Fuck you for making me do this," Abner told him between rushed breaths. Eddie's answer came in the form of a berserk roar and spear-led charge. Abner lashed out with a one-handed parry to send Sarkisian's spearhead shooting past him. He added a spin, and then a sprint as well, to gain some ground between himself and Sarkisian. When he looked back, Abner discovered that Eddie had not followed him across court. Instead, the sweat-soaked officer settled himself down to adopt a stalking pose, hunched over at the waist, legs bent slightly with his weight firmly on the balls of his toes, the spear held out before him in a staggered two-handed grip.

Then, slowly, Sarkisian began to make his way to Abner's position, all the while adjusting his angles to try and trap him in a corner. Abner caught onto the tactic quick enough, and with its understanding, came the release of any final lingering inhibitions. Abner snapped into fight mode, into the time-warp, into the battle-inebriation. The time for talking was well and truly done. Abner's warrior spirit understood that fact, if no other part of him did. He let that spirit take over him now. It was like flipping a switch that couldn't be found for the asking but was always right there for the needing.

Abner barged directly at Sarkisian, leading his attack with a wide, looping, one-handed slash of his war hammer to parry clear Eddie's spear darting in to meet him. The momentum of his charge brought Abner crashing into his enemy. He met Eddie with a precisely aimed right shoulder to his foe's sternum that sent Sarkisian sprawling backwards. Abner knew it was a good blow; the air escaping Eddie's lungs in a harsh exhalation could be clearly heard. Plus, he'd seen the look in his eyes as he went ass-over-teakettle, nearly losing his grip on his spear in the process. So Abner charged once again at his slowly recovering opponent as soon as he regained his own footing. Sarkisian was on his knees when Abner got within range to launch a looping slash at Eddie's head with the spike of his hammer. Amazingly, Sarkisian managed to flick his long spear up in time to deflect the mortal blow before it could land. Eddie even used the momentum of the parry to spin to his feet and dart a few yards up court.

Abner was set to charge right after his retreating opponent but held off at the last moment, letting Eddie turn around and square off to face him. Abner started to whirl his war hammer around in his right hand while gesturing with his left for Eddie to charge him. The slowmo battle fever fell over the world like a thick, wet blanket. Abner was able to make out every last wrinkle of tension and spasm of muscle in the face of his enemy fifteen yards across the court, and beyond him another five yards, the faces of the crowd. Each told their own unique story, yet all had one thing in common: they were staring back at him. Then the faces blurred, and his focus resharpened back to the near, pinning the oil-slick, shimmering edge of a spear blade piercing through the air and heading straight for his heart.

Snap. The rubber band of time lurched back to full speed. Abner whipped the war hammer out, catching just enough of the spear shaft to parry the blow. Though perhaps the parry was not truly *enough*, for when Abner looked down at his right arm where Eddie's spear blade had just grazed past, he saw a three-inch tear in his white shirtsleeve. Then, even as he watched, the pristine white fabric of his sleeve surrounding the gash quickly sopped up an ever-spreading red stain. There was no pain. Pain always came later. The battle-inebriation can get you through anything. He tore his eyes from his painless wound to look up at his attacker a few yards in front of him.

Sarkisian was in the process of drawing back the spear for another thrust when, like some god hitting the half-speed button on his DVD-player-of-time's remote control, the wheel stretched its elastic band once again. Abner cared naught for the faces in the crowd this time. No, this time he took advantage of the time warp to launch an offensive of his own. Abner bent down low at the knees and lunged his war hammer out toward Eddie's stomach. Sarkisian went for the feint, abandoning his spear thrust to lash down a quick parry to meet Abner's lunge. But Abner's lunge wasn't there to parry. He had burst firmly off his planted left foot while bringing his war-hammer-wielding hand back up to eye level. Sarkisian had been thrown off balance by the quick change of direction, and it was almost too easy for Abner to then launch back off his now planted right foot and bring the blunt-nosed hammerhead squarely and savagely down atop Eddie's left hand gripping tightly around his spear shaft.

"Aghhhhh!" Eddie cried out over the sounds of a half dozen bones in his hand snapping like dry twigs. He quickly hauled his injured hand out of danger's way, cradling it against his chest. The pain-induced and ill-advised action turned his body so that Sarkisian now had his back to Abner and only one hand left clinging to the long spear, whose blade still dripped with a few small blots of Abner's red blood. Time had snapped back to full speed, but even still, it seemed the simplest thing in the world for Abner to whip a one-handed smash with his war hammer, spike end first, into the small of Sarkisian's back. Abner could feel several of Eddie's spinal discs shatter through the ringing of his war hammer as it pierced his former teammate's flesh. The long spear fell from Sarkisian's hand as slowly and sorrowfully as an ancient redwood felled for kindling. Then his arms went flying up like a man born again along a riverside. The war hammer's spike had sunk three inches deep into Sarkisian's back but came out with only a slight tug when Abner went to pull it free after his friend and teammate crumpled to his knees.

Sarkisian fell flat on his face as soon as the hammer was yanked loose. Abner instantly whipped it back for another blow. *Victory!* His warrior spirit shouted at him. *Quick, claim it while you still can!* He spun the war hammer in his hand as he stepped towards his downed foe. It was already completing its deadly arc just as Abner arrived alongside the head of Eddie Sarkisian, so he wouldn't have been able to stop the blow even if his one-time friend's helpless state had moved him to mercy.

It hadn't done, so whether he could've stopped the blow from landing was irrelevant. In that moment, Abner had only been thinking about victory, about finishing his opponent, about winning. In that moment, he was no better than any of them. In that moment, he was terrible. In that moment, he was vengeful. He was wrath incarnate. In that moment, there was only his hammer and the foe, so that when the war hammer landed on the back of Eddie's skull, it was imbued with enough force to cleave through bone, brains, and blood alike, to crash straight through the woeful face on the other side, and then bury itself two inches into the hard-packed turf of the Tournament grounds.

Abner rose back to full height with deliberate movements, leaving the hammer sunk stiffly in the dirt. He stumbled backwards a few paces once he'd fully stretched back to a standing position, and after regaining solid footing, used his shirtsleeve to clear a blotchy red veil from his blinking eyes. It was then the hideous horn blast of fight's end called out. It served to instantly snap Abner clear of the persisting fog of battle. The mad fever passed, and the rubber band of time suddenly had no tension. With their passing came sudden weariness and pain, both physical and psychological. The lifting of the combat fog laid bare before him the stark reality of what he'd just done, and once Abner's eyes fell to the mangled remains of bloody flesh that had once been Eddie Sarkisian's head, he could not look away again. Reaching across his body with agonizing weariness, he clamped his hand over the still bleeding and sharply painful gash on his right arm, wishing all the while that he could clamp tight the far fiercer pain inside his tortured soul. And when his anguish was utterly impossible to endure another moment, he finally allowed himself to raise his eyes from the gory evidence of his ignominy.

Abner was facing the open end of the bleacher horseshoe, so when his vision cleared, it was that section of silent crowd where his focus landed. And when his oddly vacant mind, apart from shame and guilt, finally caught up with his vision enough to resolve with some lucidity what his eyes were taking in, he wished he'd just kept on staring at the friend he'd dispatched in the most brutal of ways. Unbelievably, Stevie was right there, standing in the front row in the same hastily cobbled together garb she was wearing when he left her. His wife had come, here, to this place. The last thing Abner ever thought to see was Stevie, just one more gawker to the sadistic show, but there she was. His vision was crystal clear now, and there was no denying what he saw. Stevie's face was plain before him, yet also oddly strange in ways. If it was anguished and forlorn when he'd left her this morning, then it was morose and disbelieving now. Their eyes locked across the length of the court for a few horrible seconds. Horrible in that Abner was able to read the anger, disgust, pity, shame, and stupefaction brimming inside those soft blue orbs, and the dreadful knowledge that they would never again look upon him with the same love and adoration they previously bore.

Then a scream drew his eyes from his broken wife's. "I challenge!" Jasper Montrois' shout was so loud it could be heard throughout the entire breadth of that near silent, gargantuan dome. And when Abner's eyes locked with his former commander's, he read in them some of the same emotions Stevie's carried. Fury, rage, stupefaction, and disgust were all plainly there, but a different disgust than Stevie's eyes bore, a disgust rooted in disloyalty and betrayal. Abner knew going in that Monty would most likely challenge him if he defeated his first opponent, and he'd felt sure he could deal with the prospect. He felt no joy in its possibility, but there was a certainty that he would be able to push away the unruly emotions such a bout would stir, and center himself enough to defeat the bigger man. Only now, looking into the eyes of Montrois, as he reiterated his intentions to fight Abner to the death, his certainty crumbled and died. He felt only pure desolation of soul, only utter regret.

It wasn't long before keeping up the eye contact with Monty became intolerable. He turned back to find Stevie, desperate for some spark to burn away his bitter chill. All he saw was her back. She was shoving her way through the still mostly silent crowd standing in a dense pack at the end of the bleachers. Abner watched as his wife made her exit, rooted to the ground beneath him, frozen by surreal circumstance.

Then, only moments after she melted into the crowd and disappeared from his sight, the derisive jeers started raining back down on him in fits and starts. Although, once the taunts got going, they seemed to carry a thousand times more passion and acrimony than they had pre-fight. Abner never heard a word of it though. He did feel the rage thick in the air around him and saw the vehemence in many of the faces in the crowd, but Stevie and shame, and Eddie and shame, and shame, and shame, and shame were all that occupied his consciousness. He wept then, falling to his knees. And after the tears came the vomiting. All the pent up bile of pure misery spewed out like a firehose. And when his stomach was empty, and the gagging had ceased, he raised his eyes to the shimmering heavens hanging just above the bright dome. He searched desperately, but in the end could find no comfort in the endless promises there.

With a sudden lurching jump, Abner clambered back to his feet. A new kind of madness had him then. Not a battle madness, but rather a madness of misery. And without really knowing what he was doing or saying, he began to shout into the roiling cacophony, "Stevie! Stevie! Wait! Stevie!" The crowd started to hush a notch with each new shout. "Stevie, wait! I'll forfeit. I will! I'll forfeit! Stevie, please! I'll forfeit! I will! I– I– I do! Yes, I do!" In his new madness, he'd made the sudden decision, though it was the antipathy of a resolve he'd held iron-firm only minutes earlier. Abner turned to direct his next shouts at his friend of countless years and missions, "I forfeit. I yield to you. No more, Monty. Let it end. I forfeit!" He shouted out into the now whisper-proof silence the two words he thought to never say back-to-back. Then he threw down his war hammer to erase any lingering doubts about his intentions.

"You don't get to just kill Eddie and walk away!" Pedro Alvarez' shout came from only five yards behind him, but in the fresh silence of The Meadow, and with the amount of rage and animus with which it was spoken, along with the sheer ear-piercing decibel of the shout, he'd have heard it from 500 yards. Abner didn't turn to face his enraged former squadmate though. He lacked the will to even make the attempt. "Don't you let him, Monty!" Alvarez demanded of his commander.

"You think we're letting you leave here on your feet, you fucking traitor?!" Abner kept his head and eyes downcast but knew the angry question had come from the gravelly voice of the lantern-jawed Officer Steve Schwambach, whom he'd elbowed in the head only a few hours earlier during his escape from the rec room.

Then, in no time flat, he was hearing similar shouts from all six members of the security staff present. Only their commander remained silent amongst them. The crowd kept its hush as well, eager to hear every word of the drama playing out before them. Abner kept his eyes firmly on the ground at his feet. The weight of his shame was too great to even lift his head, much less respond to the taunts and demands to fight from his former colleagues. Abner never saw it, with his head down, but he assumed Monty must've raised his hand for silence because the outraged shouts of his one-time fellow officers quickly died away. Then he heard Monty's voice once more, "We swore to abide by the rules of this tournament, my friends. In those rules, a man has a clear right to forfeit. So we shall honor Abner's request."

A fragile hush held sway in The Meadow after those words. Until Schef shattered it, "Then we have a champion!" His voice carried a cheer that felt grossly out of place. "Ladies and Gentlemen, I give you the victor of the Final Tournament." Schef and Monty had left their front-row seats during the chaos at fight's end, and when Abner finally worked up the courage to raise his head again, he found them standing a few feet apart from each other, and only a half dozen yards from where he stood with rigid dejection. Even as he watched, Schef gestured towards Monty with the flair of a circus ringmaster.

Monty did not at all seem pleased with the gesture, however. He seemed determined to continue with solemnity, for the sake of the fallen Eddie Sarkisian, and the bubbling rage of his officers, if nothing else. "We have not called for a challenger yet, Harclay," he scolded the survivor.

"Right," Schef said, trying to recover some of his dignity in the face of the withering look Monty had fixed upon him. He pulled out his microphone from a back pocket and flipped it on, "Well then, do we have a challenger for Commander Montrois? Or can we end this unfortunate but sacred tournament and rest easy in the knowledge that the best man among us is set to take the reins of power, set to steward humanity until we may be once again free to flourish back in our hallowed garden we call Earth? Shall I raise the arm of Jasper Montrois so that we may all return to our critical duties?"

Schef made a big show of spinning around after that and pretending to seek for a raised hand of challenge in the encircling crowd. After all 360 degrees were completed, he brought the microphone back up to lips stretched tight in the smarmiest of grins. But before he could speak, a slightly wavering voice called out from the crowd, "That's all I want, Mr. Aponyashcefski. That's all any of us truly want: to end this farce." the voice grew in confidence with each word. Abner turned to the voice's source and saw Dr. Perry Sagal step down from the righthand set of bleachers and stride with a mixture of weariness and determination onto the court.

"Well," Schef began slowly, "let this *farce*, as you name it, end then. Step off the court, Dr. Sagal. Speeches are only going to delay the process."

"If only words could find their rightful power up here, I would never stop speaking. But all my pleas have fallen on deaf ears, Mr. Aponyaschefski, sad to say. So I won't waste anymore on long speeches here."

"Then what is it you want, doc?" Schef asked with impatience.

"To challenge, of course," Perry Sagal answered bluntly. The entire crowd released a collective gasp with that answer. Abner would've joined them, had he the power to break free of his frozen stupor to say or do anything. Instead, he could only look on while Sagal continued, "I don't want this, Mr. Aponyaschefski, don't misunderstand me, but you know as well as I do, at least on some level, that you and Monty are too damaged to bear this responsibility. Your propaganda is strong, sir, no doubt about it. Some of it is even true too. We are humanity's last hope, for instance, and we do need to endure up here. But *together,* good sir. You are a quintessential fascist, Mr. Aponyaschefski. You've turned people's fears into a stepping stone for your own aggrandizement. And so, I have to stop you."

"It's not I who's won here today, Dr. Saga—"

"Don't pretend like you didn't organize this whole thing to end just like this," Sagal interrupted the survivor. "You've gotten just what you've wanted since the day you stepped aboard Cardinal's Nest. I'm not about to just roll over for you like all the rest of my fellow residents."

Schef had no answer for that. He fought for one, that was plain, but after a few seconds of attempting responses only to stop them stillborn, he shook his head in bafflement. It was Monty who answered the doctor, "Please don't do this, Perry," he said with obvious despair.

"Spare me it then, Jasper," Sagal responded in a now unwavering and crisp voice. "Forfeit now, and let's end this. You and I can set this right. Yield to me, and I'll make sure there is no retribution for any of this. We can get back to the work of saving the goddamn world."

"They killed my wife and daughter, Perry! As well as the rest of the fucking world. They are a cancer. I can't let you give them back their power." There was only unabashed commitment in Monty's deep voice as he answered the doctor. "If you want to go through with this challenge, you will have to fight me, my friend, and I will not hold back."

"This is all your choice, Monty, all your doing, not mine," Sagal answered.

Suddenly, Abner's stiff, frozen limbs thawed enough to allow him to rush over to Sagal's side. "Don't do this, doc," he whispered to Sagal in a hurried voice once there. "Trust me, it's wrong. There's no winning here."

Sagal broke off his eye contact with Monty to glance over at Abner clutching tight to his arm. "That may be," he agreed, "but we've come too far to turn back now."

"Dad?!" A young voice called out into the hushed atmosphere. Abner and Sagal both turned to the spot in the bleachers the doctor had come from to see Maisie, Perry's daughter and Stevie's fast friend. But the contented smile that Abner was used to seeing was nowhere to be found. Her face was a mask of panic and confusion. Abner turned back to Perry to watch him treat his daughter to a sad smile.

It seemed that was all the reassurance she would receive, for the doctor then quickly turned back to stare Abner square in the eyes, "If we don't face down these fascists here and now, then we are lost forever, Abner," Perry told him. "*You* have ensured it's come to that, and now you've lost the spine to see the thing through to the end. So I must." Sagal strode away from Abner, leaving him alone once more with nothing but the heavy, crippling weight of shame.

Sagal slowly marched his way towards Schef and Monty standing now at center court. Abner stayed where he was, and though the crowd was still mostly silent, Monty spoke to Sagal in such a low whisper that Abner was unable to clearly hear. He didn't really need to though. It was plain what was happening. The pleading and cajoling were evident as gravity. Sagal remained unmoved, however. He barely responded to Monty's gestures and articulations, only nodded his head now and again in a repeated confirmation of his intentions.

Finally, Monty threw up his hands and seemed to wash them clean of Sagal. He ripped the microphone from Schef, bringing it to his scowling lips. "It seems we have a challenger," he said. "But I do not believe the man to be in his right mind, and so, our fight will be postponed for today. We will resume again in the morning, unless the good doctor comes to see the light, that is."

The crowd let out a mixed groan of frustration and confusion. Sagal spoke loud enough for Abner to hear him over the groaning, "Are you free to bend the rules as you like? Are my fears well founded? Have you all been rigging this tournament all along to give yourselves power over the rest of us?" He continued, not allowing Monty a chance to answer any of the allegations. "If so, have the courage to admit it, and we can end this mockery. I'll withdraw my challenge, and we can all face our new realities and go from there. So go on and admit it, if that's truly what this whole *Final Tournament* bullshit was for." Monty seemed too angry now to answer, while Schef seemed cowed out of speech all together. "Or do you really intend to stay true to the oaths you say you've all sworn?" Sagal shouted the question loud enough for all the officers on sentry to clearly hear. "Will you truly respect the authority of the champion? If you all reaffirm your sworn oaths once again, here and now, I will accept that, for I do, in my heart, believe you all to still be honorable men and women. Swear your oaths before all these assembled residents, and I'll agree to the rescheduling of our match for tomorrow."

Monty was first to comply. "You have my oath, Doctor," he said with his eyes locked on the unwavering Sagal. Alvarez was next to supply his oath. Then Schef, even though he was no true officer. The five remaining officers quickly followed suit. Sagal simply nodded once at Monty after the last of his officers' oaths faded from the air. Without a glance in Schef's direction, the doctor then turned on his heels and marched off the court. Abner watched him all the way, wanting desperately to run to the man and shake sense into him, as no one was able to accomplish for him, but the crippling weight of copious shame once again had him fixed firmly to his place upon the killing grounds. So instead, Abner Hyun did nothing as the dead-man-walking rushed past the crowd, across the footbridge and through the neon-orange archway of The Meadow.

CHAPTER 14

PERRY

Alice Stark pulled him along with a firm grip of his hand. She'd grabbed hold of Perry as soon as he'd turned onto Alleyway XI in Orange Corridor. The auburn-haired greenhouse tech had been propped up with her back against the interface censor of one of AOA's Holographic Interface Information Kiosks. The alleyway had been all but empty so no one else was witness to the faux pas, though Perry was certain they wouldn't have given one shit about Alice's obstructive perch. With AOA locked out of their own system, there wasn't any information in the kiosks to access. The bulky machines had been reduced to nothing more than expensive obstacles in the flow of pedestrian traffic, so when Perry had turned the corner onto Alleyway XI, Alice was in such a position that she was unable to miss him, and as soon as she saw him, she'd taken solid hold of his hand.

She hadn't let go yet. Without a word spoken between them, Alice had laced her soft and stubby fingers, tipped in perfectly manicured, brightly colored, inch-long fingernails around Perry's long, skinny, and sweaty digits. Then, with a tug of his arm, she'd started marching towards Annex VI, and Alleyway XII beyond, where the Sagal's domicile was carved neatly into a bend halfway down the winding alleyway. Perry hadn't argued with her. He let Alice lead. The view of her soft, curvy body beneath tight black joggers and a delicate floral-print blouse made surrendering to Alice's shepherding a rather rewarding decision in the end. But now this goddess of a

Sherpa had guided him to the summit. They stood before his living quarters hatchway. Alice still had a firm grip of his hand, and after Perry had paused in silent reflection for a long enough time outside the door to annoy her, she gave the hand clasped within her own a good, stiff shake.

"What?" Perry mumbled. "Huh?"

"The door, Perry," Alice told him in exasperation.

What she wanted from him did register in Perry's mind, but somehow, he still found himself frozen in place. Alice gave up and released her grip of his hand as she threw both of hers into the air. "Step back," she told him.

Perry complied and Alice stepped up to the keypad. She punched in the code with no delay. Perry was left wondering how she knew it while the automatic door swooshed open. Alice reached back for his hand once again to pull him through the open portal, and a sudden memory of a late night, a bottle of the priest's harsh wine and a few whispered promises exchanged while entangled in each other's arms came flooding back to him. It was that night that he'd given the sweet, rosy-cheeked, thick-legged and firm breasted cherub now leading him into his own home the code to these living quarters. Perry shook his head in light exasperation at the recollection. Alice could talk him into anything, it seemed. *And boy has she.* Memories of ecstasy and opprobrium swam in on that thought's tide.

Alice had become as much his shame as she was his joy now. What they had been doing to Helena was cruel and reprehensible, but every time he saw Alice, every time she held her soft, smooth hand in his, he could hardly resist the pull to have her, to be with her, to be in her, and right now was certainly no exception. Alice let go of his hand once the hatchway had swished closed behind them. She turned back to the keypad set in the wall and started to quickly dial in some protocols Perry had never seen anyone use before. "What are you doing?" he asked as she turned back to face him.

"Locking the hatchway so nobody's code can open the door," she responded before going about his residence and shouting his son's name. It didn't take her long. Perry's living quarters were just like all the others, in both dimensions and layout. Only a few knick-knacks here and there, and a dozen or so framed photographs scattered on surfaces, and hung from the walls, along with the antique cher-rywood rocking chair that had belonged to Perry's mother let you know it was the Sagal residence. When Alice was satisfied with the negative result, she walked back down the cramped passageway leading to the bedrooms to where Perry now stood in the middle of his living room.

"What are you doing?" He asked the same stupid question again.

"Making sure no one is here," she told him, still darting glances into the living quarter's shadowed corners.

"No one's here," he assured her. "Elias is with a couple I know down the alleyway that didn't attend the tournament. I dropped him off on my way and told him to stay till I came to pick him up. I only wish I could've forced Maisie to stay with friends so easily."

"Right, Maisie," Alice remembered. "She's probably on her way here now, isn't she?"

"Probably," Perry guessed. "I left the goddamn place in a big hurry, and I'm a little ashamed to admit that I kinda forgot I brought her in the first place. Jesus, I hope she's okay. I hope those bastards didn't take her or anything, God forbid. I'll never fucking forgive myself if some-thing happens to her ... or Elias."

"Then we don't have much time."

"Time for what? "Perry was treated to a side-eye capable of melting stone after that question. Alice reached a hand up to Perry's cheek, and as he gazed down past her tortoiseshell glasses and deep into her swirling green eyes, all the tumult of his recent choices and slim future melted away, leaving only a burning desire to take her into his arms.

"Time to be together, before it's too late," she told him.

Perry was helpless then. He bent to kiss her soft, moist lips and taste the wet and longing tongue within. Bringing his hands up, he placed them to either side of her gorgeous, round face, cupping her warm, rosy cheeks ever so softly. Alice wrapped her arms around him, pulling him tight against her voluptuous frame. Her lips left his, and slowly began working their way down his neck. Each kiss upon his throat elicited a new chill. Unfortunately, one such shook free a treacherous thought. At first, he tried to ignore it; he fought it, but even-tually it completely removed him from the passion of the moment.

So he gently pulled away from the much shorter woman to stare down into her eyes, and while the madness of courage lasted, asked a question, fearing the answer. "Is this all just some attempt to guilt me into yielding tomorrow?"

"What?" Alice asked with light indignation. "How could you ask me that? You know me better than that by now, don't you?"

"I'm sorry, it's just … this is wrong, and you've always felt guilty before and afterwards. We've only ever stumbled drunkenly into this before, and now you're all over me with no reservation, and I… I–"

"We don't have time for all of that now, Perry," Alice interrupted him. "Your daughter is probably on her way right now, along with lord knows who else. I didn't come to find you to try and talk you out of challenging tomorrow. I know you made the right choice, despite how scary a prospect it is for me. I know too that you are the best man here among all of us for stepping up and making that choice, and I know you deserve a reward for it, and I want to give it to you, while I still can, for myself as well as you." Alice placed her hands on Perry's cheeks. "I love you, Perry. I know that now in spite of how much I hate myself for betraying Elle, even though she is turning into a fucking *hard line party member* right before my eyes. But you see, none of that baggage prevents me from feeling for you the way that I do. So before it's too late, I want to be with you. I want you inside me at least one last time." Alice slid her soft hands up the front of Perry's untucked shirt with that plea. Her long nails scraping across his torso left goosebumps in their wake.

In heartbeats, Perry's shirt was completely off, as well as Alice's shoes, bra, blouse, and pants. They moved in tandem steps to the navy-blue couch in the corner of the living room, their bodies pressed firmly against one another, their arms roaming every surface of their partner's pale flesh. Alice shoved him down and jumped atop him, straddling his legs and pressing her exposed soft, yet gratifyingly firm breasts full in his face. Perry slowly shook his head back and forth, rubbing the skin of Alice's tits against the rough skin of his nose and cheeks. Then he began working his way with soft, wet kisses towards her dark pink nipples. As he took each one in his mouth and swirled his tongue around their budding tips, he felt them grow stiffer and stiffer with each wet circuit.

Alice screamed then, the pleasure of the act causing a sensitivity too great to sustain. Perry raised his head from those heavenly pillows and Alice dropped her lips down upon his. They kissed with an urgent, mad sort of passion while Alice used her hands to unzip Perry's jeans and pull out his fully stiff manhood. She kept one hand gliding up and down on him while using her other to pull her panties to the side and expose her glistening wet sex. Still maintaining a passionate kiss, Alice slid herself down him and the two of them broke off their kiss to gasp in unison. Perry brought his hands up to cup her glorious breasts as Alice squeezed firm around his cock, sliding slowly up and down its length. She threw her head back, fighting to suppress a scream. Perry reveled in a grin when he saw Alice's face etched in exultation.

That slice of Eden may have lasted for minutes, or perhaps only seconds even, but never before had a more satisfying and unifying event ever happened in Perry Sagal's life. Even with his late wife, Perry had never felt so alive, so connected to every fiber of himself. When the pinnacle of his pleasure finally burst upon him, Perry felt a supreme gratitude just to be alive and able to experience such bliss. It was only a few moments later, as Alice rested atop him, with their hearts beating out a fast and simultaneous rhythm, that his joy at being alive turned to ashes in his mouth. He remembered then what he had sworn to do tomorrow, and he feared. He feared to never again share another perfect moment like this with Alice. He feared to lose her ... and Maisie, and Elias, and ... his life. *God get me through tomorrow's fire,* he thought, feeling like a pretender, only believing when convenient. He felt entirely undeserving of any special attention from a benevolent and just god. The soft, sexy, half-naked and fully-married woman in his arms cried out testimony to that truth.

Then the hatchway hailing bell chimed its deep, sonorous song three times. With each new chime, Perry and Alice gripped each other all the tighter. "Shit," Perry finally said, uselessly.

Alice snapped into motion in the blink of an eye. She rolled from atop him while simultaneously snatching tissues from a box of Kleenex off the end table. Once back to her feet, and as gracefully, and with as much dignity as was possible, she used the tissues to wipe clean his warm white seed from her inner thighs. The sight brought to Perry a wave of both hope and shame, in equal measures. It distracted him from attending to his own redressing.

The greenhouse tech was already back in her pants and shoes, fluffing out her blouse to pull back over her head, by the time Perry finally got himself tucked away and back into his long sleeve heather-gray and soft-purple Northwestern University t-shirt. He glanced her way once his head was through his shirt and instantly knew she wasn't pleased with his lackadaisical effort. Alice waved her arm toward the hatchway with impatience. Perry quickly got the message and ran his fingers through his hair and beard stubble on his way to unlock the hatchway.

Once there, he paused, unsure of how to accomplish the feat exactly, as the hailing bell sang out its ominous sound once more. Perry made a quick decision to not bother Alice with asking how to undo her magic. Instead, he simply did, in reverse order, what he'd seen Alice do when they'd first entered. And his skill of recall, it seemed, was just as sharp as ever; the door swooshed open in the instant after he smashed down the final key.

Maisie dashed inside just as soon as the gap was wide enough to fit her short and graceful frame. And before Perry could form the words of greeting, Helena Heathcoat stepped in right after her. "Helena?!" Alice exclaimed with barely suppressed shock. "What are you doing here?"

"Funny, Alice, my darling, that was about to be *my* question," Helena said in a voice full of equal parts righteous fury and heart-breaking knowledge. "Tell me, *sweetie*, why was the hatch locked?"

Perry figured Helena's black turtleneck and matching skinny jeans were a hint to a dark mood. Alice must've picked up on that as well, or it could've been one of the hundred other clues Helena was currently supplying. But judging by her dismayed face, Alice knew damn well Helena Heathcoat was not happy. Alice could only splutter when she tried speaking. Perry watched her for a few nerve-racking seconds. She only spluttered more. He could tell she was struggling desperately to not adjust her tossed and wrinkled clothing. Maisie saved them all by suddenly sprinting to Perry, burying her head in his chest and wrapping her arms snugly around him. "What the hell, dad?!" She cried in a muffled voice. "What were you thinking?"

"I had to, baby. I'm so sorry for leaving you there," Perry told her in a soothing voice.

"Well, Alice," Helena prompted in a tone unmoved by sentiment, "have you got nothing to say?"

"Nothing to say about what, Elle?" Alice managed to ask.

"Just what in the hell are you doing here, Alice?!" Helena shouted the question in a way that made it plain she knew damn well what. "It's plain enough what *I'm* doing here: I'm looking for you!" She shouted, marching further into Perry's quarters toward the edge of the living room where Alice currently stood.

"I heard about Perry challenging, that's all," Alice reassured her wife.

"Perry?" Helena picked out the use of his first name to battle over.

"Dr. Sagal," Alice conceded. "I heard that he had challenged, and that they were postponing the fight until tomorrow. Then I ran into him in the alleyway, and I figured a lot of people would probably end up meeting at his living quarters anyway, so I just decided to walk with him the rest of the way."

"You just happened to be walking around in some back alleyway in Orange Corridor, two corridors over from our place in Blue?" Helena was having none of it. "And that doesn't explain the locked hatch."

"Can we discuss marital squabbles at a different time?" Maisie asked before Alice could answer.

"Maisie!" Perry scolded his daughter with empty sincerity.

"I'm sorry, ladies," Maisie directed her response to the wives, "it's just ... I'd kinda like to have some time with my dad before he goes and fights a former friend to the death. So if you could just take whatever *this* is elsewhere, I'd really appreciate it," she ended, bold as you please.

"Maisie!" Perry shouted at her again, not knowing what else to do.

"I'm sorry, Dad, but you and I gotta talk," his daughter informed him.

"It's okay, Perry," Alice said. "We'll go. You're right, Maisie. You deserve alone time with your father. Helena and I are sorry for bringing our business into your home. Aren't we, Elle?" Alice asked her wife with a scowl.

"Yeah," Helena conceded after a time. "Sorry for barging in on you like this, Doctor ... I guess."

"It's nothing at all, Helena. I appreciate yours and Alice's concern, and I'll take comfort into tomorrow knowing you two are pulling for me," Perry told his lover's wife, somehow managing to keep his face from cracking out in guilt.

Clearly Helena didn't know what to say to that. She just nodded a couple times after a few seconds and turned to her spouse, "You ready then?"

Before Alice could reply, the hailing bell chimed out yet again. Maisie was closest to the hatchway. She spun around and smashed the open key. She didn't need to undo Alice's magic, as Perry had; the lock was off now, and the door instantly swooshed open. With no audible invitation or welcoming gesture, Father Boyd strode into Perry's quarters. Two steps into the foyer, and in popped Dolly Duchesne just behind him, with her goofus of a husband Gabe in tow. Maisie threw up her hands in surrender. She instantly switched to host-mode and began ushering the newcomers toward the dining room. "Come on, people," his daughter spoke out in a commanding voice. "I guess there's no getting rid of ya, so we'll gather in the dining room, and maybe together we can figure out just how big a bone-head my father truly is."

The priest chuckled a little at that, allowing himself to be led by the arm. Perry stayed rooted to his spot for a good few seconds, just watching his daughter take charge of the room, so he was still in the foyer when Alice and Helena attempted their quick getaway. They stood no chance; Dolly Duchesne spotted them right away. She broke off from her stroll to the dining room to turn back and accost the two women, "Hey, where you gals headed? You need to help us speak some sense to this fool," Dolly said, pointing with a thumb in Perry's direction. "Or at least help me to understand the fool's reasoning."

"Oh, we were gonn–" Helena began.

"You're right, Dolly," Alice interjected. There was a sudden defiant brightness in her gentle face that hadn't been there only a moment before. "I think I kinda see Perry's point ... a little ... maybe, but some chit-chat with you and Gabe, and maybe a bottle of wine, will surely help me understand it all a little easier."

"Maybe two bottles even," Dolly added with a laugh.

Helena had a look of pure loathing on her face, but Perry was wearing a wide smile. *I should've told her I loved her too,* he thought, wistfully remembering Alice's watery green eyes churning like storm-tossed seas and shimmering before him as lodestars to his soul while she admitted her true affections. Before Helena could quell her rage enough to articulate some excuse for ducking out, Alice grabbed her by the forearm and pulled her bodily towards the dining room. After that, it was only Perry left in the entry of his domicile. He took advantage of the momentary solitude to shake loose his pent-up jitters. From head to heel, Perry twitched every muscle of his every limb for a few seconds. Finally, one last deep breath, and he headed toward the dining room. And for every single step of the short distance, Perry fluctuated from confident to surely incompetent.

As he crossed his dining room's threshold, a grin born of sheer discomfort stretched its treacherous tentacles across his burning face. He gazed down at his antique oak dinner table. The table was so large it left little space to maneuver around the massive piece of furniture. All his uninvited guests had taken up residence in one of the eight oak chairs staggered around the heirloom. Maisie sat at the table's head, directly across from where Perry now stood. To her left, sat Dolly Duchesne, while her disheveled husband slouched to Maisie's right. The priest left a chair's gap between himself and Dolly. Across from him, Alice sat with a mask of normality pulled down her face. Her wife sat to her right, brooding.

Maisie gestured to the chair directly across from her own at the table's opposite end. Perry complied with the invitation, all the while trying not to let Maisie see him smile, for Perry understood he ought to be upset with her presumption over these past few minutes. Try as he might though, he just could not bring himself to feel anything other than pride at what a unique and strong-willed person his daughter had become. She was going to be a fine woman someday, that was for sure. *Joan would've been so proud.* Carried on the tails of that thought were a thousand bleak avenues Perry definitely did not have the time to go strolling down just now, so he pulled himself away from them by posing Maisie a question. "Have you offered everyone refreshments yet, sweetheart?"

"No, Dad," Maisie answered, her hazel eyes dancing in the light of the modern art globe chandelier hanging three feet above the antique table. "We just sat down before you finally decided to grace us with your presence. I haven't had time yet." She pushed to her feet and gazed around the table, "May I get anyone a refreshment? Coffee, perhaps?"

"No need, Mais," Father Boyd spoke up. "I brought a bottle." He leaned back to unzip his gray hooded windbreaker and pull out a one-time two-liter bottle of some kind of soft drink, but which was now chock full of the priest's famous dark red wine. He withdrew the bottle with such ostentatious flair that Perry was afraid the old, recycled bottle might crack when he seemed about to bring it slamming down on the tabletop, but the fallen priest halted the slam at the last instant to rest the bottle gently down in front of him. "We probably will need some glasses though," the priest allowed.

Maisie twisted in place, heading for the kitchen behind her with a wry grin of her own plain on her face. A silence hung over the crowded room at her departure. So much so, Perry was sure he could hear his analog clock, mounted on the wall of his living room, ticking each second away with painful lethargy. He decided, about fifteen seconds in, to just plaster a knowing grin to his face—nothing too flashy or arrogant—and to, most importantly, avoid eye contact with Helena Heathcoat at all costs. Then, returning from the kitchen after what seemed an eternity, like the first flower of spring, Maisie reappeared with eight glasses, a lightness of foot, determination in her eyes and a wise smirk on her lips.

Maisie handed out the goblets as Gabe Duchesne broke the silence, "So just what in the hell makes you think you can beat Montrois, doc? What makes you think you belong anywhere near the same freaking league as that dude?"

Dolly groaned at her husband's impertinence, but Perry raised a hand to calm the cheerfully sweet, soft-edged woman. Then he turned to face Gabe opposite her, "I have faith in myself, as well as my cause."

"Faith?" Gabe asked with utter condescension.

"Faith can move mountains, Gabriel," Perry said, not fazed by Gabe's mocking tone. "I know I'll win because I have to. There was hope, so long as we stayed united, of not indulging in the security staff's sick tournament, but Abner Hyun, God love him, destroyed that hope. He played their game and legitimized it. I was there, Gabe, you, and a few of you others weren't. The people have lost themselves, completely. Well, enough of them anyway. They bought the product Aponyaschefski, and Montrois, and the rest of the aptly abbreviated *SS* have fed them. They've swallowed it whole, my friends. They can't spit it up now, they'll gag. It's staying down. They belong to this dirty plan to install a medieval dictator with their whole hearts. But that belief, burning in the minds of so many of our fellow citizens, is both the thing we have to fear most—now that Hyun has burned our bridge of appealing to them through morality and reason—yet it is also now our one key to ending all of this. The champion of the Final Tournament must be obeyed, or their entire belief system crumbles from the inside. The fires of belief will all be extinguished if they fail to commit to the hell pact they've all sworn themselves to. And that fire is all they've got now. It's immoral and destructive, and clinging to it burns up all the rest of yourself, until the fire is all you are. Winning this tournament is all there is left to us now. Those people there today, my friends, I looked in their eyes; the fire has already consumed them. Abner pushed the balance over the edge. I had to challenge."

"Okay," Gabe didn't back off his condescending tone in the least, "What makes you think they'll stop rolling trained and experienced close quarters combat warriors out, one after the other, to challenge you in the one-in-a-million chance that you actually defeat Montrois?"

"Gabe!" Dolly said, scolding her husband, much the same way Perry had scolded Maisie just a few minutes earlier. "You don't gotta sound like such an ass to him, for cripe's sake. And sit up straight in that chair, you freaking bum!" She finished with an undeniable finger-wag. Gabe sat up straight then, albeit with a grumble.

"It's a fair question, I suppose, Dolly," Perry broke in. "The reason I think the nightmare scenario your husband just laid out won't happen is simple: they don't have the men."

"There are eight of 'em!" Gabe shouted at him like he was an idiot. "Once Polly Dobechek recovers, that is," he added in a half mumble.

"Yes, there are eight of them, but there are a whole hell of a lot more of the rest of us: 487, if I'm remembering correctly," Perry spoke now in his lecturer voice. "That's a lot of people to keep under control, even with all the guns in the world. Eight people only have eight trigger fingers, after all. They're only able to keep a relative order around here now because of the distraction of the Final Tournament. Once that's over, they'll have a problem on their hands. They can't afford any losses, the way I see it. I'm sure that's why Commander Montrois challenged in the first place. They can't risk losing any more officers, so they sent out their best fighter to end it. If I beat him—no, *when* I beat him—the other officers will, of course, want to take retribution, but I have a strong feeling they'd find out soon enough what a bad idea that would be."

Everyone had a full glass of the priest's wine by that point, apart from Maisie. Though she had brought herself out a glass, the priest was wise enough not to fill it in front of Perry. Boyd raised his filled glass to his lips and gulped down a long swig. It drew the attention of the table. When he brought the glass down, his upper lip was smeared with red. Using the sleeve of his windbreaker to wipe it away, he began to speak, "*Whatever thou doest, do it in conjunction with this, the being good, and in the sense in which is properly understood to be good. Keep to this in every action. Do not have such an opinion of things as he who does thee wrong, or such as he wishes thee to have, but look at them as they are in truth.*"

"Is that from a book of the New Testament, Father?" Alice asked the priest after a short, confused silence had taken hold.

"It's Marcus Aurelius. From Book Four of his Meditations," the priest answered in an oddly indecipherable tone before taking another swig of wine.

"Well, what the hell is it supposed to mean?" Gabe asked with impatience and revelatory ignorance.

"It means, we can't beat them by playing their game," Boyd said looking directly over at Perry now. "Not when their game is immoral. There is no way it won't corrupt you, doc. Just look how fast it took that understanding to dawn in Abner's head today, after he brutally murdered a man he had called a dear friend only days earlier."

"The road to hell is paved with good intentions, Daddy," Maisie told him before Boyd could speak.

"Precisely," the pompous heretic quickly concurred with Maisie, wearing the look of a proud mentor.

Perry's anger flared and nearly showed itself on his face, but at the last moment he calmed himself with a certainty, *He hasn't taken her from me. Maisie has always had her own convictions. In Father Boyd, she's merely found an echo chamber.* Perry loved Maisie's brilliance and steadfast morality, but he knew he had to stick by his convictions, no matter how proud his eldest child made him. So after a small sip of sour wine, he posed the priest and his daughter a question, "We just do nothing then?" After they stayed silent for a beat too long, he pressed, "Is that what you are proposing? We just let them loose to do as they please around the station, and to all of us?'

"I simply submit that it is better to do nothing than to do the *wrong* thing," Boyd once again used that even tone. "There is always tomorrow, after all. Despots never last long. I suggest we simply bide our time, doc."

Perry swallowed back anger before responding, "Well, I'm sorry, Boyd, but your way is bound to get good people killed, or worse. You better believe these guys will be coming for their retribution once this tournament is over. Retribution against me, most likely, and my family, not to mention every other resident who hasn't burned up their humanity over the poison pyre of Aponyaschefski's unrighteous cause. I am not going to let all that happen while we wait around with our thumbs up our butts for some perfect option. I'm sorry, Boyd, but I have to go through with this."

"I said nothing about *perfect options*," the priest showed the first hints of emotion in his voice. "I'm just saying that choosing an immoral path, no matter how noble the reasons, is always a bad decision."

Perry almost told him to stuff it up his ass. He almost told him he was a drunk fraud who didn't know what the hell he was talking about. He almost screamed a hundred things, but in the end, Perry Sagal took a deep breath and simply cracked a black-humored joke, "I think you just don't believe I can beat him, father."

Boyd had his glass to his lips for another sip just then and choked back a bit of the sour red as a laugh struck him. With a cough, the square-shouldered gentle giant regained his composure. "Well, can you?" He asked with an impish grin.

Perry let a couple soft chuckles bark out into existence, but that was all. He quickly forced his face to become serious again. "Don't worry, Boyd, you'll find I'm pretty capable. I got a few tricks up my sleeve; I'll be just fine," he promised the self-righteous booze peddler with a confidence that Perry was certain must appear ludicrous to him, and everyone else, everyone save Maisie, anyway.

"Seems to me like the priest is just trying to talk you out of the right choice for the sake of his liquor store, Dr. Sagal," Helena spoke up. "He just don't want the credit flow interrupted, I'll bet." Perry looked over to Helena with everyone else and saw the strangest of smiles cemented to her face. It was almost a sneer, almost a grin, yet somehow wholly neither. She turned then to look Perry straight in the face, and quick enough, he was pretty sure why Helena was speaking now, and where she was going with it. Then, right on cue, she said, "I say give 'em hell, Perry. I believe in you." Helena didn't seem to care that her predator eyes and smug smirk greatly undermined that claim. *She's picturing your death, my man,* Perry thought of that enduring smirk.

"Do you need a refill or something, Elle?" Boyd responded to Helena's accusations with an uncaring nonchalance to accompany his quip.

"Fuck you, Boyd!" Helena had only rage in her voice now.

"Elle, what the hell!?" Alice scolded.

"We're leaving," Helena answered, rising to her feet. "Come on, Alice."

She reached down to grab her wife by the forearm, but as soon as Alice was able to overcome her shock and understand what Helena was trying to do, she pulled it back out of reach. "What the hell are you doing, Elle? Don't be fucking grabbing at me!" Alice yelled, still trying to evade Helena's grasp.

"Don't do this here, Alice. Let's just go, please."

"Seriously, Elle, what the hell is wrong with you? You look insane right now."

The deep chime of the hailing bell sang its note once more, just before Helena could find a response. "Who the hell is this now?" Perry blurted out in nervous frustration.

"It's probably Jed and Larry, and maybe Patel." Dolly's voice sounded as appropriately awkward as the situation around her would suggest. "I'm sorry, doc, but I messaged 'em earlier on my tablet when we was headed here, and they said they were going to come here just as soon as they finished a few things down in the module garage."

"No need to apologize, Dolly; the bell just caught me a little off guard is all," Perry assured Mrs. Duchesne, a woman he liked and admired a great deal. She was a bright and witty sweetheart. He only pitied her that spineless cretin of a husband she was stuck with. "Maisie, do you mind?" He asked his daughter, gesturing toward the hatchway. Maisie complied without an argument. She was wearing her hostess hat and jumped to it eagerly. *Probably wants to escape the tension as much as me,* Perry thought of his eldest's haste.

Everyone in the room seemed to freeze in place after Maisie's dash to answer the door. Helena made no further grabs for her spouse's arm, though they remained locked in a death stare. Dolly and Father Boyd made neither move nor sound. It was only Gabe who seemed immune to the solemn and awkward freeze, belching out a long, lip-flapping burp after a deep chug from his wineglass. Then the slob must've figured he needed even more slouching space because he began to scooch back in his chair until its back was touching the wall. The legs of his chair had dragged across Perry's flawless, special request, faux wood floor in a loud, grating scrape the whole way, making Perry wish for a moment that Gabe could be his opponent tomorrow, rather than Monty.

Maisie reentered the dining room on the heels of that cruel thought, and Helena instantly broke off her icy staring contest to point an indignant finger at the men who followed Perry's daughter into the room. "No!" she screamed, as if in answer to an unasked question. "No way. We can't be here, Alice!" Helena cried, her voice turning desperate and plaintive. "It was bad enough hanging around giving encouragement to Montrois' fricking opponent, but now you expect me to risk being seen at the same meeting as the fricking AOA? Oh great, President Rafferty's here too," she said after the last man stepped out from behind Hubert Harrington giving Helena a good look at his face. "Oh my god, Alice, this is crazy. We gotta go, now."

Helena made one last grab for Alice's arm, but it too was evaded like all the others.

"Go home, Elle," Alice told her wife with stern patience. "I'll give you time to cool off, then I will come back, and we can talk. We *need* to talk. Go now, please," Alice added a finger pointed toward the hatchway for emphasis, "before you embarrass me any further."

Perry thought that last barb might've been a bit too much. It seemed to him the kind of comment that demanded a retort. Apparently, the dynamics of Alice and Helena's marriage were different than that of his and Joan's; Helena carried out her spouse's order without a delay of any kind. Perry kept his eyes on the tall, regal-looking woman in the black turtleneck as she made her way out of his dining room. Helena kept her face neutral the whole way, refusing to even glance back at Alice. Once her shuffle around the table was complete, Helena turned sideways to slide between AOA's CEO and the United States of America's President standing in the room's archway, being sure to avoid touching either man on her way through.

As soon as she was clear, Perry looked over to Alice. Their eyes met, and he felt the weight of all her current emotions as he took in her beautiful face in its present, distraught state. He used eyes and expression alone to convey his sympathy and support, and after a short enough time, Alice returned a slightly reluctant *I'm okay* nod. Perry then looked over to his daughter. Maisie seemed to understand what he wanted right away. She moved herself a few paces to her left to gain a view of their hatchway. In what seemed no time at all, Maisie nodded to signify Helena had left the quarters. The woman obviously hadn't lingered. Perry figured her long legs were eating up the yards at a rapid clip on her way back to Blue Corridor even now.

Rising then, with Maisie's confirmation, he turned to face the two formerly powerful men in his quaint dining space. However, it was Gabe who decided he had the right to speak first. While leaning against the wall behind him and rocking Perry's antique chair on its back two legs alone, he blurted out both a question and a comment to the two newcomers, "What the hell are you guys doing here? I thought the security staff had you all locked up tight in your VIP quarters back in your luxury branch."

Hubert Harrington aimed his sarcastic, million-dollar grin directly at the inconsiderate moron. "This is our station, sir; we designed it," he told him. "We built it. We know our way around it. There are shortcuts and passageways all around this facility that you know absolutely nothing about."

"Well then, if you're so slick, how'd you lose control of the station in the first place?" Gabe asked, with grating snark.

President Rafferty's calming Louisiana drawl broke in then, commanding the room's attention the way only a politician can, "Please, let's not argue. That's not why we're here," Rafferty was surprisingly short when you met him in person, but his piercing blue eyes and high-cheekboned, worldly face, with its soft age lines conveying hard-earned wisdom, demanded respect. Accordingly, the room fell silent, and Gabe had the decency to plant four chair legs on the floor and slightly straighten his slouch.

Perry finally found a moment to pose his most pressing question, "Why are you here, Mr. President?" Then, of the AOA CEO he asked, "Mr. Harrington, boss, what brings you two to my home today?"

Before either gray-haired, patriarchal leader could provide an answer, Gabe decided to pile another question of his own on top, "And why don't you have time?"

"The bastards check on us," Hubert Harrington muttered with scorn in his voice, choosing to answer Gabe's question, it obviously being the easier of the two.

"Well then," Perry said loudly and quickly, before Gabe had a chance to butt in, "what has made you evade your captivity and come you to my humble quarters?"

Rafferty stretched his mouth into a grin so smoothly and easily that, had Perry a bit more yokel in him, he might've been fooled, but being the educated and experienced man he was, Dr. Sagal didn't buy it for a second. The smile was an art form for men like President Daniel Raferty. Though, for the wary, it served as an indicator that every word that floated out from beneath was sure to be a beautiful lie. The president raised an index finger for pontificational purposes, and the bullshit began, "We felt it necessary to show our support and gratitude for your actions today with some sort of gesture to prove our humble appreciation. Mr. Harrington and I, along with our colleagues, Prime Minister Rivington of Canada, Chancellor Hoffreyer of Germany, Prime Minister Antoneson of Great Britain, Presidents Anatoly, Chen and Bergevin of Russia, China and France respectively, and Prime Minister Enomoto of Japan, came to the unanimous decision to risk our confinement and send emissaries to you to signify our unification of purpose. Being your fellow countrymen, Mr. Harrington and I were chosen thus for the honored duty."

"*Our unification of purpose?*" Perry asked.

"Yes," Rafferty answered, his smile never wavering. "To quell the security staff's unfortunate rebellion, of course. We failed to properly monitor the mental health of Commander Montrois, and it has proven a critical error. We hope to set it right with your help, Doctor," Rafferty locked eyes with Perry directly now. "Once you defeat Mr. Harrington's wayward employee, we can begin to hold the guilty parties in confinement for future trial and get back to our important work in the labs. I know you can't wait to return to the microscope either, Doctor. So we have come to lend you whatever assurances we can that all will be taken care of upon your victory. And it is our hope that our small gesture and these assurances will serve to ease your mind of one fewer burden during your upcoming match. I was also asked by the other world leaders to pass on their thanks and let you know they shall be praying for you tomorrow."

In other words, you came to make sure you're getting your titles back if I win. They already lost one champion in the form of that Secret Service agent. You'd think they'd have given up hope of backing a winner in the Tournament. Goddammit, these bastards and their special agent are just as much to blame for legitimizing this freaking tournament and forcing my hand as Abner Hyun. Hell, maybe even more so. He struggled for a few moments with whether to say just what he really thought of his president's pitch, but ultimately held off. He settled for returning Rafferty's obnoxious grin with a crooked eye and a sneering lip. The old politician's smile did flicker for a moment, but only just. It held up in the end to Perry's best silent menace. Finally, he was forced to use his words, "Tell us there is no truth to what Aponyaschefski has been telling everyone."

"What?!" It was Harrington who answered.

Perry pressed on, not caring about his boss' warning face, "If I'm risking my life to get your station back for you, then I think I deserve the truth. I believe we all do. If you want tomorrow playing out the way you all hope, you're going to swear to all of us, here and now, that there is no truth to Aponyaschefski's claims. Tell us you had nothing to do with the spread of the infection. Tell us the Alpha theory isn't some elaborate hoax you've cooked up to pull the wool over my eyes. Say all that, and I will kill your wayward security commander for you tomorrow."

Harrington stepped up, chest puffed, and face flushed with indignation, "Neither my company nor my government investors had absolutely anything to do with this goddamn infection!" he said in a deep voice meant to intimidate, yet failed horribly. "We are all just extremely lucky to have had this facility to retreat to when the infection spread. You're welcome for that, by the way," he added, condescension to his voice now. "If we hadn't employed you and let you in on the secret of this safe haven, you'd all be dead ... or Damned. You'd think we'd get a little fucking gratitude for that, but no, we get fucking suspicion!" He finished with a shout.

"Just how did you manage to build this safe haven?" Perry asked, throwing Harrington even more off his game.

"That's classified," the CEO managed after a few moments.

"Classified?" Perry asked in disbelief. "That isn't exactly reassuring, Mr. Harrington. Surely you can see that."

"It's the protocols and restrictions you all agreed to when you signed your contract," Harrington told him menacingly. "Just you win tomorrow, Doctor, then focus on helping the science team in the lab. The rest is above your station."

Rafferty placed a calming hand on Harrington's arm and pulled him back a few paces until they stood shoulder to shoulder. "You'll have to forgive Mr. Harrington He's been struggling with maintaining the secrecy of this facility for so long ... and recent events haven't exactly been easy on him either. We've all been dealing with a lot, I'm sure," the president added. "I wish it were possible to say more now, but these kinds of things get their classifications for a reason I'm afraid. It's up to us, as responsible citizens, to trust the system and abide by its restrictions. But, rest assured, Mr. Harrington speaks truly.

We had nothing to do with the infection. And if we can get the lab back up and running, we will crack the code of the Alphas and find our-selves synthesizing vaccine in no time, I'm sure of it. So," Rafferty said turning to leave, "with that hopeful thought, we will leave you. We have to be back to our quarters before the security staff's next inspection. Good luck, Dr. Sagal," he added before flapping his suitcoat on his way out of the dining room.

Perry moved to where he could see the president and CEO exit his premises. As the door slid slowly open, both Rafferty and Harrington looked back at Perry, and so were surprised by the two large men they ran into at the threshold, enough to elicit a simulta-neous shout. The gray-hairs bounced off the two men and didn't recover their footing for a few paces. Then they took a further step backwards when two more men stepped into the foyer.

Steve Schwambach and Hopkins Masterson parted enough to allow Jasper Montrois to step freely past. Once beyond his men, their commander paused, leaving two yards between himself and the two escapees. "I'm not surprised to find you here, gentlemen," Montrois told them. "I expected it, really. I know you have blueprints with uncharted passageways, secret underground annex tunnels and alternate operations platforms. We know about everything, Harrington." Hubert Harrington wanted desperately to spit back a witty retort, it was plain, but apparently none came to the executive. He seemed to settle on a snarl. Montrois was unperturbed. "You run on back now," he told them. "Take your secret way, if it makes you feel special, I don't give a shit. Just be back in your quarters before my men search it in thirty minutes."

Harrington and Rafferty shared a quick, uncertain look before ducking around Monty, Schef, and their two big bodyguards on their way through the hatchway.

"Hello, Perry," Monty said to Sagal once the door slid closed behind the suits. "Rude of me to just enter like this, I know, but we were friends once, were we not? Even barge-in friends, I dare to say."

"We were that once indeed, Monty. Can't say it's still so, sadly," Perry responded.

"Well then," Monty said with a resigned and somber visage, "I mourn for what was, and I apologize. I was just hoping we might speak."

"Go back out and try again then!" Maisie edged her way around Perry to shout at Monty.

"I'm sorry?" Montrois answered in confusion.

"You ain't king yet, Jasper," she yelled at him. "If you want to speak with my father, then go back out and ring the bell, and perhaps we will choose to let you enter."

Perry let his daughter's wrath burn. He watched Schef all the while, waiting for the man to dare make a demand of him to control Maisie, or perhaps even insult her. Perry was even kind of hoping for that, a little. Unfortunately, Schef seemed as timid as Perry had ever seen him. He remained by the hatchway and didn't say a word. It was Monty who was speaking today. "I apologize again, Maisie, the door opened in front of us, and I suppose me and my men were a bit over-eager. I will go out in the alleyway to play out the act of ringing the bell, if you like. But I think today seems like it might be an occasion where we could, perhaps, ditch all that nonsense. What do ya say?" Monty asked Perry's daughter.

In that moment, for some strange, serendipitous reason that wasn't worth digging into just then, Perry thought of the two books that sat atop the end table in his reading nook, and an idea struck him. "Let's talk in private, Monty," he suggested. "My room down the hall would probably be best." With a wave of his arm to get Monty to follow, Perry immediately set off for his room. "Sorry about my daughter," he apologized for Maisie's behavior as soon as Monty begrudgingly turned to follow him. "She can get a bit passionate at times," he continued. "She really loved your Roxanna and Carrie though, that's for sure. She misses them like crazy, thinks about 'em all the time. Just as much as she thinks of her own mother, really, my Joan. Elias too, of course. He speaks of Carrie all the time." Perry looked over his shoulder to lock eyes with Monty, "She had quite the impact on him, you know? I'm sure it will just kill Elias to learn we are at odds."

Monty remained silent, avoiding the topic of his family as he stepped into the room ahead of Perry. *He's blocked his wife and daughter from his thoughts completely,* Perry thought of the 260-pound gorilla of a security commander. Lost in thought, he stepped on Monty's heels and had to immediately dodge around the big man to avoid a collision. Monty had pulled up short upon entering to gaze around the room.

Apart from the AOA supplied bed and dresser, the only other furniture in the master bedroom was a pair of twin forest-green lounge chairs, positioned right next to each other with a small dark maple table separating them. Every available inch of wall space in the bedroom was covered over by oak bookshelves, while every centimeter of shelf space was occupied by a pristine hardcover book, fraying paperback, or anything in between. "I've come, of course, to try and speak some good sense into that stubborn head of yours," Monty finally said, still gazing about the room.

"I'm afraid I'm quite beyond your fatalistic notion of good sense, Jasper," Perry responded in a thick voice. "I am committed to walk the path I've laid before my feet. I will not be moved to stray from it by any words of yours, my friend."

There were two books extracted from their places in the bookcases. They currently sat, one atop the other, upon the narrow surface of the little table. After a scoffing huff in response to Perry's pronunciation, Monty stepped further into the room, right towards the two books. Montrois seemed to not be able to help himself. He plucked up both books and held them out before him in one big, meaty hand. Perry knew which two they were. He'd taken them down recently, after all.

Well, one of them anyway. The other one was almost always placed there on that table in his reading nook, just so. It was rarely ever actually read anymore, but it elicited from Perry a mild form of OCD whenever it wasn't resting right there, in pride of place. The freshly extracted book could often be found on the end table as well. It was chicken soup for his soul. He always turned to it in times of turmoil. Needless to say, recent events qualified, and he'd plucked it from the shelf last night in search of some salve for his anxiety. He'd passed out with it in his hands, in fact, and hadn't been absolutely certain that he'd placed it back on the end table as he stumbled off to bed. So Perry felt mild relief to see it, a thin red book of poetry by Rudyard Kipling, its bookmark set to page twenty-three, and the very start of Perry's favorite of the legendary author's poems, "If."

The other book was fairly thin as well, though it was in a great deal worse condition than the Kipling. Its cover was white, faded, battered, and scuffed, with a black smudge lining a torn corner, speaking of fire. Its basic, no-nonsense, straight-to-the-point, the-essence-of-brevity title was printed in a black, bold-faced plain font halfway up the cover page. It read, "U.S. Army Special Forces Medical Handbook," and as soon as Monty read that title, he glanced back at Perry. Without a word, Perry walked to a tall bookshelf to his right and opened a small cedar case resting between two piles of books upon a waist-high shelf. He stepped to its side to give Monty a good look at his Special Forces tabs resting on the soft red felt within. The tabs were positioned alongside his Army Medical Command Badge, while two Purple Hearts and a Meritorious Service Medal were nestled firmly in place beneath the unit badges.

"I know you served, doc," Monty said. "You can quit the show."

Perry was taken aback for a moment. Then he scolded himself, *You dumbass, of course he would know now.* "I take it you have access to AOA's files then," he said, begrudgingly.

"We know what we know," Monty answered, evasively. "I'll admit I was a bit surprised to learn you had prior service experience though."

"I don't like to talk about it," Perry answered, saying words he'd said too many times before, so much so, they were starting to sound braggadocious despite themselves. "I've held too many brothers as they drew their last breaths. They're the ones who deserve the veneration. They're the ones that made the sacrifice and truly earned it. Plus, in my later years, the righteousness of my involvement in some of those things has become a bit of an evolving proposal. So I prefer to ride my achievements as a healer into whatever success I earn in life."

"Funny," Monty dropped the two books back on the end table as he turned to add, "you don't have no problem flaunting your service in my face right now."

"As fair warning, Monty," Perry told his old friend in all seriousness.

"Very well, Perry, consider me good and warned," Montrois answered Perry's solemnity with sarcasm.

A deep breath and a shake of the head had Perry ready to speak again, "Maybe you ought to pick that Kipling book back up. I got a mark on page twenty-three. It's where my favorite poem starts. You'd like it. It's short, simple, and sweet, and even a bit pertinent, if I dare dissect literature. You should give it a read. Do it before tomorrow," Perry pressed him, "as one last favor to me."

Monty allowed the faintest of grins to curl on his thin lips as he nodded his head and picked the book of poetry back up. "I'll give it a read, I'll promise that much, but this'll be the last of my favors."

"Could you at least tell me what this is really all about?" Perry pressed him, seizing on a momentary receding of his firm communication wall. "And please don't give me any of that bullshit you told the priest, about how that horde down in Millstone clarified your purpose when you saw it or what not. I think I know you pretty well, or at least I *knew* you pretty well, and I've seen a cold look in your eyes ever since they left your wife and daughter to die. I hadn't known what to make of that look really, but now, I think I'm finally starting to understand it."

Monty's face grew dark, almost physically so. His eyes appeared to withdraw behind a thick fog. His mouth grew hard, and his chin jutted out in anger. "Yeah, Perry," he finally said. "I think maybe you are ... maybe. My motivations will just have to remain a mystery in your mind. I'm sorry, my old friend, I truly am, for Elias and Maisie's sake, if nothing else."

"I guess that means we really are fighting tomorrow then?" Perry asked sadly. Monty only had an affirmative nod for answer. "I guess challenging really was the right choice. Perhaps I can try and scrape some cold comfort from that knowledge," Perry added, off-handedly.

Monty was done talking. The parlay was over. He shoved Rudyard Kipling's paperback of poetry into his back pocket and strode toward the hallway. *How has it come to this?!* Perry wanted to yell at the big grief monster trudging out of his bedroom, but he stayed silent. So silent, his mind played with him, and he swore he heard the screech of the Final Tournament's alien yowl of a buzzer far off in the distance.

Perry followed Monty out shortly, but by the time he made it back to his dining room, the security commander, Schef, and their two silent bodyguards were gone. Replacing them were Jed Redding and Larry Holderman. Apparently they'd arrived while Perry had been speaking with Monty in that short and unfruitful meeting. A handful of competing conversations died away the instant he entered the dining space. Perry Sagal said nothing. He simply walked two paces to his vacant chair and picked up the still full glass of wine perched on the tabletop. He threw back the sour concoction in a few deep gulps. Then, with a resigned smile, and secret wink for Alice, he held out his empty glass before him and indicated for Boyd to pour a quick refill. "I'm going to need at least one more before I face tomorrow," he said.

CHAPTER 15

CAINEY

The round shield's hide-covered pine boards soaked up the dragon's flames long enough for Nate Novocaine to slash out from beneath its protection and slice his broadsword clean through the soft powdery-green flesh of the mythical beast's underbelly. The monstrous serpent instantly broke off its lancing fire. A scaly and muscular neck 15' long began to writhe and twist as the dragon threw its arrow-shaped head back to screech and snarl in awful pain. Cainey did not hesitate. He saw the opening, and flinging his burning shield clear, he charged the beast, sword arm outstretched before him, the heavy blade's point aimed straight towards a gap in the massive monster's thick and craggy chest plates. Then, a mere inch from his blade plunging home, the Interactive Gaming System suddenly froze.

Flickering between his sword's point and the green dragon's chest was a command Cainey had programmed to flash at him in warning: "SIMULATION PAUSED, CURRENTLY 0105 ST … YOUR PROGRAMMED ALARM HAS REACHED ITS ACTIVATION TIME … CURRENTLY 0105 ST … SIMULATION PAUSED." Then a pop-up box suddenly appeared just below the alarm warning, reading: "DISMISS ALARM." And a box just below that, reading: "END SIMULATION." With a disappointed sigh, Cainey used the motion capture glove encasing his right hand to depress the "end simulation" box.

The frozen dragon and keen-edged broadsword before him immediately blinked out of existence as total darkness fell upon the world. Then Cainey pulled the elastic strap of his matching maroon and silver IGS Sim Specs up over his head to remove the glasses that were much akin to dark swimming goggles. The IGS pod's shining walls, with their distinctive, small, alternating concave and convex white and pale gray tiles instantly greeted him with their harsh brightness. The pod walls always made him blink tears from his eyes whenever he removed the goggles after a long session in the gaming simulator. Today was no exception. Cainey had found the IGS Lounge in the Rec District almost empty when he'd first arrived here around 2100 ST to log some gaming hours. No one seemed in a gaming mood aboard the station the last few days. Cainey was pleased to let their timid reverence be his gain and was able to book a pod right up until the very moment this night's clandestine meeting was set for.

He hadn't actually planned on using all that time, but luckily he had set an alarm for himself before he started his simulation because he wound up engrossed and captivated by the awesome realism of the IGS system, and the amazing capabilities of its interactive gameplay. He would've fought dragons and slayed orcs right through his meeting if not for the alarm. But as it was now, he had about nine or ten minutes to make it to the billiard lounge just a few stops down one of the Rec District's many alleyways. So he felt no undue rush in picking up his backpack and AOA tablet, nor in returning the goggles and gloves to the IGS Lounge's attendant. Soon enough though, he was on the march.

Cainey strolled past the casino to his right, which trafficked in Cardinal's Nest credits alone, and then the theater, with its massive 40' x 75' IMAX projection screen, on his left. A few more of his short strides and he found himself standing just outside the billiard lounge's archway. Cainey peered into the poorly lit chamber, scanning for three specific individuals.

Locating the three proved a difficult task. The gigantic hall's only form of lighting was the green hooded lamps swaying four feet above every one of the twenty-five billiard tables arranged in orderly rows throughout the hall. So, needless to say, the hall had plenty of dark corners. But after a few moments spent fruitlessly peering into a few of them, Cainey remembered that Sergeant Marge Hamill had told him she and the pilots would be playing a game of pool at one of the tables. Another quick glance over the assembled players, and Cainey finally located his quarry, third row from the right and two up from the back.

Cainey took a moment to remind himself of his upcoming task, and its stakes. *Just play it cool, Nate. If you're going in, just grab a cue and walk right up to their table. Don't make a big deal, just casually play the game and never actually look any of 'em in the eye. We're gonna be most likely watched the entire time.* Hamill had laid out those same ground rules for this upcoming meeting, and given him that warning, in a rushed whisper at dinner earlier today.

She had sneaked over to his table in the Main Cafeteria as deftly as a tiger stalking its prey. Cainey had been mouth-deep in a cheeseburger when he suddenly felt warm breath on his neck. He had been certain it was one of the many women up here who were constantly making eyes at him. Most of them were married, so Cainey figured a sneaky approach and a whispered rendezvous was something to be expected. But as soon as he recognized the voice and the tone it carried, he knew his hopes of a little secret sexual tryst were way off the mark. He knew Marge Hamill wouldn't be talking to him if she had any other choice. That told him two things: that his services were critical to accomplishing whatever she was cooking up, and that whatever that thing she was cooking up turned out to be, it was sure to piss off the security staff.

Cainey had no idea what he would say at this meeting Sergeant Marge invited him to, or really even which side he would choose to back. Cainey was in no way a fan of Montrois or any of his staff officers, loyal or otherwise. He had no illusions about what kind of oppression would be in his future in a world ruled by them. But he had no wish to stick his neck out only to have his head lopped off for the effort. So he had remained unsure about this rendezvous all day. He'd hoped a clear choice would suddenly reveal itself when he finally saw the billiard lounge's crowd and scoped out the hazards. If there were too many security officers lurking around, that might decide things for him. Sergeant Marge couldn't really expect him to risk meeting to plot a seditious act with a half dozen officers staring at them. The security staff already had him under suspicion as it was. Cainey was sure of that.

He'd caught Pedro Alvarez looking over at him just after Marge finished her whispered instructions in the Main Cafeteria. The look on his face told him the officers were dead serious, and that they did not at all trust him. He was just happy Alvarez hadn't looked over in time to see Marge whispering. If he had, Cainey might not have even come *this* far. It would've been just way too risky. Marge Hamill was asking enough of him as it was.

But, for whatever reason, Cainey had indeed come. The meeting place had seemed like a safe enough choice, he supposed. He knew Marge had been spreading the word around station that everyone's living quarters were most likely tapped by the security staff now. Cainey had figured that out for himself days before, though nobody cared to listen when *he'd* tried spreading that word. But whatever, he wasn't surprised she didn't opt for a quiet get together at one of their quarters. He figured the billiard lounge was really the only logical choice to avoid their conversations being picked up and monitored in some way. It would be too loud in there, as well as crowded enough that a gathering wouldn't be seen as abnormal.

The billiard lounge had become the station's unofficial drinking hole over the last few weeks. Residents gathered there in droves with bottles upon bottles of the priest's liquor to socialize and numb the world's insanity. It was an adults-only club, unofficially. The stipulation was enforced by the adults through a sort of collective unspoken agreement, and it quickly took on a bar-like atmosphere. Only a few folks ever really played serious billiards in there anymore. Most just talked and drank and dicked around. So his bumping into Sergeant Marge and the two Star Hawk pilots might not look like anything nefarious to any watching security staff at first glance, or likewise if they were overheard by any of his fellow residents looking to score points with Montrois by way of some juicy gossip. Instead, most residents and officers would hopefully see it as nothing more than a chance meeting in a crowded drinking hall, *if* they played it right, *if* they followed Sergeant Marge's instructions. Cainey trusted himself and Marge to possess the necessary levelheadedness to pull off the meeting without attracting unwanted attention, but he wasn't sure he could say the same of Gillian Gerwitz and Barry Calvin.

Cainey had not at all been comfortable with the chosen meeting time though. It seemed a bit too late and would end up negating all the place's benefits. A part of him, which he wasn't willing to admit existed, was actually kind of hoping that was indeed the case. A part of him was hoping all his other reservations about meeting with the sarge wouldn't need to be the deciding factor in his not attending the furtive meeting. A part of him hoped he'd look in on the lounge and see it all but empty. Marge would have to agree then that it was just too big a risk to meet under those circumstances. But, as he looked in now, he realized his hopes on that end were completely dashed. *No wonder the IGS Pods were all empty, everybody's in here,* he realized. The billiard lounge was often crowded, that's true, but this crowd was truly surprising. Not only was it late at night, but there was also a bloody revolution still currently unfolding aboard station.

Maybe that's the frickin' reason they're all still in here, Cainey thought with morbidity. *Maybe they all need to get good and drunk with someone to bitch and whine to while they do it.* Cainey had figured everyone aboard station was going a little crazy lately, each in their own way. He was just fine, himself. Cainey always assumed the worst in folks, so the security staff reaching for power came as no shock to him. He'd learned to brush off things that might once had driven him mad. Apathy, some folks called it, but Cainey Barker simply called it his *sanity pill.*

Cainey had found out what corrupt and incompetent assholes the security staff all were on that mission they dragged him along for. He knew Montrois was an asshole never to be trusted after that. *And the sarge knows I know that too. That's why she's turned to me for help.* Cainey fought off an out of place smile at that thought. Just then, out of the corner of his eye, he suddenly noticed a man staring at him. Cainey turned his head and immediately locked eyes with Pedro Alvarez standing in a shadowy alcove ten yards into the lounge.

Shit, Cainey thought as soon as the man's cold and curious features registered in his consciousness. Cainey suddenly felt his legs moving, unbidden by any direct order of his own. It was fear moving him. Cainey was screaming internally for the fear to turn him around and march on back to his quarters, but for some ungodly reason, they were moving him ever deeper into the cavernous hall, straight towards Sergeant Marge's billiard table. He scanned the lounge with each stride, his head swinging back and forth in an overt and obvious manner that he could not at all control. Halfway to the sergeant's table, he spotted a second security officer. Cainey's eyes stayed locked on the man for a beat too long. Steve Schwambach's searching vision landed on Cainey, and he was only then able to quickly and conspicuously dart his eyes down to the floor. *Shit,* Cainey cursed himself. *Get your shit together.*

Feeling Schwambach's dark-eyed gaze locked on his back, Cainey stepped up to a rack of pool cues. With forced deliberation, he withdrew one. The rack was between two others just like it. They were part of a long line of racks spanning the width of the lounge and dissecting the hall into halves. Marge's table was only ten yards from the dividing racks, so Cainey paused to mentally rehearse his approach. He needed it to look casual. A beeline directly for the sergeant and the pilots would be too suspicious. He would never throw off Schwambach's attention that way. Cainey figured Pedro Alvarez was most likely watching him right now as well. Though with his back facing the man, he couldn't be sure.

Fuck, this is going to be hard, he thought, unhelpfully. *At least it's just the two officers in here. God, why in the hell did you walk into this shithole in the first place, you moron?* Cainey couldn't answer that. He knew it was too late to turn back though. At this point, that would look more suspicious than going through with the secret meeting. So he decided to casually inspect his cue and stroll toward Marge's table. Once there, he would wait for one of them to gesture in a way that would be obvious they were asking him to join their game. With them only having three people gathered around their table, his joining them to even out the teams would seem natural.

With his strategy set, Cainey decided to set the plan in motion, but found that fear had him in its stony grip once again. This time it was pinning his feet to the spot, rather than forcing them to stride into hostile territory. *Get a hold of yourself, man,* Cainey silently scolded his cowardice. He couldn't believe how badly his will was losing its battle with his fear. He was normally so brave under fire; Cainey prided himself on that. He ended up having to physically slam a fist into his leg to get it moving toward Marge's table. All the way there, he struggled to shove his wounded pride, uncertainty of allegiance, and thousand other worries to the back of his mind and focus on the task ahead. *Act natural, man,* he was telling himself just as he arrived alongside the sergeant's table.

Cainey was instantly triggered red with indignant anger at first glance of the sergeant and her pet pilots. Each of the three conspirators stood there, cue in hand, with the dumbest looks in the world slapped across their guilty faces. Not a one was lining up a shot. None of them were engaged in conversation or sipping a beverage. Nothing. Instead, all three were just staring at him with their moronic looks plastered to their ugly faces. *Be cool, you fucking jackasses!* Cainey wanted to scream at them. *Don't they realize there's two security officers in this lounge, and they're both watching my ass?* Finally, one of the buffoons remembered the plan and indicated for him to join their game.

Cainey stepped forward on treacherous, shaky legs. Without a word, he walked up alongside the table, positioned himself behind the cue ball and began lining up a shot. "They're freaking watching me, you assholes," he told Marge and the Star Hawk pilots in a voice pitched so only they could possibly hear. "Play it cool. They got it out for me." Cainey slammed his cue into the white ball with that. He didn't give a shit where it was headed, and immediately looked up to lock eyes with Marge before the shot had even finished playing out on the green felt. "I would've warned you about that if you gave me a chance to respond to this summons you whispered in my ear, but you just ran away before I had a chance to say a goddamn word. You're lucky I am here at all."

Marge stepped up behind the now settled cue ball. After a moment, she bent down over the table to line up a shot of her own. "You're here 'cause you got no other choice," she said while sliding her cue stick back and forth, measuring out her speed. "Don't kid yourself, Cainey."

He was standing tableside, leaning his weight slightly on his thin cue stick as if it were a wizard's staff. His back was still to both officers, and he was glad for it because a sneer crossed his lips at Marge's accusation that in no way spoke of pleasant or sporting competition. Cainey caught himself before any outburst could make its way out his lips, but he still cursed himself again for the lapse in character.

Gerwitz spoke up before Cainey had composed himself enough to give the sergeant the retort she deserved, "You're going to overcome your fears, Novocaine, and help us out."

"Screw you, Gillian!" Cainey yelled in a voice too soft to convey the proper scorn it demanded.

The sergeant just missed a kiss shot off the rail after Cainey's attempted shout. Barry Calvin was next to approach the cue ball. He picked up a cube of blue chalk and twisted it around the point of his stick while he spoke, "We'd just as soon not involve your shaky ass at all, Cainey. But circumstances are dire. So let's not draw out this whole fucking song and dance any longer than we have to. Just shut up and play the game. Marge will tell you what we need from you while you do. Then, afterwards, you can nod your fucking head and slink off back to your quarters, or wherever the hell a creep like you hangs out."

Cainey probably would've shot the son of a bitch right then and there, had he a gun. Instead, he marked Barry Calvin down in his mental black book and simply complied with his orders. Marge didn't start speaking until Calvin finished his shot and Gerwitz approached the table. "We need a lookout, Nate," she told him. "You are going to do that for us. Not only 'cause it's the right thing to do, but also because it's the only way to ensure Montrois and the rest of my fellow officers don't get the power they're after. We all know damn well how scared of that prospect you are. None of them have forgotten our last mission to Earth, Novocaine. Every one of 'em blames you for Sarah Bristol and Donny McGuinness, I can promise you that. You are going to do what we need you to do for your own damn sake. So let's skip all the drama of us trying to talk you into joining up with our plot. You are already in, and everyone at this table knows it. Just nod your head yes, Cainey," she demanded.

Cainey swallowed a hard lump of fury in his throat as he stepped up to take his turn in the game. He wouldn't give Sergeant Marge the nod she'd asked of him, he decided. Instead, he kept a little pride while still giving her what she was after, "I'm in," he said over his shot.

"Good," he heard Marge respond softly. A comment meant for herself alone, most likely. But Cainey heard it. His ears were as keen as every other part of him. They hardly missed a thing. He was glad of that just now, as Marge's soft-spoken comment revealed that she wasn't nearly as confident in Cainey's support as the three of them were pretending. He squirreled that knowledge away just as Marge launched into her spiel, "You will attend the Final Tournament tomorrow morning, Novocaine. Make sure a few of the officers see you there too. Then, when the match starts, everyone will be distracted, and you will use that moment to slip out of The Meadow." *Will I now?* Cainey thought with skepticism as Marge carried on, "A trolley will be waiting for you right outside the archway. We've paid off the operator, so all is taken care of. If you've any concerns, rest assured they've been addressed. I don't care to hear them here and now. So stow it, if you got any." Cainey did have concerns, many, in fact, but he decided he wouldn't give Marge and the two smug pilots the satisfaction of voicing them. So, once again, he swallowed rage and simply played his part of the casual pool player. "The trolley will take you all the way back to the depot," the sergeant continued. "You will jump out there and hustle your ass to the security staff's rec room. Gerwitz, Calvin, and myself will be waiting around a corner for you. Just as soon as we see you, we will move out, hauling three utility hand trucks, and meet you in front of the rec room. The hand trucks won't fit through the hatchway, so you will stay in the alleyway with them and serve as our lookout."

"And what the hell will *you* be doing?" Cainey blurted out. Marge's withering glare chased his eyes back down to the table in front of him, the shame of which forced another knot of anger to be choked down.

"Procuring something of value," Marge answered him in a controlled voice. "Once we come out with it, you will then serve as our scout as we make our way to a secure location."

"Which is where?" Cainey couldn't help his blurting now.

"Somewhere secure," Gerwitz answered him, patronizingly.

"You'll find out tomorrow, Cainey," the sergeant promised him. "Just don't miss that trolley."

Cainey stepped back from the table. He cast his gaze between the sergeant and the pilots for a few seconds before working up the nerve to dart a glance behind him to ascertain whether or not Alvarez and Schwambach were still interested in him. He didn't see them lurking anywhere close by, but in the crowded lounge that didn't mean much. He turned back to his three coconspirators to see their dumb looks had turned to pitying scowls. Cainey thought for a good few seconds that this next lump of rage he swallowed was sure to be the one to gag him, but somehow he choked it down too.

"We're done now, Novocaine," Calvin informed him. "You can go."

"Won't that look strange?' Cainey asked with a sneer. "I mean ... no one's even won this game yet."

A wormy grin crawled across Calvin's mouth in answer to that. He bent down to the table, and with almost no hesitation at all, sunk home a double-boarded shot solidly into a side pocket. The cocky pilot proceeded to clear the table of all remaining striped balls within seconds, and in no time flat, found himself with a cross-table shot at the eight ball. Cainey barely had enough time to register the shot's difficulties before Calvin sent the cue ball on its way. The white ball kissed the black at just the perfect angle to allow the match-ending sphere to slide between the three ball and two ball and drop softly into a corner pocket. "Okay, Cainey," Calvin said, stretching back to his full height, "*now* you can go."

Cainey heard Gerwitz's muffled chuckles as he spun around and turned his back on their table. He marched off toward the rack of cue sticks and only then remembered to act casual. Cainey darted a quick glance left, then right, trying to spot the two security officers, but Nate Barker was a short man and the goddamn billiard lounge was so crowded that he could only see the people just ahead of him. He nearly let the frustration of that fact overwhelm him, until he realized his height might actually prove of some benefit in this particular circumstance. *Maybe I can make my way unseen all the way to the archway,* he thought with sudden hope. Cainey picked his way there carefully, plotting out his path dozens of steps in advance. The diligence paid off. He made it there and didn't spot any sign of either officer when he spun around in a circle to check for a tail. Cainey congratulated himself on a successful covert meeting and tactical withdrawal before strolling through the archway to seek a quiet spot to grapple with what he should do about the instructions he'd just received.

Beyond the billiard lounge's archway, echoing silence reigned supreme. The murmuring, chattering thunder died completely within the first ten yards, so that the pitter-patter of tailing footsteps halfway down the alleyway could be clearly heard as soon as he came within about 200 yards of the Central Hub, despite the stalker's obvious attempts at stealth. Cainey had a pretty good idea who those footfalls might belong to. He took a quick second to begrudgingly commend the man for his efforts up to now. Cainey had both ears straining for stray sounds ever since exiting the billiard lounge, but those half dozen footsteps were the first signs his tail had given.

Unfortunately for his stalker, the rest of the station was a bit of a ghost town. Some noise was unavoidable when traipsing through Cardinal's Nest's alleyways and annex tunnels. It made a little cover noise a necessity when performing tailing work. But the stalker had no cover at all to speak of, and Cainey had easily pinned him down with those few overheard footfalls as a single man slinking along the alley walls, trying to stay in the shadows.

The stalker was probably about fifty feet back from his current position. Cainey Barker had a choice before him: either press his luck and try and make it to the Central Hub, and then lead his tail on a merry chase through the maze of alleyways in the living quarters' corridors beyond, or duck into the oval gray maintenance hatch coming up on the right. Cainey was pretty sure the tunnel beyond the hatch led to the Fishery and Dairy, Pork and Cattle Farms. *That might be a good place to lose this asshole tailing me,* Cainey thought of the huge, crowded, and convoluted farming facility.

Then the decision was taken from him. The maintenance hatch suddenly swung open just ahead of him and Security Officer Dontavious Woodson ducked through. Cainey was frozen in place when the man's features crystallized in his consciousness. It wouldn't have mattered if he had reacted quickly. The alleyway leading from the Rec District to the Central Hub, where they currently stood, was wide, with high ceilings, but the stalker had rushed up behind him in the same instant the maintenance hatch had swung open, so Cainey would have gotten nowhere even if he had tried to flee. It still forced yet another lump of rage to be choked down his gullet, nonetheless. Cainey Barker was really letting himself down this evening. *Well, no more,* he silently swore. *I ain't giving these assholes anything ... no matter what they do to me.*

Cainey had just finished swearing that oath to himself when Dontavious Woodson placed his hand on the handle of the 9mm pistol slung on his right thigh and stepped in close to Cainey. In that same instant, the stalker stepped up behind him and just to his left. Cainey hadn't wanted to give the stalker the satisfaction of turning to see who it was, but instead, he added one more failure of courage to the night. And unnecessarily too, for it was exactly who he expected: Steve Schwambach, the dark-eyed silent brooder among the security staff. Cainey gave the man a look of derision before quickly turning back to face Woodson, but a new pitter-patter pricked his ear, stopping his turn dead in its tracks. Cainey's head snapped all the way back over his shoulder to see Pedro Alvarez materialize out of the shadows. Cainey kept his eyes locked on the security squad team leader as the man stepped up between Woodson and Schwambach to effectively box him in against the wall.

"What's this about?" Cainey shamed himself even more with the squeak in his voice.

"We require a minute of your time, Novocaine." Cainey hadn't spoken his question to any of the three officers in particular, but it was Woodson who had decided to answer him. Cainey locked eyes with the young, lean-faced officer with the broken nose. He had no idea what expression his own face was showing at that moment, but he was honestly shocked to see the scorn and cruelty that lay in the dark brown eyes of Dontavious Woodson. Just weeks before, this man was trading jokes and shooting the shit with Cainey, cordial as you please, on the ride from Earth back to Cardinal's Nest. *Abner Hyun put an end to that with his big fucking mouth though, the bastard,* Cainey thought, remembering the source of all his current woes. It didn't seem to matter to any of the security officers that Abner was now their public-enemy-number-one; they all still believed the lies Hyun had shouted about him. Cainey's culpability was set in stone in Montrois' mind especially, and that seemed to be all that really mattered around this place anymore. "Pedro and Schwambach tell me they saw you shooting some pool with our old sergeant," Woodson spoke with a tiresome grin. "Sergeant Marge won't speak to any of us anymore, and quite frankly, we're all a bit concerned for her wellbeing. We was hoping you could fill us in on her health and such."

"We'd sure appreciate a verbatim resuscitation of y'all's conversation, for example," Pedro Alvarez interjected in a voice that made it clear he was taking command of the situation. "Woodson knows of a private little maintenance hut tucked away down that access tunnel beyond that hatch." Alvarez used his chin to indicate the open maintenance hatch. "Us four are going to head there all nice and quiet like. Then we're gonna pour you a mug of the priest's best moonshine and sit ya down in a nice, comfy chair. And then, Novocaine, you're gonna tell the three of us every last word our dear sergeant said to you back there."

Cainey was boxed in. He was unarmed. The officers all had visible sidearms, in ready holsters, along with who knows how many unseen weapons. Those simple facts made up his mind. The choice gave him no joy. In fact, it brought with it a lump of anger so large Cainey truly could not swallow it. He gagged and spat up a little on the floor of the alleyway in front of him. Steve Schwambach grabbed his arm mid-gag, unmoved by the pathetic display. He heard Alvarez's scoff but never his order to move out. First thing Cainey knew, Schwambach was shoving him toward the open maintenance hatch. He didn't even have enough time to wipe the spittle from his lips before the brutish officer shoved his head down so he wouldn't bash it as he was manhandled through the portal.

CHAPTER 16

ELIAS

Each of his hands gripped tightly to a clutch of the beast's shaggy fur. Elias had been staring the dark-eyed wolf beast down one moment, watching it lope towards him on six long ash-gray legs, and in the next, he'd found himself astride the monstrous, snarling creature. He wasted no time trying to recall how, Elias simply found a firm seat in the arch of the creature's seven-foot-long torso and clamped his legs tight to the wolf's flanks. With his firm grip in the beast's shaggy gray fur just below its neck, his control of the powerful, folkloric steed was absolute. Elias shut his eyes and heard the giant wolf howling inside his mind. What's more, he actually understood the strange canine language. "Run with me," it was saying. "Hunt with me. *Kill* with me."

Elias didn't hear himself speak, nor howl, but somehow the wolf heard him. And somehow, he *knew* the wolf had heard him. "Yes," he had told the beast, with full-hearted desire.

They were racing across the countryside now. The massive creature ate up yards with a powerful gallop. Elias watched as first a rolling pasture, lit by a full, twinkling moon, passed by in a blur, and then a dense, dark forest whipped speedily past him. Suddenly, the trees thinned, and Elias and his mount leapt a wooden post-and-rail fence in a single bound to land safely in a freshly planted farm field. The wolf stopped there, rearing up on its hind legs to howl a slow, mournful cry at the face of the moon shining high above. Elias added his voice to the howling cry as man and beast bounded about the field in a wild, liberating release of frenzied emotion.

A mighty crack cut short the howls of Elias and his wolf. A snapping sound whizzed past his ear an instant later. Elias tugged on the tufts of his beast's fur, gripped tightly in untiring hands, to face the source of the noise. Elias could only just make out a dark figure across the field outlined in front of the fence. Then, suddenly, another crack and snapping hiss reverberated into the still night. The sound was accompanied by a spark of light just in front of the dark figure. The wolf growled low, and when Elias heard more cracks and saw more sparks before the figure, he let the beast's will reign supreme. Elias gave himself over to the fury bubbling inside the gigantic mythical creature.

His wolf ate up the ground even faster than before. In no time, they were leaping through the air at the dark figure. Elias heard a pitiful scream followed by a final crack but did not see the final spark; the wolf had engulfed the figure. A burning pain was suddenly burrowing its way through him, though some part of Elias was aware that it was not his own pain, but the wolf's. Elias howled out, feeling the giant creature's flaring rage as strongly as he did the sharp sting. His wolf's fangs tore deep into soft flesh, and the hot, coppery blood that filled his beast's mouth tasted glorious on his own tongue. It tasted triumphant. Finally, when the wolf had sated its hunger and reared back to howl at the cold and distant moon, Elias eagerly joined in the call.

A sudden snuffling and panting noise cut through the sound. They broke off their animal call and came back down on all four padded paws. The wolf, and the boy atop its back, turned to see a colossal bull, 9' at the shoulders, with horns 11 feet wide from tip to tip. The bovine behemoth emerged completely from the shadows a hundred paces from them. Elias could see its dark brown hide lathered with white foam. He had no idea where the sudden certainty came from, but somehow, Elias knew the bull had been running towards them for miles and miles. It had been running towards them forever. The bull was their doom. Their response was rage, red, red rage. It burned away their pain until it was but a faint memory far back in his mind.

Elias kicked his heels into the flanks of his other half. The giant wolf instantly responded, leaping forward to meet the bull's charge head-on. Elias watched from his mounted perch as the bull ducked his head down and to the right in the last few paces before the wolf was on him. He knew right away his wolf's leap was a mistake, but it was too late to stop. He could do nothing but watch as the bull whipped its head back up and to the left. A horn, four feet long and thick as a ten-year-old pine sapling, slammed like a freight train into the side of the wolf just below the neck. The point of the horn, fortunately, was above the wolf's back, so the creature wasn't pierced, but the impact of the mighty blow still sent the wolf flying sideways a dozen yards into the farm field.

Elias managed to jump free of the wolf's back just before it impacted the ground, avoiding being crushed, but the hard impact still knocked the wind out of him. His subsequent rolls and bounces along the dirt were no picnic either. Even so, Elias was back to his feet before the wolf. His other half was lying on its side, motionless. Only the shallow rise and fall of its chest gave testimony against its total demise. He glanced back to the bull. It had bounded around in a wide circle, tearing up the dirt and whatever crop was planted within, and was now lined back up for a charge at Elias' helpless wolf.

"No!" The boy screamed, so loud he had to recoil from the lingering echoes within his skull. Without a moment's further hesitation, he sprinted to intercept the charging beast. Elias arrived in its path with the bull still twenty feet from him and sixty from the wolf. At first, it seemed the bull wouldn't halt its charge. Its impossibly muscled legs kept churning up the field beneath it for a dozen feet. Then, abruptly, the bovine beast pulled up before him, tossing its head back and snorting furiously.

"Traveler, come on home. Traveler, come!" A distant voice drifted to them from somewhere in the vacant darkness. The sound floated clear to his ears. The bull must've heard it too. It snorted at Elias before turning to find the source of the shout. "Come on home. Come on back, Traveler," the voice called out once more, and this time there was something familiar in it. The sound of the voice suddenly made Elias think of warmth and lost hopes. It made him think of his favorite meal and his mother's hugs. He took a step toward it, along with the mighty bull. He couldn't help it.

Then he heard the wolf in his head once more. It was angry. It needed to kill, to feed on the flesh of a fallen foe. Elias felt its pure fury in every fiber of his being, in every molecule of his soul. He stopped walking toward the voice, everything that had called him forgotten in one quick breath. Elias suddenly looked down to his right hand. It held a jagged-toothed, eight-inch hunting knife, and even as he squeezed the spongy wood of the knife's grip, Elias could not recall how it arrived there. The wolf howling for blood inside his head seemed to make the question a moot point. Elias answered his beast's call without a sound, simply stepping one pace towards the mythical bull and thrusting his knife deep into the join at head and neck. Elias didn't cower from the act, driving the dagger in deep, ripping and tearing through ludicrously dense tissue until his entire arm was soaked from shoulder to fingers in bright red bull's blood.

The howl of the wolf left his mind in a flash, and once more the beckoning shouts of that eerily familiar voice reached his ears. "Traveler, where are you?" it called with bright, blossoming hope. And then, like a cloud before the sun, it changed, "What have they done to you?! What has *he* done to you!?" it demanded, before a cry came that shattered him, "Elias, no!" The once warm voice took on a horrible chill with that screech, a chill so icy cold it jolted Elias clean from the nightmare.

He sat up fast and regretted it immediately, as his forehead bashed into the ventilation duct hanging three feet above his sleeping cranny. "Ahh, dang it!" Elias' pained shriek echoed down the twisting access tunnel. He reached a hand up to his mouth but pulled it away quickly as he realized the childish futility of the gesture. *Get it together, man,* he admonished himself. *God, what was that dream though?* he thought, scooching clear of the low-hanging duct. With a groan, he rolled a few feet to his left and fell down from his sleeping perch atop a boxy piece of ventilation machinery lining an access tunnel. Elias landed on the metal grating of the tunnel with a deal more force than he'd intended, and once more cringed as evidence of his location went echoing down the winding passage. *Dang it, Elias, get yourself together.*

That nightmare really had him rattled. He stood up on the walkway and glanced down the path behind and ahead of him. As soon as he was sure no one was close by, he leaned against the tunnel's rail and drew in an extended nervous breath. Elias took a few moments to try and capture the unsettling dream's story in his head, but it slipped through his mind's eye just before he could remember it with any firm definition. All he knew was that whatever had disturbed him in the dream was still with him somehow. He felt its cold fingers all over his destiny.

Elias shook his head clear of what he couldn't unravel and tucked his trusty blue ball cap back in its accustomed place atop his skull. Then he whipped his tablet out from his back pocket. *Oh, no,* he thought in horror at first glimpse of the clock in the lower right corner of the pocket tablet's homepage. Like a striking cobra, Elias launched himself down the access tunnel. The path weaved first left, then right, and then right again before he came to a screeching halt, even sliding a little on the metal grating like some Looney-Toons character. The hatch he needed was right above him, set right into the access tunnel's ceiling. Elias approached the ladder rungs protruding from the bulkhead leading up to it, and only then did he realize his pocket tablet was still clutched tight in his hand. Tucking it back in its usual place in his back pocket, he instantly started the climb.

He was late, very late. *God, why didn't I set an alarm?* He'd certainly meant to. *I suppose with all the craziness of last night, and all that freakin' running around I did, I just passed out in my hiding spot before I remembered to set it.* That made a lot of sense to him, but it brought no comfort. All he could think about as he spun the handle of the ceiling hatch above him was how he should've been doing this very thing thirty or forty minutes earlier. Day 3 of the Final Tournament was set to begin at 0900 ST. And even though it was only 0855 right now, Elias had wanted to be in place a good while before most people would arrive. He couldn't afford someone spotting him as he made his climb to his viewing spot. His father would never let him stay if he found him there.

So he was cursing himself as he ascended the rungs of the vertical access tunnel beyond the opened ceiling hatch. He was going to have to pick his moment if he wanted to climb up that big, gnarled, old oak he had discovered in the Meadow's forest. Elias figured it was really the only way to see any of the action on the tennis courts from the forest. If he had to stay low and hide behind some shrubs or something, he'd never see over the bleachers. He had to climb up that old oak and sit in that conveniently placed fork in the tree about twenty feet up its trunk, or not bother at all.

Elias reached another ceiling hatch at the top of the vertical access tunnel and paused there to catch his breath. He thought about what he was about to do and the surreal absurdness of what this day promised to bring. Even now, he could barely believe any of it was actually happening. The last thing in the world Elias had expected his father to sit down and tell him yesterday, after he came and plucked him from that creepy family he'd dropped him off with, was how he had challenged Commander Montrois.

The news seemed as unreal then as it still did now. *How could Dad fight Mr. Montrois?* he wondered, leaning back against the wall of the tunnel while keeping one hand on the rung, and not for the first time. It made no sense to him. Both he and Maisie had told their father countless times, over and over again, about how much they owed everything to Carrie Montrois. Her actions on that launchpad were the only reason he and Maisie were still alive. *And dad is going to try and kill her husband?* The notion was illogical to the fullest extent. Worse yet, it was a betrayal. It was dishonorable. Elias had screamed as much at his father last night, but Perry Sagal wouldn't listen. Instead, he was going to save the world by killing Elias' honor. He was going through with it. Nothing Elias had said made any difference. "You're too young to understand," his father had told him.

"Eli, this is what dad feels he's got to do. He don't want to, but he feels he has to. We need to get past our doubts and fears and give him our support," Maisie had added in her most patronizing voice, which was worse still. *It was her damn life Carrie had saved too, for cripe's sakes.*

He'd simply stared back at his family in bewildered disappointment, and when his father had made to grab his arm to lead him off to his room "to calm him down," as he had put it, Elias had spun away from him. His sister had made a grab for him as well, but he evaded her with an easy side step. He'd even added a nasty scowl as he blew past her, just for good measure. Elias made it through the hatchway and was forty feet down the alleyway beyond before his father's head and shoulders had emerged from the portal. "Elias! Come back here! Elias!" he had shouted, standing helpless in the open hatchway.

Elias had no intention of going back. He knew what his father had intended. He and Maisie would watch over him all night, and in the morning his father would drop him off with that boring ass family—whose name he never even bothered to learn—and force him to stay there all day until his father came and got him, *if* he came and got him. Elias would have to just wait and see.

Well, he'd be damned if he was going to let that happen. If his father wouldn't call off the match, then no way was he going to stop Elias from watching the fight his entire future rested upon. So he'd quickly formulated a plan as he darted down the twisting alleyways of Orange Corridor. He knew he had to avoid his father and whatever minions he may employ to search for him, so he definitely needed to stay hidden, which meant he couldn't be exposed for long tomorrow as he made his way to his viewing spot in the Meadow's forest. After only a few seconds reviewing the endless tangle of alleyways, ante-chambers and access tunnels of Cardinal's Nest Station weaving their way through his mind, Elias settled on the perfect hiding location. And seeing as how he'd awoken undiscovered in that very spot this morning, it obviously was a smart choice.

But even now, resting beneath the ceiling hatch, Elias was still uncertain about what exactly he hoped would happen in this upcoming fight he'd hidden himself away to watch. He definitely didn't want any harm to come to his father, but neither could he stomach the thought of his own family member slaying the love of Carrie Montrois' life. One more look at the clock on his pocket tablet told Elias he had no more time to work it out.

Stuffing the tablet away, he set to work spinning the handle of the ceiling hatch. The hatch popped loose after five rotations. It was spring-loaded, so swung up and open smoothly and slowly. Elias had discovered it weeks ago, along with a similar hatch in the desert, and even one in the middle of the meadow itself. This hatch opened up on the peak of a slight rise in the forest floor right between two gigantic elms. The top of the hatch was completely covered over with turf and forest litter. Similarly, the hatch in the desert came up right in the center of the oasis, covered by an artificial rock that blended into the surrounding landscape. The hatch in the meadow had a thick layer of sod atop it and popped open, unseen except from directly above, right in the center of a patch of wild raspberries. Elias had spent an entire afternoon lying on his back in that patch, munching juicy raspberries and staring up into the milky blackness above.

He'd remembered the hatches in that mad dash away from his family's living quarters and knew instantly they were going to be the key to his plan. The forest hatch would get him into The Meadow without a soul seeing, provided there was no one in the forest. He'd almost decided on sneaking into The Meadow last night and hiding in the forest until morning. But when he remembered the hatches, he realized he could sleep in a warm cranny he knew of close by and slip into the forest just a few dozen minutes beforehand. He could've easily slipped up into the fork of the oak a half hour ago, with only the first few people arriving. Only, now that he was late, Elias wasn't certain he could make it to his viewing spot without being noticed by the packed crowd.

Well, you'll just have to risk it, won't ya, Elias? he told himself with resigned determination as he popped his head up through the hatch to peer around the dim forest. The coast was clear, just as he expected. So he clambered up out of the access tunnel and stayed low, ducking from tree to tree most of the way to the old oak at the edge of the forest. He realized the behavior was a bit foolish after fifty yards or so, seeing as how he was completely alone in the damp woods, so jogged warily the remainder of the way to the big tree.

Here is where it gets tricky. As soon as he started the climb, he would be exposed for at least the first fifteen feet. After that, he could tuck himself completely out of sight behind the towering tree all the way to his viewing spot. He risked a peek around the oak to discover if any eyes were pointed his way and instantly realized he could be wearing a bright orange vest while blaring disco from a loudspeaker and no one would notice him on his climb. For one thing, two of the sets of bleachers faced completely away from him. Plus, the people on the other set, along with those milling around at the open end of the horseshoe, had eyes only for the two combatants standing at opposite ends of a black-lined tennis court. *Oh, Dad, what are you doing?* Elias desperately thought, scurrying up the oak with no regard for stealth.

He pulled himself up into the majestic tree and adjusted his position until he was comfortable. He wanted to have his back against the trunk and also clearly see without any limbs bending through his field of vision. He achieved the ideal position and location just as Harclay Aponyaschefski raised a microphone to his lips down on the court. Elias was a good eighty yards away from the action, so he couldn't exactly make out the microphone as anything more than a black smudge, but when he heard the survivor's voice boom out from a speaker somewhere, he figured it was a pretty good assumption. Conversely, the slim-shafted morningstar his father held loose in his right hand at his starting position was clearly visible from this distance. It was the end of the court nearest Elias, yet it was still about 65 yards away, but even so, the weapon was plainly recognizable. Elias had been researching medieval weapons ever since he'd first learned they were what the combatants of the Final Tournament would be using in their battles. Elias had been spellbound by all the pomp and reverence surrounding the Final Tournament. He knew his father had originally opposed the fights wholeheartedly, so he kept his interest in the tournament-style battles, and the awesome weaponry a secret from him and Maisie both.

When Elias had first heard about the Final Tournament he had instantly remembered lying on the floor in the priest's quarters and staring at the survivor with wondrous curiosity. He remembered thinking then that the man presaged something momentous. He'd felt like the skinny survivor brought their future with him up here from Earth. Elias wanted desperately to know why the man thought The Final Tournament was the path to that future. Something inside him wanted to hear the survivor standing before an enraptured audience, preaching his beliefs. The idea kindled within him hope for a grand purpose or noble goal. He couldn't say why exactly that might be, no more than he could deny the fact that he was almost giddy now as the man spoke, "You both know the rules and you've accepted them," the survivor said, with that same spark in his voice that had so intrigued Elias back in the priest's liquor lab. "In so doing, you have sworn yourselves by your very lives to abide by them," he continued as Elias leaned forward, straining to hear. "And so, let your battle begin."

The survivor jogged slowly off the court, and Elias couldn't help but feel a bit disappointed. He lifted his gaze from Aponyaschefski in time to catch Montrois take his first step toward his father. The weapon the commander carried, though another 25 yards further than his father's, was easy to make out from his viewing spot as well. It was a simple device. His father's chosen weapon was attached to a 3' steel staff painted matte-black, with yellow tape wrapped around the lower fifth for a grip, exactly like Montrois'. The only difference being the device grafted to each staff's end. Perry Sagal's was tipped with an eight-inch steel ball with at least nine or ten arrowhead shapes welded around its circumference. Whereas Montrois' weapon's head was a simple device, familiar to most everyone in the known world. Montrois wielded a battleaxe. The shaft of his axe was just as long as that of Perry's morningstar, though the axe handle curved backwards slightly, about halfway up. The axe head itself was also matte-black, apart from an inch-wide band at the edge that Elias could see gleaming silver with sharp promise all the way from the forest. The axe may have been recognizable for what it was, but it was still foreboding in appearance, nonetheless. The blade stretched eighteen inches, Elias guessed, from tip to tip, and jutted out from the handle a good ten inches as well. There was just the one head, however. Elias had heard rumors of earlier competitors wielding double-headed axes, but apparently, Montrois felt the single-bladed version of the weapon was the way to go. Elias figured the man knew best. His confident stride sure seemed to shout as much.

Elias looked to his father to see how Montrois' confidence was affecting Dr. Perry Sagal. His father stood firmly in place, the morningstar still held low in his right hand. He knew his dad was one cool customer, with all those countless operations he'd needed to perform over the years, not to mention the military service he had in his background—which he refused to ever tell Elias anything about—but even still, he thought his father would show some sign of nervousness as the mean-mugging, hulking, square-shouldered security commander lumbered toward him, axe held at the ready. Instead, his dad's resoluteness seemed to visibly redouble. He brought his shoulders up once and rolled his neck. Then, just before Montrois arrived in front of him, Perry Sagal darted to his right two paces before quickly adding five more up court. Montrois turned to face him and a bemused look that was plain even from Elias' vantagepoint dozens of yards away popped up on the commander's broad, scruffy face.

Elias could understand why he wore it. He too was curious as to why his father was making his way to center court with his free arm raised high above his head. Perry Sagal began rotating once there in a slow, patient circle, all the while shouting something to the crowd. Elias couldn't make out a word of it, but it was apparently inflammatory to some folks; the rush of enraged, unintelligible taunts, and shouts that quickly rippled out from the surging crowd was evidence of that. When Montrois added a bellow of his own and charged his father at full speed, any lingering doubt about his dad's plea to the assembled residents was put to rest.

Listen to him, you jerks, Elias silently begged the recalcitrant residents, and Montrois himself, Montrois most of all. *If dad refuses to back down from this fight, you're my only hope left, Mr. Montrois.* Elias let his gaze drift up from the match for a quick second to send a prayer out to his friend Carrie through the seamless glass of Stargazer Ceiling and the inky twilight beyond. *Please tell your husband to lay his axe down at my daddy's feet somehow. Please,* he prayed, *my dad will take care of him after, I promise he will. I'll make sure nothing bad happens to him. Please,* he pleaded, more apologizing rather than praying now. *I couldn't make my dad drop out. I'm so sorry, I tried so hard. You gotta stop your husband now. It's the only way.*

His eyes flicked back to the action on the tennis court in time to see his father duck a looping slash from Montrois' axe. Elias' dad rolled forward and wound up five yards behind Montrois before the massive man could bring himself to a stop and change directions. He clearly had fury still bubbling out of him, but he held off from any further charges. The security commander stretched out his weapon instead, pointing it straight at Perry Sagal's chest. Once more, Elias could tell some words were being spoken, but could not hear them. He took advantage of the reprieve in action to dart a few quick glances around the edges of the Final Tournament's battlefield. The crowd was mesmerized, almost down to the very last man. Then he noticed a number of parents in the crowd clutching tightly to children no older than himself. His anger and indignation at the unfairness of the sight was soon forgotten though, when he noticed that he could only see four of the security officers standing around the tennis court's perimeter.

He had expected to see all six remaining officers pulling guard duty for the fight. Or five of them at the very least. It was possible Officer Dobechek was still laid up in his father's spiffy hospital down Branch 1. Though, he'd assumed she'd be out of there by now. Newton Hospital was like that, no one stayed there long. Elias' father had marveled every night over his finger of smuggled Pappy Van Winkle about the feats they were performing in its surgical wing, with various trials and simulations, and in actual practice in a few cases. He raved and raved about the exotic equipment they were working with in the labs too. "I'm playing catch-up with the science from one minute to the next, kid," he had said. "I swear, Eli, I don't think I'm ever gonna actually understand the capabilities of some of the medical equipment we're working with in there. It scares me a little." His father had speedily changed the topic after that, and Elias had drifted off to sleep on their comfy tan couch. But the impression had been made. Newton Hospital was capable of miracles. So Dobechek ought to have been recovered enough to stand sentry by now. Only, his focused study had turned up no sign of her. *Maybe she got hurt worse than people figured,* he guessed.

That still left one other officer unaccounted for. Elias couldn't be sure who that officer might be. He had taken a strong interest in the security staff since day one aboard station. It wasn't only because of Jasper Montrois and how much he revered him simply by proxy for Carrie. He held them all on a pedestal of sorts in his mind, like they were professional athletes, or action stars, or comic book heroes. So he should've been able to recall which face was absent. He thought he'd known everything about them. He repeated their bios to kids on The Meadow's ballfield, like stats on ESPN. It made him angry that he couldn't place the absent officer. He was their biggest fan, after all. In fact, what Elias really wanted, if he was being honest with himself, was to be one of them. *But they'll never let me join up if my dad kills their commander.* The thought was unsettling. He couldn't make heads or tails of what he was actually pulling for in that scenario. *Of course, joining the security staff to make good on my promise to earn Carrie's sacrifice in Commander Montrois' eyes isn't more important than dad's life, right?* He asked himself, and the doubt that gripped him in response was shameful.

The action on the court started up again and Elias was able to step aside from the turmoil in his heart; even the puzzle of the missing officer's identity was quickly forgotten. The combatants seemed to abandon words and charge in the same instant. They met with a thunderous clang of morningstar on axe, then instantly withdrew their weapons to aim another swing. His father flicked his morningstar low, but Montrois stepped back to meet the blow with ease. Perry Sagal went right into an overhead looping smash aimed at the commander's head. The giant man was all over it; this time stepping right as he parried to provide himself room for a counterstroke. Elias' father saw the blow coming, however and spun quickly to his left, opening up a small gap between the two men. The crowd noise filled Elias' ears then. He couldn't be sure if they'd been screaming all along, or only now took up their chants. *Jesus, have I been holding my breath too?* He pondered before the fighters charged each other again and all questions evaporated.

It was Montrois who went for the legs this time. His father was not expecting it. Too late to parry, he leapt over the axe blade as it sliced through the air his legs had occupied only milliseconds earlier. The jump was so sudden and desperate that Perry Sagal wasn't able to land with any grace whatsoever. He avoided tumbling to his knees but was still wildly off-balance as Montrois' axe came whizzing toward his face. Elias was certain he could see the hairs on the back of his father's head sheared in half as he ducked just in time to avoid a hideous death. Montrois arrested his follow-through and butted the end of his axe handle into the top of his dad's head.

Perry Sagal was knocked backwards, landing on his ass with Montrois lurking right over him. The commander whipped down a one-handed slash that his dad was only just able to avoid with a quick roll. Then the good doctor managed to get his morningstar in the path of the commander's next slash, buying him time to spring back to his feet. His father dodged and weaved in retreat from an onslaught of wild swings after that until Montrois finally pulled up short, huffing with exertion.

The crowd noise once again invaded his concentration. It was just as loud as last time, only now it seemed like he could actually make out a few of the shouted phrases. The cruel suggestions and ungodly taunts revealed to Elias the obvious fact that Perry Sagal had been in the extreme minority in his opposition to the security staff's overthrow of AOA and their imposition of the Final Tournament. *They're all rooting for the commander, at least the loudest people are anyway.* Elias' confusion, doubt, and accompanying shame flooded his soul again with that observation.

He was hoping the action would snap free the weight of those feelings once more, but as the battle on the tennis court flared back to hot, the gravity of their presence remained. His father charged this time while Montrois held off, letting Sagal come to him. The doctor never broke his stride, bringing a one-handed smash flying in at the commander's head as he arrived in front of him. Montrois didn't move to parry. His axe-wielding right arm stayed still. Instead, with his left, he simply snatched the morningstar's shaft out of the air two feet from his face. Perry Sagal had put a great deal of effort into the blow, and Elias' father was a strong man, but Montrois had stopped it dead. It left his dad off-balance yet again, and as he stumbled to his left to keep his feet; the gorilla-man wrenched the wicked weapon from his grasp.

His father wasted no time in darting up court to put distance between himself and the man who now held a medieval instrument of war in each of his two massive hands. Montrois didn't chase him. He turned to the crowd to raise his new trophy high above his head. Elias could see his lips forming words, but still couldn't hear them. Whatever they had been, the people approved. Cheers seemed to ripple through every corner of the assembled mass of wide-eyed residents. Montrois turned to face his father after a few moments of basking in the cheers and very deliberately tossed the morningstar a few yards away from him.

Elias was panicked. He was engrossed. He watched on with terror. He watched on with anticipation. He felt sick to his stomach. He never felt more alive. He was a burning ball of confusion on a collision course with clarity. Then, Montrois charged his father, and all those emotions redoubled.

Perry Sagal stayed poised and ready for the charge. He ducked under the first slash the commander launched and dodged the next two by dancing right then left. Then he stepped back from an arcing slash aimed at his chest. Letting the axe whip past him, he stepped in toward Montrois and clasped both his hands on the giant man's axe handle. The commander tried to yank his weapon free, but the doctor went with him, clinging firmly to the battleaxe. Another yank brought his dad shoulder to shoulder with Montrois, and without hesitation, he snapped in a solid headbutt, catching the taller man on the side of the face.

The commander's head did bounce back a few inches, but only that. One might've expected the look on his face to be a bit dazed as well, but it was only calm fury that filled his eyes. Elias could see it plain from a quarter of the way across The Meadow. Fear and wonder warred in his mind as he watched the big man endure yet another powerful headbutt from his father. The commander's head didn't move a centimeter this time. A smirk tugged at the corners of his mouth instead, as he brought up his free hand, covered Perry Sagal's face with it and shoved. His father lost his grip on the axe and went stumbling backwards. He managed to stay on his feet until Montrois charged him. The commander collided, shoulder first, into Elias' dad's chest, launching him through the air a good four yards.

Perry Sagal wound up a foot in front of the black line along the open end of the bleachers. Montrois might've ended it then and there. Yet, oddly, the man strolled back to center court. Refraining from addressing the hungry, begging crowd, he simply turned to Perry Sagal, climbing back to his feet, and waved for the doctor to charge him. He even nodded to his right at the morningstar lying on the turf a few yards from him. Elias understood the commander was daring his father to make a grab for his weapon so he could connect a deadly blow as he bent to retrieve it. His father must've understood that as well because he charged straight for the commander rather than the morningstar. Montrois might have been caught off-guard for a moment by the decision. He certainly seemed to react a good deal slower than his capabilities would suggest. His first reaction was, in fact, a backwards step. That alone was unprecedented.

By the time Perry Sagal was within striking distance though, his composure was fully restored. Montrois slashed at the charging doctor, but Elias' father anticipated it, ducking under the swing to slide right on past the burly security commander. A twist and another looping slash forced Elias' dad to dash backwards to avoid disembowelment. In the blink of an eye, Perry Sagal changed direction, launching off his back foot and closing the gap between himself and his foe. Montrois was stepping back from him, trying to bring his axe to bear on the doctor's side when Perry Sagal's elbow smashed into the side of his neck with a thud that Elias was sure he heard over the crowd noise all the way up in his high perch. He knew as Montrois brought his free hand up to cover the fresh injury, reeling backwards a few paces, that he should feel ecstatic about his father's sudden change of fortune, but as Perry Sagal hounded the commander's retreat, he felt only his sick confusion all the stronger.

Montrois tried to buy time to recover and catch his breath by flicking his axe towards his pursuer, but Elias' father snatched the weapon just under the blade with his right hand. He tugged on the axe, forcing the commander to extend his arm, and then jumped up a few inches to bring his left elbow crashing down on his opponent's stressed and outstretched arm. Elias didn't hear his snarl of pain, though it was plain to read on his face. The axe tumbled from his grasp as he snatched his arm back. He held it cradled against his chest as the doctor whipped a bicycle kick at his legs. As that impact bent him sideways one way, Perry Sagal danced the other to bury a fist in the commander's side just below his ribcage. Elias' father didn't wait to see what damage the blow caused, instantly following it with an elbow to Montrois' jaw. As the imposing security commander was forced backwards a step from the blow, Perry Sagal stepped into a mighty right jab that connected solidly into Montrois' solar plexus.

Elias' heart was in his throat as the towering commander fell to one knee, clutching his midsection and gasping for breath. Perry Sagal seemed to skip into a tremendous right hook. Elias figured it would knock Montrois clean on his back; he could see the corded muscles in his father's shoulders bunch through his sweat-slick red cut-off tee. Only somehow, the commander managed to flick his arm up to block the punch with ease. He was back to his feet in the next heartbeat, and the left hook that Perry Sagal countered with after his first had been thwarted so abruptly was captured in Montrois' gigantic right hand.

He tugged on the captured arm, and with a display of strength so ludicrous it touched Elias even through his fog of confusion, the commander flung his father across the court. What's more, he'd done it with his freshly injured arm. *Incredible*, Elias thought with awe and terror. The doctor had landed in an undignified heap five yards away. Montrois was right on him. Perry Sagal was in the process of rising to his feet when the commander grabbed a clutch of his thinning hair to hold his head steady as he smashed a gargantuan fist into the perfect ivory teeth of Dr. Perry Sagal.

No! Elias wanted to scream, but something kept him silent. Not so the crowd. The uproar at the sight of his father's bloody teeth flying loose like shrapnel from a grenade as Montrois smashed home three more devastating blows was deafening. The commander loosened his grip on Perry Sagal's hair and clasped it around his neck. Montrois lifted him bodily off the turf with his injured arm, and once more, flung the doctor across the court. His father's landing was no more graceful than his last. He rolled to his back quickly though and began to scramble backwards like a crab as Montrois stalked toward him. Elias might've been the first to see it, but the crowd's audible reaction wasn't far behind his own realization; Perry Sagal was scrambling right towards his fallen morningstar. He was between the weapon and Montrois, blocking the commander's view of the nasty killing tool, so the hulking brute kept right on heedlessly chasing the scrambling doctor.

The crowd suddenly hushed just as his father's hand brushed against the yellow-taped handle of his weapon. Montrois must've been too in the moment to notice, and whether Perry Sagal knew what his hand now held was anyone's guess. He had to be dazed and woozy, with possibly a broken jaw, but he didn't hesitate to slash the weapon at the face lurking just above him. The blow wasn't the strongest of the fight, it might even have been classified as feeble under other circumstances, but it had enough behind it to tear a bloody path across the tanned, scruffy, hard face of Jasper Montrois. Elias could see four distinct gashes starting just below the commander's right ear and running up and across his right eye, two of which seemed to cut directly across the eyeball itself. The four lines didn't last long. In a heartbeat, the blood sheeting from the slashes blended together, leaving him looking as though he was about to star in a darker, redder version of The Phantom of The Opera.

Montrois' hand shot up to his face to staunch the flow as he lurched away from the still seated doctor, trying to wipe the blood clear of his eye to no avail. Elias' father stood, spitting teeth and globs of bloody phlegm. The silence in The Meadow was absolute, but Elias didn't know that until he screamed, "No!" His father had pulled back his morningstar to crash it into the side of the half-blind commander's head, when the shout had escaped his lips. The simple exclamation carried all the way to the killing grounds. His father had definitely heard it. Perhaps it was because everyone else was silent, making the shout perfectly clear and distracting, that his father pulled up short with his swing, or maybe he'd recognized his son's disloyal screech. Elias would never know. Montrois took advantage of his father's distracted state by charging headlong into him.

The two went down in a tangle of limbs, but it was the commander who wound up on top of the smaller man. Elias might've screamed "No," again, he couldn't be sure. Everyone else in the crowd was seemingly screaming "Yes," drowning out whatever he might have shouted. In a blistering fury, Montrois hammered down punch upon punch, blow upon blow, straight into Perry Sagal's already damaged face. A dozen blows in, Elias watched his father's legs go limp beneath his gigantic attacker, but it was another six or seven punches before the security commander stopped his assault.

Montrois lurched to his feet, straddling the limp figure of Dr. Perry Sagal, both of his massive fists covered in red as he raised them high. His right was held a bit lower—a result of his fresh injury—but he opened them both to the heavens above as he let loose a snarl so ferocious it would put any lion to shame. It was those blood covered hands raised high, along with the accompanying howl, that made Elias suddenly recall his nightmare. *Oh god ... I ... I killed him. The bull's blood is on my hands,* he understood, with a heart so heavy it could crush diamonds.

Half-blind and staggering slightly, Montrois started walking towards his battleaxe across the court. The crowd hushed as he approached it, perhaps in anticipation of an address of some sort. Montrois simply bent over and snatched up his weapon of choice. Silently and purposefully, he staggered back towards the still limp doctor with the pulped face. The commander paused for a long, stretched out heartbeat, hunched over the unconscious body. Elias didn't understand, and judging from the tense silence pervading The Meadow, neither did anyone else.

Without warning, the commander abruptly whipped his axe down toward the beaten man at his feet. Elias watched in dumbfounded horror as Jasper Montrois severed his father's head in four fast, heavy chops of his black battleaxe. He flung the axe to the ground afterwards, bending down to Perry Sagal's decapitated corpse. And when he stood back up, palming the gore-dripping skull in one massive, bloody hand as an NBA Power-Forward would a basketball, Elias was frozen stiff with grief and shame. Montrois then began to spin in a slow circle at center court, face half-covered in a sheet of red, splattered chest to heel in the blood of his fallen foe and snarling with triumph.

The silence in The Meadow remained as Montrois tossed the head of a once proud doctor back towards its sprawled out body. "Who challenges now?!" The commander bellowed in a voice so deep and powerful it floated clear to Elias' ears. The continued silence of the crowd certainly helped as well. "Who's next? Come on," he taunted. "Come on and kill me. Come on, who challenges? Speak now. How 'bout it, Mikkelson? You got any other ringers to send my way?" Mikkelson either wasn't present or chose not to respond, so Montrois pressed on. "Come on, who challenges my right to lead us? Huh? Which of you wants to die today? Huh? Anyone? Anyone? Come on, who wants to die?" His voice was cold with promise, a promise no man or woman present was willing to test. The crowd remained dead silent as Montrois made a slow circuit in place. "Remember this day," he finally told them after it seemed he'd let the moment stretch on forever. "Remember this feeling. Remember who I am."

With that, the security commander stalked off the court, never once breaking stride the whole way across the turf, over the footbridge and through the archway. His officers and Aponyaschefski fell in alongside him, and it was only after their echoing footfalls had fully faded from the giant dome that people began to speak again. Slowly at first, then all at once, the dam broke. The place seemed to explode like a hornet's nest, yet the buzz of chatter that drifted up to Elias in that ancient oak barely registered. Elias' eyes had wandered back to his father. They were locked there on a headless lump of carrion in the center of a pool of spreading blood, glimmering with reflected starlight. His father was dead, and he and his idol had killed him. The world would never be the same again.

CHAPTER 17

PEDRO

"Let me speak to her!" the bound Star Hawk copilot demanded of them. "That was the deal, ya bastards! She ain't taking off before she hears from me."

Pedro Alvarez knew the bruised and fearful man strapped to a rolling desk chair before him wasn't wrong. After all, he was the one that had offered the deal to the copilot and his cronies. Though in truth, most of him had wanted the two pilots and his treasonous former sergeant to reject the offer. His blood had been up for the past few days. How could it not? He'd been standing just a few feet from a half dozen brutal death duels, not to mention the fact that he'd actually been only a second or two away from challenging in the damn tournament himself, several times in fact. All of it had Pedro Alvarez craving a release. He had hoped Marge and the pilots would give it to him, but, sadly, they'd meekly flung the feeble weapons they'd managed to scrape together for their failed heist to the floor after only the briefest of reflections.

"You'll hear from her when we get the okay from the Commander," Pedro told the whiny copilot in an emotionless voice. Barry Calvin rolled his eyes in response until a frown quickly spread across his lips when Steve Schwambach began chuckling at his pathetic state. Steve was standing right next to the chair on which the copilot was strapped down with duct tape, lurking over Calvin with unrelenting menace in his eyes, even as he laughed. "For now, just sit there comfortably as you can and keep silent," Pedro added when Calvin's attention had once more fallen back to him.

"Where the hell is Sergeant Marge!" Barry Calvin shouted back, defying Pedro's instructions. "What've you done to her? Huh? I want to speak with her too," he demanded through split lips. "Gillian ain't gonna take off without hearing from her as well as me."

"That wasn't the deal, Barry," Pedro told him, a little annoyed.

"Fuck you and your deals!" The copilot added a pitiful attempt at spitting in Pedro's face on top of his outburst, and Schwambach backhanded him alongside his head.

Barry Calvin had nothing but unintelligible groans to say to that. Pedro and Steve broke out with tepid laughter at the treacherous worm. "You'll speak to Gerwitz when we say," Pedro told the dazed man. "And you'll tell her what we want you to tell her."

Calvin managed to raise his head back up and unscramble his eyes enough to focus on Pedro just in front of him, leaning casually against the Commander's desk in the security staff's rec room. "Tell me why you're sending her back to Earth," the battered Star Hawk copilot managed after a few moments. "I thought the point of y'all's overthrow and the damn Final Tournament was to stop the missions back to the planet."

"There's something down there we need," Pedro lied. "Don't worry about it. Worry about the pain from another of Steve's smacks to your ear if you don't shut the hell up."

"Who?" the petulant prick asked with condescension.

Lieutenant Schwambach, Pedro almost shouted the name at Calvin until he suddenly realized, with a shock of shame, that he hadn't been using the Witenagemot council names, as they'd all sworn to, not really anyway, not on the inside, where it counted. He vowed then and there to change that. *I gotta remember to call him Lieutenant if I want him calling me Captain Alvarez. Steve is dead with all the others, as well as Pedro. It's just Commander, Steward, Captain, Supervisor and Lieutenant now.* That thought was a strange one, so he shook it off and answered the insolent fool taped to the chair, "Lieutenant Schwambach is an honored councilmember of the Witenagemot, but he is not above beating a man to death," he told Calvin with no hint of humor. "Mock either one of us again, and you'll discover that truth for yourself."   "Fine then, Captain Alvarez ... is that your new name?" Pedro nodded. Barry Calvin returned the gesture with an irritating, little grin. "Very well, *Captain Alvarez*, why are you really sending my partner back to Earth?"

The captain's answer came in the form of a nod to Lieutenant Schwambach, and Steve–*Lieutenant Schwambach*–lashed out with another backhand to the ear. The copilot's pathetic whimpering groans that followed were particularly satisfying. Captain Alvarez didn't want the man probing into the motivations for Gillian Gerwitz' mission down to Earth in one of Cardinal's Nest's two Star Hawks. It was a weak point in their plan, and the Commander and Aponyaschefski–*I mean, the Steward*–had both pointed out that fact to the Captain when they'd first outlined their plans for him to lure the pilots and Sergeant Marge to the rec room by very conspicuously moving the PRZVL-33's and the other heavy guns they'd hid away for the Final Tournament back into the weapons locker. The Commander knew the sarge couldn't resist a chance to seize the weaponry. He knew they'd come for it. Captain Alvarez needed only spring the simple trap when they arrived and then keep them locked up until what they had in mind for today.

"Just hit him and keep him dazed," his Commander had told him this morning before he left for The Meadow. "Don't let the son of a bitch press you. None of what we have been doing lately makes sense to the treacherous bastard; one more thing won't be that concerning. We only need him to confirm his condition to Gillian or she won't take off. So just keep him quiet and relatively comfortable until then. So, I guess ... don't hit him too hard," he'd added with a smirk. Barry Calvin would give Gillian Gerwitz that sitrep, Pedro–*I mean, Captain Alvarez*–would see it done, and then the part he was looking forward to most would come.

Captain Alvarez would see it all done. He was as dedicated to his Commander and their new Witenagemot as any of his fellow members. He would not fail them. After all, his job wasn't all that difficult really. But he knew it was important, and that was some balm for the sting of knowing he'd have to miss the Steward's speech to the assembled residents in The Meadow. A speech that was set to kick off in just five minutes, he realized with a gaze at his pocket tablet. /

hope Polly and Burg—I mean, Lieutenants Dobechek and Gregson— are in place, he thought of the team handling the other component of today's plans. *Maybe I ought to hail them and find out? Na, Lieutenant Dobechek would be pissed as shit,* he thought with an inner chuckle.

Lieutenant Dobechek and Lieutenant Gregson were supposed to be in position just outside of Branch 2 and the transport craft garage and lunar dock with a captive Sergeant Marge in tow. Which left Lieutenants Dirks, Woodson, and Masterson with Aponyaschefski—*the Steward, get it right, man*—and the Commander, the Final Tournament's grand champion, at The Meadow. All three teams were linked on an open comms line through their tablets. Captain Alvarez stared at his, hoping to hear the crackle of static preceding his orders to set the plan in motion buzz out from the device. He was a bit nervous about today, if he was being honest. The Steward had made it plain that the Commander's authority wasn't fully secured until today's plans had been carried out. Captain Alvarez was eager for that moment.

He did not think himself a power-hungry man, nor cruel, nor irrational, or anything like that. Captain Alvarez felt he was a *practical* man. He knew Jasper Montrois assuming power as the Commander was the only practical way to keep life churning in a relatively livable condition. He didn't need the Steward's brilliant observations and speeches to understand just how lucky they were to have Cardinal's Nest Station, nor what a responsibility to keep the human race alive was on all their shoulders due to that good fortune. He also understood, long before they even found the survivor, that the security staff was being sent off to die on useless missions. So he was all in favor of whatever means were necessary to ensure that stopped, and the safety and security of the station were maintained. There were few lingering doubts in his heart that the Commander would take good care of all of that. Even now, as he stood over the pathetic copilot, the man's bloody and bruised face seemed only earned, in the Captain's eyes. *The sergeant and these pussy-ass pilots are fools not to see the pure pragmatism of the Commander taking charge up here,* he thought, gazing down at the traitor.

"What about Cainey?" the piteous copilot asked him. "What did you do with him?"

Lieutenant Schwambach moved to smack the man once again, but Captain Alvarez raised his hand to stop him before the blow connected. "It's okay, Lieutenant," he told his fellow councilmember with a smirk in his voice. "Why would you care about the fate of your betrayer?" He asked Calvin.

Captain Alvarez couldn't keep the grin from stretching across his face with that question. Cainey had been easier to flip than either he or any of his fellow interrogators could've imagined. He'd needed only to see their weapons before the scrawny little pig-faced fool was spilling the beans on the mission the Captain and Lieutenant Schwambach had watched Sergeant Marge and the Star Hawk pilots *covertly* explain to him over a game of pool in the billiard lounge only a few minutes earlier. The ploy was as pathetically constructed as it was obvious to anticipate. The Commander had sent Captain Alvarez—then still just Pedro—along with Lieutenant Schwambach— before he'd adopted that title—to the lounge to scope for Cainey after Pedro had reported seeing Sergeant Marge whispering something to the little coward at dinner in the Main Cafeteria Hall earlier that day. It had been all the clarification either he or his Commander had required that the fools had indeed swallowed the bait. And when the dumb little shit had stumbled up to the sarge's billiard table to hang around for a game all of five minutes long, there had been absolutely zero doubts left.

And sure enough, they were right. The fools planned on storming the rec room to steal the surplus sidearms and ammo, and had even secured some hand trucks to haul away the two massive tri- pod-mounted PRZVL-33's. The 33's were Gatling guns on steroids. The most devastating squad assault weapon ever invented by man in Captain Alvarez's humble opinion. Their power sources burned through pretty fast though. Currently, they were down to seventeen of the battery packs, for the only two PRZVL's in the universe, and no one was going to be making any more of them anytime soon.

That was the reasoning AOA had given for not allowing the security staff to take them on their recons to Earth. The captain had only ever fired the damn things once in training before AOA realized how quickly they were burning through the battery packs and put a stop to it. The "space-machineguns," as Hopkins Masterson had unimaginatively nicknamed the weapons, didn't fire bullets and so required no re-loading. They were still a two-man weapons system though. But once the bulky beasts were mounted, the second man could stand by with his finger up his nose until it came time to switch out a battery pack. Captain Alvarez wasn't exactly sure just what it was the machine guns did fire. *Some sort of plasma projectile, or some such nonsense.* Captain Alvarez had majored in Sociology at Cal Tech, and while that naive kid was there, he did his best to steer clear of the science wing. So the physics of the deadly machines were well beyond his capacity to grasp. All Captain Alvarez knew was that the 4' high, 12' long, stubby, black barreled behemoths could bring Cardinal's Nest to an explosive end in seconds.

The sarge and the pilots planned on coming for the guns during the Commander's fight with that stupid-ass doctor in the hopes that all the officers would be at The Meadow performing security for the match. Sergeant Marge had actually tried to break in by herself the day before. It was a half-assed attempt at best, really. Captain Alvarez guessed she was looking to confront the Commander more than actually making a play for the weapons vault; she'd been so animated delivering her pleas and condemnations to the Commander that Captain Alvarez had understood it to be her true intentions. *For that day at least.* She had made it all the way to the weapons vault censor pad before he and Lieutenant Dobechek—*then Polly*—had stumbled into the room and caught her. So the idea that the sarge would make another play for the vault wasn't a hard one to cipher out. And her obvious cohorts were the knucklehead pilots who had showed up to drag her away from the rec room kicking and screaming after the Commander had made it plain that he would cut her throat if they didn't. And Nate Novocaine Barker was an obvious ally for them as well. The little module garage maintenance worker knew damn well how much the Captain and all the former officers hated his guts, as did everyone else aboard Cardinal's Nest. It only made sense that the sarge would use that knowledge to get the treacherous bastard to help her, and thus it had been no accident that Pedro Alvarez was glancing Barker's way during that dinner to catch the sarge whispering in the ugly little fucker's ear.

The Commander knew you'd try and use the little clown, Captain Alvarez thought with pride for his leader as he stared down his nose at the battered copilot. "Don't worry about poor little Nate Novocaine," he told Calvin. "We let him go. We made a deal, and he held up his end. We are men and women of honor in our Witenagemot, so we released him back into the population, free as a bird. The little bitch will lay low and keep his mouth shut today. So, if you got a sudden hope of the weaselly bastard rallying some folks to rescue you, go ahead and think again. You ought to have known what an unreliable worm Novocaine Barker was, and never involved him in your plans in the first place. Thankfully for us, you and Gillian and the sarge are dumbasses as well as traitors." Lieutenant Schwambach barked with laughter at that, and even the Captain had to chuckle at his own wit.

They were dumbasses, he thought, remembering the sarge and her pilot pals' half-assed attempted heist yesterday. The bumbling nitwits had been so loud hauling those hand trucks they'd brought to load the PRZVL-33's down the narrow alleyway that the idiots probably would've been caught even if Cainey wasn't working for them. But, as it happened, Cainey had indeed tipped them off.

Pedro Alvarez and Polly Dobechek had been waiting for Marge and her two pet pilots when they burst through the rec room hatchway. They had each held an M-4 rifle in one hand and an M-9 pistol in the other. The sergeant and the pilots had entered the room with nothing but makeshift clubs in their hands. Even still, they might've resisted, trusting on their fear of firing a weapon inside the station, but after Pedro had holstered his pistol and withdrew a Shock Disc from a pocket of his tactical vest, the three would-be thieves must've instantly known their plot was foiled. They all surely knew the capabilities of one of those tiny little gray discs, anyway. Toss it at the ground and anything within a 10' radius would be instantly zapped painfully into unconsciousness by the arcing voltage that shot up and out from the harmless looking puck. Clearly, none had the stomach to endure that pain. And after Pedro had offered them the deal he had been instructed by Jasper Montrois and Harclay Aponyaschefski to offer, they had thrown down their quaint weapons and raised their hands in surrender.

Maybe the traitors really believed they would let them go free after they did what was offered. Their easy capitulation had been yet more evidence to Pedro and his fellow officers that they were all doing the right thing. Only the weak willed and feeble minded among the residents were resisting the Commander's takeover. After all, if you thought about it for even a few moments, you'd realize his offered request for Gillian Gerwitz to fly solo down to Earth really didn't make a whole lot of sense. But he'd promised they would keep Barry under guard until she returned, and that Gillian would be able to confirm his condition every step of the way, and that they would all be held safe and secure in the rec room until she left on that flight the next day, so the fools must've been blinded by the selfish hope of survival, and so, eagerly accepted the terms. They'd been too eager to even question what was to become of Sergeant Marge who'd been conspicuously left out of the deal he'd offered. *Pathetic pussy-ass retards,* Captain Alvarez scoffed to himself before turning his attention once again to his pocket tablet.

Jed

He'd been staring up through Stargazer Ceiling at the brilliant, twinkling conglomeration beyond, so Jed didn't track exactly when Maisie had shoved her way into their conspiratorial huddle. First thing he knew of the recently bereaved young girl's arrival was her pleading voice desperately trying to elicit information from Jed Redding and his gathered friends.

He had turned his head up a few moments earlier, searching for an escape from the previous monotony of useless what-do-we-do-now questions and infuriating I-don't-know answers. Most of those I-don't-knows had come from the priest, while most of the what-do-we-do-nows were voiced by Larry Holderman and Gabe Duchesne, both of whom were currently sandwiching Jed in the circle. The priest stood with slouching shoulders directly across from Jed, crowded between Dolly Duchesne and Alice Stark, with Stevie Hyun jammed in between Alice and Larry. The uselessness of the group's question-and-answer game had driven Jed to the point of madness.

It was one thing to plot against the asshole security staff and that bastard Montrois, who'd cut the good doctor's goddamn head off, but it was another thing entirely doing it in broad daylight right under the security staff's fucking nose. The fact that their whispers were so utterly pointless drove home the absurdity of their behavior. Jed had wanted to run, to distance himself from his foolish friends, but he knew Larry would never forgive him, and Jed could not live with that. So he stayed and stared up at the stars. But Maisie's voice had brought him back to the conversation. "Have any of you seen Eli?" she asked in a tone that was all at once frightened, earnest, broken, and eternally strong.

"No, sweetie, I'm sorry," Dolly was the first to answer.

"We've only been here a few minutes, Mais," the priest told her. "It was as packed as this when we arrived. He could be anywhere in here."

Father Boyd was certainly right about that. The place was indeed packed. Well, packed around the dais the security staff raised in the center of The Meadow's soccer field, anyway; The Meadow itself was impossible to pack. But the station had been once more ordered to skeleton crew protocols and all off-duty personnel were ordered to attend some sort of ceremony/speech-type-thing the security staff was planning. So the sheep had all crowded the dais, shoulder to shoulder. Elias could be anywhere amongst them.

Jed and his circle of whisperers were at the far back of the mass of residents and could only see the backs of the first few rows of people directly in front of them. The dais itself was raised ten feet off the ground, so the survivor Aponyaschefski and security commander Montrois, with his four fresh scars slashing across a milky-white right eye and a black axe clutched tightly in his right hand, along with an officer Jed knew as Millicent Dirks, were plain to make out atop it, even from his rear vantagepoint.

There were also two other officers lurking in the back of the crowd. They were on opposite ends from each other and only about twenty yards from Jed's group of friends directly in the middle. Jed hadn't noticed them right away. It took a minute to actually see their faces before he remembered they were officers. They were in their black tactical pants and blouses, but they were very conspicuously unarmed, apart from a club in their right hands and a sheathed axe or bat handle slung over one shoulder. During the Tournament, every officer had been armed to the teeth with assault rifles and pistols galore. It was strange to see them stripped bare, so to speak. Stranger still, Jed couldn't locate any of the other four officers any-where in The Meadow.

"I know it was him yesterday that shouted "No!" just before dad … just before dad … just before Monty killed dad," Maisie said in a heartbroken voice. "I need to find him," she added with somber determination.

The girl was impressive, that was for sure. She was only a single day removed from watching her father's friend decapitate him in front of almost the entire population of humanity, but somehow, she was focused on her brother's state. It was really amazing to see. Amazing and soul-crushing, for Jed could offer no balm for her worries. He agreed It was most likely Elias who had shouted out yesterday. He didn't know the boy's voice that well, but he was certain the shout had come from The Meadow's forest, and he knew what an explorer of the station the kid was. Plus, they hadn't found him the night before when Jed had joined up with a team of about a dozen other trusted residents to search for the boy. They'd all come up empty and called the search off after a few hours.

Yet, when he realized the shout had come from the forest, he remembered that area had gone unsearched by his party. He'd quickly put two and two together and understood Elias hid out in those woods all night and had been watching his father's death match from the trees. *No child should ever have to see something like that,* Jed thought. Maisie seemed to be handling it as well as could be expected, but Jed knew Elias was another case all together. He understood the boy to be the least emotionally stable of the Sagal crew. Jed knew the doctor and Maisie had both taken great pains to care for the little explorer, even though he was but a year or two younger than Maisie herself. So Jed understood the boy's absence to be a reason for great concern. His eyes went up once again to the stars above, and though Jed probably would never admit as much, he prayed to God for the boy's safety and sanity.

Dolly stepped across the circle of conspirators to wrap Maisie in a bear hug. Jed wished he had the gumption to do the same, but feared the rejection that might come with such an act. *You're really just a coward deep down, ain't ya, Jeddy?* He asked himself rhetorically. "I'm so sorry about your father, Mais," Dolly told the brave young girl. "We're all here for you, sweetie. And I promise we will all help you look for Elias just as soon as this nonsense is finished," she promised.

"Yeah, Maisie, we'll look together." Stevie Hyun had strolled into The Meadow sans husband. She had joined in their circle without a word, keeping her silence until this moment.

Maisie seemed well pleased by the small redheaded woman's pledge. Perhaps she knew the inner turmoil Stevie was dealing with herself and knew that any gesture from the woman meant doubly as much because of it. Jed's heart went out to Stevie as well. She'd tried to stop her foolish husband from challenging and ensuring this whole terrible mess they were now in. Jed gave her credit for that. Though he knew some folks, his partner Larry Holderman included, were livid with her husband Abner Hyun for forfeiting and forcing Dr. Sagal to be killed in his place. Such people were shamefully lumping Stevie in with that choice. Abner found that monstrously unfair. He was no fan of Abner Hyun and his baffling decisions, but he kept enough of his objectivity to realize his wife was not at all to blame. He'd told Larry as much, several times, but the fool was blinded by anger. His navigator was definitely more open to reason than most residents of Cardinal's Nest currently were, that was for sure, but his reason didn't seem to stretch quite far enough to give Stevie Hyun a break. So Jed had been pleased when his partner hadn't shouted for the innocent woman to leave as soon as she'd joined their circle. *Maybe the gruff old fool is coming around,* he'd thought.

"Thanks, Stevie," Maisie told the freckle-faced woman.

"I still can't believe we aren't gonna do something to stop these assholes," Gabe spoke out in a tone that showed he felt Maisie's intrusion into their conversation to be a nuisance.

"What is it exactly you think we ought to be doing, Gabe?" Father Boyd asked with annoyance. "None of us here are any less frustrated with the security staff than you are. So, if you got an idea, we are all ears. If not, hold your tongue and have some decency. Maisie has just lost her father after only recently losing her mother, and now her brother is missing. This is something we can actually deal with here and now. So, unless you want to help with that, drop the whole angry man-against-the-world-act and shut up for a while. We are all well aware of what a shitty situation we're all in. Your frantic questions aren't helping anyone."

"So, we're just gonna do nothing?" Gabe could not be cowed. "These assholes are about to cement their authority, priest! That's what this whole summons is all about. I mean … come on, you got to see that. This is our last chance."

"Our last chance for what?!" Father Boyd shouted at the pudgy, pink-cheeked clown. "What are you suggesting I do? What, more violence? Is that what you're advocating here, Gabe? Should we all plot out how best to sneak into the officers' quarters late at night to slit their throats. Is that what you think we ought to become?" The priest broke off his rant to allow Gabe time to answer, but the man simply crossed his arms over his potbelly. "Well, I won't be a part of that," the priest went on, "or anything of that nature. We don't beat madness by joining in with it. I tried to explain that to Dr. Sagal last night." He broke off to look at Maisie directly. "I'm sorry I couldn't persuade him, Mais. I'm sorry I'm such a lousy priest. I'm so freakin' sorry for everything. But your father was wrong to fight. I loved him, and God rest his soul, but it was wrong. We won't beat them by playing their game. I ain't trying to piss on your father's memory, by any means. He was a great man, and we will miss him sorely, but he was wrong to fight."

"I know you tried, Boyd," Maisie said in a soft voice. "His mind was set and there was no moving him. I just wish it played out differently." A tear broke free from Maisie's otherworldly poise, trickling slowly down her cheek.

"We all do, Mais," Alice Stark added in a cracking voice.

"Oh, sweetie," Dolly said, drawing her in for another warm hug.

"I'm sorry I don't have answers for you all," the priest addressed the whole group now. "Little as it pleases me to say, I think our best option now is to lay low and work from the inside out. We will look for opportunities and do our best to stay vigilant in order to fight against whatever atrocities are in our power to prevent. We shall make it our mission to wake our fellow residents out of their fear and help them to remember what it was to be civil and reasonable. This madness will pass, my friends. We just have to ride it out."

"For now," Maisie added in a strange voice.

"What?" The priest asked her, a bit confused.

"For now, we will wait, and keep our heads down," she answered him with conviction. "For now."

CHAPTER 18

HELENA

Dawn of the Witenagemot

Oh, *thank god,* Helena thought with shuddering relief. She'd made direct eye contact with Officer Millicent Dirks, and even received a return nod from the tall, dead-eyed, knife-faced officer. *They've seen me. Thank god, they've seen me.* Helena had arrived a full hour before the order required, but she still had to force her way through an obnoxious and smelly mess of her fellow residents to secure her spot directly in front of the newly raised dais. She was extremely pleased to see her persistence pay off. Helena Heathcoat desperately wanted to demonstrate her commitment to the new regime. She had thought about little else since fleeing the bastard doctor and his meddling little bitch of a daughter's quarters last night.

Word had spread quickly that Montrois and Aponyaschefski had caught them all there with Hubert Harrington and Daniel Rafferty right after she had left. Helena's fury at her wife had quickly fled at that news. Fear had been what replaced it, fear and determination to be seen on the security staff's side. She knew it would most likely put her at further odds with her betraying wife, but she felt it was Alice who'd driven them down that road, not her. Alice had made her choices. Helena still loved her. She knew that was what fueled the broiling hate.

She'd never hated anyone as much as she hated Alice right now. Helena had never before been anything close to a hateful person, and so hated Alice for driving her into becoming one. Alice's treachery had changed her entire being. Helena guessed a part of her would forever hate Alice for making her hateful. So coming to terms with siding against her and doing whatever she could to aid the security staff, and demonstrate her loyalty to them, wasn't really all too difficult in the end, despite her persistent love for the treacherous wife she hated so very much.

Alice will come running back to me soon enough, Helena told herself for the gazillionth time. *And maybe I'll even forgive her.* She flashed then on Commander Montrois rotating in a slow circle at center court yesterday with the head of Dr. Perry Sagal in his outstretched hand. Disgust and horror reared their ugly little heads, but they paled in comparison to her satisfaction. *God, who am I becoming?* Helena wondered for a panicked second. *No, no, the bastard deserved it,* she assured herself. *Stealing my baby wasn't bad enough; he'd brought down destruction on this station. No way the people would let him hand power back over to Harrington and his AOA now, not after everything Aponyaschefski has opened our eyes to.*

A screech of microphone feedback cut through Helena's thoughts, bringing her eyes up to the man himself, Harclay Aponyaschefski. Microphone in hand, the survivor looked out over the crowd with the scarred Commander Montrois to his left and Officer Millicent Dirks to his right. He stood two paces in front of the two security officers with a somber posture and visage, and as he spoke, the tone of his voice was equally reverent, "Ladies and gentlemen, please settle down so that we may begin." The survivor hadn't lost the knack he had shown for crowd control during the Final Tournament; silence gripped The Meadow in a matter of seconds. "We would like to thank everyone for coming here to such a hastily assembled gathering."

"No problem," a drunken, slurred shout bellowed out from the middle of the dense mass of residents.

Schef did not allow it to break his solemnity. He simply held his hand up to quell the few laughs that followed the shout. "I'll start by reminding you of all those billions of lives lost to the infection, to the dozens killed on the launchpad on that first day of the Infection Event, to the seven security officers sent to their pointless deaths by Harrington and the government council, and the six brave souls that perished in the sacred Final Tournament. I believe their memories deserve your respect and your silence. Please take that under advisement." Sufficiently chastened, the crowd fell completely still. "Last night," the survivor continued, "the commander, his officers, myself, and a delegation of staff supervisors outlined our plans for Commander Montrois' reign. Today, I will relay some of the details agreed upon during that meeting. Further instructions and necessary rules and regulations changes will be made available to you all within the coming days. For now, know that, as of this morning, AOA and the government leaders have all been moved out of Branch 1. Their quarters will be occupied by us. Harrington and his friends will be settled in one of the many available living quarters throughout the various colored corridors. Now, we understand that this may look like a vain and selfish grab by us, and perhaps it may even persuade you to think we have gone through all of this blood and sacrifice for our own personal gain, but rest assured, it is a move based in necessity. We must maintain security over the control room, and so, we will stay close and guard it tight." Schef broke off and seemed to swallow a lump in his throat before bringing the microphone back to his lips. "Occupying quarters down Branch 1 will be members of Cardinal's Nest Lunar Station's new ruling regime. We are the Witenagemot. The security officers are now, from this moment until their last, Lieutenants of the Witenagemot. They will be forever known as Lieutenant, and then their last name. For instance," Schef said, turning to his right to point at Millicent Dirks, "Officer Millicent Dirks is no more. She is to be addressed as Lieutenant Dirks. Any resident who does not comply with this directive shall face a penalty, the details of which will be released soon, as I stated earlier. My title will be the Steward. I, like my leader," he said, indicating Montrois, "have abandoned our former names all together, as a symbol of our commitment to humanity. We have given ourselves wholly over to its care. So, I shall be addressed as the Steward and, from this moment until his last, Commander Jasper Montrois will be referred to only as the Commander."

The Commander, Helena silently repeated the name of her new leader with awed reverence. She was glad to hear how seriously the security staff was committing to protecting the station and humanity. She dragged her eyes from the mesmerizing Steward as the man paused to draw in a deep, soothing, and centering breath. There wasn't much she could see beyond the few faces surrounding her, but the majority of those seemed to be sharing Helena's awe at the Steward's pronouncements.

Her gaze fell back to the survivor just in time to see him continue his speech, "We have also accepted, as full councilmembers in the Witenagemot, all fourteen staff supervisors, including their former boss Ian Mikkelson." *No*, Helena thought, flabbergasted. Those were the first sour words she'd heard the Steward speak. *Don't tell me they forgave that fat bastard.* "Labor Supervisor Mikkelson has seen the error of his ways. He has realized his fruitless defiance gained nothing but the death of men who might otherwise still be alive today. He has repented this folly and sworn a sacred oath to forever commit to the Witenagemot with absolute loyalty. In return, we have agreed to let him take up his old position as leader of the staff supervisors, as well as award him a seat in the Council of the Witenagemot. However, all this is contingent on one more condition."

The Steward turned then to the side of the dais. Helena tracked his eyes and saw a huge man waddling up the stairs leading to the platform. The silence in The Meadow remained unbroken but for the fat man's booming footfalls across the surface of the dais as he marched towards the Steward, Lieutenant Dirks, and the Commander. Mikkelson stopped directly in front of the Commander and a pang of fear for her new leader swept through Helena. But the man only struggled down to his knees, wheezing and huffing all the while. The Steward kept him there for a few long heartbeats before bringing the microphone back up. "Labor Supervisor Mikkelson, do you pledge your fealty to the Witenagemot, and the supreme authority of the Commander?"

Helena's earlier consternation over Mikkelson's inclusion in the Witenagemot evaporated as she realized what the Steward was doing. They were humiliating the man, making the whole station watch his capitulation. Helena understood they were all being treated to the belligerent man's defanging. So she wore a smile as Mikkelson responded to the Steward's question in a thin, pathetic voice, "Yes."

"Say the oath in full, Mr. Mikkelson, and you may rise forever as Supervisor Mikkelson, the Witenagemot's Labor Director and Supervisor Chairman."

Helena smiled at the look of utter surrender in the face of the kneeling man as he looked up to lock eyes with his master. "I swear to be forever loyal to the Witenagemot, and deferential to the supreme authority of you, the Commander," the thing that had once been Mikkelson recited.

"Very well, Supervisor Mikkelson, rise and stand beside Lieutenant Dirks," the Steward told him in a bored tone. "Supervisor Mikkelson will also be better able to focus on the needs of all of you, Cardinal's Nest's dedicated workforce, now that we have relieved him of one of his most taxing duties. He will no longer monitor the credit system, for their will no longer *be* a credit system." A ripple of shock fizzled its way through the crowd with that pronouncement. Helena had looked back to Mikkelson and was glad she did. She'd caught the surprised look, followed by the immediate scowl, that flashed across the bulbous man's face. *They got you good and defanged now, you fat bastard.* Helena thought with delight. "The credit system was designed for a thriving station with a full complement of residents, when resources would inevitably need to be conserved," the Steward went on. "As it is only the 500 or so of us up here aboard station, the credit system will not be necessary. We have more than enough to sustain ourselves, and you are all welcome to any and all of it. But, be warned, you will be expected to work for that privilege. Work will keep us focused as we wait for the infection to end, and for our triumphant return to Earth. We all, from this moment until our very last breaths, if need be, share the same sacred mission: to keep this station running as smoothly as possible. We must all do the work of 3000, so there will be no tolerance for slackers. But fear not, we have no wish to uproot the lives you've made up here. Your workload will stay the same as before. We have been doing a wonderful job keeping Cardinal's Nest going with just our small band, and we will keep that going. But lose heart, and fail in any of your assigned tasks, and you will be stripped of the privileges this station offers us. And again, the details of what will be expected from each of you will be issued within the coming days."

"Maybe we ought to search for more survivors like you and bring them up here too," a high-pitched voice called out from somewhere in the crowd. "We have the extra space, after all, like you said."

The Steward's face grew stern, only an eyelash away from angry. "There are no more survivors," he told the anonymous voice. "We have settled all that. The Commander's ascension has closed the door on the old world. All any of you need to concern yourselves with is ensuring the future for the new. This is not an open debate, ladies and gentlemen, let there be no confusion here. This is merely an orientation for Cardinal's Nest's new order."

Helena couldn't help but glance at the Commander. The man hadn't moved a muscle since the Steward began speaking. Even when Mikkelson went to his knees before him, he had maintained his casually stiff posture and flat, emotionless face, with his fresh scars and milky eye adding gory menace. Both his arms hung loose at his sides, but his right hand clung tightly to the shaft of the black battleaxe he had used to decapitate Perry Sagal. Helena smiled at the weapon. The Commander had plainly cleaned the blade, but she liked to think she could see that bastard adulterer's blood still dripping from its gleaming edge. The axe appeared heavy, yet the Commander held it as effortlessly as a baby's rattle. Helena might've guessed he'd been chiseled from stone, if she didn't know better. The Steward was pronouncing his new authority as leader of the human race and the Commander looked as if he were pulling guard duty at a rock concert.

"Each one of the Witenagemot's six Lieutenants will be assigned as Warden of one of the six Living Quarters Corridors," the Steward continued. "All residents will take any civil disputes that may arise to their Corridor Warden. If the Lieutenants, aka Corridor Wardens, cannot handle the dispute themselves, they will take the complaint to Captain Alvarez. He will hold the title of Regent of the Corridors within the Witenagemot. If Captain Alvarez—as you all shall address him— cannot handle the situation, he will bring the issue to me, and I will take it before the Commander, if need be. And so it will go. Each corridor warden has hand-picked their own footmen to act as their eyes and ears throughout their corridors. Those chosen will be pinged on their pocket tablets once this orientation wraps. Many of you have been drafted into new assignments and roles within the Witenagemot and will receive a ping on your pocket tablets at the end of this orientation as well. Those who do receive notice will remain here as the rest of you good residents will be sent on your way to do as you please. Now, where was I?" The Steward paused to ponder for only the briefest of seconds. "Ah, yes," he said with a raised index finger. "Each staff supervisor, as a full member of the Witenagemot, will be addressed as Supervisor, and then their last name. Like Supervisor Mikkelson, for example. They will each have authority over all matters under their specific purview. They will handle all labor issues and will have authority to bring issues directly to me. Their authority, just as the lieutenants' and captains', will not be questioned." He stopped there to glance at the Commander. Humanity's leader moved for the first time since Helena had been watching him. It was only a simple head turn, followed by a slight nod, but it was movement. The Steward turned back to the crowd after the gesture, wearing his first hints of a smile. "And now, my fellow residents, we have prepared a demonstration for you."

The Steward dropped the microphone to his side with that and looked back to Lieutenant Dirks. He gave the lieutenant a small nod and received a return gesture from the tall blonde woman. Lieutenant Dirks stepped back a pace and turned so her profile was toward the gathered crowd. Helena watched as she tapped on her pocket tablet a few times before speaking into the device. Judging from the pause and response pattern, Lieutenant Dirks must've been communicating with someone, or multiple someones. Helena felt every eye in The Meadow locked on the slender lieutenant. They all watched on as she stayed silent and stared down at her pocket tablet for a long time. Finally, she spoke a short, inaudible sentence and then stuffed it back into a vest pocket. Lieutenant Dirks crisply turned back to face the crowd and gave the Steward another small nod.

"I now direct your attention above us," the Steward said, pointing directly over his head. Helena followed his finger and saw nothing but the twinkling Milky Way.

Others must've been as confused as she, as a grumble rapidly spread through the crowd. Before the collective consternation had time to crescendo, a dark flash trailed by white fire, streaked out into the expanse. It raced into view from the corner of Stargazer Ceiling covering the far third of the desert and went rocketing up until it locked on a steady path right over the center of the massive and flawless glass ceiling. Helena could make the black flash out clearly now. *It's a Star Hawk!* She was certain of that despite having never actually laid eyes on one before. AOA only had two types of interplanetary craft. The E-11 Transports she had seen up close, both inside and out. That left only the Star Hawks.

"That's one of this station's two remaining Star Hawks," the Steward added, confirming her identification of the ship. "Piloting that Star Hawk are two traitors ... Barry Calvin and Gillian Gerwitz. They, in cahoots with Sergeant Marge Hamill, attempted to raid the weapons vault during the Commander's fateful match against the valiant Dr. Perry Sagal." *Valiant my ass*, Helena thought as the Steward continued, "They failed, thankfully, due to the decisive actions of Captain Alvarez. They would've armed the weakest and blind amongst you to murder the wise and awoken. Their planned uprising would've spelled doom for this fragile station. It would've spelled doom for humanity. But, instead, it was foiled by the good, diligent work of those of us who've given our lives over to our collective future. No one is truly secure up here until all resistance to the Witenagemot's rule is eradicated. The firearms stocked aboard this station with us are the biggest threat to that safety and security. With them out of the way, we may all rest easy, safe from the potential of their destructive capabilities. So, with that in mind, we packed every last heavy weapon, assault rifle, pistol, and shotgun aboard station on that Star Hawk with those two traitorous pilots. You may notice Lieutenant Dirks and the other lieutenants around The Meadow are lacking their usual compliment of projectile weapons," the Steward said. "Not even the former security staff remain armed. Every single firearm is aboard that Star Hawk ... along with something else," he added, pulling out a small device from his jacket pocket that Helena could only guess was a detonator.

He held the device high above his head. The crowd was murmuring slightly as he moved his thumb toward a red button in the center of the device. The hush had once more taken hold in The Meadow as his emaciated thumb arrived above the red button.

Helena glanced at his face and saw mischief swirling alongside the determination in his eyes. After a slight hesitation, the Steward depressed his thumb, and thousands of feet beyond the seamless glass, the Star Hawk vanished in a brilliant flash of light that crumpled back in on itself an instant after flashing into existence. Helena blinked, and when she opened her eyes again, there was only an ever-shrinking arc of sparks, each evaporating within a beat of blossoming.

"Those were the last two residents of this station trained to fly the Star Hawks," the Steward said in a voice still every bit as reverent as it was before he blew up two people in front of hundreds. "No one in this station will be allowed to train in the simulators to fly the remaining Star Hawk. Don't worry, once the Earth is cleared for our return, we will train a few of you to fly that Hawk. Right now, there are eight certified E-11 pilots and copilots aboard station. Each one of these good folks has come to an agreement with the Witenagemot to refrain from passing on their knowledge and from going anywhere near the two E-11 Transport Cruisers on the lunar dock. Compliance with that last demand will be made easier for those transport pilots by our next demonstration. For that, we direct you all now to your pocket tablets."

The Steward looked to Lieutenant Dirks, and she once again stepped back to fiddle with her tablet. Helena reached for hers, tucked away in her back pocket, and felt everyone around her doing the same. She tapped on its screen to bring up the homepage, but Helena found nothing of note when it popped up. She glanced back up to Lieutenant Dirks just in time to see the corridor warden finishing a response to something before tapping her screen a few more times. Helena's pocket tablet's screen flashed, drawing her attention back down to the device.

The whole screen was now displaying a vid-feed from a camera in the Grand Rotunda just outside of Branch 2, and the transport craft garage and lunar dock beyond. Helena looked at her screen with confusion at first, not knowing exactly what she was looking at, seeing as how no Branch hatch had ever been drawn closed before. She hadn't even really known the Branches had hatches to be closed off. Looking tiny beside the massive, closed hatchway were Lieutenants Dobechek and Gregson. Helena had made it a point last night to memorize every security officer by name and face, step one in her quest to ingratiate herself. The two officers—now Lieutenants—standing alongside Branch 2 might've been tiny on her screen, but after her quick study last night, she knew them well enough to place each officer at first glance.

On the screen, Lieutenant Dobechek faced the distant camera and gave a thumbs-up before pointing at the closed Branch. Instantly, the image on Helena's screen flashed to a new camera's perspective. She recognized the surroundings the image displayed; she'd walked down that alleyway before. It was one of the first parts of Cardinal's Nest Helena Heathcoat ever saw. She was looking through a lens inside the alleyway running down the length of the transport craft garage, specifically, the section just beyond the currently closed mega-hatchway. Racing from much smaller locked hatchway to locked hatchway down that stretch of alleyway was Sergeant Marge Hamill. Helena didn't know the sergeant very well, but she'd seen her around the station enough to recognize her right away, in spite of the frantic state of the woman. Sergeant Marge had never appeared anything less than cool and collected in the past. The woman on every screen of every pocket tablet in the station was a desperate soul, however. *She probably doesn't know she's on video,* Helena thought absently.

"Keep watching," the Steward called out into the silence. He needn't have bothered with the directive. Helena could feel everyone around her just as glued to their tablet screens as she was. On screen, the sergeant suddenly stopped her frantic search for an unlocked hatch. She fell to her knees, clutching her throat with both hands. Helena didn't understand at first. It wasn't until a few loose papers and lighter detritus went flying across the alley that she caught on. All of the oxygen was being sucked out of the garage. Helena looked on as Sergeant Marge Hamill struggled against the tremendous power of the sucking vacuum. The sergeant was being smashed by a steady stream of airborne debris while being dragged across the alleyway, all the while clutching her neck, desperate for a breath.

The athletically built and extremely virile sergeant took a long time to die. The crowd stayed silent for every last second of it. When at last her struggles ended, the image on their tablet screens shifted back to that of Lieutenants Dobechek and Gregson in the Grand Rotunda beside Branch 2's closed giant hatchway. Helena watched as, on screen, Lieutenant Dobechek glanced up from her own pocket tablet. She looked at the camera in the Grand Rotunda and gave another thumbs-up. The two Lieutenants on the screen stepped up to what Helena took for the controls of Branch 2's currently closed hatchway. The controls were embedded into the nearby wall. Helena figured a similar control panel was embedded near every Branch, but she'd never noticed them before. She was making a point to seek them out next time she was in the Rotunda just as Lieutenant Gregson drew out the axe sheathed across his back and smashed an over-head slash straight into Branch 2's hatchway control panel. A gasp was released from hundreds of throats all around her as Lieutenant Gregson hammered home six or seven more devastating smashes. When he and Lieutenant Dobechek stepped away from the deci-mated panel, everyone knew it was out of operation for good.

Helena's screen went black, and her eyes instantly went back up to the Steward. "Fret not, the hatchway can still be operated from the control room," he told the enraptured crowd. "And it will be opened again someday, when Mother Earth is ready for us. The transport craft and remaining Star Hawk will be perfectly preserved for us until then. For now, we need everyone here to know that this is your home. There is no leaving and no endangering our safety for your own selfish whims. And now any temptations our interplanetary craft may have provoked in you has been eliminated. You're welcome." The Steward showed a full grin now. "That ends today's orientation, my fellow resi-dents. Those pings I spoke of earlier will be issued now. If you receive one, please stay for further instructions. If not, the Commander asks that you kindly and orderly disperse and return to your lives in what-ever way you so choose."

Helena heard a ping close by and eagerly looked down at her tablet screen, hopeful as a kid on Christmas. Unfortunately, her screen remained blank. Helena gazed around to see who the lucky nearby resident had been. The crowd thinned out around her, revealing Maddie Aranzono standing a few yards away, with her tablet in hand, and a pleased look on her flabby face. Maddie glanced around and eventually locked eyes with Helena. Her lip rose in an instinctive snarl, but it quickly died when Helena took the first step towards her.

Maddie was clearly wary as Helena approached her, so she adopted a smile that Helena hoped conveyed her peaceful intentions. "You got pinged?" Helena asked when she arrived beside Maddie.

"Yeah ... so?" Maddie answered in a voice that started hostile but faded to confused.

Helena kept up the smile and even added a pat on the shorter woman's shoulder. "Congratulations," she told Maddie.

"What do you want?" her old enemy asked.

"I know we've had our differences, Maddie, and I'm sorry for that," Helena said in an earnest voice. "I've been a fool up here these past few months; I realize that now. We gotta take care of this place. It's our duty. And I'm glad to know the Witenagemot chose you to help them with that."

"Okay," Maddie answered, still very wary.

"I know you don't owe me nothing, but I was hoping you might put in a good word for me with the Witenagemot, and the Commander especially. I'm willing to prove myself. Can you tell them that for me? "Helena's voice turned plaintive. "Please tell them that."

Maddie Aranzono looked her old rival up and down for a few moments before a smirk cracked the corners of her mouth. "I'll see what I can do," she said through the grin.

The vague promise was as much as Helena might've hoped for. She hustled her way out of The Meadow after receiving it. The residents who didn't receive a ping had been told to leave The Meadow, and Helena wanted to be seen following the Commander's orders. She had no wish to be the last ping-less resident through the giant neon archway.

Captain Alvarez

The new Captain looked up from his pocket tablet to lock eyes with Barry Calvin. He knew from the indignation on the bruised fool's face that his own grin was definitely showing. Captain Alvarez couldn't help it. The plan had gone off without a hitch. the Witenagemot had done it. He was Captain Alvarez, Regent of the Corridors, in actual practice now. *Captain Alvarez,* the title had a tangible weight to it, as he spoke the name to himself, in a way it hadn't only minutes earlier. *Just one step left,* the Captain reminded himself, still grinning at the copilot.

"What?" Calvin asked him. "Just what the hell were you watching on that tablet?" After a few beats passed with no answer forthcoming, he tried a different tack, "Let me speak to Gerwitz. You said we could stay in touch every step of the way. I said just what you wanted in the pre-launch check-in, just what you asked, and nothing more, now just let me talk to Gillian, alone. And the sarge too. I want to hear from both of them. Come on, Captain, that was the deal. Let me talk with Gillian."

Captain Alvarez chuckled softly a few times as he looked back down at his tablet. He played with the vid player for a couple dozen seconds before turning the screen around so Calvin could see it. "Watch this for me." He hit play and watched the copilot watching the screen.

Captain Alvarez had pulled up footage from an exterior camera mounted on a transmitter dish near The Meadow. It was showing a five-second loop from just before the Star Hawk exploded, turning Gillian Gerwitz to scattered atoms, until about three seconds after the spectacular disintegration. Barry Calvin's face, pale and weak only moments earlier, had now flushed red with fury. Captain Alvarez let him stew in it for a while before tapping the screen to bring up the next clip he had prepared for the copilot. This one was the same fifty seconds of footage every pocket tablet in the station had displayed just minutes earlier. On screen, Sergeant Marge broke off a frantic search for an escape hatch to bounce and roll along the alleyway in a cruelly slow, agonizing death.

The bright reflection from the screen's light dimmed on the copilot's face and Captain Alvarez knew the footage had ended and the display had gone black. Nonetheless, he held the tablet facing the bound and helpless man. "Shall I play it again?" he asked Calvin with glorious sarcasm. "I can narrate, if you like."

Lieutenant Schwambach barked out laughter as the copilot made another attempt to spit at him. It was Captain Alvarez himself who forestalled the insult this time, with a backhand of his own to the copilot's ear. The man didn't wail or whimper though. Calvin's rage must've supplanted his pain. He snapped his head back to lock eyes with Captain Alvarez. "Fuck you!" he shouted impotently. "I'll kill you for this! I'll kill you all!" he promised, struggling against the duct tape to little avail. "You bastards are humanity's true tragedy. The infection was a catastrophe, but what you're doing is worse. It's deliberate and false, you fascist fucks! You'll destroy us all!"

"No," Captain Alvarez interrupted the blasphemous rant, "not all … just you." Rising to his feet on that promise, he locked eyes with Lieutenant Schwambach. "Destroy this man, Lieutenant."

The lieutenant's smile was sinister, and nothing about that made Captain Alvarez the least bit uncomfortable. "Roger that, Captain," he said, stepping up to the traitor in the chair. Calvin haltingly turned his head toward the lieutenant, and as he brought his eyes up to meet the smiling corridor warden's, Lieutenant Schwambach wrapped his meaty, long-fingered paw around the copilot's slim neck. Calvin fought the throttling as best he could, but all it amounted to was some useless jerking. Eventually, his tongue came lolling out of his mouth and his eyes rolled up in his head. Lieutenant Schwambach released his grip and stepped away from the man.

"Well, Lieutenant, I guess that's that," Captain Alvarez told his fellow Witenagemot councilmember after a few reflective seconds.

"I guess so," the lieutenant agreed. "So, what now?" he asked after a dozen silent breaths in the still room.

"Now we take our power, my friend," Captain Alvarez told his subordinate with a smile in his voice. "Clean this up," he ordered, pointing at the fresh corpse in the rolling desk chair. A euphoric sense of belonging filled every corner of his soul as he marched from the rec room. Pride and clarity of purpose swelled within him, buoyed upon a golden sea of dedication to his Commander and their Witenagemot.

EPILOGUE
CAINEY

Cainey Barker spotted Maisie Sagal passing through the towering entrance archway into Cardinal's Nest Station's colossal collector module docking garage at a casual stroll. She cupped her hands to her mouth and shouted across the enormous gulf to a nervous and impatient Cainey, "What ya got for me, Nate?" The high-tech garage was currently as empty as the docking port, or any other nook or cranny of the massive lunar station, thanks to Cainey cashing in on a couple dozen favors. It was no easy feat to clear the garage and arrange this clandestine meeting party for the collector module Jed and Larry were about to pull through the gates of Docking Bay 17, and Cainey was proud of his achievement. He had chosen bay 17 for both its availability and its semi-seclusion in a far corner of the mammoth docking port. Maisie Sagal was casually disregarding the reasons for this choice, as if their lives didn't hang in the balance should some unfriendly eyes or ears join them at this meeting party. Cainey waved his arms frantically at Maisie and began to jump up and down with his index finger pressed firmly to his lips. *How can she be this dense? Shout it from the rooftops, why don't you?*

"What?" Maisie shouted, though not quite as loudly as before.

"Shhh!" Cainey stage whispered while waving in an excessively animated fashion for Maisie to stop her shouting and hustle on over to his side.

Maisie seemed to get the hint; she started jogging across the seamless gray concrete floor of the docking garage, dodging stray equipment and docked modules in the process. Soon Maisie stood just a few feet from Cainey, huffing and puffing slightly from her exertion. Only slightly, she was a very fit and lithe woman after all. Cainey couldn't keep his eyes from roaming all over an otherwise oblivious Maisie, struggling to define just how and what he felt whenever he saw her.

Maisie was one of those people who is hard to put your finger on. Someone asks you to describe her and you beat around the bush with metaphor and simile, but you never actually quite capture her. That was Maisie Sagal to Cainey Barker. It wasn't the physical description that was difficult. Well, it was, and it wasn't. Maisie was pretty. Cainey had always thought so, most folks did, as far as he knew. It wasn't that Hollywood pretty, as one might say, and it wasn't that cute girl-next-door kind of pretty either. It was, again, hard to put your finger on; she was slim, yet well-toned, not tall, but not short either, she was young—maybe twenty or twenty-one, but she had an ageless, commanding maturity in her hazel eyes. Her dark brown hair fell in a cascade to her shoulders and was definitely one of Cainey's favorite things about her. It had good bounce. Cainey was always a sucker for a head of hair with good bounce. But it was her eyes that made her what she was: a good leader, a great leader even. He couldn't deny that even if he had wanted to. Which, he wasn't at all certain he did.

Maisie had always seemed to make Cainey a little uneasy though, a little unsettled. He was very aware of that around her. As much as he hated to admit it, it was so. He had always had a problem with authority. That's what made him the rebel he was. It's what kept him in an endless loop of rooting for the underdog. That's what currently had him taking orders from the likes of Maisie Sagal and the Priest. Maisie was one of the unofficial leaders of the few station residents actively resisting the Witenagemot. That made her an authority figure, whether or not either of them liked it. She wasn't really that bad, as far as authority figures went, if Cainey was being honest with himself. She was just careless. *I mean … what is she thinking, shouting like that across the length of the docking garage? Somebody could've easily* come back to the port, favor or not and caught us red-handed trying to dock a module without following proper procedure and protocol. *The negligence was bordering on gross*, he thought. *And before you could say "Jack Robinson," the Commander would be swinging that ugly, old black shafted battleaxe of his down on the back of our necks.* But Maisie Sagal was who she was, and if anything was to ever truly change around Cardinal's Nest Station, Cainey was going to have to work with her. *With her and the Priest, and all the rest of them zealots,* he told himself.

"What ya got for me, Novocaine?" Sagal whispered in a patronizing fashion.

"Didn't Patel tell ya?" Cainey retorted impatiently.

"He told me to get over to the module docking garage, that you had something I was going to want to see for myself. He was his normal cryptic self, in short, and I didn't get much more out of him. I did head straight over here though, with no delay. I knew you wouldn't send up a warning signal without a damn good reason. So, what's up, Cainey? What's so important you cleared out the garage for?"

Cainey couldn't help but feel a little complimented by Maisie's trust that he wouldn't bring her running to him for no good reason. "Well, I got a pretty amazing call over the coded comms channel from our pal Larry Holderman," he told her with a grin. "It seems he and Jed Redding picked up a hitchhiker on their way back from their latest collection run."

"They did what?!"

The shock on Maisie's face was as greatly satisfying to Cainey as her trust had been. He knew how big a deal this was going to be, if half of what Larry was babbling over the comms turned out to be true, that is. He couldn't help but feel pride in being at the center of what was sure to be their big break. "They picked up a hitchhiker," he stated in a deliberately bland manner.

"What the hell are you talking about, Nate?" Maisie asked, exasperated.

"Larry and Jed were on their way back to the station when they came across an abandoned Star Hawk along their path. It had seemingly crash-landed and come to rest in the lunar dust alongside a slight hill about twenty or thirty miles northwest of the Kepler

Crater. There were footprints leading away from its opened emergency hatch. They followed the tracks and came across the pilot trudging towards the station. She was pretty beat up from the crash, and only a few minutes from running completely out of her oxygen supply. They hustled her aboard their collector module and sent out the word on our encrypted comms line. I happened to be monitoring the encrypted channel at that time, so I took the call. I knew you and the priest would want to see this pilot before the Witenagemot got their hands on her, so I called up about a hundred favors and secured us this private rendezvous, off the books. Then I sent Patel to hunt you down and bring you back here. I told him to find the Priest and tell him too."

"I sent Patel to the Priest after I spoke with him," Maisie said absently, with an incredulous look plastered across her normally stoic face. Cainey watched her search for words. "Are you saying someone piloted a Star Hawk from Earth and crash-landed on the moon? Were they headed here? To the station? Who is she, this pilot? She's a woman? Well, obviously. What's her name?"

"I haven't the slightest. I shut Larry up before he could really get going. Those encrypted comms channels aren't quite as secure as we might hope. You spend enough time chatting openly on one of them channels, and even the Witenagemot may have some bumbling comms tech in the control room with enough brain cells to hack in and listen. All I know is they are on their way back." Cainey lifted his wrist to inspect his trusty watch. It was an old piece he'd had since as far back as his memory went. The glass over the face was cracked and splintered, the green fabric of the strap frayed to the point of structural failure, but it never failed to tell the time. "They should be here any second, as a matter of fact," he said, with another grin.

It wasn't quite the as-if-on-cue moment Cainey was hoping for, but it was close. A few seconds wait, and the airlock indicator lights on the giant bay door turned green as a rush of air blasted out from the seal at the door's base. The top of the huge number seventeen painted in black with orange trim against the white surface of the bay door disappeared into the ceiling of the garage as the door rolled slowly open. The smog of compressed air thinned, and sure enough, there was Jed and Larry perched up 15 feet off the ground on the cabin bench seat of their collector module, creeping it slowly into its docking bay after yet another collection run. The two men always made for a slightly comical sight in the cockpit, in Cainey's mind. Larry slouched like the messy, short, rotund, middle-aged, balding white man he was, whilst Jed never failed to appear alert and on the ball. His tall, slender, long distance runner's figure, coupled with his caramel skin and salt and pepper hair and beard, made for a farcical contrast that never failed to bring a smirk to Cainey's lips.

This time, however, there was a wrinkle to his deja vu. Sitting in between the two men was a third person: a dark-haired stranger, an outsider. It was incredible. Cainey had to blink, he couldn't help it. He knew what to expect, but expectations were one thing, and actually seeing her was quite another. Cainey could hardly take his eyes from her. Even with the top of her head wrapped in a crude bandage, her stunning beauty sent a shockwave through Cainey's chest, knocking the breath clean from him.

He kept right on staring at the beautiful woman seated between the two station veterans as he and Maisie approached the module. Jed performed his hard-docking procedure with the protruding power connector located in the center of the floor of the bay. The 50' long beast of a collector module instantly began to power down its massive dorsal-mounted engine.

It felt a little like life happening in slow motion for Cainey when the pilot began her descent down the three-rung ladder below the driver-side door of the module's cabin. She set both feet on the floor and spun around crisply, almost militarily, to face Maisie and Cainey. The angelic outsider quickly set to stripping out of her VLSE gear, as did the two collector module operators. It was odd to see the two men suited up, but Cainey realized they must've struggled into the cumbersome equipment when the mystery pilot came aboard. He glanced up into the collector module's cabin and noticed three VLSE helmets perched in a neat row on the bench seat. *Must've been too cramped to clamber out of the rest of the gear in there.* The innocuous thought was quickly thrown off as soon as Cainey turned back and got his first glimpse of the pilot sans VLSE gear.

Cainey's slow-motion euphoric state increased ten-fold as her true majesty was fully absorbed. She appeared to be in her early thirties, though she looked as fit and spry as any college track star. Cainey could see that plainly, even through her baggy olive flight suit. Her flawless brown skin was the shade of heavily creamed coffee. Big, round, and beautifully haunting dark eyes flecked with gold flakes were spaced with flawless symmetry in a slightly heart-shaped face. Cainey could not seem to tear his own away from them. Under her bandage wrap, she wore her hair in a business-like, no-nonsense fashion and stood as proud and rigid as any military man or woman he had ever seen. Nate Novocaine was eternally and hopelessly in love before the pilot had ever spoken a single word.

Larry came around the front of the module to make the introductions. "Jordana, this is Maisie Sagal," he said, holding his open hand out in Maisie's direction. Then, almost as an afterthought, he shifted his arm to point at Cainey. "Oh ... and this is Nate Novocaine. He's one of the docking garage's maintenance guys."

Cainey didn't appreciate the casual, throw-away nature of Larry's introduction. He was flailing for some way to articulate this to him when the navigator barreled on obliviously, "Maisie, it's my pleasure to introduce Miss Jordana Revere, a former British Royal Air Force fighter pilot." *I knew she was military,* Cainey thought. "I have a feeling the two of you are going to want to have a long talk," Larry finished with a mischievous grin.

Maisie stepped up to Jordana, taking the pilot's hand into her own and drawing her attention away from the gargantuan domed ultra-advanced facility around them. "Ms. Revere, it certainly is a pleasure to meet you. Please forgive my initial shock in seeing you here with us. It's just ... it's been such a long time since we've seen a strange face. Not that I'm saying you have a strange face, you understand. It's just ... we were told... we were told... well hell, we've been told a lot of bullshit over the past nine years, Ms. Revere." Maisie barked out a nervous laugh and plunged right on, "I'm sorry, I'm sure you have a million questions of your own to ask. I promise there will be time for all that, but right now I need you to trust me. We don't have much time here, I'm afraid. Cainey has done what he could for us, but this place will be buzzing with workers again before too long. I need you to come with me. We don't have far to go, but we will need to stay out of sight."

Cainey watched the mysterious pilot look Maisie up and down. He could almost picture the mental calculations she was making. She was wondering about all the secrecy. It clearly confused her. She must've known she didn't have much choice but to trust them. She certainly couldn't get back to her ship. *Well, maybe she could steal some oxygen packs and skip slowly across the surface back to her crashed Star Hawk. But then what?* Cainey asked himself. It came down to whether or not she decided to believe in Maisie's bumbling appeals for trust, or else start shouting, and hope that whoever came to help was in a better position to do so. Finally, Cainey could see Jordana come to a decision. She didn't speak; she simply nodded her head very slowly, and only once.

"Great! Oh, that's great, Ms. Revere. Thank you so much," Maisie gushed over Jordana as she once again took her hand into her own, shaking it excitedly.

"Jordana. You can ... uh ... call me Jordana," were the first words Cainey Barker ever heard the goddess of a pilot speak. Her voice was melodic and sweet, her accent comforting and regal.

Maisie was still shaking Jordana's hand as she said, "And I'm Maisie Sagal, like Larry said. Could you give me one second? And then we'll get you some place a little warmer, and a great deal more hospitable."

"Ugh, yeah, of course, I suppose. Whatever you've got to do," was Jordana's tentative reply.

"Thanks. Guys, could you join me over here for a second?" Maisie asked as she waved for the three workmen to join her a few paces away from the awe-struck Jordana. Cainey managed to drag his gaze from her innate majesty after a lengthy struggle and moved to join Maisie, Jed, and Larry milling a few paces away in a rough semi-circle. "Okay, guys," Maisie began authoritatively. "What did you tell her so far?"

Jed and Larry glanced at each other before shrugging their shoulders simultaneously. It seemed that Larry was the only one of the pair who currently had a working voice today. It was he who finally spoke up, "Not much, Maisie. She was curious about us and the station, that's for sure, but we was almost back to the Nest long before she was close to finished telling us her story. She had a lot of questions and everything too, but I got away with not answering most of 'em, especially after we got within visual range of the station. I'd forgotten just what an awe-inspiring sight Cardinal's Nest can be to fresh eyes. Anyway, the sight must've done something for her, 'cause she kinda shut up after that and ain't really said much since."

"She told you her story?" Maisie's wonder once again revealed itself in her voice. "Where is she from? Who sent her? What's her mission?"

"She told us some. I feel like she was holding more than a few things back. But anyway, she says she's here to recon the station, to confirm whether or not it's habitable, and to learn what she can about the station's occupants. Us, in other words." Larry paused to allow for a response from Maisie that didn't come. "Apparently, she's a member of some kinda brotherhood of survivors back on Earth. *The Bruderschaft*, I think she called 'em," he added after a couple heavy breaths. "She says the leader of this *Bruderschaft* used to work for AOA and knew about a top-secret alternate AOA launch platform site in Wyomin–"

"An alternate launch site? No kidding? Incredible," Maisie interrupted out of sheer astonishment.

"Yeah … so this Bruderschaft leader apparently knew about Cardinal's Nest Station, as well as the alternate launch site. I think she said the guy's name was Arlo, maybe. Yeah, that's it. Arlo uhh … Bailey, I think she said. He's some London born and bred Oxford guy with a bunch of engineering degrees. He got fired by the AOA for something. She didn't really say what. I got the impression he'd uncovered something at the company he wasn't meant to see, you know. Or something like that anyway. So, this Arlo guy was back in London when the Infection Event went down. Jordana says this Arlo fella rallied a group of survivors over there in Europe and they made their way to the launchpad in Wyoming. This Arlo Bailey managed to convince a bunch of terrified survivors that he could get them to a safe haven. He managed to rally quite the large group, the way the pilot lady tells it."

"Incredible." Maisie sounded like a toddler watching Barney teach her to spell. "We'll take Jordana to The Clubhouse to see the Priest," she said, pointing to Larry and Jed. "You guys can scout the path ahead and do whatever blocking may be necessary for us. We can't have anybody spotting her in that strange flight suit." Maisie turned her focus to Cainey. "Novocaine, you stay here and make sure all our tracks are covered up, so to speak. Come to The Clubhouse when your shift ends. I'm sure Boyd will want to talk to you."

A tiny nod of acknowledgment was all Cainey could muster up for a response. Maisie and the two collector module crewmen turned away from him, breaking their conspiratorial half-huddle. And just like that, the stunning pilot that had so captivated Cainey was gently guided away from the module garage by a hand from Maisie pressed softly in the small of her flawless back.

Jordana

Having been swiftly escorted from the gigantic garage, with wide passageways, cramped tunnels and chambers of all different dimensions passing by in a blur too fast to fully take in, Jordana was doing her damnedest now just to keep up with her guide. Maisie was five or six paces ahead, weaving her way through a dimly lit maze of an antechamber they'd entered off of a brightly lit passageway, which Jordana's eyes hadn't adjusted to in time to achieve any clear visual information about whatsoever. Jordana assumed she was in a maintenance tunnel of some kind now. She was able to make out piping and tubing running haphazardly throughout the dark tunnel. Down below her feet, Jordana could see a tangle of electrical wiring under the metal grating of a footpath that cut a weaving trail through the madness of machinery all about them.

After a sharp turn, which Jordana definitely did not see coming, she collided into the back of a suddenly stationary Maisie. Jordana muttered an apology as she stepped back to gain a better look at what had caused this sudden halt in their journey. The curvy, yet slender young woman was turning a metal wheel attached to a hatch set a foot off the floor and encircled by a jumble of snaking pipes, tubes, and wires in blacks, blues, and reds barely discernible in the gloom. A few more revolutions of the wheel, and the hatch swung open. Maisie turned back to face Jordana. "After you," she said, gesturing for Jordana to be the first to enter the brightly lit chamber on the other side of the open hatch. Jordana could tell that Maisie registered the hesitation in her body language. "It's okay," Maisie said with a warm smile. "Really, you can trust me."

Aghh, bloody hell, I've come this far. No point turning back now, Jordana thought. She looked over her shoulder one last time before scooting past Maisie and stooping through the open hatchway. Jordana stepped into a chamber she did not at all expect. The space was a great expansive rectangle roughly 50 feet long and maybe 30 wide, with a 15' ceiling. It was pleasantly warm and comfortably furnished. The hidden room was just one large chamber, but its furniture arrangements created the illusion of four distinct rooms.

In the far right of the chamber, chairs of every sort, from recliner to stool, were arranged around a large, central oak coffee table. Oak bookshelves overflowing with hard cover and paperback books covered half of the far wall from floor to ceiling. The area was well stocked with bright lamps, creating an inviting atmosphere for either conversation or a little reading. The central space of the chamber was split in half by a large blue couch adorned with an abundance of colorful blankets and throw pillows. Behind the couch was the dining room, where a long red cedar table surrounded by intricately carved red cedar chairs sat atop a large maroon, blue, gold, and silver oriental carpet. A dozen feet in front of the couch was a colossal flatscreen television. Two blue Lazy-Boy recliners sat at either end of the couch. Another coffee table, this one with ashtrays and a few empty liquor bottles atop it rather than books, sitting on an enormous black carpet dotted with white stars and blue galaxies, flanked by two antique bronze lamps, all did great service in bringing the living room together. It created a homey space that must make everyone who saw it immediately want to make themselves cozy. Jordana certainly did. To her left and encompassing about 300 square feet from the back of the chamber all the way to the front, was a welcoming little kitchen boasting a matching refrigerator, dishwasher, stove and range-top decked out in a modern matte ebony. Its outer boundary was established by the black-trimmed white island countertop positioned in the kitchen's exact center. A half dozen wooden stools with white legs and black seats surrounded the large, square island.

From the kitchen, a mouthwatering aroma gently floated its way toward Jordana. It was so heavenly rich it nearly overwhelmed the processing capacity of her olfactory nerves. Jordana swore that she could actually see the scent, wafting in misty waves through the comfortably warm air of the chamber. In front of the industrial-size, eight-outlet range-top, a woman in a white apron stood facing the stove. Jordana took another step toward the kitchen and its resident chef, but she couldn't make out much beyond the woman's short blonde hair and greasy, well-used apron. She felt like sprinting right up to that mystery cook tending those heavenly smells to beg for scraps. Every fiber of her being seemed to be calling out for it, but somehow, Jordana stayed rooted in place.

"Smells good, don't it?" Jordana whipped her head towards the voice to see a middle-aged man with a bright and lively face seated on one of the wooden stools beside the kitchen's island cabinet. *How did I miss him?* She wondered. The man was dressed casually in dark blue jeans and a black hoodie. Despite this, being that he was the only man in the chamber, Jordana took him for the Priest she'd heard Maisie and those module crewmen mention. He wasn't quite what she had been expecting when Jed and Larry had first told her about the Priest. She had the classic image in mind: an old, bald white guy, with liver spotted hands, constantly pushing back thick, ugly glasses as he smugly pontificates. This supposed priest on the kitchen stool did not fit the picture in her head at all. He was roughly 50, maybe 55. His dark hair had one or two stray streaks of gray, but hung in loose curls, almost down to his shoulders. His skin had a dark tan somehow, which only added to Jordana's confusion. Hiding most of his lower face was a scruffy brown beard a couple inches long and dense as a bird's nest, which he was currently stroking thoughtfully as he leaned one elbow on the countertop. He did not at all have the figure of the stereotypical meek priest, either. The man in the black sweatshirt seated before her had a physique more reminiscent of a rugby hooker or prop.

"Dolly's the best damn cook in the whole station. It's why I married her," the Priest added.

The woman at the stove was apparently Dolly. She turned around and blew a kiss in the Priest's direction, allowing Jordana to catch a quick glimpse of her face. She appeared roughly the same age as the supposed holy man but had one or two more age lines to show for it. She wore her sandy-blonde hair cropped short around her chubby, round face. Her blue eyes matched the blue sweatshirt she wore under the white apron. The sweatshirt made it difficult for Jordana to gain a firm impression of her figure, but she guessed Dolly was maybe a couple dozen pounds overweight, give or take a few. The older woman wore the extra weight well though, with it seeming to add to her charms, rather than diminishing them. Jordana watched as Dolly turned back to monitor the food in her skillet. The buxom chef swayed her curvy ass back and forth in a playful manner that brought a smile to the Priest's face.

Jordana was at a total loss for words. The day's unbelievable events kept claiming their costly toll on her wits. Behind her, Jordana felt Maisie enter the chamber and take a few steps into the living room. Jordana looked over at Maisie, who favored her with a warm grin.

"Dolly really is a fantastic cook, Jordana, and you really should eat. I'm sure that hike across the surface drained you. Not to mention that bash on the head. You gotta be woozy, I'm sure. Some nice, hearty breakfast will do ya good." Maisie began walking towards the refrigerator as she continued speaking to Jordana. "Dolly does the best bacon and eggs I've ever had, and I ain't just saying that to be nice."

As Maisie opened the refrigerator, Dolly playfully swatted her on the shoulder. "Oh, don't act like you never complain about my cooking, Maisie Sagal. Don't you recall what you said about my meatloaf last week? I sure do. Something about my love affair with garlic had taken on uncharted heights, or something to that effect," Dolly said, keeping up the playful tone.

"I didn't want to give Jordana another worry to have to deal with," Maisie half chuckled as she reached into the refrigerator to grab two bottles of water.

The young brunette tossed one of the bottles across the room towards Jordana. The quick toss was unexpected, forcing her to make a clumsy, last-second catch. She quickly twisted off the cap and lifted the bottle towards Maisie in recognition. "Thanks," Jordana muttered.

Just then, Jed and Larry clambered their way through the open hatchway. "Close the hatch behind ya, fellas," was the Priest's only greeting for the two module crewmen.

Larry left the hatch closing duties to his partner Jed and walked over beside Dolly in the kitchen. "Where's Patel?" he asked no one and everyone.

"Left just after delivering his message," Dolly answered him. "You know that man, always on the move."

Larry grunted in acknowledgment and then peered over Dolly's shoulder. "Bacon and eggs?" he asked, instantly receiving a nod of confirmation from Dolly. The stout navigator pulled out a brown leather flask from his coat pocket with a smile. After the red-faced lush helped himself to a lengthy swallow of whatever lay within the drunkard's calling-card from which he sipped, he asked Dolly a further question about the upcoming breakfast, "Where in the Sam-hell is the sausage gravy for the biscuits?" Then he made a point of glancing around the kitchen before adding, "And where in the Sam-hell are the biscuits?"

Dolly used the wooden spatula in her hand to smack his arm. "You get what I make," she scolded.

"Or you get nothing at all!" the Priest added in a tone that cut through the playful mood in the kitchen.

"Jeez, I was only joking, Boyd. Relax," Larry responded, sounding a bit hurt by the sharp condemnation.

The Priest didn't respond for what felt to Jordana like a very long time. Finally, when the tension seemed heavy enough to bury them, he spoke, "Did anyone follow you and Jed back here?"

"No, of course not," Larry responded sharply, tucking his flask back in its holster. "There weren't even Footmen patrolling this sector. There ain't never any."

"Did you see any resident, or worker, or anybody at all spot Maisie and our new pilot friend as they made their way here?" the Priest pressed.

"No! Like I said, all the alleyways and maintenance tunnels were deserted all the way here. Nobody saw us in the module docking garage neither. Novocaine did a good job of clearing it out," Larry said, balking against the Priest's accusing tone.

"Okay, how about the cameras in the garage and along the alleyways? She must've been captured on video."

"They only got two guys at most in the control room, and not a one of 'em is watching live vid-feeds anymore," Larry told him. "The operators let the Wardens, Supervisors, and Footmen do as they please in their sectors. Nobody wants to be looking over their shoulders. All of the Witenagemot's operators are cowardly tech nerds. They keep their noses out of it. But even so, before you yell at me anymore," Larry quickly added when the Priest's chest began puffing up to release an acidic retort. "Cainey set off a video scrambler in the module garage just before we arrived," he continued. "If, by some miracle, the Witenagemot had someone watching, alls they saw was snow."

"Well, won't that seem a bit suspicious?"

"Oh, come on Boyd," Larry's voiced nearly cracked. "It's like I told ya, all them operators down Branch 1 are too scared shitless to even monitor the vid-feed anymore. Not to mention, the scrambler only lasted for the few minutes we was in there. If anyone was watching, they'd be satisfied that it was just some technical glitch now that it's back up and running properly."

"I wish I had your confidence, Larry old boy. Although, it would most likely come with your naivety as well, so perhaps I'll save my wishes." The Priest paused for a moment to let his inferior stew in the silent aftermath of his cutting insult. *Not very priestly at all,* Jordana thought. "So, where is Nate *Novocaine* Barker?" the Priest broke his self-constructed silence to ask. "I want to have a talk with him before he goes running his mouth to anyone else."

"I told him to finish his shift and keep his ears open," Maisie spoke up. "He'll be here when his shift is over. I trust him to keep his mouth shut. Well ... till then at least."

"How sure are we that the Witenagemot's operators in the control room weren't alerted to our new friend's crash? Or her emergency broadcast?" the Priest addressed Larry directly.

"As far as we can possibly know, the Witenagemot is in the dark completely. Ms. Revere told us she never achieved a firm link with the control room when she attempted to hail them," Larry assured the

Priest. "And Cainey and Sheffield both swear by the secrecy of the encrypted comms channel. They promised me no one is listening in without their knowledge. We should be good ... but who the hell knows with those two."

"What about you, Jed?" The Priest addressed the tall module pilot now seated at the dinner table. "You're awfully quiet over there. Can we trust you to keep your mouth shut about our visitor?"

It was then that Jordana's impatience finally wore thin. She had been rattled ever since she'd first heard that impossible noise coming up behind her as she futilely bounded and leaped her way across the moon's surface. Registering the sound had stopped her dead, though she couldn't bring herself to turn and face the preposterous noise right away. Jordana was sure her oxygen had been running lower than her suit levels were registering on her face shield display. Hallucination was the only explanation. She was on the bloody moon for Christ's sake. Cardinal's Nest was all but dead. There was no possible way that the rumbling at the edge of her hearing was truly the ululating moan of an industrial-grade motor. There was just no way the stuttered flicking noise accompanying the moan was the sound of bulky tank tracks treading across loose lunar dust. There was no way she was hearing those things. It was just impossible.

So it had taken her a good few seconds to finally allow herself to turn around and face the noise. When she'd actually laid eyes on the particle collector module, Jordana became certain her oxygen was running dry. She'd nearly sat down right then and there, so confident in her belief that the massive box-on-treads headed straight for her was a hallucination, but thankfully, something had kept her up. Maybe it was hope; she couldn't be sure. All Jordana knew was she had still been on her feet when that massive gray module with its streaks of silver and maroon had finally pulled up alongside her.

Arlo had talked about the collector modules many times, but Jordana had never thought to actually see one out and about collecting hydrogen and oxygen atoms from the thin lunar dust.

She had sat quiet for the bulk of that awkward journey to the station on that cramped cockpit bench seat alongside the two collector module crewmen with absolutely no idea what surprises were in store for her when they arrived at Cardinal's Nest. She tried during that relatively short trip to prepare herself for anything, hallucination or not, but this calm and seemingly off-topic banter of these supposed rescuers of hers was grating at her powers of comprehension. It had all just gotten to be too much. Her mind couldn't keep up with the questions her eyes and ears were demanding. Jordana could no longer go another second without answers.

Before Jed could respond to the Priest, she burst loose with all the questions that would no longer stay contained, "Will someone please tell me what in the bloody hell is going on here?! I mean ... what is the reason for all this secrecy? What the bloody hell is going on up here exactly? None of this makes sense. There were no detectable signs of life, besides a few lights flickering, and a few essential operations running. We had scans and satellite data. There were only supposed to be a few of you up here at best, and barely hanging on, as far as we could tell. How is this place all lit up like this? How are all the systems operating? And you all say there are hundreds of you up here? How is any of that possible? Did the shuttles make it up here with the AOA execs and the government officials after all? But that's not possible. We had the data. The launchpad was overrun. The shuttles never lifted off. No one made it out. This station was just supposed to have a few dozen prep crew left aboard, at best. We were so certain. None of this makes sense. Who in the bloody hell are you people?!"

"It's true then," Maisie said quietly to the seated priest. "Spurnberg's theory."

"Sounds like it," the Priest concurred with Maisie's strange statement.

"What's true? What in the bloody hell are you talking about? What is going on up h—" The panic in her voice shamed her, and even though she had a thousand more, Jordana cut her questions short.

"We've heard rumors, going all the way back to just after the Infection Event, that the Witenagemot have been cloaking the station from all known forms of detection," Maisie said in a frustratingly calm voice. "Tom Spurnberg—he was once a fighter in our early resistance, and a former computer engineer for AOA—well, he told everyone long ago that he stumbled across blueprints for the cloaking tech hidden away in an encrypted file in AOA's central mainframe. Although, there are apparently some limitations he failed to mention, or else was unaware of, seeing as how your people were able to tell this station was still operating. But anyway, if Spurnberg's cloaking theory turns out to be true, then it's no stretch from there to imagine they could alter satellite data to say most anything they want it to, and even erase any knowledge of the evacuation from the mainframe as well, along with any existing operating systems left on Earth or in orbit. They did blow up those platform satellites by remote all them years back, after all. Most everybody just ignored poor Tommy's report though. And anyway, AOA and the world leaders have always maintained that it's nothing more than a myth."

"Myth or no, it hardly matters," the Priest broke in. "It don't change our plans."

"It might," Maisie posited. "If the residents found out for sure that the Witenagemot is lying about monitoring Earth in search of evidence of the infection's end but were instead hiding us away up here and disguising our condition from detection just to ensure their authority, it might be the straw that broke the camel's back."

"It's a tempting dream, Mais, don't get me wrong, but you don't really believe that it could work any more than I do," the Priest said calmly. "We've got a plan, a solid, well-analyzed plan. Just 'cause it ain't the quick fix we all dream of, don't mean it's not the right one."

Jordana took in a deep breath to calm herself and force some coherence into her voice, "I don't mean to sound ungrateful for the rescue out there on the surface, but before I was rushed out of that giant garage, I believe you promised me answers when we got somewhere more hospitable. Well, this room is certainly a great deal more welcoming, so I think it's time you told me who you people are, and why it's so important that no one apart from you knows I'm here."

"I'm sorry, Jordana. You are absolutely right," Maisie said apologetically. "I can't even imagine how confusing this all must be for you. None of us can. But it's a bit of a long story, and it wouldn't be exaggeration to say our lives hang in the balance if we are discovered here with you. I promise to tell you everything, but Boyd is right to make sure all our ducks are in a row before we start up with all that. We can't afford any loose ends."

"I'm Boyd, by the way," the Priest said, rising from his perch atop a kitchen stool and offering up his hand. "Most folks around here call me the Priest, for reasons I'm sure you can guess," he said, with no hint of sarcasm.

"I'm Jordana. Jordana Revere," she said, struggling to repress her utter confusion. Finally, the awkwardness of the moment became too much to take. She felt her mouth forming words without her leave as she gripped the hairy man's fat paw. A graceless question tumbled off her tongue, "I'm sorry, did you say you were a priest?"

"That's right," Boyd responded flatly, serving only to increase her tense confusion further.

"But I thought you just said that she was your wife," Jordana pointed towards Dolly, unable to stop herself.

"I did."

"But I thought it was illegal ... or whatever ... for ... for priests to get married..."

"For the first 1100 years of the Catholic church, the lesser clergy were allowed to wed and procreate as they saw fit. It wasn't until enough sexually repressed Cardinals got together in the twelfth century to take out their carnal frustrations on the rest of us and declare the sensual touch of a good life-partner a sin, without one word of input from Jesus or his father, by the way. It happens to be just one of the many pieces of arbitrary church dogma I find it necessary to rebel against. You don't hold it against me, do you, Ms. Revere?"

"Uh ... no. Well ... I'm not Catholic so I ... I don't reall—"

Boyd spared her any further stuttering embarrassment as he indicated the stool beside him. "Never mind, Ms. Revere, never mind. It's not important. Please sit down."

Jordana was a bit hesitant, but ultimately, she decided to take the Priest up on his offer. She stepped a few nervous paces across the chamber, and in as dignified a manner as she could muster, climbed atop the indicated stool. "I take it you people aren't in charge up here. Perhaps I should be dealing with whomever is." Jordana took pride in the calm delivery of this potentially incendiary statement, especially in the face of her bursting confusion.

"That would be a mistake, Jordana," Maisie interjected. "I know it's asking a lot to just trust us about that, but it's true."

"If the Commander stumbled across you first, Ms. Revere, he would've buried you out there on the surface and blew that Star

Hawk of yours down to its constituent atoms." The Priest spoke in such a matter-of-fact tone that Jordana found herself believing every word he said. "And anyone besides the Steward who knew about you would wind up buried in the dust right alongside you. All the collector paths would be diverted away from your crash site, and any trace you ever crashed on the moon—or even existed at all—would be washed away forever."

"We will explain everything, Jordana, like I said," Maisie once again interjected. "But first, we need to know how you got up here and where you came from."

Jordana looked around the chamber at the faces of the station residents and quickly realized they weren't going to tell her a damn thing until they knew more about her. She knew that Larry had recounted to Maisie what she'd told the two collector module crewmen about her mission when they'd stepped away from her back in that cavernous module garage, but apparently, they wanted the firsthand account. So, resigned to her fate, she drew in a deep breath and launched into a retelling of that story, adding as much detail as she could remember. Well, pertinent detail anyway. She wasn't about to spill any Bruderschaft secrets, after all. She basically kept it to only the necessary and obvious parts: traveling from Europe in a group to Wyoming where her group's leader, a man who used to work for AOA, knew a secret launchpad was located, and how, with her flying background, Jordana was chosen for the recon mission to inspect the state of the lunar station. However, she said nothing of the Bruderschaft's intentions upon her mission's completion.

A silence fell over the room for a few moments after Jordana finished her story. It was cut short by the sound of a ceramic plate plopping down on the countertop in front of her. The plate was piled high with golden, fluffy, and best of all, *cheesy* scrambled eggs, along with a heaping helping of crispy bacon. "Eat up, honey," Dolly said with a genuine grin as she placed a few pieces of freshly-toasted home-made white bread atop her eggs.

Jordana watched Maisie and the Priest exchange simultaneous nods just before the casually dressed clergyman swiveled in his chair to face her, "Yeah, you go ahead and eat up, Jordana. Whilst you do, Maisie will tell you the story of our lives here at Cardinal's Nest Lunar

Station, just like she promised." The Priest swiveled back on his stool to face the handsome young woman, "Go on, Maisie, tell her all of it. Start at the beginning."

Maisie gestured towards the food on the plate before Jordana, "Go on then, Jordana, eat up while it's hot."

Slowly at first, still a little wary, Jordana snatched up the fork and set to work on the bountiful breakfast before her. After the first bite, a billion tense thoughts and an immense suffocating weight fell instantly from her shoulders and chest. Suddenly, there was only the meal before her. It was heaven. *Fresh eggs, for god's sake ... and bacon, real freaking bacon,* she marveled with ecstatic madness. Every bite was as unreal as the last. For the life of her, Jordana could not remember the last time she ate something that wasn't straight from a tin can or a plastic MRE bag. In what seemed to her to be no time at all, the bacon was nowhere in sight and the scrambled eggs were down to a few scraps, which she set to mopping up with the last piece of warm and crispy white toast.

Maisie cleared her throat, bringing Jordana back to the moment. She stared up at her uncertain rescuer just in time to see her begin stuttering out a few halfway comprehensible sentences. Jordana knew from the look on the bright, captivatingly hazel-eyed woman's face that she was building up to what was sure to be a very long story.

To be continued ...

BOOK CLUB QUESTIONS

1. Is it nature, nurture, or circumstance that makes a person?

2. Maisie's moral certainty is often put to the test. Does it ever waiver unjustly?

3. Is it purely experience motivating Harclay to manipulate the security officers?

4. What is AOA's actual culpability with regards to the infection's spread?

5. Was Abner justified in his challenge? Or was Gerwitz right when she said he simply made a rash decision in anger and was too proud to back down?

6. Is absolute order actually necessary on a delicate lunar station?

7. Will years of authoritarian rule break Maisie's resolve?

AUTHOR BIO

Andy T. Hanson is just your average mid-Michigan native and Army veteran who, in his own words, "discovered a way to travel the universe without ever leaving the comforts of home. It's a bit like magic in that way, a fantastic sleight of hand. I only regret waiting until my thirties to get started." Residing in Bay City, Michigan, Andy is an avid Detroit and Michigan sports fan. In between Lions games, golf, grilling, and chilling with his big family, in particular his lovely wife Lauren and son Teddy, and devouring science fiction, historical fiction and fantasy novels, he writes sci-fi novels of his own, inspired in large part by George R.R. Martin, Stephen King, Bernard Cornwell, Lee Child, and Sara Rosett, with a bit of Stephen Fry, Richard Dawkins, Kurt Vonnegut, Neil Gaiman and Craig Allanson for spice. Andy is attracted literarily to well-fleshed-out characters, especially gray characters, while his favorite part of writing is simply being present as the story grows of its own organic volition. Calamity: Book One of The Despot Chronicles, a dystopian, apocalyptic epic is what grew from those twin joys.

Discover more at
4HorsemenPublications.com

10% off using HORSEMEN10